SOMEONE'S WATCHING

She stopped. Worked her hand in an arc toward her body. Waving for him to cross.

Why didn't she come closer?

Hesitant, James took a quick look up and down Mill Road. No cars he could see, but the street disappeared around a curve no more than half a block away in each direction. He checked back. Yes, she was still gesturing, urging him to hurry.

'Okay,' he said. 'Ready or not, here I come!'

Breath held, he descended the grassy rise and started across the street. He felt a swell of jubilation at the thought of all that waited over that ribbon of blacktop: lunch, hugs, TV, chocolate chip cookies, a warm place to pee.

But then his ear caught a breath of danger. Suddenly, it was hot on his neck. Searing. He tried to run, to back away. No use. He was stone. Scared stiff. It was on him in an instant. All over him in a white, hot, shrieking wave.

And then nothing.

Also by Judith Kelman

Prime Evil
Where Shadows Fall
Where Angels Sleep
Hush Little Darlings

Someone's Watching

JUDITH KELMAN

Mandarin

A Mandarin Paperback
SOMEONE'S WATCHING

First published in Great Britain 1991
by William Heinemann Ltd
This edition published 1992
by Mandarin Paperbacks
Michelin House, 81 Fulham Road, London SW3 6RB

Mandarin is an imprint of Reed Consumer Books Ltd

Copyright © Judith Kelman 1991

A CIP catalogue record for this title
is available from the British Library
ISBN 0 7493 0992 X

Printed and bound in Great Britain
by Cox & Wyman Ltd, Reading, Berks

This book is sold subject to the condition
that it shall not, by way of trade or otherwise,
be lent, resold, hired out, or otherwise circulated
without the publisher's prior consent in any form
of binding or cover other than that in which
it is published and without a similar condition
including this condition being imposed
on the subsequent purchaser.

For Ed: helpmate, soulmate,
and personal shopper.

Special thanks to Peter Lampack,
agent extraordinaire,
and to Kate Miciak, brilliant editor.

Thanks also to Dr. Harry Romanowitz
and Dr. Lew Siegel.

1

The school bus was two stops away. Malcolm Cobb pictured the squat yellow capsule stuffed with boisterous children. He imagined the dizzying pulse of their energies and felt a sympathetic surge of adrenaline. His mouth parched and a fierce tingling shot from the nape of his neck to his groin.

Snapping alert, he was assailed by harsh sensations. There was the throbbing glare of the sun. The shiver of the car's idling engine. Fumes hovered like a gnat swarm in the frigid air.

Time for the final inventory. He mentally reviewed the procedures. All was in readiness.

The preparations had been painstaking. Exhausting. For days, he had used each spare moment to observe the child. Studied his every tic and nuance. Planned the moment of his taking breath by breath.

As always, Cobb's vile job had been the largest obstacle. When he'd most needed to concentrate on his strategy, there was always a fresh crisis at work. He detested the wretched calls and intrusions. Loathed all the mundane tasks and responsibilities that came with his repulsive livelihood. He was nothing but a repairman, a fixer of ruined parts, a lowly mechanic whose days were spent sloshing in the most monstrous filth.

But soon, he would be beyond all that. After this was done, he would be free to pursue his true calling.

One stop away now. The shrill was a summons. A heraldic cry. Cobb yielded to its pull. Easing his cramped foot off the brake pedal, he let the car roll toward the elbow of the road. His pulse was already bound to the child beyond his vision.

He imagined the boy stepping down. Looking this way and that. He savored the image of the child's buoyant

1

stride, the flush of health, the boundless vigor Cobb would soon claim as his own.

Two more minutes.

Most often, the seconds seemed a promise dangled before him, only to be wrenched away. Stolen. But now time's passage seemed a meager sacrifice. He eyed the limp ruin of his left arm. Caught sight of his grotesque visage in the windshield, shapeless as a mass of pummeled dough.

This was the only path to salvation. He would take what he needed and be healed.

2 James Merritt clambered down from the kindergarten bus and watched it slither away like a snake on fire: flashing red, whining. Fifty yards up Mill Road, it veered out of sight around a hairpin curve, belched a plume of exhaust, and was gone.

Alone, James gazed across the street at the entrance to Tyler's Grove. Squat stone pillars with broken tops marked the neighborhood's border. Once, an older boy with bubblegum breath had sworn that the pillars were the remains of the original grove owner's twin sons.

As the story went, Mr. and Mrs. Tyler's boys had perished over a century ago in a storm of unfathomable intensity, so fierce the winds had screwed their feet into the ground and wrenched off their heads.

A callow four-year-old at the time, James had seen no reason to challenge the tale. For months he'd been careful not to glance at the pillars, fearful that the calcified Tyler boys might still retain the capacity to bleed. Or worse, to come alive again and chase him in a headless rage all the way to the Kasden's house at the far dead end on Pumpkin Patch Drive.

Now, of course, James was older and far more discerning. In open defiance, he crossed his arms, trained his eyes directly on the stone columns, and stared at them for a minor eternity without blinking.

One was capped by a crushed Coors can and the gutted remains of a sack lunch from Burger King. On the other Fluffy Goldblatt lay sleeping in a fat cinnamon tangle, his signature tail trailing on the insistent wind.

Beyond was a scatter of houses set in no particular order on irregular one-acre plots. Most were clapboard colonials of indeterminate vintage and sparse imagination. There

3

were several boxy raised ranches and a few jarring cedar contemporaries.

Some parts of the community, like the Merritts' own expanded farmhouse two houses in from the pillars, were remnants of the Tylers' original homestead. So were the old well in front of the Podhoretzes' and the dilapidated gazebo near the DeRosas' and the majestic stand of chestnuts at the border of the Pavans', which had once produced bushels of delicious nuts and now yielded a bumper crop of worms shaped like rice kernels.

The air thrummed with hickory smoke and the hazy glare cast by a ferocious sun. There was the buzzing of a chainsaw, a motorbike revving, the shrill of barking dogs. James squinted through the glare, searching for someone.

He was a sturdy child, shaped like a fireplug, with blunt limbs and a square torso. His coppery hair capped curious blue eyes and a squash-blossom nose salted with freckles. The cold had polished his cheeks, and he sported a rakish fruit-punch mustache from the morning snack. James was a good-looking child. Almost a child's drawing of a child, rendered in clean lines and pleasing angles.

Still no one.

Restless, he deposited his Batman backpack in a hillock of dried leaves and started kicking twigs and stones onto the rutted pavement. Goal kick. Go, Merritt! Atta Boy!

James was the star goalie for the purple and white team in the lollipop division of the Stamford Youth Soccer League. Entrusted to defend the critical area between the two orange traffic cones that served as the goal, James had pioneered a fail-safe strategy. When there was a serious threat from the offense, he simply shoved the cones closer together.

'Attaway, Jamie boy! You show 'em!'

Practising now, he was careful to keep the toes of his blue Nikes safely back on the grass. James was forbidden to cross Mill Road alone, an edict he soundly endorsed. Cars whipped around the blind curves, overshot the narrow lanes, recoiled without warning from the poorly banked shoulders. Wavering shadows played over the sur-

4

face in an eye-fooling kaleidoscope. There had been frequent accidents. Abundant near-misses. At least two people had been run over in James's memory, and he was only, as he liked to put it, pushing six.

The first, a teenager named Mark something who'd been visiting his cousins on Melon Patch Lane, had been killed, squashed flat as a stomped bug from what James had overheard. And Laurel Druce, a skinny second grader from down the block, had broken her leg in a collision with the U-Haul coming to deliver the McMurrays' lawn furniture. As rumor had it, the shattered bone had pierced Laurel's shin, and the doctor had been obliged to use carpenter's tools to coax it back into its proper position. Some kind of pliers, James had assumed, thinking it inappropriate to ask.

Run over. James shivered and zipped his denim jacket to the chin. His worst and most frequent dream was the one where he was run over by a giant locomotive. He'd be dead asleep, and suddenly tracks would materialize. Enormous metal worms invading his bedroom, coursing through his bed. He couldn't move. Couldn't get away. The train bore down. Closer and closer. There was the thunderous wheeze of pistons, the screaming whistle . . .

His heart was doing a drum roll. James forced the train dream from his mind and resolved to focus on lunch instead. As usual, he would ask his mom for a chocolate chip cookie sandwich on white, and she'd ask whether he preferred mustard or mayonnaise. He'd say ketchup, and she'd ask if he wanted lettuce and tomato. He'd say spinach and banana, please, and they'd both laugh even though they told the same joke in precisely the same words every day. Then she'd make him his regular: peanut butter with an ooze of grape jelly cut in crustless triangles. And a mammoth glass of ice cold milk.

Afterward he'd have a mountain of chocolate chip cookies for dessert. He would consume them in the timeless manner of the toll-house connoisseur, chips first, nuts neatly excised and deposited in an artful arrangement on the plate. There was a subway rumble in his belly. Hunger. And his bladder was starting to complain.

Come on, somebody.

Usually, his mother was already standing beside Fluffy's pillar when the bus pulled up. He could picture her now, eyes downcast, reading a book. He imagined the way her face would change when she spotted him. Her mouth would move in an exaggerated circle of greeting and then spread in a smile.

Once in a while, when she got stuck late with one of her speech patients at the hospital and couldn't meet the bus, Dad would duck out of the recording studio he'd built in the cottage behind the house and see James safely across Mill Road.

On those days James got to eat his sandwich while he watched a demo session or the laying of background tracks for an album cut. He loved sitting on the throne stool next to the studio's huge electronic sound board, chewing to a bass beat as mysterious as Australia.

James hoped he wasn't going to be spending the day with Mrs. Zielinski, a neighbor who sat for him in a pinch. Mrs. Z was nice enough, but she smelled like bathroom spray. And she insisted on zapping his milk in the microwave to get the chill out even though he'd patiently explained any number of times that he much preferred the chill undisturbed. When she wasn't paying attention, James would sneak a couple of ice cubes into his glass. Then he'd be forced to take mouse sips to avoid any telltale clinking.

The pressure on his bladder was building. James felt the first stirrings of fear. What if they forgot about him altogether? What if he had to stand here until he froze or starved or peed on himself like a two-year-old baby?

No way.

That's the way Todd Holroyd would probably react to the situation: cry and go crazy and wet his pants. Well, James was no sissy wierdo like Odd Todd. Not even close.

If no one showed up in a couple of minutes, James resolved to fly across the street. He'd simply slap his palms together, take a giant leap, and land next to the broken pillar that was alleged to be the decapitated Tyler twin who'd been born first by three minutes.

James was not afraid to fly. There was almost nothing he feared except getting run over so his bone stuck through his skin like Laurel Druce's. And the train dream. And while he didn't see it as the same brand of fear, he did have a healthy regard for his monster.

James's monster had sour breath, stringy hair, and a stomach filled with hot, green poison. The unsightly creature had taken up residence in James's closet shortly after the Merritts moved to Tyler's Grove from their apartment near the turnpike when James was pushing three. For several weeks, he had felt the heat of the demon's eyes boring into him as he lay in bed. He'd fought sleep, instinctively aware that this particular monster's tastes ran to slumbering children, especially boys. James had many ambitions, but none of them had anything remotely to do with becoming a meal.

When sleep threatened to triumph, James had dragged himself out of bed and slogged into his parents' room, seeking asylum. But neither his mother nor his father would acknowledge that he was in serious jeopardy. One or the other would ply him with empty assurances and shepherd him back to his room.

The issue might have gone unresolved indefinitely. But one night, in frustration, his father had slammed the closest door before ordering James to sleep. At once the child could sense the monster's impotence. The grotesque creature was incapable of opening a simple door.

Salvation.

Several times after that, James had attempted to evict the thing with pleas or admonitions. But the monster was unyielding. Eventually, resigned to cautious coexistence, James had named the monster Vinton after two infamous sixth graders, Vincent Scanlon and Tony Friedberg, who carved unthinkable words in the cafeteria tables and deposited fat wads of used gum in the water fountains.

In school James avoided Vincent and Tony by dawdling

near the teacher until the bullies had selected another diminutive subject for their torments. Nights, he avoided Vinton by following scrupulous precautionary procedures. Before the lights were doused he insisted on being covered to his ears, kissed three times on his forehead, and having the closet door closed until he heard the click. Then his mother had to intone, 'Stay, Vinton!' in her most authoritative voice. The ritual had proved effective. Each morning, he conducted a cursory check, and not once had there been so much as a tooth mark.

Come on already!

James was starving and cold and so impatient he could almost hear his insides rattle. He wanted to pee for an hour and eat a hundred chocolate chip cookie sandwiches with the crusts off. He wanted to tell his mom about how he'd been chosen for the power kids group with a real reader and a spelling book. He wanted to tell her about the shadow man . . .

Maybe if he did his trick.

When James desperately wanted something to happen, he coaxed the benevolent spirits by closing his eyes, holding them shut for precisely five seconds, and opening them very, very slowly. It was a power he reserved for dire emergencies and singular requests.

He forced his lids together until he saw a riot of yellow sparkles dancing on an ebony ground. Determined to make no mistake, he took a deep breath and counted the seconds aloud: 'One, Mississippi . . . two, Mississippi . . . '

'Five.' On the final beat, he released his cramped lids. A flood of brilliant light made his eyes water and reduced the autumn landscape to a blur.

Had it worked?

He struggled to focus. Peered across the undulating blacktop. Wished.

Yes! He spotted her walking toward him. Plodding over the farmhouse lawn. Coming closer. Indistinct in the glare, but definitely her. He could tell by the puff of curly brown hair, the blue coat.

She stopped. Worked her hand in an arc toward her body. Waving for him to cross.

Why didn't she come closer?

Hesitant, James took a quick look up and down Mill Road. No cars he could see, but the street disappeared around a curve no more than half a block away in each direction. He checked back. Yes, she was still gesturing, urging him to hurry.

'Okay,' he said. 'Ready or not, here I come!'

Breath held, he descended the grassy rise and started across the street. He felt a swell of jubilation at the thought of all that waited over that ribbon of blacktop: lunch, hugs, TV, chocolate chip cookies, a warm place to pee.

But then his ear caught a breath of danger. Suddenly, it was hot on his neck. Searing. He tried to run, to back away. No use. He was stone. Scared stiff. It was on him in an instant. All over him in a white, hot, shrieking wave.

And then nothing.

3 Cinnie Merritt jotted a final note in the chart and tucked it into the file drawer marked 'inactive'. Satisfied, she replaced the testing materials in the supply closet nearest the door and shrugged into her coat.

Her office at the Fairview Hospital was on the sixth floor in the freshly renovated rehabilitation wing. The space was generous and cheerful with its sleek furnishings, primary accents, and warm lighting. Most often, it was a perfect foil for Cinnie's optimistic nature. She had inherited her mother's flair for divining scraps of light in the bleakest circumstances and her father's gift for smoothing life's ruts with humor.

The combination had helped her through a recent string of difficult years including her mother's slow, cruel death from Lou Gehrig's disease, her father's precipitious remarriage, and most recently, the difficulties with Paul.

Cinnie couldn't deny that their marriage, product of a romance launched in junior-high-school homeroom, was falling apart. Fraying and unraveling in ways they both seemed powerless to define or arrest. Lately, he'd taken to sleeping most nights in the cottage behind the farmhouse, which he'd spent years and a fortune converting into a state-of-the-art recording studio.

Paul's moving out seemed oddly anticlimactic. He'd been gone, in a palpable way, for months. But Cinnie could still sense the resonating hum of his presence in her bones. And she still ached for the remembered connection between them that had once been as easy and natural as a breath.

But none of that was the cause of her present unease. Something she could not identify had been prickling at her all day, nagging like an invisible burr. It was one of those inexplicable feelings she had from time to time. A splinter of the world out of place. A beat missing. Annoying as a crooked picture on a crooked wall. And as impossible to set right.

She paused at the broad, plate window and spotted Dal and TeeJay walking out of the hospital and across the parking lot. They were holding hands, their matching caps of cropped ginger hair ruffled by the wind. TeeJay's little legs worked like a windmill as he tried to keep us with his mother's exuberant stride. Dal was gesticulating with her free hand and talking nonstop. Everything back to normal.

Dal, Cinnie's closest friend, had called earlier in a panic, certain TeeJay had developed a serious problem. She'd declined to describe the symptoms over the phone. 'You have to see for yourself, Cin. And as soon as possible. It's awful.'

Cinnie had told Dal to bring him in at noon, right after her last scheduled morning patient. Hanging up, she'd felt a hard tug of anxiety. After all of Dal's breathless false alarms about her little boy, maybe this time the crisis was real. Maybe that was the source of Cinnie's crooked picture.

She'd decided it made sense to see them at the hospital. If whatever it was proved to be out of her field, she knew she could find the right specialist at Fairview for a quick consultation. Dr. Ferris, the pediatrician they both used for their children's routine ailments and inspections, had no skill in managing Dal's hysteria. He would simply tell her not to worry, which was about as effective as ordering someone not to think of an elephant.

Cinnie had called Paul in the studio and asked him to meet James at the bus stop at twelve. He'd sounded distracted. Distant. But that was standard for the new model Paul. The stranger.

The sky was glazed with sunlight and a shimmer of frost. Shading her eyes with cupped fingers, Cinnie watched as Dal unlocked her gray Jeep and strapped TeeJay into his car seat.

Terrific little boy. Bright and eager with the perfect

pinch of silliness. He had caught his father's passion for football and now refused to leave the house without rolled-sock shoulder pads and a plastic helmet. From six storeys up, he resembled a travel-sized can of spray deodorant. Adorable kid. And perfectly fine.

If only Dal could relax and enjoy him.

Cinnie felt a twinge of guilt. She knew that living in Tyler's Grove was at the root of Dal's problem. The neighborhood was a rich breeding ground for maternal insecurities. There was an unhealthy, unforgiving spotlight on the children. Which was best, brightest, biggest? The kids were scrutinized like fruit in a grocery bin. Only perfect would do.

Soon after she and Paul moved in, Cinnie had been buffeted by the undertow of jealous comparisons. Casual talks between the mothers tended to turn mean and ugly. That one's daughter couldn't make friends. This one's son was doing terribly in school. Had she noticed that the other one's little girl was getting fat?

Cinnie had tried to pass it all off as petty nonsense, but on some level, she knew it was more than that. There was a desperate edge to the nastiness here. It hung like a poison vapor in the neighborhood's tranquil air.

Still, when Dal and Rick had talked about buying a house in the area, Cinnie had done everything in her power to sell them on Tyler's Grove. She'd wanted so badly to have Dal nearby, she hadn't allowed herself to consider how the venom of envy might affect her friend. After all, she rationalized, Tyler's Grove was no better or worse than any other family neighborhood. Certainly they hadn't cornered the market on bitchy, insecure women who polished their children and set them out on display.

Cinnie knew you didn't have to let it affect you. She'd managed to find her way around the minefield of jealousy. When the women were at their worst, she could tune them out like radio static. Simple. All she had to do was focus on that luscious little boy of hers. No contest.

But honest, vulnerable Dal was a frequent victim.

This morning's mock emergency had to do with TeeJay's

repeating an occasional word or syllable. Dal had convinced herself that the little boy was doomed to a life of severe stuttering, struggling to communicate, each word a physical and emotional ordeal.

As usual, Lydia Holroyd, a neighbor of Dal's and Cinnie's, had planted the bomb. Lydia took obscene pleasure in preying on Dal's apprehensions. Nothing that hideous woman enjoyed more than studying TeeJay and commenting on his imaginary deficits in her overblown British accent. She sounded as if she'd been born with a whalebone tongue and nostrils sewn shut like the pockets of a new suit.

'Stuttering, my, my,' she'd told Dal, shaking her head in mock sympathy, 'poor thing must be suffering from dreadful stress and tension. Perhaps you put too much pressure on the boy, Dahlia.'

It had taken Cinnie about thirty seconds to confirm that the 'stuttering' was an innocent, common phase in language development that would disappear on its own in a month or two. For good measure, she'd put TeeJay through an abbreviated battery of speech and language tests. No doubt Dal could use tangible reassurances like high scores and enviable percentile rankings. It was the first time in ten years on the job that Cinnie had conducted an evaluation on a child wearing a Giants' helmet complete with chin strap and face cage.

Afterward she'd settled TeeJay on the waiting room floor with a heap of toys and tried to put her friend at ease.

Dal was pitched forward in the visitor's chair like an expectant pinball. 'It's serious, isn't it, Cin? Be honest with me.'

'Very serious. Poor kid has a crazy mother.'

'But Lydia said . . .'

Cinnie puffed her disgust. 'First, it was the bedwetting, then the invisible rash, then his brain was going to turn to tapioca from watching cartoons and he was going to perish because you don't hand-grind his peanut butter. When are you going to stop listening to that woman?'

Dal dipped her opal eyes like a chastened puppy. 'You're right. I know you are. But she gets to me.'

'So don't let her. When she starts in, think about that wonderful kid of yours. The truth is Lydia would give anything if Todd could be two percent as normal and delightful as TeeJay.'

Todd Holroyd, Lydia's only child, was a pale, nervous, bookish boy, a year older than James. Already, the neighborhood kids had taken to calling him Odd Todd. They shunned him in the way children instinctively revile anyone or anything too difficult to understand. Unfortunately, no amount of hand-ground peanut butter or television avoidance was going to remedy Todd's predicament.

'You're sure, Cin? He's really okay?'

'He's better than okay.'

Dal drooped with relief. 'I don't know how to thank you. Promise you'll send me a bill.'

'TeeJay already paid me. Two hugs and a helmet kiss.'

'Come on. This is business.'

'All right. My standard consultation fee is either fifty thousand dollars or a lunch for two at the Pancake House.'

'Lunch it is. How about right now? We can stop for James. I'll call the office and tell them they'll have to muddle along without me for another hour or two. Give them a chance to realize how indispensable I am.'

'Today's not good.'

'Today's wonderful, Cin. I'm scheduled to run a focus group on a peanut butter substitute made out of tofu. Does that sound like a must miss or what?'

'Sorry I can't bail you out, kid. Tofu and jelly? Yuck.'

'Yuck is right. And since you won't save me from it, I'm going to punish you with a sample.'

Cinnie watched the Cherokee drift out of the hospital parking lot and turn onto Prescott Street. Long after the car had disappeared, she stood staring. Searching for something.

She was startled by a rap on the door. Without waiting for an answer, Oliver London twisted the knob and propelled his wheelchair into the doorway. Cinnie smiled.

14

'Hi, Mr. London. What's up? I was just on my way out.'

London growled and smacked a fist on the padded arm of his chair. He was a sallow, square-jawed man whose face had been parted down the middle by a recent stroke. One side was normal and fluid, the other frozen in a permanent grimace. The paralysis extended to his right arm and leg, which he held at odd angles. Also warped by the stroke were his language abilities. London was afflicted with expressive aphasia. He could understand everything he heard but could not put his thoughts into words. At least, not yet. He cast his good eye at Cinnie and bashed the armrest again.

Cinnie checked her watch. 'Sorry, friend. I really have to go now. We have our usual appointment tomorrow morning at nine-thirty. I'll be glad to hear all about it then.'

A playful grin tipped the working side of his mouth, and he folded his operative arm over the one affixed to his chest like a latched shutter.

Cinnie suppressed a smile. 'Come on now. Don't tell me we're going to play hostage again. You know I have to get home to my little boy.'

London checked the brake locks holding his chair in place and recrossed his arm. He was in the center of the doorway, leaving no more than a couple of spare inches on either side. The man was obviously accustomed to getting his way, whatever it took.

Cinnie sighed and settled against the edge of her desk. 'All right. You win. What's the gripe this time?'

London looked smug. He rapped the chair arm twice and issued a guttural grunt.

'The food again?' Since London had gotten well enough to propel himself around the ward corridors, he'd appointed Cinnie as his personal complaint department. She was able to understand him when no one else could. In certain ways, she found London as articulate as anybody else. Maybe more so.

He hitched his eyebrow and made a noise like cat nails raking a screen door.

15

Cinnie sighed. 'You want me to bring you *another* pastrami on rye? Look, you know you're on a low-salt, low-fat diet. I could get fired for sneaking in contraband deli. I could lose my livelihood. Tell me how I'm supposed to feed my young son then, Mr. London. How am I supposed to save for his college?'

London's grin broadened and his voice rose to a mischievous squeak.

'How about a compromise? What would you say to a nice, big turkey on rye with Russian dressing and a side of coleslaw?'

Three raps and an indignant growl.

'A turkey club then? Think of it . . . crisp lettuce, red ripe tomato – oozing juice, a luscious slice of bacon . . . ' She rubbed her stomach and slurped. 'Mmmmm.'

A mute, murderous look.

Cinnie lost the stare-down and conceded with a studied frown. 'All right. Pastrami it is. But only on the condition that this is absolutely the last time. And I'm ordering extra lean. And positively no sour pickle.'

A pounded fist.

' . . . Half sour, and that's my final offer. Take it or leave it.'

London nodded, clearly pleased with himself, and backed out of the doorway. He made a chivalrous sweep with his arm, inviting Cinnie to pass.

She shook her head at him and made a face. The whole point of the game was letting him feel in control. The dietician and London's doctor had both agreed that the psychic benefits far outweighed any potential harm from an occasional pastrami lapse.

Three months earlier, when London was first brought in after his stroke, he'd been a blown eggshell of a man – hollow, fragile, dark eyes glazed with fear and defeat. There had been no trace of the legendary forty-year veteran of the Stamford police force. From what Cinnie had heard, he'd been a fiery curmudgeon with a short fuse and a long memory who'd kept entire generations of community children on the right side of the ledger. London had been known as a cop's cop. Never one to bend or back away, even when his own leathery hide was on the line.

Cinnie was delighted to witness the gradual return of the original bullheaded London, even though he was fast becoming the textbook impossible patient.

Unfortunately, she had no way of knowing where or when his forward motion would stop, or whether there might be a serious backslide. These things were so unpredictable. So much hinged on attitude, the marvels of motivation, luck. In the past year alone, two patients as severely afflicted as London had made near-complete recoveries. And then each had suffered another stroke. One fatal.

Cinnie shuddered. More doom and gloom. What was wrong with her today? She was accustomed to the sour taste of her own attitude, but the nagging sense of impending disaster trailed her onto the elevator and out the door.

Slipping into her ancient blue Volvo wagon, she was cheered by the sight of James's Hulk Hogan doll propped in the passenger seat between the child's weekly complement of library books and a solitary Spiderman mitten. The other one was probably warming his pocket, she thought. James was already at the age where warmth and comfort took a second seat to image. Overalls had gone first, then hats, now mittens. Soon, she thought, with a flicker of wistful amusement, he'd refuse to be seen in public with anything as mortifying as a mother.

Driving north on High Ridge Road, she tuned the radio to a light-rock station and sang along with a chorus of 'Celebration'. Next was a Beatles medley. Cinnie felt the gloom lifting, veil by veil.

By the time she turned onto North Stamford Road and began the winding course of country lanes toward Tyler's Grove, her standard good humor had been restored. After lunch, she would let James talk her into a hot game of Old Maid. Or maybe they'd do some baking. Her two o'clock appointment had canceled, which meant a bonus of extra time with her little boy before Cinnie began seeing her private afternoon clients in the office over the garage.

Nothing James liked better than helping her concoct his

favorite toll house cookies. She could imagine him floured and streaked with chocolate, wearing the intent expression of a miniature mad scientist.

Delicious kid.

The boys from Liverpool were singing 'I Wanna Hold Your Hand'. Cinnie turned up the volume and felt the rhythm of the music thumping in her veins, the words propelling her through time and place to the junior high gym in Rockville Centre, Long Island. She could see Paul gyrating opposite her. Feel the explosive enthusiasm of a hundred flushed, sweaty teenagers trampling out the invisible fires on the polished floor.

'I wanna hold your ha-a-a-a-and. I wanna ho-wold your hand.'

The song ended as Cinnie approached the juncture of Cascade and Mill roads. Slowing as she neared the stop sign, she flipped off the radio. There was a breath of silence. And then the calm was pierced by terrible sounds: wailing sirens, the strident squawk of police-band radios, a cacophony of shocked voices.

A snake line of cars was stalled along Mill Road. Up the street near the entrance to Tyler's Grove, Cinnie spotted a pair of uniformed cops standing in front of a makeshift barricade. They were deflecting traffic from the scene. Beyond them was a tangle of flame-capped emergency vehicles: fire, police, ambulance, EMS.

Cars were retreating from the logjam. Cautiously circling on the narrow, grassy banks on the side of the winding street, they were heading up the road toward the neighboring hamlet of New Canaan. Cinnie checked behind her. All clear. She could back down Cascade to the nearest driveway and turn around. There was another approach to Tyler's Grove from further north on High Ridge.

But as she was about to execute the maneuver, she noticed that the clot of cars in front of her was breaking up. A van edged forward, leaving a hole in the traffic line, and impulsively Cinnie turned onto Mill Road. She'd explain to the police that she had to get through. She could see the farmhouse from here, still and inviting.

Three cars from the barricade now. Two attendants were lifting the victim into the back of the ambulance. Cinnie saw the stretcher frame, a form swaddled in sheets.

She looked around. Strange. No mangled cars. No wrecker. What kind of an accident? She thought of the others, and her throat closed. Not another kid. Please not another kid.

Only one car from the barricade. Cinnie gazed through the broken pillars at the scatter of familiar houses. She was eager to get home, aching to give James a long, loud, serious hug.

The car in front of her mounted the grassy shoulder and executed an awkward pirouette. Cinnie inched forward and stopped at the wooden barrier. One of the policemen sauntered over to driver's side window and hitched his thumbs in his belt.

'Sorry, ma'am. Been a bad accident here. You'll have to go around.'

'I understand, Officer. But I live right over there, and my little boy's waiting for me. Can't I please go through?'

He frowned and pulled a slip of paper from his pocket. 'Name?'

'Merritt. Cinnie Merritt.'

He kept his eyes averted, and his craggy face registered a pinch of pain. 'Better come with me, Mrs. Merritt. I'm afraid it's bad news.'

4 Brittle with fear, Cinnie sat beside James on a stiff bench in the rear of the ambulance. Behind her, the doors were slammed shut from the street, locking out the world.

Inside, a burly black attendant presided over a row of bleeping monitors. Every few minutes, he depressed a red button over the squawk box and spoke to the driver or the hospital in clipped tones. 'Boy's stable now. Ready four pints O positive and a neuro consult. We're coming in.'

The driver was a disembodied voice beyond a stainless steel divider. Seconds after the attendant gave him the go-ahead, the engine coughed and came alive. Turning sharply, they sped away. Lights flashing. Siren piercing the stillness like a scream.

James was strapped to the stretcher frame by broad bands of woven green nylon, his head was bound in place by a leather strap. His lips were dusky, his face as white as the sheets bandaging him to the chin. The only visible damage was a clean bull's-eye bruise on his left temple.

A worm of tubing connected him to an IV rigging that dripped a steady beat of clear fluid. His heart sounds were registered on a narrow strip of paper that spewed from one end of a clacking monitor and settled in a wire tray. Another electronic device recorded the rest in skittish green digits: pulse, blood pressure, respirations.

'James?' Cinnie said in a whisper. 'I love you, baby. Don't be scared.'

She ran a fingertip over his pallid cheek. Cool velvet. Too cool. 'You'll be okay, sweetheart. Everything will be okay.'

The attendant stepped between them, set a pair of half glasses on his nose, and checked the child's lines and tethers. Finished, he caught Cinnie's eye and nodded. 'You can hold on to him, Mother. No sign of any fractures this side.' He loosened the sheets and extracted a boneless arm.

Cinnie cradled James's small hand in hers. It was a dead bird, limp and weightless. She stroked his cupped fingers. 'James? Can you hear me?'

She detected a hopeful breath of change, a tightening in his forehead, his lips tensed. 'James?' There was a hint of movement in his fingers. 'That's it, sweetheart. Wake up.'

He grimaced, and there was a flutter under his lids.

'That's good. That's my boy. Can you say something?'

His chest filled, held a moment, then collapsed like a pierced balloon. Snap, and he was gone. Cinnie swallowed back a lump of panic, then smoothed the band of his forehead visible beneath the strap.

She caged James's hand between hers and stared out the window. They were speeding down High Ridge Road now. Passing familiar strips of shops and office buildings. The high school. The library. All of it streaming together in a dizzy whirl.

Again, she replayed what the officers had told her, trying to make some sense of the nightmare. Whoever hit James had taken off. No witnesses yet, but they were hoping someone would come forward soon with useful information. Or the perpetrator might reconsider after the initial panic and turn himself in.

Unfortunately, James had been knocked to the shoulder, and a number of cars had gone by before someone spotted him and called nine-eleven. Any helpful skid marks or tire prints had been obliterated by the time the police arrived. No broken glass or metal fragments they'd been able to find. Of course, a team from forensics was on the way up, and if there were any clues left at all, they'd be uncovered. The officer shook his head as he spoke, obviously convinced the search would be fruitless.

Cinnie grappled with several, nagging questions. How could this have happened? She knew her son. Knew he was not the kind of child who violated absolute prohibitions like the one about crossing Mill Road alone. Especially not after what happened to the little Druce girl.

James had prattled on about Laurel's broken leg for weeks, still mentioned it from time to time in reverent tones. 'That street's a menace,' he would remark, mimicking the somber adults who'd gathered months ago in the Merritts' living room to work at petitioning the town for a traffic light. The effort had fizzled after a few unsuccessful attempts, the urgency of the street's hazards dimmed by time and fresher outrages.

Still, she was certain James would never have ventured across that street alone.

And where in the hell was Paul? He'd promised to be at the bus stop. Cinnie discarded the impossible notion that he'd simply forgotten. There had to be some reasonable explanation.

Could something have happened to him, too? Cinnie's heart squirmed like a beached fish, and there was a vicious hammering in her head.

She closed her eyes. *Please let my baby be all right. Please let him wake up and be fine.*

A sound.

Cinnie's eyes shot open, and she stared at James. His lips were working. There was a breathy rattle in his throat. She bent closer. 'What, puss? Tell me.'

His eyes forced half open and his face tensed. 'Mommy?'

'Yes, sweetheart. Everything's going to be fine.'

He winced. 'Hurts, Mommy. Burns.'

'I'm sorry, baby. You hold on a minute, and they'll give you some medicine to make you feel better.'

'So sleepy, Mom.'

'I know. But try to stay awake. Okay?'

His face was full of struggle. 'The shadow man . . . Blue . . . coat lady. Have to pee, Mommy.'

His voice was fading, falling to dust. ' . . . Saw you wave. . . . But the man came. Pop the weasel. Flying green tunnel. All gone.'

'James?'

He smacked his lips and tasted the air. 'Don't forget, Mommy. Three kisses and no more . . . Vinton.'

22

'Don't you worry, James. Mommy won't let anyone hurt you.'

'Stay, Vinton! Get back. Make him go way, Mommy. Make him stop. Stop him!' His voice rose to a desperate wail, clawing at the air. His hand fisted, body clenched in spasm, arched against the restraints.

And then he went limp. The cardiac monitor shrieked its terrible alarm and, as Cinnie watched in helpless horror, the darting needle slowed and settled in a flat, dead line.

5 Malcolm Cobb could feel the mute progress of time. The steady thrust of the universe resonated in his pins and fibers. Moved metronomically with the rhythm of his firm internal tides. Undulated like the hips of an exotic dancer: seductive, mesmerizing.

Soon.

Often, the coming of the moment filled him with an acid dread. But today he was eager to begin. Brimming with confidence. Reveling in the heat of his own infusing strength. His cheeks were fevered. Limbs tingling. Heart thumping with the virile insistence of a tropical drum.

Almost time.

Knowing it was unthinkable to start early, he paced the square front room of his cabin. The floor was harsh beneath his bare soles. Cinders. Ash. Vile residue. He must remember to sweep it clean before her visit.

And to bathe and change into suitable costume, he thought, making a mental list. His blue coat and club tie perhaps. Or the dark silk smoking jacket and silver flannel trousers. He mustn't forget to polish his black tasseled slippers. Everything had to be precise, perfect. Nothing to spark her displeasure.

He paused and filled his lungs. The air smelled of pine and tallow. There was an unpleasant taint of spent matter. A tinge of rotting leaves. Dust. But not a trace of the charred, repugnant scent. Not a hint of the bitter blue vapor.

Wonderful!

The enemy had been thwarted. Permanently, he was sure. There would be no threat to distract him when she arrived. He would be free to savor her presence, bask in her affection and approval. Slather her honeyed words on his soul and surface like a balm.

He could feel the tingle of anticipation, taste its sweetness. Soon she would be here beside him, redolent of sweet sunshine. He imagined the rustle of her black taffeta dress, the airy tapping of her heeled sandals, the coy wink of tiny diamonds in her ears. His mind filled in the satin slick of her dark hair, the laughter in her gray eyes. The porcelain skin – soft as a sigh.

A gleeful twitter escaped him. He felt the electric swell of excitement. But when she arrived, he would not yield to it. He resolved to maintain a calculated pace. Not a breath of hurry. All would proceed in due course. They would enjoy a slow, easy greeting. And then would come the smooth flow of idle chatter. Any incidental gaps in their conversation would be filled with a gentle, spreading warmth. A natural rejoining of their fates.

He would wait for the perfect moment to show her what he had written. Offer it as a delicious surprise. How she would exult! How she would celebrate his sweet liberation. His gift winged and soaring again at long last. It was for this that he had been created. Not for the vile enterprise that was his daily labor – his wretched work.

Reverently, he scanned the row of framed treasures on the rough-hewn wall opposite the window. Tributes. Stellar reviews. 'Clever,' they gushed. 'Sparkling.' 'A fresh voice.'

His heart ballooned with the adulation. He craved more, the yearning riper than lust. And now, it would be satisfied. At last he had commenced a flow of perfect words. An endless beginning. An unstoppable start. How pleased she would be!

Perhaps he should warm some brandy.

There was, after all, much to celebrate. He plucked one of a dozen, identical, slim volumes from the center of the crammed bookshelf over the sooty stove. With enormous care, he caressed the crackling binding, ran his callused palm over the dust jacket. It was soiled, worn dull. His name all but obliterated, his picture on the flyleaf stained the color of smoker's teeth.

He stared at his own younger image: a boy slender as

thread with pale, frightened eyes and a mouth that failed at defiance. A stern nose, elfin ears. Skin the tone and texture of paste. The shirt was over-starched and too short in the cuff, so his pale arms extruded like gobs of caulk from which his hands hung, limp and apologetic. The shoulders were angled and uncertain. The hair a dull tangle.

But what Malcolm Cobb saw was magnificence. Triumph! Beautiful, brilliant boy, he thought, his heart overflowing. He remembered her approbation when the book was born, the glow of pride and pleasure in her eyes. Those eyes, a gleaming mirror for his soul. Her words a treasure. His throat went taut with feeling, and he issued a wrenching sigh.

Brandy it would be.

Before she came, he must remember to wash the crystal snifters and polish them dry. He must ready the silver tray and rummage through the storage bin for Mother's crocheted doily. So much to do. But he would not allow it to distract him.

The time was nearer. Nearer still. He shivered with anticipation.

Absently, he stripped off his white coat and blue chambray shirt and ran his fingers in a teasing tickle along the tops of his naked arms. Long snakes of hairless flesh. He could feel the ripple of lithe muscle underneath.

Shivering, he drizzled his fingers through his hair. Ribbons streaming to his shoulders, spilling over. The chill trickled down his neck like rivulets of spring water.

Raising his hands to his hairline, he traced the ridge of his brow, the velvet lids, the taut seam of his lips. The chin.

The chin had once been his nemesis, girlish and given to emotional display. But it felt firmer now, filling to a suitable square. Exactly as he wished it. As he'd planned. And plan he could. For he was to be the product of his own deliberate design. A dark moon, round and fulsome. Radiating brilliance.

Just as she'd predicted, as she'd promised. A smile claimed his face, spreading like a stain.

Slowly, he tickled down his chest and abdomen. Dipped his hand below his belt and pleasured himself with light, deliberate strokes.

In a ragged whisper, he commanded his own visceral obedience. . . . Eyes closed. Body gripped in total absorptive concentration.

Control!

. . . Cerebral sector disengaged by lever of will. Somatic sector climbing the crest of controlled dominance. Rising. At the precipitous peak. Beyond. Facing the dark drop to blind oblivion. Mustn't cross. Danger!

Abruptly, he stopped. Wrenched away his fingers, and constricted them into claws. Fisted his limbs in deliberate spasm until the pain consumed him. Held fast until his muscles screeched and surrendered, falling away in dead, rubber strips.

Cerebral sector restored. Somatic sector disengaged by lever of will . . .

Control.

He was still. Satisfied. And she would be as well. He must remember to defrost her favorite pastries and wrap them in a fine linen cloth. Spoon the peach preserves into a porcelain dish. Settle the filigreed jam spoon in the crook.

So much to do. But all of it would be pure delight. As soon as he completed his exercises, he would ready things for her visit. He conjured her light floral scent. The silken weight of her hand on his, telling him all was forgiven. Right again. Healed.

It was more than a week now since that dreadful scene between them. He could still see her face, flushed scarlet and twisted with rage. Still feel the pounding of her words and the blade of her voice. Calling him useless, a mockery. Telling him she wanted nothing more to do with him. That he was dead to her. Forgotten.

The memory ignited a fury in him. The sparks leaping. Threatening. He had done exactly as she'd asked.

Everything. And still she'd been cold, dissatisfied. Still, she'd shut him out. Reviled him!

A mockery. Sentenced to dark oblivion for a crime of her own invention. Impossible.

How he'd suffered. He'd stood at her door, keening, debased, begging her to let him back inside. He pounded on the cruel wood frame until his precious hands were broken and bloody. His cries rent the black silence. Useless. Still he'd pleaded and wailed until he felt the acid etch at his throat. And tasted the bitterness of his own despair.

But she'd been deaf to him. Refused to acknowledge his pleas. Cruel, unfeeling . . .

Tonight, he had to make her see what she'd done. It was imperative that she understand. Repent if necessary.

Yes, repent absolutely. She owed him apology and more. Warmth. Concern. She owed him, and the debt would be repaid. Malcolm's chin quavered with the need. The outrage.

Stop!

Must retain control. Lever of will engaged. Cobb measured his breaths. Ordered his pulse to a steady, sympathetic beat. He would not think of her now.

Now he must focus. Absorb himself in the task at hand. The moment was here. And today, he would achieve perfection.

He collected his things from the narrow maple cabinet beside the door and arranged them on the round oak table.

Perched on a ladder-back chair, the raffia seat harsh against his thighs, he slipped a finger into the nearest volume and stared at the open page for precisely thirty seconds. Slamming it shut, he positioned the leather-bound tablet in front of him, uncapped his pen, and squeezed the rubber shaft until the nib bled a fine bead of ebony dew.

Ready, he opened the tablet and began writing.

Oedipus the King: Chorus

Sweet-voiced daughter of Zeus from thy gold-paved Pythian shrine.

Wafted to Thebes divine, What dost thou bring me? My soul is racked
and shivers with fear . . .
He wrote without pause, pen flying. Mind a vibrant reel.
Lord of the death-winged dart!
Your threshold aid I crave . . .
When he reached the bottom of the right-hand page, he crossed to the left and wrote right to left, bottom up, backward, recreating the original Greek.

Soaring. Unstoppable!

He was slick with sweat. Hair matted to his neck. Cheeks aflame.

But not yet finished. He felt the rumbling restlessness of powers yet untapped.

Turning the tablet to a fresh page, he selected two other volumes at random. Gardner's *Fundamentals of Neurology* and *The Cacti of Arizona* by Lyman Benson. He perused each for precisely sixty seconds. Flipping pages so quickly the print jiggled, and he raised a breeze.

His breath was coarse and shallow, pulse racing.

Stop!

He closed both volumes, opened a second pen, and tested its ink supply. Beside the leather tablet, he positioned a spiral binder filled with lined paper. Setting his internal timer to five minutes, he drew several deliberate breaths. Three hundred seconds precisely. Starting . . .

Now!

With his right hand, he wrote an essay on the leather-bound tablet on the microanatomy of the nervous system detailing the neuroglia, ependyma, and neurilemma. He discussed the distinction between true fibrous astrocytes and their pretenders, which could be found in the pituicytes of the neurohypophysis. Structure and function, purpose and pathology, embryological precursors. Analysis and synthesis. Contrast and comparison.

At the same time, his left hand filled the spiral binder with page after page of data on the new taxa and nomenclatural recombinations of cacti including the general opuntia, cereus, echinocereus, mammillaria, epithelantha

... He included graphs and charts on geographic distribution by species and a brief treatise on the species composition and geologic history of floras in the nine American regions of natural vegetation.

Time . . . up!

Panting, dripping sweat, he sat back. His neck ached, head throbbed. His fingers still clutched the pens in steel spasm.

Closing his eyes, he edged into a gentle descent. Emptied his mind and filled the void with feathery wisps. The low sputter of white noise. A light bath of neutral ions.

Five minutes precisely.

Cobb yawned. His ears popped. He rubbed his eyes and sought his place in a world washed clean. Gleaming. Lovely.

He drew himself upright and surveyed his work.

Perfect. magnificent! He was restored. How pleased she would be!

He ached to let her know, to contact her. But that was not the way. She had rebuked him. Cast him aside. Refused to answer his pleading letters, avoided his calls. She had to make the first overture.

Nothing to do but wait.

He stood at the window, peering out at the woods. His breath fogged the glass as he stared down the long, slender footpath toward the road. Occasionally, a car passed. Cobb could sense the tug of air, the drawn cloud of disturbed molecules in the distance.

Where was she?

Restless, he paced the room, stopping at intervals to straighten a picture or plump a pillow.

After seven circuits of the small space, he forced himself to sit in the rocker near the door. He passed a moment flipping through the binder and the tablet, perusing his exercises again. Flawless. Then there had been no doubt.

Perfect exercises, the manifestation of his renewal. Proof that he had done her bidding. He had sent her a note, telling her that it would be today. He'd explained his plan for taking the child – elegant in its simplicity, perfectly executed. But still there was no sign of her.

Panic nipped at the border of his mind. What if she did not feel the healing aura? What if she never came?

But no, that could not be. He had done everything. All she'd asked and more. By now, she must know. She must have heard!

With trembling fingers, he crossed and retrieved the local newspaper from a jumbled heap of reading matter in the corner of the room. Yes, it was there. He exulted at the oversized headline and the prime position of the story on the front page. It had been the day's most critical event. The focus of the entire community. Center of the eye of the world. So she must know.

Dusk consumed the silent sky and cast snips of shadow on the cabin floor. With his keen inner ear, Cobb listened to the muted thunder of his heart, the lapping tides of his circulating blood, the sizzle of his mounting fear.

He ached for the distant flicker of her approaching headlights, the sight of her looming shadow crossing the stone patio. But with a growing weight of anguish, he realized it was not to be. Not today.

What was that?

A sword of heat slashed the base of his neck. He felt the inexorable draw of the bitter blue vapor. Draining him.

No!

He strained against it, but he could feel his power seeping away. Impossible. It was too soon. Getting worse.

He struggled to maintain his control. There was a way out, he soothed himself. Salvation. He would take what he needed from the child.

The child was his.

6 Cinnie stared through the frosted glass panel separating James's bed from the nurses' station on Fairview's pediatric intensive care unit. She was mesmerized by the wavering silhouettes and darting shadows. Something distant and comforting in the scene. Like gazing through the window of a diving bell at a hushed, liquid universe.

Nothing to do with her.

She was numb with exhaustion. Insulated. In the five days since the accident she'd become one with the deadening rhythms of the ward. Another piece of machinery.

James was stable. A hopeless term for interminable waiting. No change. No progress. But at least there had been no further incidents of cardiac arrest. With a shudder she recalled the three times the first day when the green line on the cardiac monitor had gone flat, and he'd needed resuscitation.

Her heart had stopped with his while the massive needles were jabbed into his chest, the paddles positioned. She could still feel the sympathetic jolt as the current passed through him. And she relived the terrible moment before the flat line wavered and danced again on the black screen.

Dr. Ferris had stopped by and tried to explain the episodes in his cool, clinical way. No brain damage was evident, but there might have been some insult to the brain stem. Only temporary, he'd said. They would watch James closely, but Ferris was confident that the cardiac crisis was over. Cinnie had clung to the doctor's assurances as if to a life preserver. They were all she felt she could trust in a world turned on its head and jumbled beyond recognition.

Stable was far from the worst thing, Cinnie thought. Be *grateful*.

Her breathing was tuned to the steady beeps and hums

of James's mechanical aids and monitors. The sounds were an itch at the far edge of her consciousness, irritating and yet oddly comforting like an intractable drip from a familiar faucet.

From time to time she forced herself to look at her little boy. With shock-induced detachment she noted the steel pin anchoring his fractured leg to a traction rig, the medley of tubes and fluid sacs suspended from a metal pole that provided him with nourishment and medications.

Every so often, she stood to pace the stingy span between the cubicle's walls. Three steps over and three back to the single straight-backed chair.

Only parents were permitted to visit on the unit, and only for five minutes each hour. While she waited outside, the time seemed impossibly inadequate. But once she'd stepped back into the cubicle, taken her first anxious look at James, and confirmed that things were exactly the same, she was left with nothing to do but pace or sit staring through the glass divider.

When her five minutes were up, she would drift out to the waiting room, an airless, overlit square filled with anxious people and prehistoric magazines. There, other parents asked solicitous questions in tender tones. She answered with as much accuracy as she could muster. 'Hit by a car,' she'd say. 'No, they're not sure about anything yet. We'll have to wait and see.' They would nod in reply, their eyes filled with knowing sorrow. And then they would tell her about their own impossible circumstances in voices frosted with disbelief.

She could sense the instant closeness between the huddled knots of strangers in that awful room. It was a feeling she missed. She couldn't seem to remember the way to connect with anyone. Even her bond with James seemed fragile, a brittle filament where once there had been a massive steel cable.

Friends and relatives came, stayed for an anxious while, and disappeared. Paul couldn't bear the place for more than a few minutes at a time, and Cinnie found it easier not to have him around.

The accident lay between them like a gaping wound. She could nether blame him nor forgive him. The sight of him, once enough to melt her bones, now left her chilled and empty. She was startled by the changes in him, changes she hadn't noticed before. There was a rough, wary edge to his once-boyish features, and much of the magnetic glint in his hazel eyes had been webbed over and dulled like a long neglected room. Cinnie found herself irritated by the habits she used to find endearing: the way he fiddled with his sandy hair while he talked on the phone, the tilt to his head when he was listening, his distracted humming when he wasn't.

She kept going over the first impossible conversation they'd had a couple of hours after the accident, when he'd finally showed up in the emergency room. Cinnie recognized the signs of recording studio overdose. His eyes were ringed with exhaustion, his face smudged with whisker stubble, and he trailed a stale scent of used air and tobacco.

'What happened, Cin? Is he all right?'

'I don't know yet. They're still working on him. . . . Where the hell were you, Paul? Why didn't you meet the bus?'

'The studio clock was an hour off. There must've been a power outage during the night. I didn't realize until . . .'

'You didn't realize – ' A mob of angry questions were pressing at her. How could he make such a mistake? Why hadn't he checked his watch? How could he be so careless? James could have been killed. Still might not make it. She clenched her fists and felt the furious words jam in her throat like stones. They were too unthinkable to let out. Too dangerous.

For once, she was glad to see Lydia Holroyd, who came barging into the waiting room like a sudden storm. Her hair was pulled back in a taut chignon that sharpened her already stern features.

'You poor, poor dears. I came as soon as I heard.' She clacked her tongue. 'You look dreadful, the two of you. Well, not to worry. I'm going to ring up my friend Walter

Kampmann in administration and make sure James is being seen to properly. Walter adores me.'

Cinnie and Paul watched Lydia's performance on the pay phone in the corner of the waiting room. She spoke in a grand, theatrical aside. 'Yes, Walter, dear. That's lovely to hear. I knew I could count on you, darling. Certainly, I'll tell them.'

Lydia hung up with a flourish. 'All taken care of. Walter will see to it that James has the best of everything. He said you should ring him right up if there are any difficulties at all. Now . . . '

She started pulling things out of the large black canvas tote she carried: plastic stacking toys, popbeads, a busy box. 'It occurred to me that James might enjoy some of Todd's old things while he's here.'

Baby toys. Leave it to Lydia. Woman had an uncanny talent for insensitivity. But Cinnie was too numb to be hurt by Lydia or anyone else. Too terrified.

For Cinnie, most of the other visitors blended in a blur of vague impressions. There was Dal's pillowy hug. Paul's parents leaning together in a human tepee. Cinnie's father and his new wife, Madeline, holding hands. There were endless doctors armed with studied expressions and legally correct remarks. A parade of brusque, efficient nurses referred to James as the hit-run in three. A reporter from the local paper stopped by to tell Cinnie that a number of local groups had posted a sizable reward for information about the hit-and-run driver. He proudly displayed his paper's cover story about James's accident. The headline had hit Cinnie like a blow: 'Fresh Tragedy Strikes Tyler's Grove.'

One of the few who stuck out in her mind was Charles Allston, deputy chief of detectives from the Stamford police force. Allston had been put in charge of investigating the hit-run, but he seemed far more eager to have the case done with than solved.

Cinnie had disliked him on sight, with his arrogant carriage and bloodless aristocratic face. And he'd confirmed her negative impression immediately. The creep was convinced that James was responsible for his own injuries.

'Let's face it, Mrs. Merritt,' Allston had said. 'Five-year-old boys are impulsive. He probably ran into the street without realizing a car was coming.'

'James would never do that. You don't know him.'

Indulgent chuckle. 'My wife is the same way. Never thinks those kids of ours can do any wrong. Women.'

Allston had so irritated Cinnie that she'd called Chief Carmody to ask if someone else could be put in charge of the case. Carmody had done a tap dance. Cinnie was left with the clear impression that this particular assignment was beyond his control. Apparently, Deputy Chief Allston had friends in very high places.

Politics. Even in intensive care, you couldn't escape them.

Two precious minutes remained before she'd be asked to leave the ICU for this hour. She checked her watch for the thousandth time and made a fresh resolution. James would wake up by this time tomorrow. No later than five p.m. sharp. He would rub his eyes and tell Cinnie he was starved. Then he would ask her if it was time for his favorite show: reruns of *Little House on the Prairie*. They would watch together while he ate. It would be a happy episode, she decided, definitely not the one when Mary went blind or the time the baby died in a fire.

She wondered if they'd start him on a liquid diet. She considered that he might be too weak to feed himself and she would have to find a way to help him that didn't bruise his fragile sense of big-boy dignity. Those were the worst possibilities she allowed herself to entertain.

The charge nurse, a perky cheerleader type named Amy Lyttle, poked her head in and told Cinnie it was time to leave. Dal was in the waiting room. Even now, Cinnie was cheered by the sight of her friend's flashing blue eyes and puckish expression. Everything about Dal was generous: heart, smile, shape, affections.

'How's it going?' Dal said.

'It's not.'

'Did you have it out with him?'

Cinnie met Dal's firm gaze and looked away. 'Paul, you mean? No. What's the point?'

Dal sighed. 'The point is to get the whole awful business off your chest before it suffocates you. Telling *me* how you feel isn't enough, Cin. If Rick pulled a stunt like not meeting TeeJay's bus on time, I'd kill him. I'd poke his eyes out and kick his butt around the block and tell his mother all his secrets. And that would be for starters.'

Cinnie's eyes welled up. 'It's different with us.'

'Different, shmifferent. Paul screwed up, and James got hurt. Yell at him, Cin. Let him have it, and you'll feel better. You'll both feel better.'

'It's not that easy. Anyway, that's not what's bugging me. I just keep thinking about all the kids who've been hurt in the Grove. All in the last year and a half. It's so crazy, Dal. How can there be so many?'

Dal's face went grave. 'Look, you need a break, Cin. You're getting paranoid. Go home for a while. Take a nap. Soak in the tub. Get a decent dinner. I'll stay here.'

'I can't.'

'Yes you can. It so happens I can pace and worry every bit as well as you can. Better in fact.'

Cinnie's lip quivered. 'I know. It's just . . . '

Dal wrapped her in a hug and rubbed soothing circles on her back. 'I know, Cin. It's impossible.'

The damned anguish swelled and spilled over. For the first time since learning of James's accident, Cinnie gave in to her grief. She stood in the warm circle of her friend's arms until the sobs had gentled to a syncopated pulse.

'Thanks, I needed that.' She plucked a tissue from the box at the reception desk and blew her nose with a honk.

Dal's eyes crinkled. 'Now that's the Cinnie I know and love. All class. Go on now. Take a break. You won't be any use to James if you get yourself sick.'

Cinnie was stuck in place. She'd been sleeping on one of the waiting room's stone couches, showering in the cramped patient bathroom. She was terrified to leave

37

James alone in this place. Afraid the feeble link between them would snap to nothing if she did.

'I'll be right here,' Dal said. 'I promise.'

Cinnie nodded. Dal was the only one who seemed to understand. James had to be protected.

'Okay, I'll get some air and be back in a couple of minutes.'

'Two hours – minimum. If Paul's not here, I'll sneak in for the five minute visits.'

'A half hour, Dal. Be reasonable.'

'Don't be a wiseass, Cin. I'm bigger. Now scram.'

She ran into Dr. Ferris at the elevators. As always, the pediatrician was perfectly groomed and immaculate. According to his receptionist, Ferris spent the first twenty minutes of each day locked in the office restroom, scrubbing as if for surgery. It fit with the man's unimpeachable image of calm, professional control.

'Mrs. Merritt,' he said with a crisp nod. 'On your way home?'

'No. Just taking a break.'

He nodded, his expresson inscrutable. 'I've seen James's latest blood values. Everything's coming along nicely.'

'That's good.'

'He's doing fine, Mrs. Merritt. I would tell you if he weren't.'

Cinnie felt relieved. Ferris was not one to offer empty praise or encouragement. Cinnie had an urge to hug him, but she imagined he'd turn to salt if anyone tried to slip inside his flawless professional shell. She remembered trying to explain her loyalty to Dr. Ferris when she'd recommended him to Dal. 'He's a terrific doctor, but not exactly the warm, fuzzy type.'

'Then why use him?'

'I told you, he's superb at what he does. Solid, thorough, up-to-the-minute. You want TeeJay healthy, you go to Ferris. You want cuddly and affectionate, you call your mother in Florida.'

Standing under the concrete awning at the hospital's main entrance, Cinnie drew her blue coat tighter around her and turtled into the upturned collar. She was cold. Sore. Overwhelmed by the vibrancy and volume of this alien world. The air was thick as cream. The wind a shriek. Someone had turned the streetlights up so high the glare made her eyes water.

With no particular plan or expectation, she began walking. Down the long, circular driveway. Past Prescott Street and over toward Summer. As she crossed the four-lane street, cars materialized out of the ether, twice missing her so narrowly she could feel the angry heat of their exhaust. Horns blew. And a disembodied voice was hurled like a brick from a car that screeched to a stop half a block away, 'Crazy broad, you trying to get yourself killed?'

She passed the Ridgeway Center strip mall, where the lot was jammed and a steady stream of early holiday shoppers passed like a current from store to store. Lights gleamed from a triple strand of condominiums. A truck clattered out of the delivery drive for the Tara Hotel.

She turned onto High Ridge Road, one of a pair of meandering arteries that linked sleepy North Stamford to its distant urban core. Paul liked to say that Stamford was the best of all possible places to live. Where else could one find all the crime and punishment of a big city combined with all the parochialism and inconvenience of a small town?

Still, neither of them had ever been inclined to move. They liked the city's multiple personalities. Enjoyed the rambling patchwork of neighborhoods. They'd picked Tyler's Grove for the farmhouse with its endearing eccentricities and affordable price. And they'd convinced themselves that the neighborhood was no better or worse than any other.

But increasingly, Cinnie was forced to consider that the tranquil enclave of dappled lawns and coddled houses masked an inexplicable dark side. The newspaper headline had picked up the thread. 'Fresh tragedy . . . '

There had been so many.

In the past eighteen months, one neighbor child had fallen through thin ice on the community pond and suffered brain damage. Another had lost two fingers and an eye when a firecracker he'd found exploded in his hand. An eight-year-old on Strawberry Patch Lane had disappeared on his way home from school, sparking a massive search and rumors of a madman on the loose. The boy had been found a week later, dazed and filthy, wandering in the arboretum a mile away. From what Cinnie had heard, he'd been unharmed physically. But he rarely spoke anymore, had to be schooled at home, and suffered hellish nightmares. Late nights, in her half sleep, she sometimes thought she heard his screams. The crazed keening of a trapped animal.

And now, this string of traffic accidents. A boy killed. Little Laurel Druce, who still walked with a rolling limp and a gleam of pain in her eyes.

James.

Cinnie's mind filled with his giggles, the curious tilt of his head, his unbounded enthusiasms. She could see him kicking a soccer ball, hair flapping, tongue burrowing in his cheek. She pictured him doing his Bruce Springsteen imitation in a T-shirt and tight jeans. She could see him wielding the toilet paper tube he used as a microphone, wiggling a little backside shaped like twin parker house rolls, doing a squint-eyed lip sync to 'Born in the USA'.

She was not about to lose that priceless child. Not without a gargantuan struggle. With a fresh charge of determination, Cinnie turned and headed back toward the hospital.

It had never been her way to go gently. For the first time since the accident, she felt a sense of purpose. She had to find a way to get through to her little boy.

First, she would go back to where it had happened. Stand in his place. Feel what he felt.

The Volvo sat in the center of the hospital lot where Paul had parked it for her three days ago. The old bomb was cranky with the cold and neglect, but Cinnie pumped and prodded until it came reluctantly alive.

She drove north on High Ridge and maneuvered through the maze of narrow streets toward the Grove. She deflected the terrible memory of the last time she'd made the trip. The police, the shock. Living it again wasn't going to get her anywhere. She angled through the broken pillars and parked the car.

Across Mill Road she stood at the exact spot where James's bus driver always pulled over to let him off. She peered at their farmhouse, second building past the pillars on the right, looming cold and still as drifted snow.

Knowing it was what James would have done, she mounted the grassy rise opposite the stone columns. She spotted the trail of rake marks the evidence squad had made in the frigid soil. Her feet crunched in the mounds of dead leaves. A twig snapped. The chill climbed her legs like a platoon of frozen spiders and settled at the base of her spine.

There was an icy stillness. Cinnie imagined what James must have thought. Nobody there. No one coming to get him. What had he felt? Hunger? Cold? A twinge of worry?

From High Ridge Road over two miles away came the steady whoosh of passing cars. Not a hint of anything approaching closer to where she stood.

She stared at the stone pillars. Slipped into James's skin. Looked with his eyes. At the time the bus had dropped him off, no one had been around. Likely all he had had for company was the Pavan's rangy pair of Afghan hounds loping back and forth on their run and the Goldblatt's lazy calico snoozing on the left stone pedestal he had claimed as his own. James must have waited for what seemed to him an eternity. Still nobody coming to meet him. So he'd decided he had no choice but to cross on his own.

Cinnie could almost hear him thinking it through. Can't stand here forever. Have to get home one way or another. Maybe they forgot. Or maybe something is wrong at home. Someone sick . . .

She could picture him drawing a deep breath, squaring his shoulders, and lifting his chin. I'm a big boy. I can do it, he'd say, working hard to convince himself. I'll just be very, very careful. And then he'd take a deliberate look in both directions the way Cinnie had instructed him a thousand times. She could see him clearly, cocking his head to listen, checking a final time to make sure there wasn't a hint of crouching danger he'd overlooked.

All clear.

Go!

She imagined him moving into the street. One step, two. and then from nowhere . . .

Cinnie could hear the scream of brakes. Feel the jolt of terror. The paralyzing shock. No!

She waited for her pulse to subside, the roaring in her head muted to a distant rumble. She imagined James lying in a crumpled heap on the frozen ground, ringed by a halo of spattered blood. She pictured the driver fleeing in a mindless panic, leaving James hurt and alone.

What if he hadn't been seen by a passerby? What kind of a monster could have abandoned her hurt baby like that? Her gut roiled with murderous rage. She desperately wanted the driver caught and punished. But all the police had come up with so far was one sketchy witness account.

The bus always delivered James at twelve sharp. On the day of the accident, Lydia Holroyd had driven by a few minutes past noon on her way to pick up Todd at school for a dentist appointment. Approaching the corner of Mill Road, Lydia had heard a car stop short, and then she'd seen a maroon sedan speeding toward Cascade. Nosy Lydia had noticed that the car had New York plates. A youngish man with blond hair was at the wheel. If only she'd known at the time that James was lying injured on the road bank. If only she'd paid better attention.

Cinnie stared at the somber sky. Dense clouds denied the faintest gleam of starlight. No amount of fevered hoping would speed the end of this nightmare, Cinnie realized. All she could do was be there for her son.

7 Cinnie went through the farmhouse, collecting James's most critical possessions in a pair of shopping bags. She tried to ignore the musty scent of the place, the creepy stillness. She hadn't been back since the accident, and the house had taken on an alien, uneasy feeling. Paul had left things in a shambles: crumpled napkins, soiled plates, glasses puddled with milk. Cinnie ignored a spark of anger. This was far from the worst mess he'd made.

Methodically, she packed a pile of story books, part of James's stuffed bear collection, a battered GI Joe doll, Snoopy pajamas, Yankee slippers, a Walkman, Speak & Spell, GoBots, wrestling posters of Andre the Giant and Randy 'Macho Man' Savage, and a Lego space station kit. There were a number of things she couldn't find: James's favorite T-shirt from the Los Angeles Hard Rock Cafe, the superhero cape she'd bought him for Halloween. In vain she searched for his precious backpack. She made a mental note to ask the police if it had been found at the scene and claimed for evidence.

On the way to the hospital she stopped to pick up a few other things for James. She wanted to surround him with everything he loved. Half an hour later, she entered the ICU waiting room burdened with a medley of paper bags. Dal took one look at her and left happy. Clearly Cinnie was on the brink of returning to her normal exacting standard of lunacy.

When it was time for the next five-minute visit, Cinnie arranged the bears at the foot of James's bed, stowed the books and toys on the carts supporting the monitors, taped the wrestling posters over the glass partition, and blew up a cluster of Mylar balloons. Satisfied, she sat on the bed beside him and took his hand.

'No more of this tuned-out lazy business, James Lucas

Merritt. It's time for you to wake up and get ready for some serious playing.'

She stared at him. Searched for a hint of response. But aside from the occasional tic or grimace, he was stone.

'Come on, Jimbo. I've got big plans for us. First we'll play sumo wrestlers. You get to throw the salt in the ring and sell tickets to the invisible crowd. I'll run the imaginary popcorn stand and do the announcing and declare you champion of the universe. What do you say?'

Nothing.

But she couldn't bring herself to give up. 'How about a blind cookie tasting then? I picked up a half pound of assorted from Mrs. Fields and a half pound of mixed macadamia, pecan, and double chunk from David's. I'll smuggle in some root beer for a palate cleaner, and we can really go to hell with ourselves.'

His head was lolling off center. Gently, she repositioned it and smoothed a ripple of tension from his forehead. 'Tell you what. You wake up right now, and I'll throw in a bedtime moratorium. Think of it, you can stay up forever if you want. We can watch *Arsenio Hall* or *Letterman*, and then we'll find a couple of old flicks to take us right into *Sunrise Semester*. I bet you've never seen a single thing starring Lionel Barrymore or Jimmy Stewart.'

She watched him, willing a response. A sign. 'This is a limited-time-only offer, James Merritt. Better hurry on down.'

There was the rasp of a throat clearing behind her.

Paul.

He looked weary and rumpled. His face was pale, his eyes shot with veins and sunken with exhaustion. The wind had tossed his sandy hair and left a stray wave lolling over his forehead. She felt a swell of affection that was quicky displaced by anger.

'How's he doing?'

Furious words leapt to her tongue, but she bit them back. 'Coming along.'

'I ran into Dr. Silver in the lobby, Cin. I asked him

to tell me what we can expect – honestly. . . . He wasn't encouraging.'

'Silver's a troll,' Cinnie said and turned back to James. 'Tell you what, Jimbo. You wake up right now, and I'll throw in a weekend at Hershey Park this summer and a whole week at Disney World over next Christmas vacation. Every man has his price, right, sweetheart?'

Paul touched her shoulder. She stiffened until he took the hand away. 'We have to be realistic, Cin. Silver said the longer he stays in a coma, the less chance he has for a full recovery. Silver said at this point we'd better prepare ourselves for the worst. He may not come around at all. And if he does, chances are he'll be brain damaged.'

'No. James is going to be fine.' *James*. She noticed Paul couldn't bring himself to use their child's name. Always saying 'he'. Was he feeling so guilty he couldn't bring himself to acknowledge this wounded little boy as his son? Or maybe he thought a damaged child was like a troubled marriage or an imperfect recording – something to be thrown away and forgotten.

'What if he isn't? What if he can't walk or talk anymore, Cin? What if he's severely retarded? God, Cinnie – '

'Stop it. He doesn't need to hear things like that.'

Tears puddled in his eyes and a drop trailed the hollow of his cheek. His lip trembled. 'I wish . . . '

She stoked James's forehead. Her voice was trembling with rage. 'Tell your daddy that Dr. Silver is a board-certified jackass who specializes in overcharging. Tell him that even the best doctors don't know everything. Tell him how you intend to show all those Dr. Buttbrains that you are the one and only James Lucas Merritt – man of steel.'

'Please, Cin . . . '

Cinnie swung around, eyes blazing. 'Please what, Paul? Please act like he's a hopeless case because you say so? Please give up? Well, I'm not giving up on James. If that's what you want to do, go do it someplace else. The last thing he needs right now is someone to drag him down. . . . Now, Jimbo, let's get down to business here. Books or radio? Okay, then, which book would you like me to read first?'

She heard Paul hesitate behind her. She couldn't look at him. Couldn't find any more words. The silence was so enormous, she feared it would swallow her whole if she moved or took a breath. She was stuck in place until he left.

Cinnie picked a book out of the pile, *Alexander and the Terrible, Horrible, No Good, Very Bad Day*. Perfect.

By the time she turned the final page, her five precious minutes were up. The charge nurse passed from cubicle to cubicle, inviting visitors to leave. Cinnie found Paul waiting in the lobby. He had the same whipped puppy expression that claimed James's face when he knew he'd done something naughty.

James had always been so much like Paul: looks, temperament. In a way, both of them were little boys trying too hard to play tough and independent. Couldn't be an easy act to keep up. Cinnie could see the toll it had taken on Paul. Sympathy blunted the remains of her anger.

'Don't listen to Silver. He's just covering his behind. He's afraid we'll sue him if he commits the mortal sin of optimism.'

'I hope you're right, Cin.'

'I am. I have to be.'

Their eyes locked. She felt an impossible mix of emotions: love, hurt, sorrow, terrible loneliness. 'Think you can spare a hug for the hug-starved, mister.'

Funny what a perfect fit they were, even now. Everything solid, warm, and achingly familiar. Her cheek settled in the hollow of his shoulder, his cheek pressed against her hair. She wished she could sink in the feeling and disappear. But nothing was ever that simple.

Visiting hours ended at nine. After Paul left, Cinnie curled up on the blue couch in the corner of the waiting room and drifted into an uneasy sleep. She dreamed James was playing basketball, charging up and down a polished court.

Crowds of feet trampling. A tangle of straining arms. Taffy strips aching skyward. James stretched tall and lanky. Face beaming. Little-boy face on a lithe body. Nothing he can't do. Go James!

'Mrs. Merritt? Mrs. Merritt? Wake up.'

Cinnie started. A plump, growl-faced nurse with a halo of kinky gray hair was standing over her. Her mouth went dry. A vicious pulse rose in her temples, and she tensed for the worst.

'What's wrong? Is it James? Is he . . . ?'

A grin softened the woman's harsh features. 'James is fine, Mrs. Merritt. In fact, he's asking for you.'

8

When the phone rang, Jeremiah Drum had Booker two pawns down and was closing in on a critical rook.

Booker shot him a look of tepid curiosity and resumed studying his position. His elbows were planted on the dining room table, palms cradling his jaw.

Another ring.

'Ain't for me,' Booker said with a hitch of his slim shoulders.

'*Isn't* for you, hotshot.'

'Like I said.'

Drum took his sweet time sauntering across the room. Two more rings. Probably someone trying to sell him carpet cleaning or get him to contribute to the Committee to Save the Onion Bagel.

Damned phone had been ringing all night. Nothing but robots or robot imitators on the other end. Everyone wanting something. And Drum was in no mood for distractions. Chess required total attention. So did a kid. He stood with a hand on the receiver, stalling.

Booker's chocolate skin was freckled with pins of light from the crystal chandelier. His onyx eyes gleamed like a mirror in the dark. There was a hard set to his mouth.

Same look he'd sported when he'd tried to sell Drum the hot Rolex. Hard to believe that was almost a year ago already.

At the time, Drum had been working undercover on a sting operation. Fat real-estate scam. An enterprising syndicate of local greediest cases had been peddling shares in a giant mall project. Would've been fine except for a little flaw in their arithmetic. The sold portions already added up to two hundred and sixty percent, and the principals were still looking to lure more pigeons into the deal.

Shares were going in the half-million range, minimum,

so Drum knew he had to pass for a high roller. Chief Carmody had squawked plenty, but Drum had managed to squeeze him for the custom cashmere suit, Ferragamo wing tips, and silk accessories that were, as Drum had patiently explained, bare necessities. Carmody had also blown for the hundred-dollar haircut and the rented Mercedes 560 Drum was lounging against when the kid sidled up out of nowhere hawking the watch.

Kid had big eyes. Cold as buckshot. Drum knew the look and the feeling behind it. 'Only three bills, Mister. No tax. Big bargain.'

Drum had taken a long, hard look. The Rolex was real: real gold, real diamonds, real hot, as in grand larceny. The kid was something else: lean, quick, and cagey. Junkyard pup. Couldn't have been more than eight or nine from the look of him, though Drum could also tell from the look of him that they'd been eight or nine hard ones.

Drum had done the only thing possible under the circumstances. He clamped a hand on the kid's scrawny wrist and flashed his shield. 'Jackpot, junior. You're under arrest.'

Kid didn't flinch. 'Okay, okay. Make it two-fifty then. Special cop discount.'

The little crook had balls. But those weren't near his best assets. Drum had pegged him right away as redeemable. Not like certain dead-eyed punks who tried to pass themselves off as children in the worst of lousy neighborhoods. Some of them were way beyond saving by this kid's age. But this one was still in the play. Spunky. And plenty smart. Which, Drum knew, could work for or against him, depending.

For a couple of nights, the country had put the kid up in a pip-squeak detention center. Not a good place, but probably way better than Booker was used to. At least there he got hot meals, clean sheets, a talking-to when he needed one. Drum had dropped by a couple of times to see how it was going, and even with the parade of strangers and the uncertainty, the boy's pluck showed no signs of wilting. Drum admired that in a kid. In anyone.

When social services finally came in with the background report, there were no surprises. Poor little gutter rat had a jailed druggie mother and no known father, which, Drum figured, was why he chose to go by first name only. He'd been living with a grandmother who'd died after a brutal mugging a couple of years back.

As Booker had explained it to the social worker, the punks weren't satisfied with the couple of bucks the old lady was carrying when they grabbed her purse. So they'd expressed their disappointment with the business end of Louisville Slugger.

Next morning, Booker had found what was left of her outside the door of their apartment. She'd managed to make it that far before she collapsed. The kid had called nine-one-one, though he could see there was no more emergency. In that neighborhood, you got to know what dead was at a tender age.

Soon, the tenement had been crawling with uniforms. Booker had taken advantage of the confusion and disappeared. Last thing he wanted was to go 'on the state'. Which was a sentiment Drum could more than appreciate.

Since then, the kid had been scraping by on his own. Living here and there. Running errands. Doing odd jobs. No bad stuff, as Booker was quick to assert in his own defense. The worst he ran were betting slips, he said with an expression that reeked of innocence. The direct sales business was a sideline. He only brokered what fell his way, and he only dealt in life's wholesome necessities: gold chains, fancy watches, exotic leather goods.

Bottom line was he handed most of his earnings over to a two-legged, half-ton reptile predictably known as Tiny. In exchange, Tiny had allowed Booker to keep on breathing his minimum daily requirement of air.

The rest was predictable. Medical neglect, malnutrition. Chronic truancy. And those were the high points. Drum had read the sad story cover to cover and decided to hold on to the kid himself until someone managed to arrange a decent, permanent home.

Otherwise, he knew Booker would be tossed like an

undersized fish into the foster care system. He'd be shunted from place to place until he aged out or ran away or some of both. Drum knew the script by heart, and it was nobody's idea of a comedy.

Stella had pretended to be furious when Drum showed up with the kid in tow. 'Jeez, Jerry,' she said. 'Not another one of your strays.'

But Drum could see she was melting behind the frown. Her eyes smiled as she inspected Booker's nails, checked behind his ears, and ordered the kid to take a long, hot bath.

'Don't be stingy with the soap, mister. And then we're going shopping for some new clothes. And you look like you need a cheeseburger, fries, and a milkshake badly.'

Stella was Mother Earth. Thick-hipped and steady. Bosom you could get lost in for days. Watching her with Booker, Drum regretted that they hadn't been able to have any kids of their own. Woman was made for a houseful of noisy kids.

Booker had responded to Stella's mothering with his baby pimp swagger and a burst of hip, angry muttering under his breath. Kid obviously wasn't used to being treated like a kid. But Drum could see it was going to be okay. Stella had a knack for bringing out the best in people. Woman could find the single sugar cube in a truckload of horseshit. She'd even managed to see something worth salvaging in Drum. And that had to have taken a pile of imagination.

Anyway, Brooker would only be with them for a little while. Drum kept telling himself the kid would be placed in a real home in a week or two.

So it hadn't turned out to be as easy as Drum had expected. So what was?

Booker moved his threatened rook and crossed his arms. 'That's check, Mr. Drum.' The kid's face lit up like a Roman candle. 'I got you in mate in three moves. Resign?'

'Like hell you do. Don't you touch that board. Put those sneaky little paws of yours where I can watch them.' The phone had quit for an instant and started up again. Drum gave in and answered.

'Drum? Dan Carmody here. Hope I'm not interrupting anything.'

'Dan Carmody? Sorry, the only Dan Carmody I know is the chief of the Stamford police department. And no way that sonavabitch would be calling an excommunicated useless scumbag such as myself.' He winked at Booker. Kid rolled his eyes.

'Okay, Jerry. Have it your way. I got something for you. But if you're not interested . . . '

Drum hesitated. But not for long. He'd been on unpaid suspension from the force for three months. Three more to go, and already the unpaid bills had taken on a life and unpleasant personality of their own.

'I might be. Depends what it is.'

A chuckle. 'Something right up your alley. Trust me.'

'Said the snake.'

'All right, mouth. You want to be mad at me for putting you on ice for a while? That's your privilege. I did what I had to do.'

'So did I, Carmody.'

'You knew the rules, Jerry. You don't go around busting people up, no matter how hard they're begging for it. You especially don't bust up people named DiBiasi. Half the town was breathing down my neck after you trashed those punks. Screaming about police brutality like those boys were fresh from the altar at St. Leo's. I had no choice about the suspension, and you know it.'

Drum smoldered in silence awhile. Pissed him off when Carmody was right. He knew he should have been content to simply collar those two turds when he caught them working a crack franchise in one of the elementary schools, but his fists had gotten in the way of his judgment. Old story.

'I know, Carmody. You suspended me for my own good. And I'm grateful, really.'

'That's nice, Drum. So you interested in a little work or not?'

'I said depends. What's the gig?'

'Not now. Never met a phone I could trust. I'll meet you at the place where we nailed the thin man. You know where I'm talking about?'

'Yeah, okay. Half hour?'

'Check.'

That word again. Drum winced as he hung up and locked eyes with Booker. 'What'd you pull, you little weasel? You scamming me?'

'No way, man. You left yourself wide open. You figured I'm going with a Sicilian defense, I'm playing by the book, right? Last thing you figured was a two-pawn sacrifice. You ask me, you wasn't paying good attention.'

Drum examined the board for a few minutes, shook his head, and tossed a buck on the table. 'You know you could throw a game my way once in a while, hotshot. I'm an old man.'

'You ain't that old.'

Drum patted the kid's head and pinched his cheek. Filling out nicely now that Stella was stuffing him like he was a turkey two weeks before Thanksgiving. 'Okay then, I'll roast your rump fair and square tomorrow. Right now, I gotta go out for a while.'

'Where you going, Mr. Drum? How 'bout I go with you?'

Drum hesitated. The kid's eyes were full of pleading. Runt knew how to make a case.

'Stella wouldn't like that, Book. You know how she feels about you turning in early on school nights. How about I call that foxy Mary Ellen from next door? Bet she'll come over and tuck you in and give you a fat smooch good night, you lucky creep.'

Booker wasn't buying. 'Mrs. Drum's out singing at that lounge place in Norwalk tonight. Bet she'll be there singing 'til way, way after we get back.'

'Can't count on that, kid. And even if she is, you can't get a damned thing past that woman. Believe me, I've tried.'

Booker had on his blue down jacket already. He zipped

it halfway up and flopped on the hood. 'I'll take my chances. I'm going wth you.'

'You'll be grounded. We'll both be grounded. Probably for life.'

'I ain't afraid. You?'

Drum grabbed the kid by the scruff and led him out to the garage. Booker was fizzing over like a fresh-tapped keg.

'Who we after, Mr. Drum? Whose bad ass we gonna fry?'

'Ours, kid. I told you. Stella finds out I let you come along with me, she'll shoot first and ask questions later. You don't want to cross that woman, Book. She gets fierce like you can't imagine.'

'How 'bout we stop on the way back at the A and P and get Mrs. Drum some of those real nice pink flowers she likes so much?'

Drum laughed. 'Good idea, hotshot. You're buying.'

'You gonna let me start the car, Mr. Drum? You gonna let me work the radio? I'm your deputy, right?'

'Right. Only when I talk to the chief, you gotta make yourself real scarce, okay? Invisible. He wants this thing kept strictly under wraps. Top, *top* secret, you dig?'

'Yeah, I ain't no big mouth. What you think he's got cooking, Mr. Drum? You think maybe his wife's fooling around on him and he wants you to go nail the guy?'

They drove down High Ridge Road, across Washington Boulevard, and out through Booker's old neighborhood. Drum stole a peek at the kid, wondering if he felt lonely for any of it.

Plenty of local color. They passed hookers in bayonet heels and spandex skirts the size of Band-Aids, a bustling open-air drug market, packs of fidgety kids idling on street corners. There was a body: dead, drunk or both, lying facedown on the sidewalk in a puddle of something Drum chose not to consider. The broad plate window fronting an appliance shop had been smashed. Third store tossed on the block this week according to the local rag, and it was only Monday. No place like home.

If Booker felt nostalgic, it didn't show. He was glued to

the third-grade spelling list. Mouthing the words, closing his eyes and playing them back in his mind. Kid was determined to win the upcoming citywide bee. Now that he'd had a taste of winning, hotshot wanted to do it all the time. Weird how he could read in the dark.

They drove under the Connecticut Turnpike and through a maze of side streets toward the slice of the city nestled along the shore of the Long Island Sound. Strips of factories and warehouses yielded to condo complexes, restaurants with ferns, and trendy surfside boutiques. Drum could remember when this was miles and miles of all the nothing you could ever want. Anyone could own it then. Or think they did.

Drum wanted to warn Booker about thoughts like that. Kid didn't have to make the same mistakes Drum had. Seemed only right he should get the chance to make new ones of his own.

Drum killed the lights as he aimed the Mustang through the broad gap in the wire fence at Intell Industries, a think tank serving several of Fairfield County's fat-cat corporations. As Drum understood it, companies paid hefty fees to rent Intell's resident brains so they didn't have to put a strain on their own.

And people accused him of scamming.

He swerved the car around to the back of the main building, a soaring cement box overlooking the frothy gray surface of the Sound. Tomb with a view.

The last time he'd come to this place, it was to pick up a load of trash named Drew Whittaker, a tall character so emaciated you could read his veins like a road map and count his ribs through his overcoat. During the investigation, the cops had taken to calling him the 'thin man'. Joke around the station was that Whittaker was nothing but three hundred bones and a boner.

The thin man had been one of Intell's top minds. Turned out that when he wasn't cooking up ideas for his client corporations, his thoughts turned to the little girls he abducted at knife point and brought to Intell's parking lot after hours.

Chief Carmody's unmarked was idling in a dark delivery bay, spitting fat lines of exhaust. Drum edged into the sliver of remaining space in the bay and flung open the Mustang's door so it kissed Carmody's Town Car hard on the cheek. There was the sharp crunch of metal biting metal.

Carmody yelped. 'Shit, Jerry. What the hell was that about?'

Drum stepped out and inspected the driver's side of his black beauty, vintage 1969, low mileage, original engine. Despite his scrupulous care, he'd noticed lately that the finish was fading and showing a few tiny moles of rust. With the suspension, he had no bucks for bodywork. He hadn't been able to figure how he was going to get his sweetheart fixed up, until now.

'Tsk, tsk, Danny boy. Looks like the department's going to have to spring for a little paint job on my buggy here. No hard feelings, but next time be more careful how you park that pig of yours, will you?'

Carmody lumbered out of his car. The wind caught the ribbons of khaki hair he used to mask his bald spot and sent them flapping over a florid ear. As he moved, his jowls wobbled and his gut shimmied so he reminded Drum of a walking Jell-O mold. No surprise considering old Dan was the type who considered cheesecake a yellow vegetable.

Carmody glumly surveyed the damage on both cars. 'You're really pushing it, Drum. You want to get back in good standing, you're going to have to keep more than that temper in gear. We've talked more than once about how you play fast and loose with your expenses. And what the hell's that?' He pointed a fat finger at the glistening eyes sunk low in the Mustang's front seat.

'Stray cat. Don't worry. Her hearing's not so hot, and she only speaks French.'

Carmody squinted and frowned. 'Hey, it's a kid. Where in hell did you get a kid?'

'Going out of business sale. Look, Dan, I'm a busy man. You got something for me or what?'

Carmody sniffed and smoothed back his hair. 'I told

you, Jerry. This has to be between you and me. Strictest confidence or forget it. This gets out, I'm going to have a lot of embarrassing explaining to do.'

'Okay, fine. I understand perfectly. You take care, Chief. Pray regular and all that.' He stuffed his hands in his pockets and started toward the Mustang.

'Wait, Drum. Take it easy.'

Drum kept walking.

'Come on now, Jerry. Don't be that way. I hate it when you get like that.'

Drum's hand was on the door. Fingers squeezing the handle. Drum had known Carmody most of his life. The chief had been in the same rookie class as Drum's old man. Most of the time, Drum knew how to play the guy with his eyes closed.

Carmody sighed. 'Okay. You made your point. No more games. This is no joke. I'm up to my ass in this hit-run thing and sinking fast. There have been six kids hurt or killed in Tyler's Grove in the last eighteen months. Not only are the neighbors after scalp, and mine will do nicely, but Charlie Allston is hell-bent on using this mess to sweep me out the door.'

'So why'd you put that nazi on the case, Carmody? You don't seem like the suicidal type.'

The chief held up his palms. Empty. 'No choice. You know Allston's got Mayor Schippani in his pocket. Those two go back practically to the womb together.

'Soon as this case hit the fan, Schippani himself called and asked me to put his buddy Charles Allston in charge, which gives Allston exactly the opportunity he's been looking for.'

'I don't get it,' Drum said.

Carmody sighed. 'It's easy, once you've got Allston's playbook, Drum. My bet is he'll scuttle the investigation and blame the failure on poor management from me. Then he'll plant a bug in Mayor Schippani's ear about how I've failed to deliver on several other explosive cases, especially the one where that Wilder kid disappeared from the Grove last year. Kid was missing six days, then turned up with his brains scrambled. I put half the force on it, but still no suspects. Not exactly the kind of results you write home about.'

'So where do I fit in?'

'You've always had a way of getting to the bottom of lost causes like this, Jerry. I don't know how you do it, and I have a feeling I don't want to know. But I need that driver found. I want this thing to go away quickly. And I think you're the Houdini who can make it disappear.'

Drum took the compliment. Banked it. 'So reinstate me.'

The chief sniffed. 'You know I can't do that. And I can't put you back on it officially, but I'm willing to deal if you are. So what'll it be?'

Drum turned, grinning. 'You just said the magic words, Dan old boy. Now tell me what you've got in mind, and I'll tell you what I want. And I bet at least one of us is gonna leave here real happy.'

9 Carmody pulled away first. His Town Car lurched over Intell's rutted drive and angled out onto the four-lane road. Drum held the Mustang back. Black beauty had a way of straining at the lead, especially when she was in a real good mood.

After Carmody's taillights evaporated in the distance, Drum eased his car through the gate, shifted to third gear, and let the Mustang have her head on the ghost strip of deserted roadway. The speed shot through him like an electric charge, jolting him alive.

Booker grabbed the door handle and whooped his approval. Drum squeezed on the brakes and eased back to the speed limit. For a second, he'd forgotten the kid was around. Took a load of getting used to, having a kid.

'A car's no toy, Book. You got that?'

'Got it, Mr. Drum.'

'Say it. The whole thing. You know.'

'A car's no toy. A vehicle is a powerful tool and a big responsibility. Anyone goes around speeding and acting like a cowboy behind the wheel's a major fool.'

'Right, hotshot. Exactly right.'

They drove awhile in a silence diced by the syncopated tick of the dashboard clock. Drum tuned to the steady rush of wind and the hum of the pampered engine. Nice.

Then, passing under the turnpike, he was assailed by the clatter of cars and trucks traversing the metal span overhead. The noise jarred him. Drum was full of rotten associations. Noise equaled trouble. Trouble had a heavy foot.

Through the underpass, he saw that the action was escalating in Booker's old neighborhood. While they stood idling at a red light, there was a pop of gunfire. Drum spotted the shooter, a ferret-faced young Hispanic, charging toward an abandoned elementary school. He was brandishing a semiautomatic with a visible halo of heat.

The guy vaulted the chicken-wire fence girdling the school and started weaving in a frantic dance through the littered playground. With the car window cracked open, Drum could hear the crunch of broken glass under the shooter's feet. Jerk was in a big hurry to get where he was going, which was exactly no place. There was the wail of approaching sirens.

Drum remembered how it felt to run like that, trying to escape your own terminal stupidity. Muscles on fire, lungs screaming, heart a pumped balloon on the brink of rupture. Running on nothing but poison fumes of fear. Nowhere to go. No way out.

He resisted an urge to stop the car and help bring the shooter in. Carmody had warned him he'd better lie low until all the bad blood about his little run-in with the DiBiasi boys had a good chance to cool off and get forgotten. Lie low or be kept on iceberg watch indefinitely. Easy choice. He drove on.

Booker was silent until they passed the dark hulk of Bloomingdale's – the great divide.

'You gonna catch him, Mr. Drum? You gonna fry that badass creep who trashed the little kid and took off?'

'What's it to you?' Drum hid his amusement. Booker must've read Carmody's lips. Some trick since the chief had stood with his back to the Mustang and whispered so the kid wouldn't be able to hear. No use. Boy was like Stella. Nothing got by him. The runt was going to go far, Drum thought, in whatever direction.

'Little kid's from my school,' Booker said. 'He's in Mrs. Biondi's kindergarten. I see him in the E.L. program.'

E.L. stood for extraordinary learner. Booker had been at Davenport Ridge Elementary School for about five minutes when they'd realized the kid had extra large brains. Ever since, he'd been up to his eyeballs in advantages. Special programs, computers, field trips.

'Good kid?' Drum said.

'Yeah. He's cool. You find the creep who hit him and

took off. You haul that guy's chicken ass over to the deep fry and drop it right in, Mr. Drum. Anyone can do it, you can. You're the best cop in the business.'

Drum ruffled Booker's hair. He could remember feeling that way about his old man. Only difference was his old man had been worth it. Matthew Drum had the presence of Everest. Big, powerful. When Drum was a kid, he'd stand in his old man's shadow and feel as if he were under a steel bubble of protection. Nothing bad could lay a finger on him with Matt Drum around. Nothing would dare.

A couple of times, the old man had taken Drum out with him on night patrol. Drum was maybe Booker's age at the time, maybe younger. But he could still feel the cold leather seat of the old Plymouth cruiser, still see his father's keen eyes blazing like emeralds in the darkness, aimed to catch the slightest hint of trouble.

Drum had dreamed of growing up like his father. Being a good cop. Respected, steady. Never occurred to him how flammable dreams were. One stray spark and they were reduced to a stinking hill of ashes.

At least the old man had gone to his grave without knowing the worst of it. Drum flushed with shame, remembering.

Business, Drum. Get your mind on business. Carmody would see to it that Drum got the twenty-thousand-dollar reward local groups had posted if he brought in the driver. If he delivered quickly, the chief had promised to scrape a five-grand bonus from the bottom of the department budget. But if Drum came up empty, all he could count on was expenses and a lousy little per diem.

Not exactly the terms Drum had wanted, but the best he was able to swing under the circumstances. Way better than nothing, he kept telling himself. Though the truth was it could come to about nothing unless things broke his way. And Drum knew what the odds were after five days. Trail was probably cold enough to skate on by now, especially if Allston was deliberately trying to trash the investigation.

Drum ached for a smoke. Something to ease the fist

tightening in his gut. Yeah, he'd given up the weeds months ago. Doctor's orders plus Stella nagging him to set a good example for the kid. Fine in theory. Problem was, the weeds hadn't given him up. He took a deep drag on the air and let it out in a slim, lazy stream. Better.

'You okay, Mr. Drum?'

'Yeah, hotshot. I'm great. The greatest.'

He flipped on the radio and fiddled for a station. Kid liked jazz. Dizzy Gillespie, the Duke, Bill Evans. Even Clark Terry on fluegelhorn and Kenny Burrell's guitar. Amazing how they liked the same things: chess, jazz music, box kites, Three Stooges movies, anything pistachio walnut. Except pizza. Both of them drew the line right there.

They even looked alike, Drum thought. Only difference was that Drum's black was on the inside. Outside, he looked every inch the mongrel he was. Bottle green eyes like his Irish old man; whipped waves of dark, dense hair and olive skin from his Italian mother. The rest was his own contribution: the jagged scar that ran from his right temple to the edge of his mouth, the right eyelid that drooped like a hammock so he tended to look either shifty or half asleep. Time and doubt had chiseled deep furrows in his forehead, and his hair was graying in a skunk stripe. When it came to ugly, Drum was no lightweight.

What the hell did Stella see in him anyhow? Bad question. One he hoped she'd never think to ask.

Concentrate, Drum. His mind was racing around like the shooter, getting no place.

He aimed the Mustang north on High Ridge Road. Night had settled on the city like a shroud. Most of the stores were dark and caged. The parking lots were near empty. Traffic had slowed to a drip.

When Drum looked over, he saw the kid's head lolling like a flower on a broken stem. Fast asleep. Shadows played across his polished skin. Hotshot looked like a Christmas pageant angel with a tan. Drum wrestled off his topcoat and tossed it over Booker's chest.

Drum hesitated as they approached the turnoff for their

house, then decided to keep going. It would only take a few minutes to get a preliminary read on the hit-run site. Drum always played his cases the way his old man had, from the inside out. He could almost hear Big Matt's soothing bass. 'Cop work takes a system, son. Trick is never to skip a step. Never take anything on faith or promise. Only thing worth believing is what you know for yourself.'

He revved the beauty and let her out full on the dim ribbon of road north of the Merritt Parkway. Zip through a string of red lights. Racing the wind. Winning.

Turning east on North Stamford Road, Drum eased up long enough to dig in his pocket for the directions. Carmody had pressed them into Drum's palm at the close of their negotiation along with a giant pile of case reports and a few choice words: 'Gotta be quick and clean, Jerry. And invisible. I hear any talk about Jeremiah Drum nosing around this case, all bets are off.'

Drum didn't need to hear the stakes. He knew what it would cost him to lose this one. Drum hated losing. Hated it even though losing came so easy.

He memorized the rest of the route, crumpled Carmody's memo, and kicked down hard on the accelerator. The narrow road angled, dipped, and veered suddenly in unexpected directions. Drum eased into his stunt mode, clutching the wheel, unblinking, taking the curves at top speed. The Mustang responded to every nudge and nuance. Cream smooth. Sweet baby! A rush of exhilaration hit him like a bucket of ice water.

He turned up Cascade and whipped past a pristine New England church haloed in spotlight. Past the straightway, he barreled through a series of S-curves and whipped around a demon bend nestled in the tight cleavage between two plump mounds of sloping earth. Then he hustled to the stop sign like he was racing another streak of wheeled lightning to the finish line.

Past the invisible flag, he eased on the brake, not wanting to jar Brooker. Kid's eyes were working under his lids. Dreaming. Candy dream, Drum hoped.

At the corner of Cascade and Mill, Drum brought the beauty to a full stop. Time to go to work.

He turned onto Mill and eased the Mustang toward the accident site that Carmody had described on his instruction sheet. Drum absorbed the surroundings. Gnarled, naked tree branches hovered over the pavement. There was a scatter of sleeping houses. He parked on the rocky berm abutting one of a pair of broken stone pillars and took a walk around.

The wind was fanged and howling. Drum shoved his hands in his trouser pockets, hiked his shoulders, and tucked his chin against the cold.

He strode across the furrowed pavement, memorizing the ruts and potholes. On the other side, a steady stream of runoff from the angled bank trickled along the edge of the road and tracked the short route to where the blacktop veered out of sight around a curve. Drum crouched, dipped his fingers in the icy stream, and touched them to his lips. Big Matt had taught him to take nothing for granted, to trust nothing but his own instincts and senses. Hard experience had taught him that slow and steady could be the fastest way to the truth.

Mounting the embankment, his feet crunched in mounds of fallen leaves. Lifting the edge of one pile he eyed the damp, rotting underside. A reptilian creature skittered away, too quick for Drum to catch his name.

He worked the sloping ground in a systematic sweep, walking in broad chevrons that he intersected with tight Vs in the opposite direction. He picked up a muddy scrap of something he couldn't identify and stuffed it in his pocket.

Finished, he looked across the street and took in part of the sprawling community known as Tyler's Grove. He picked out the white farmhouse, two doors down on the right, where the hurt kid's family lived. In the rear was the recording studio Carmody had mentioned. Drum had the feeling he'd heard about that studio and the kid's father from Stella. If memory served, the guy was some hotshot record producer.

He eyed the neighboring houses. Spread out, prosperous and peaceful-looking. Hard to imagine bad things happening in places like that, he thought; though Drum had firsthand knowledge that they did. Rotten things. Narrowing his eyes, he filtered a certain haunting scene through the filthy mesh of his memory.

He sniffed in a rough chestful of air. There was a stale trace of wood-stove smoke, a shot of frost, and a sour blast of engine fumes. Smelled like the beauty needed an oil change. Drum wondered how he could work charging it to Carmody.

He stared at the deserted road, imagining.

The chief had reported what few scraps Allston's bumbling investigators had managed to patch together about the accident. Drum ran it through his mind. Got a picture of the victim lying at the side of the road. Drum could see the kid's face. Only it was Booker's face. Frozen in terror.

Drum rubbed his eyes to erase the image. This was as far as he could go in the dark. Slowly, he turned and trudged back toward the Mustang. He craved a stiff shot of booze, a hot shower, and a little one-round wrestling match with Stella. Didn't matter who pinned who, they'd both win. Then he'd let one of the late-night mouthpieces talk him to sleep.

Booker blinked open his eyes as Drum slipped into the driver's seat and shut the door. Kid smacked his lips and let them settle in a dopey grin.

'I was just dreaming how you was gonna nail that badass creep, Mr. Drum. I was thinking how I'd tell all the kids at school it was you did it, and they'd be blown clear away.'

'Come on, Book, what did I tell you?'

Booker's look went quizzical, then faded in a sheepish frown. 'Okay, I know, Mr. Drum. Sorry.'

'Say it then.'

'Man don't have to brag about what he does.'

'The whole thing, Book. Say it.'

Booker yawned. ' . . . Man don't have to brag about what he does. Only point of bragging is when you ain't done nothing. Then bragging's all you got. Right, Mr. Drum?'

Drum planted a hand on the kid's. It warmed him like a dose of Stella's chicken soup with matzoh balls. Warmed him nearly like a dose of Stella herself.

'That's right, hotshot. Exactly right.'

10 'To the Jameser,' Paul said and hefted his flowered Dixie cup.

'Long may he reign,' Cinnie said. She tapped Paul's cup with her own and invoked James's own variation on the standard toast. 'Chairs.'

The champagne tickled her nose and made her eyes water. Paul had gone all out for the celebration of James's improved condition: Dom Perignon, smoked oysters, a wedge of runny Camembert, and, in the patient's honor, iced shrimp with cocktail sauce. When James was three or four, he'd thought a shrimp cocktail was a mixed drink for small people. Cinnie remembered the time he'd ordered one and the look on his face when the thing was delivered without so much as a paper umbrella.

Paul sighed. 'It feels like a reprieve, don't you think, Cin? I mean, I was beginning to think we were going nowhere.'

She managed a noncommittal nod and a near smile. This was heartening progress, but it didn't change what had happened. James was still in a light coma, floating in and out of consciousness.

Still, she realized there was much to celebrate. No more intensive care. James had been moved to a sunny room on the pediatrics floor. Dr. Ferris had pulled strings to get him into one of the few private rooms on the unit. Usually, those were reserved for kids with contagious illnesses, but somehow Ferris had convinced the powers that be that James would be better off by himself.

Most of the pediatric patients were packed into four-bed mini-zoos with four competing televisions and a steady procession of boisterous visitors. Headache central. In a rare attempt at humor, Dr. Ferris had quipped to Cinnie that the pediatrics floor was specially designed to drum up business for the psych department.

There were no more monitors. And the fractured leg had healed sufficiently to be set in a cast. So, aside from the IV rigging and the hospital pallor, James looked like his regular self.

Paul was trying so hard. Despite herself, Cinnie smiled as he made a great show of tuning his air guitar and launched into a medley of the songs he'd written years ago to mark certain milestones in James's development. There was 'Moving to a Big-Boy-Bed Blues,' 'He's Not Gonna Hit the Bottle No More,' and Cinnie's personal favorite, 'Don't Mess With James, He's Potty Trained.'

She loved Paul's voice and the way the music took him over. He sang with his eyes half closed, his expression rapt and edged with serenity. He'd always been happiest when he was writing or playing his own songs, even the playful, private ones. So what that he'd had to scramble for work and they'd been forced to subsist for months at a time on macaroni and chunk light tuna? Those things tasted every bit as good as shrimp and smoked oysters when they were spiced with a few teaspoons of contentment.

Then he'd hooked up with a young band during an amateur night at a local club. He'd helped them put together a demo tape, and they'd hit it big. So Paul had developed an instant reputation as a hot record producer. And he'd been offered the contracts and fees to match.

At first, he'd claimed he was too busy to keep up with his own music. Later, he'd devoted every spare second to planning and developing the recording studio. Having his own studio meant more work and fatter fees. He'd bought bigger, shinier toys including a tomato-red Porsche 911. But Cinnie knew that no car was going to get Paul where he wanted to be.

She'd tried to convince him to get back in touch with the work he really loved. But eventually, she'd given up. Discussing certain topics with Paul was entirely too much like getting stuck in a revolving door.

'Mom?'

'Hey, puss. How's my boy?'

'Mom? Flying green tunnel. Pop the weasel.'

68

His eyes were glazed. Cinnie kissed his forehead and patted his hand. 'Love you, Jimbo. You feeling better?'

'Big train. Cookie, Mom.'

'That's good, baby. You're trying.'

'He sounds great,' Paul said. 'Clear as a bell.'

Cinnie knew better. James's speech was on automatic pilot. The language department of his brain was a tangle of crossed wires and fractured circuits. She imagined a huge corporate switchboard scuttled by an angry employee.

Still the odds were decent that he'd recover. Three areas of the brain controlled language functions, and even if one or two were damaged, the remaining parts could be trained to take over, especially in a young child. But Cinnie knew that they were in for a long siege and a lot of tough, frustrating work.

What troubled her more was the nagging sense that James wasn't fighting to stay engaged. She watched him now, drifting off. Fading.

'James?'

He was sinking into sleep. His face went limp, and his fingers fell open like the petals of a fading bloom. There was no catch of effort. Not a pinch of strain. It was as if he craved the cover of sleep, as if he were hiding.

Sounded crazy, Cinnie knew. But that had always been James's way of reacting to stress. When he was little and a new babysitter or an intimidating stranger showed up at the house, he'd plant himself behind Cinnie's knees. During the first traumatic week of nursery school, he'd spent the majority of his time hiding in the school's Indian tepee. It had taken a birthday party with chocolate cupcakes to coax him out. And until he'd made peace with his closet monster, Cinnie had found him on several occasions, sleeping under the bed or burrowed under the blankets.

Hiding.

'Jimbo?'

He was gone again. Lost.

'More champagne?' Paul said.

'No, thanks. I'm about celebrated out. Tired, I guess.'

His eyes narrowed. 'What is it, Cin? Something's bothering you.'

'Hard to explain. I just have the feeling he's not trying.'

'Okay, I'm ready. What's the punch line?'

'It's no joke, Paul. I don't know why, but I can tell he's not fighting to tune in. Maybe he can't face the memory of the accident.'

'That's ridiculous. He's coming along fine. Better than expected in fact.' He sniffed and shook his head. 'And you talk about *me* dragging him down.'

'Look at him. He's not our scrappy little boy. Can't you see?'

'He looks terrific. Give the kid a chance. Isn't that what you told me?'

She bit her lip. Arguing wasn't going to solve this. She simply had to help him past the fear, talk him through it. But she was missing too many of the pieces. If she had all the details of the accident, she could go over the episode with James until the story lost its teeth. That had always worked with him in the past.

'Guess I'll take off,' Paul said. 'You coming home?'

'No . . . I think I should stay here. First night in the new room and all. He'd probably like some company.'

'You sure? I could use a little company myself.'

She hesitated. It would be nice to spend the night in a warm pair of arms. Cinnie knew she could use a little hiding herself. But there was still a slick, dangerous space between them that she wasn't ready to risk crossing. 'I'm sure. Just until he gets used to the change.'

He shrugged. 'Up to you. 'Night, Jameser. See you tomorrow.' He kissed James on the cheek, blew a perfunctory kiss in her direction, and left.

Suddenly weary, Cinnie tossed the party remains in a trash can down the hall. Back in James's room, she found Dr. Ferris. He had a stethoscope pressed to James's chest and a pensive look on his face. The man so rarely displayed any emotion, but still he was handsome by anyone's dictionary definition. Tall with a lean, athletic body, sensitive features, and pale, serious eyes. Cinnie was especially drawn to his hands, with their long, tapered fingers and caring touch. Artist's hands, robot's heart, Cinnie thought. Strange mix.

When he finished examining James, he faced Cinnie with his customary reserve.

'He's doing nicely, Mrs. Merritt. Why don't you go home and get a decent night's rest.'

'I want to make sure he's used to the new room.'

'Of course it's up to you. But you needn't worry. He'd be well taken care of.'

'I'm sure he would. I know it's probably silly.'

'You must take care of yourself. James will need you to be strong and healthy.'

Cinnie smiled. 'Good point. Thanks for caring. And thanks again for wangling the private room. It means a lot.'

Ferris allowed a self-conscious nod. 'It was nothing.'

Cinnie yawned. 'Excuse me. I'm afraid it's all catching up with me.'

'That's understandable. I'll be going now. You go get a good night's rest, Mrs. Merritt. It's important.'

Ferris left with the starched, regulated gait of a military drill. Funny how other women fell in love with their kids' pediatricians. Having a crush on John Ferris would be like lusting after a snowball. But ironically, the man's cool professionalism was what made him so reassuring. If Ferris said anything positive, she knew he meant it.

Cinnie felt someone watching. Looking out in the corridor, she spotted Henry Moller, one of the volunteers. Hanky, as everyone called him, was a dark young man with a lupine face and a long mop of greasy brown hair. Quickly, he averted his eyes and made a great show of looking for something on the tile floor.

Guy gave Cinnie the creeps. Always hanging around, staring. During the day, he went from room to room pushing a cart full of books, games, toys, and craft supplies for the children who were well enough to need amusement. The first few times he'd come to James's room, she'd offered a polite refusal. But Hanky wasn't easy to dismiss. He kept coming back with simpler books and new unwelcome ideas for things James might enjoy doing. Finally she'd taken to shutting the door when she saw him approaching. But she wasn't always quick enough. Hanky tended to pop up when you least expected or wanted him around. Made her want to scream.

Her bias against the guy wasn't fair, Cinnie knew. But she'd decided that she was entitled to be a little unreasonable under the circumstances.

For a couple of minutes, she debated about going home for the night. Ferris was right about her needing sleep. She even went so far as to put on one sleeve of her coat before she decided that no one had ever accused her of being sensible. Why start now?

She closed the door and settled in on the cot. Tomorrow, James was scheduled to begin an intensive rehabilitation program that would keep him busy for most of the day. Cinnie had decided to begin seeing patients again, but she wasn't resuming her full schedule for a couple of days. She'd only work with her regular clients and leave the outpatient evaluations and new admissions to one of the other therapists. She was too exhausted to be more ambitious.

Sleep was elusive. For a long time, she watched the shadows gather and stretch across James's slumbering form. Her mind was running in place, stuck on those same questions. Why so many hurt children? Why so many in one neighborhood? Was it only a bizarre coincidence, or could it be something else? She kept seeing that awful headline, 'Fresh Tragedy Strikes . . .' Was there something about the Grove?

She had to know.

She pictured all the wounded ones: limping, maimed, stuck in a web of recurrent terror. Laurel, Ricky, Michael, Billy, Jason, James. So many children.

Finally, she slipped over into a hard, black well of unconsciousness. So lost, she didn't hear the door ease open. And she was oblivious to the stalking figure as he made his silent way into the room.

11

Malcolm Cobb slipped into the room and eased the door shut behind him. Blinking away the darkness, he trained his gaze on the slumbering child. He was drawn, seduced, his need building like a malignant fever.

He padded in catlike silence toward the metal-slatted bed. His mind was ice clear, flesh tingling. So intense was his focus, he was nearly upon the boy before the ragged breathing sounds alerted him to the presence of the sleeping woman. She was huddled on a cot in the corner. A shapeless hill of dormant flesh. Hulking slab of interference.

Enraged, Cobb spat a curse. She was not expected.

Foul thorn!

She whimpered. Her face warped with fear and tensed like a drawn bowstring. Suddenly, she was tossed by a nightmare, caught in a black maelstrom of imagined dread.

Cobb held his breath. What if she should startle suddenly awake? She would likely exclaim at the unexpected sight of him. She might even scream. He shuddered at the bleak prospect of a meddlesome swarm of people rushing in to investigate. There would be questions. Suspicions gathering like noxious clouds.

True he could fabricate some passable justification for his presence in the room, but none guaranteed to keep him beyond the taint of distrust. He could not afford to raise a prickle of doubt. That would be an unthinkable deviation from his master course.

Damn her! She stood as an obstacle to his sacred mission. She was the vilest breed of enemy. A dangerous, malicious impediment.

Despite the threat, Cobb found himself drawn again to the boy. Precious thing was breathing in soft, lovely rhythm. There was a flush of sleep on his velvet cheeks. A glint of perspiration on his brow. Cobb inhaled his scent and felt a craving akin to starvation.

Frozen with indecision, Cobb stood with his back pressed against the wall. If only the loathsome woman would cease her damnable moaning and tossing, he could risk approaching the boy.

By his calculations, the night nurses would still be sipping coffee in the unit lounge. Stealing past that room on his way to the child, Cobb had seen the lot of them through a crack in the door. He'd caught morsels of their conversation. Foolish hens were so engrossed in their gossip they'd failed to observe him altogether. Not a head had been raised. Not a blink of notice.

But soon they would commence their scheduled rounds. All patients' vital signs were monitored on the alternate hour, Cobb knew. He'd taken careful note of such details during his preparatory phase.

There were only a few secure moments remaining. The danger was gathering force. Building. If he were detected future visits would be ever more perilous.

Foul, intrusive woman. Mewling like an animal.

Time was passing. Slipping away. Be quiet, fool woman, he thought. Hush!

As if his thoughts were a magical incantation, she turned on her side and fell silent. Cobb was jubilant. He bit his lip to keep from blessing his good fortune aloud. Now he could take what he needed. At last.

From his breast pocket, he extracted the hypodermic needle and a package of plastic tubing that he'd pilfered from the supply closet. Slowly, soundlessly, he approached the boy.

Almost there now. He dared not move too quickly, could not risk waking the woman. Cobb fitted the tubing to the blunt end of the needle, plucked the rubber cap from the point, and strode closer. Beautiful thing. Vessel of power and health.

The boy's eyes opened a crack, and his face lightened in a curious grin.

'Hello, James,' Cobb whispered. 'Hello, my child.'

'Shadow man.' The boy's voice was a wisp. 'Pop the weasel. Mrs Wheel.'

'You are mine, you know,' Cobb whispered. 'You belong to me now, child of my salvation. Wellspring of health and healing. Sweet servant of the dark moon.'

'Green tunnel. Mom? Mom!'

Cobb pressed a palm hard over the child's mouth. 'Sssh! You must be still.'

The boy's eyes widened. Cobb felt the struggle of flesh and sinew beneath his palm. Marvelous strength! Power of untapped humors. Power that would be his. He trembled with awe and longing.

'You must listen to me,' he rasped. 'You must do as I say.'

He had to hurry.

He attempted to pin the boy's arm and position the needle with his free hand. Too awkward. But he could not chance releasing the child's mouth. The woman might hear his summons.

'Be quiet,' he said as the small boy squirmed in his grasp. 'You mustn't move.'

Cobb heard a chirpy voice and the slap of footsteps as a nurse entered the adjacent room. 'Now why is it you're not sleeping, Abby Lee? How'm I supposed to come in here and wake you up if you're not sleeping?'

She might take several minutes with the girl, but Cobb could not linger and chance discovery. He would have to leave at once. Furious, he slipped the needle and tubing back into his pocket, peered out into the hall, and hastened toward the staircase at the center of the long corridor. As soon as he opened the fire door and ducked inside, he heard the nurse stepping into the hall and approaching the boy's room. There was the sound of the door opening and the playful rise of her voice.

'James Merritt, don't tell me you're up too, child. What's going on around here anyway? Wait. Let me guess. I bet you guys are planning a party, am I right? How'd you know my birthday was coming up?'

'Shadow man,' Cobb heard James say. 'Shadow man. Shadow bed. Pop. Mrs. Wheel.'

'Yeah right, honey,' said the nurse in a soothing voice. 'You go on and tell me all about it.'

12 During breakfast, Drum had offered to drop Booker off at school on his way to work. One mention of the case and the kid's mouth revved up to warp speed. He forgot all about eating, and Stella gave Drum a look rough enough to derail a locomotive.

Drum did his best to reverse the damage. 'Eat your oatmeal, hotshot. That's good investigator food you got there.'

'Ain't hungry, Mr. Drum. I'm ready to roll soon as you are.'

'There's no rush,' Stella said. 'Take your time and eat.'

'Tank's full up, Mrs. Drum. Got no place for more oatmeal.'

'Juice then.'

'I'm all juiced up too. Honest.'

'That I can see,' Stella said. 'Eat anyway.'

As soon as they'd climbed into the beauty, Booker started firing questions.

'You gonna talk to the little kid's neighbors, Mr. Drum? You gonna go see the bus driver? You got anybody working with you on this thing? Besides me, I mean.'

After a couple of blocks, Drum had been forced to swing over to the Mr. Donut on Strawberry Hill Avenue and stuff Booker's mouth with a blueberry-filled in self-defense. Got himself a couple of frosted crullers to keep the kid company. Sweet plan, but it didn't work. Booker was running at the mouth again before they were even out of the parking lot, raining powdered sugar all over the beauty's upholstery.

'So who you think did it, Mr. Drum? Some guy from around here, you think? You know I was figuring it could've been some dumb jerk kid gone out joyriding and hit James and too scared to admit it.'

'Could be, Book. How about I see what's what and let you know?'

'Yeah. That's cool. Hey, you think maybe it's some hot-shot celebrity hiding out 'cause he doesn't want anybody to know he hit a kid? Like maybe Peewee Herman or someone?'

'Could be, Book. Anything's possible.'

He chuckled. 'Peewee Herman. Now that'd be something else.'

Drum pulled into the meandering drive leading to the Davenport Ridge Elementary School and stopped at the broad carpet of concrete squares fronting the main entrance. 'Catch you later, hotshot. Don't forget to use those big brains of yours.'

Booker hopped out, grabbed his knapsack, and flashed a high sign. 'You too, Mr. Drum. Watch your back, man.' He raced off to join a clump of gangly kids on their way into the building. Drum watched them slap hands and toss some jive at each other. Pipsqueaks took each other real serious.

Drum pulled out of the school and back into the snarled traffic on Newfield Avenue. The day felt stale already. A nasty headache had burrowed in behind his right eye and set up housekeeping.

One of those nights. After a couple of hours of tossing around like clothes in a dryer, he'd decided to get up and use the time to better advantage.

Stella was down for the count, snoring gently. One side of her hair was still tugged back in a jeweled comb, face flushed and streaked with makeup. Looked like she'd come in from her gig too tired to do anything but dive for the pillow.

Not surprising. Onstage, Stella gave it everything she had, which was more than plenty. He pictured her framed by a bubble of light, spilling her guts into the microphone. Woman knew how to play an audience.

Drum loved to watch her set the suckers up and reel them in. Took him back to the first time she'd done it to him. One night after a day well worth forgetting, he'd gone to Tramps, a local club, for a couple of beers. Stella was in the middle of a set when he walked in, and Drum had caught her bait before his butt ever hit the barstool. Never was able to figure how to spit the hook. Not that he'd done much trying.

Now he settled a light kiss on her neck and caught the musty scent of yesterday's cologne. Not wanting to wake her, he dressed in the closet and tiptoed out carrying his shoes.

Downstairs, he brewed a pot of strong coffee and spent the rest of the night in the den reviewing the copies of the police reports Carmody had laid on him last night. Aggravating as all hell. So aggravating, he'd smoked maybe a pack of imaginary cigarettes already, and it wasn't even nine yet.

Nothing but loose threads. Dead ends. Blind alleys. If Charlie Allston was trying to botch the case, he was doing a terrific job of it. First, he'd commandeered the department dregs for his special Major Accident Investigation Squad. Drum knew the players too well: Lazy, Dopey, Grumpy, Dumpy, and Sloshed. Next, the deputy chief had made sure that nothing would be followed up or nailed by rotating assignments within the special squad so that none of the jerks was ever left walking in a straight line.

As a result, there had been no systematic house-to-house sweep of the neighborhood to ferret out reluctant or unwitting witnesses. The one witness who'd managed to make herself known, a neighbor named Lydia Holroyd, had been interviewed three times. Hat trick. Perfect way to waste the men's time and energy. Allston wasn't taking any chances that his clod squad might screw up and stumble onto the driver. Last thing the deputy chief wanted was to let Dan Carmody look good or even competent.

Charles Allston the fourth. Drum had never cared for the guy. Looked like Hitler youth and never seemed to shift too far out of park. But the character had a talent for making the right connections, and he was tight as spandex with the mayor. You had that, you didn't need much else. Truth was, it wasn't all that surprising to Drum that Allston was angling to dump Carmody and take over his job. The only surprising thing was that the mutiny hadn't gone down years ago.

When Drum finished his preliminary read-through, he scribbled some notes to himself. By the time he heard the creak of floorboards and the rush of running water overhead, he'd gotten his day planned and packed the beauty's trunk with everything he figured he'd need.

First things first. He knew from the reports that the kid was still in a light coma, but he wanted to take a look at the little guy. Get what he could from the parents. Exactly the way his old man would play it. He'd start at the center and move out until the circle was wide enough to hold all the possibilities. Then he'd draw the ring tighter and smaller until he was back in the middle holding the prize.

Reminded Drum of that old kid's game, The Farmer in the Dell. Only in this version the cheese got the rat, and the rat got the cage.

The visitor's lot at the Fairview Hospital was jammed with delivery trucks and the cars of patients with early clinic appointments. Drum plucked a plain plastic chit out of the collection of tools and incidentals in his glove compartment and used it to trigger the automatic wooden arm blocking the staff lot.

He parked the beauty between a pair of physicians' standard-issue Mercedes, popped the trunk, and spent a few minutes scrutinizing his emergency supplies.

He shrugged on a shapeless tweed sport coat over his convertible shirt and stuffed a battered briefcase with files, forms, and a costume change. Ten years of undercover work had given Drum a taste for masquerades. Lucky thing, given Carmody's insistence that Drum remain invisible.

One side of the reversible shirt was black and had a clerical collar. The other side was business white with a starched neckline and built-in club tie. It was a souvenir of a custom-auto-theft operation Drum had managed to crack a couple of years ago.

The thieves had shown the bad taste to nab the mayor's

wife's Cadillac while she was having her weekly lube and tune-up at Her Majesty's Hair Salon. Turned out that two of Carmody's boys had been eating lunch at the Szechuan place next door at the time of the heist, but neither of them had seen a thing. Three martinis and a couple of brews apiece could be hell on the eyesight.

Drum had made some discreet inquiries that led him to a baseball-card broker who dealt in hot cars on the side. Posing as a priest after an antique car to raffle in a parish auction, Drum had put in a bid for a black sixty-nine Mustang with leather interior. As expected, the card dealer had put out a hit on Drum's own beauty. When the thugs showed up to make the snatch, Carmody's welcoming committee was waiting.

Using the rearview mirror, he applied a dense layer of custom-blended Covermark to the scar on his cheek and hiked up his droopy lid with a clear thread of tape that went invisible behind a pair of thick horn-rimmed glasses. He passed a comb through his skunk stripe, and it disappeared. Industrial strength touch-up. Hell on the pillowcase when Drum forgot to wash it out. Made Stella mad enough to spank him, which was in no way Drum's idea of a punishment.

He took a final look at himself. Pitiful. Even with the camouflage that puss was enough to kill a real healthy appetite.

Not that he was after the Miss Connecticut title. Problem with his mug was it was too damned distinctive. And way too suspicious looking. Drum had the kind of face central casting would think of immediately if the call was for a serial murderer.

As soon as he'd finally finagled a place for himself on the force, Drum had begged Carmody to let him work undercover on the detective squad. But the chief had balked. Claimed the scars left him too easy to make and remember.

Drum had thought his juvenile record would be the biggest obstacle to his cop career. But Oliver London had convinced the chief to give Drum a chance. Because of his age at the time of his bust, Drum's record had been sealed. Supposedly, that wiped the scum ring from his life and left him baby clean. But it hadn't been so easy to wipe away his ugliness.

The splintered glass had forged a craggy road through the flesh on his cheek; the flames had charred the seeping wound and thinned its margins to the glistening translucence of fish scales. Spreading the edges, he studied the line of lumpy tissue in the depression. It echoed the knobby cord bisecting his eyelid.

He'd spent hours at Stella's vanity table, experimenting with the jumble of pots, tubes, and jars in her makeup case. After a number of laughable failures, he figured out how to build up layers of pigment until the scars began to fade. To make them disappear, he'd need a perfect color match.

Feeling more than a little foolish. Drum had hit the cosmetics counters at Lord & Taylor and Bloomies. When nothing in either place worked to his satisfaction, he got a referral to a makeup artist with a studio down on West Main Street.

Drum had handed her a line about planning to make television commercials for his aluminum siding business, and she'd done a complete makeover on him. Woman was a genius, so good. Drum found it hard to believe the face in the mirror was his. He'd left with a pink shopping bag full of camouflage and the videotape she'd made of the transformation so he could reproduce the results at home.

For weeks, he'd practiced until he could disguise himself in seconds. The scar, the lid, the tint in his hair, and he was remade. A stranger.

To complete the picture Drum had practiced new ways to hold his face and body: jaw jutted forward, mouth tipped up at the edges, forehead tightened, shoulders hitched so half his neck disappeared. The moves felt funny at first, but he kept at it until he could slap on the fresh expressions at will.

For insurance, he'd tested a few alternative voices. His quickest study was the weatherman on an all-news radio station. Drum broke it down to Philadelphia vowels, pre-school consonants, and a problem with chronic consti-pation. Anything was easy if you went at it hard enough.

Then he made an appointment through the chief's sec-retary, and a couple of weeks later, he showed up in Carm-ody's office posing as a recruit.

Drum was armed with a phony degree from John Jay College of Criminal Justice, a fistful of glowing forged references from midlevel Manhattan pols, and a practiced spiel about how he was itching to do his bit for truth, justice, and country. Almost an hour interview, and the chief had no clue that the earnest kid with the Yankee Doodle complex was Drum himself.

So Drum had gotten his undercover assignment. And his cover had never been cracked. Turned out his looks were the least of his problems on the job. If only he could find a way to camouflage his incendiary temper and flush this little problem he had with expense account abuse.

Not that he wasn't trying to reform. At Carmody's insist-ence, Drum had even spent a few hours with the depart-ment shrink, trying to evict his demons. It had taken only a couple of minutes for the doc and Drum to size each other up and decide they weren't made for each other.

Guy had claimed Drum's runaway spending was an attempt to substitute material things for the love he'd lost when his parents died. Doc had chalked up the temper to something he called 'displaced aggression'. The man said Drum was really mad at his folks for having the nerve to die and leave him in the care of his sonavabitch uncle.

Right there was where the doc had lost him perma-nently. Drum knew there was nothing in the least bit displaced about connecting his fist with Randy DiBiasi's fat nose. Kid asked for it, got it. Simple arithmetic.

From the stack of fake IDs in his glove compartment, Drum selected a business card that identified him as an account rep for Continental Mutual Insurance Company. Drum was the founder, president, and chief executive offi-cer. His kind of operation.

Visiting hours were not until one, and clinic patients

had to be checked in on a master list and issued a pass. There was confusion in the lobby, but not enough to get lost in. Through the glass wall flanking the main entrance, Drum spotted two burly guards armed with flashlights and walkie-talkies. Hospital security had a direct line to police headquarters, he knew. No point asking for trouble.

Instead, he took a quick hike around to the rear emergency entrance. There, the waiting room was swarming with coughers, bleeders, and squalling red-faced babies. One harried receptionist was trying to handle the flood by sticking her finger in a computer keyboard.

Drum threaded his way through the crowd, tripped the button on the doors to the treatment area, and, following the 'authorized personnel only' signs, found the back way out onto a surgical floor. He strode down the long polished corridor and passed through a glass-walled bridge to the rear elevators.

Pediatrics was on five. Drum remembered that from when Booker had his fake appendicitis attack during the summer, and they'd kept him at Fairview overnight for observation. Turned out to be an overdose of Ben and Jerry's White Russian ice cream with chocolate fudge.

The pediatrics unit was crawling with wilted staff. Drum surveyed the sea of puffy eyes, wrinkled lab coats, stethoscopes drooping like old flesh. The air was thick with coffee fumes and stale antiseptics.

A beagle-faced nurse was planted at the front desk, studying medication orders. Drum made her as the type who only crossed at the green. Suited him just right under the circumstances.

He spent a couple of seconds slipping into character. Ready, he stopped at the desk and cleared his throat. 'James Merritt's in what room, Miss?'

She came up wearing a loaded expression. But a glance at Drum and her face softened like cheese in a microwave. 'He's in five-fourteen, father. Second door on the right. You can go right in.'

Drum made a steeple with his fingers and hit her with his best Irish brogue. 'Thank you. James is a lucky lad to

84

have kind, compassionate souls such as yourself caring for him.'

A strawberry flush scaled her neck. 'Thanks. We do our best. Have a nice visit now.'

He smiled. 'Bless you, my child.'

The priest bit worked every time. On his way down the hall, he opened the Velcro fasteners on the shoulders of his magic shirt and turned the black side with the clerical collar out of sight in the back. The shirt had no sleeves, the cuffs were sewn onto the jacket arms.

He knocked at room five-fourteen, and the kid's mother opened the door. Pretty, honest face. Nice fluff of curly dark hair. Soft eyes. Still had a twinkle of good humor in them, despite all this. Looked like a kid herself.

Drum introduced himself as Arthur Kettle, one of his several drum-related aliases, and flashed his business card. He explained that his insurance firm represented the school bus company. Since they'd delivered James to the accident site, Drum had been asked to file a preliminary report. He extracted a form from his briefcase and planted it on a clipboard.

She went along, answering what she could of Drum's questions about the hit-run. She told him there was no lead yet on the identity of the driver. So far, the little boy hadn't been able to provide any useful information. He was still in a light coma, she explained. The prognosis was optimistic but uncertain. In the best case, he'd need months of intensive rehabilitation to get back to where he'd been. Drum didn't ask about the worst case. That he could see.

The day of the accident had been routine except for a friend's request for an emergency evaluation of her son's speech. Turned out to be nothing, the mother said. A flicker of pain crossed her face. Drum could imagine what she was thinking. Turned out to be nothing for the other kid. For her little guy, it was a whole different story.

While he listened and scribbled the gist of her story on his report form, Drum took a look around.

The room was cluttered with the kid's things: toys,

games, stuffed animals, a giant stack of books. Several bunches of balloons were suspended from the rings holding the privacy curtain. The bulletin board opposite the bed was plastered with get-well cards. Several were hand-lettered and illustrated in crayon. A cot was set up in the corner.

'Shadow man, shadow!'

'Sssh, sweetie,' the woman said and walked over to stroke the little guy's forehead.

'Pop the weasel. Flying green tunnel.'

She caught Drum's puzzled expression. 'It doesn't mean anything. A lot of gibberish.'

Drum nodded. Cute little guy; Dennis the Menace face. No visible injuries except for the fat, blue bull's eye over one temple and the leg that was tented in a plaster cast. Kid like that should be·out climbing trees and playing mud-magnet.

'Mrs. Wheel. Pop the weasel. Blue coat lady.'

'It's okay, Jimbo. Ssh.' She turned to Drum. 'I wish they'd find the driver.'

It was the opening he'd been waiting for. 'Can't blame you, Mrs. Merritt. You'd think the police would have managed to track him down by now.'

She looked back at the little boy's pale face. 'Yes. And I can't help but think it'll make a difference to James, to all of us, when we know who did this. Chief Carmody keeps assuring me that the department is doing everything it can. But I keep thinking there's got to be some way to hurry things along.'

'Actually, there is.'

'Meaning?'

'Well, it's supposed to be top secret, but if I can count on you not to say anything . . . '

'Of course you can. Please. I could use a little encouragement right about now.'

Drum told her that his insurance company was conducting an independent investigation. He described the firms' extensive background in accident analysis, the crack staff of field workers, the computer linkages Continental

Mutual maintained with national and international crime data banks, their network of top investigators and informants. Drum was impressing the hell out of himself.

'But as I said, Mrs. Merritt, this must be kept strictly confidential. The police brass would be furious if they found out we were on the case. And frankly, my company can't afford to alienate the police.'

'Not a word to anybody. I promise. All I want is to see that driver found. I don't care who does it.'

'Couldn't agree with you more.'

Drum gave her a diplomatic load of manure about how the police were overworked and understaffed. Naturally, his company's resources were not so badly taxed. So if she heard of any new evidence or thought of anything that might help the investigation, she should be sure to call him immediately. And if she could find the time, he'd appreciate it if she would write a detailed account of everything about that day she could remember up to the time of the accident.

'You never know what important detail the police may be missing.'

'How will it help you to know what I was doing? I was miles away when James was hit.'

'Probably won't directly. But we'll want to reconstruct the accident as best we can as part of our investigation. By taking yourself back through that day, step by step, you'll be in the best possible position to help us do that.'

Cinnie shrugged. 'Sure, if you think it'll be useful.'

'Shadow man. Mrs. Wheel.'

Funny that the kid kept saying those same things over and over again. Drum wondered aloud if any of it could possibly have any meaning.

'I doubt it. I'd know if it did.'

Drum wasn't convinced. Never paid to take anything for granted. He scribbled the odd phrases in the margin of his form. The woman's eyes were on him when he looked up again.

'Anything else you need, Mr. Kettle?'

'No. Guess that's it for now.'

'If you'll excuse us then,' she said. 'James has been very agitated and up half the night. I think he ought to rest.'

'Sure. And please, Mrs. Merritt, keep in mind that if anything comes up that you think we should know, or if there's anything we can do to help you, give me a call. Anytime.'

Drum had arranged for his number to be patched through to Failsafe Security, a burglar alarm operation with a twenty-four hour central station. When he didn't pick up the phone, his old friend Louis Packham, Failsafe's owner and full-time operator, took his messages. In return, Drum kept Louis supplied with bootlegged videocassettes of first-run movies. Turned out Drum had another old friend who'd made it big in the film pirating business. Plenty of the kids Drum had known from juvenile hall had turned out to be success stories like that.

The Merritt kid's chest heaved, his face went tight and bothered. 'Blue coat lady. Flying green tunnel, Mom. Mrs. Wheel. Pop!'

'Ssh, baby. Good-bye now, Mr. Kettle. And good luck with the investigation.'

'Thanks, Mrs. Merritt,' Drum said. ''Bye, James. Feel better, son. Everyone's rooting for you.'

'Flying green tunnel. Mrs. *Wheel* . . . '

Drum closed the door behind him and headed down the hall. Halfway to the elevator, he crossed paths with a lean, good-looking guy. Had to be the kid's father. Same face, only a lot more miles on it.

Drum stopped the guy and introduced himself. 'Arthur Kettle, Continental Mutual. We're involved in the investigation of your son's accident, Mr. Merritt.'

Guy was antsy as hell, his eyes bouncing around like he was referee in a Ping-Pong match. Drum didn't get much out of him but an uneasy feeling. You'd think Dad would be more interested in someone who was trying to get a handle on the hit-run. You'd think Dad would at least pretend to give a damn. But all the guy wanted was to cut loose. Drum watched as he ducked into the boy's room.

Five-minute visit maximum, Drum predicted. Made a person wonder.

The kid's voice pierced his thoughts.

'Pop the weasel. No more green tunnel!'

Poor kid, poor mama. Sometimes Drum wished he could make the list of the people who deserved to have such things happen to them.

He knew exactly who he'd put at the top.

13 Walking down the hall, Drum was glad to see that pooch puss was away from the desk. He could have pulled his next bit of business off as a priest, but it would have been trickier.

Pressed out of sight in the alcove that housed the fire extinguishers, he traded his tweed jacket for the lab coat in his briefcase and tucked a dummy stethoscope into his pocket. He'd lifted the thing from Booker's doctor kit. Runt hadn't shown a bit of interest in medicine.

Patient files were suspended in a skeletal frame at one end of the nurses' station. He fished out the one marked 'Merritt, James'.

With the chart tucked under his white coat, he turned into the utility room at the end of the hall and cleared a work space between the batches of mops, cleansers, and slop buckets. Using a portable copier the size of a cigarette pack, he reproduced the doctor's reports and lab findings, column by column. Finished, he tucked the duplicates into his briefcase, went back to his priest mode, and headed out.

Dog-face was back guarding the desk. He asked if he could trouble her for a drink of water, and when she left to fetch it, he returned the records to their proper slot. She watched him slug down the water. Her face was mushy with reverence.

'Thanks so much for stopping by, father,' she said, and rose to see him to the elevators.

'Sit, my dear,' Drum said and raised his palms in a gesture of benediction before turning to leave.

'Sit, beagle puss,' he muttered under his breath as he stepped into the middle car. 'Roll over. Play dead.'

Drum rode to the lobby, reconsidered, and pressed three. On the way up, he took a couple of deep breaths and tried to prepare himself. He hadn't seen the old man in over a month. The last time, the poor slob had been drooling out of one side of his mouth, and one of his eyes kept skidding around like a car on an ice patch. Drum had left with his gut tied in slipknots. Took three stiff ones to blunt the image and a week of rocky nights before his dreams were emptied of the poison.

Ever since, he'd been arguing with himself on a regular basis about coming back again. Making excuses that sounded lamer and lamer, even to his own ear. So it was time to cut the crap. Pretty picture or no, Drum owed the old coot way better than good intentions.

The room was empty. Drum tracked London to the patient lounge at the end of the hall, where the old man sat listing slightly to starboard in his wheelchair, staring at a quiz show. Drum watched him awhile and felt a rough combination of sorrow, pity, and affection.

He still remembered London from the old days, starting forty years ago, when he'd rode as Matt Drum's partner. Some pair those two had made.

'Beat 'em' Drum had been the handsome dandy of the duo. Big Matt had elegant manners and that kind of intense magnetic appeal that drove women to acts of extreme foolishness. Not that Drum's father so much as noticed. He'd married his childhood sweetheart right after high school and settled down like a deep-rooted tree.

London, still a bachelor, had been more than willing to catch Big Matt's copious rejects. But One-ton, as he'd been called, a lumbering bear of a man with a wet-cement complexion and features that drooped like soggy clothes on a line, had never been a general hit with the ladies.

Fortunately, their ties were too strong to be frayed by petty jealousies. Both men had the work in their veins. Both had steel heads and balls to match when it came to the job. And both had plenty of smarts and the bonus of good instincts. Together, they'd scraped through numerous tight spaces and managed to come out whole. It would have gone on that way until they both hung it up together if Big Matt hadn't hit that one deadly patch of rotten luck.

Drum's mother had succumbed to breast cancer three

years before Big Matt caught a belly full of lead during what should have been a routine traffic bust. Turned out the speeder had a trunk full of heroine and a loaded .45.

Until then, London had been part of Drum's family. But now there was no family. Only the pathetic pair of them were left: London and Drum.

Drum's mouth parched. 'Hey, Uncle Oliver. Hows it going?'

London blinked and wheeled the chair around to face Drum. It took a few minutes for him to see through Drum's disguise. Then he sniffed, and one corner of his mouth peaked in disgust.

'Look. I'm sorry. I know it's been a while. Where does the time go.'

London's color deepened as he struggled to speak. 'Shuh . . . '

'Take it easy, pal. Don't strain yourself.'

London's eyes bulged with effort. ' . . . Shuh-shithead.'

'Sonavabith. You can talk.'

'Shithead,' London said with a firm nod. 'Bluch.'

Drum turned up his palms. 'Okay, you're right. What can I say?'

London sniffed and wheeled back toward the television.

'Come on. I'm sorry. What'll make it up to you? Name it.'

The old man's expression went blank. He'd made Drum disappear. Poof.

'You're right. I'm a no-good, useless load of crap. But I want to make it right. Please.'

London swatted his hand in dismissal. Drum shrugged and turned to leave. London made a sharp rapping sound that caught him at the door.

'Yeah?'

London had wheeled around again, a grudging look on his face. 'Boy?'

'Booker?' Drum's grin was automatic. 'Kid's real good. Smart like you can't imagine. Scary almost.'

London nodded approval and struggled to ask something

else. 'Beh . . . buh . . . ' Drum felt himself tensing in sympathy.

The word finally popped out like a champagne cork. 'Bumps.'

Drum couldn't figure it and didn't want to ask.

'Bumps,' London said again and pounded the armrest. 'Buuummmps.'

Drum shook his head and shrugged.

The old guy frowned. Then he cupped a palm and positioned it at about a D-cup distance in front of his chest. 'Bumps?'

Drum laughed. 'Stella, you mean? Stella's great. The best. She's been singing at a club in South Norwalk. Packing the house every night. And she's nuts for Booker. Woman can't stop feeding and inspecting and bragging about that kid.'

London almost forgot himself and let a smile leak out. He clamped his teeth and forced a scowl. 'Bluh . . . blimp?'

'Carmody?' Drum was getting the hang of it now. Blimp had to be the chief. London had heard all about Drum's suspension right before his stoke, but the memory must have gotten lost in the rubble. Drum couldn't see a reason to remind him. It would only upset the guy.

The old man had been Drum's biggest advocate on the force. London had twisted Dan Carmody's arm to hire Drum in the first place. The chief had been more than a little reluctant to take on anyone with Drum's history. Understandable. But London had chipped away on Drum's behalf until the chief relented.

'Things are okay,' Drum said. 'Carmody's got me on a smash-and-dash case at the moment. The kid who was hit is upstairs in fact. Sonavabith who ran him down took off like his butt was on fire. You hear about it?'

London's good hand balled in a fist. 'Get . . . shithead.'

'Yeah. I'm working on it.'

'Go!' London ordered. 'Get shithead. Get . . . go.'

'Yeah, Unc. I gotta tell you you're making yourself perfectly clear.'

Outside, a chill wind was hustling wisps of cloud across

the polished steel sky. Drum paused at the beauty's trunk and retrieved the necessary gear for his next stop. He wanted to get the feel of the kid's neighborhood, and he needed to cover himself in case anyone questioned his prowling around.

He wrestled on a gray crewneck sweater and armed himself with a steno pad, a tape recorder, and a set of fresh credentials. From the glove compartment, he retrieved a press pass and a hokey business card with a quill pen logo that identified him as a free-lance writer, member of the American Society of Journalists and Authors, and recipient of the coveted Golden Pen Award. Seemed only fair he'd won that one, Drum reasoned, given he was the one who'd made it up.

He drove north through the clotted midday traffic on High Ridge. At the intersection before a strip mall called Fashion Plaza were two accordion-pleated cars surrounded by a halo of slivered glass. The drivers were squared off, screaming at each other on the litter-strewn shoulder.

Three wailing cruisers and an EMS van were on the scene. Drum turned his head away as he inched through the jam of cars and passed a couple of detectives he knew way too well.

All it would take was one mention of his name in Chief Carmody's hearing, and Drum would be back to full time thumb-twiddling. The suspension was hard on Drum in more ways than he cared to admit. He was a cop, or he was less than nothing. Drum would never forget the dead feeling he'd had when he thought he'd blown his chance to work on the force forever.

He sucked in a breath and held it until he was safely through the traffic tangle and breezing along the back roads toward Tyler's Grove. Certain things cost so much, you never stopped paying. He'd have to tell Booker that one too. Kid was never too young to start memorizing the price list.

14 He left the beauty running and crossed Mill Road to take a look around. By daylight, it was easy to spot where the kid had been found. The evidence techs had swept the ground clean for ten feet in each direction. He saw the fine ridges and hollows left by their tools. At intervals were his own plodding footsteps from last night. Drum knelt and sifted several handfuls of dirt through his fingers. Looked like the techs had done a decent job as far as they went. He found nothing to add to the filthy scrap of fabric in his coat pocket. Thing had probably blown onto the site after the sweep, but Drum intended to have it analyzed by his friendly private lab, just in case.

He was about to cross the road when a speeding red Porsche careened around the blind curve and whizzed by close enough to ruffle his eyelashes. Stunned, Drum stumbled back onto the grassy rise. Damned street was a death trap.

Back in the beauty, he drove through the broken stone pillars and took a meandering cruise around the neighborhood. Grove Street ran like a wiggly scar through the area's midsection. Half a dozen stunted roads led off Grove to nowhere.

The houses were set at long arm's length and projected an air of well-tended serenity. He took in the pristine paint jobs and trimmed hedges. Flower beds napped under dense blankets of winter mulch, and the latest crop of fall-planted saplings had been swaddled in burlap. Plenty of status cars and canvas-covered boats languished in the driveways. The sprawling yards boasted pricey wooden swing sets and in-ground pools dressed in foul weather gear. Toys for all ages.

Nearly all the homes looked deserted. No lights. Shades still drawn. Drum figured most of the inhabitants had hustled off to work or school before sunrise. Then this was the kind of neighborhood where everyone was in a fat hurry to get more of what they had way too much of already.

The clouds had dissipated, and a strident sun was completing its ascent to the sky's summit. Taking it in, Drum nodded his grudging approval. Day was made to order.

Still an hour to kill.

Doubling back toward Mill Road, he stopped at the farmhouse where the kid lived. It was a low, white clapboard building with forest green shutters and a red door. He noticed some obvious signs of recent neglect. Clumps of dead mums poked up from the pair of wooden window boxes flanking the front door. A crude paper jack-o'-lantern was still taped to one of the windows. A litter of rolled papers lay around the overstuffed mailbox. The handlebars of an overturned two-wheeler jutted from the base of a privet hedge. Drum spotted the training wheels. It occurred to him that now the kid might never be able to learn.

The house was dead still.

He let the doorbell ring a dozen times and, when he was certain no one was home, used his favorite set of picks to let himself in.

Place had a nice feel to it. Drum sniffed the distinctive, homey scent. Wood and warmth. He took in the broad, plank floors and the rustic cedar paneling. In the living room, a stone fireplace was piled with kindling and logs and fronted by a deep pile rug. A plump crocheted afghan was folded at one end of the down-filled sofa. There were cozy antiques: a vintage jukebox and an old wind-up Victrola complete with signature plastic dog. The coffee table was strewn with magazines. Drum detected the awkward messy feel of someone trying, but not succeeding, to keep things up. But it was Drum's kind of disorder. Snug. Made him want to curl up and catch a couple of outs.

At the end of a long hallway, he found the kid's room. It reminded Drum of Booker's. The space was crammed with dubious treasure: posters, pennants, books, ticket stubs, baseball cards, a cigar box full of carefully labeled pebbles, a vacant hamster cage, a couple of stuffed bears. Drum poked through the closets, shelves, and drawers and made a quick inventory of the rest: construction sets, more books, electronic games, puzzles, a collection of wind-up animals, a piggy bank, neat stacks of jeans, sweatshirts, underwear, sweaters, and socks.

Everything but the kid to enjoy it.

He took a slow survey of the rest of the house. His practised eye caught the places where rooms had been added and enlarged. Drum had served some time as a carpenter's apprentice on a commercial construction operation. He'd done plenty of restless roving before he was able to do the work that was in his blood.

Finished, he locked the door behind him and went back to the car. Twenty-five minutes until noon. Enough time left to do a little more digging.

He followed Mill to where it intersected Cascade Road and continued up the steep, winding course to the adjacent town of New Canaan. His eyes worked over the pavement like a minesweeper.

Nearly a mile from Tyler's Grove, he spotted exactly what he'd hoped to find. Slick patches of fresh blacktop dotted the street near the top of the hill. About a month old by his expert estimate. Having logged some time as a tar-slinger on a municipal pothole patrol, Drum knew how to read the fine print on a road surface. He climbed out and took a closer look at several of the molelike blotches. Perfect. Not a trace of tire burn on any of them. No speeder had peeled out in this direction since the pothole repair.

The neighbor, Lydia Holroyd, had seen a maroon sedan with New York plates speeding away from the scene in this direction at about the time of the accident. Definitely in this direction. She'd been interviewed by three separate detectives from Allston's Major Ineptitude Squad. Told the same story every time.

She'd been on her way to pick up her kid, a boy named Todd, for a dentist appointment when she spotted a young, blond guy speeding across Mill Road toward New Canaan.

She'd been stopped in front of the first house on the left inside the stone pillars when she made the sighting. Unaware that James Merritt had been hit moments earlier, she'd only taken notice of the car because it was going so fast. Doing at least fifty, she thought, which was more than considerable on the narrow, winding road.

Drum could see that the maroon sedan had slowed down before reaching the tar patches, which meant the driver had shown incredible cool and restraint. Interesting.

What kind of a character could hit a kid, start speeding away, and manage to get himself back in control in under a minute? Drum thought about the steel nerve professions: stuntman, test pilot, microsurgeon. Then again it could be a garden-variety psychopath. No shortage of those in anyone's neighborhood.

Drum turned the beauty around and followed the weave of roads to downtown New Canaan. Far enough for a first shot.

Heading back toward the entrance to the Grove, he cranked open his window and flipped the radio up to full volume. The beauty had a fine set of lungs: top quality Blaupunkt amp with four custom speakers coutesy of Carmody, who'd paid for the installation during a case where Drum was posing as a drummer in a rock band. The chief was one generous sonavabith. More generous than Drum hoped he'd ever begin to realize.

The music gave Drum's headache long extra legs, but he knew it was the quickest way to get what he wanted. Cruising along, he made a mental list of the three houses where curious faces suddenly materialized at the windows to check out the commotion. All possible witnesses.

He continued back onto Cascade, adding another house to his list, and kept the radio blasting until he came to a stop across from the stone pillars.

A porky cat was curled up sleeping on one of the broken pedestals. Behind the nearest house, a pair of rangy dogs were barking furiously and straining to bust loose from their run. One bared his teeth and snarled in Drum's direction. Drum snarled back. Mad dog was one language he spoke fluently.

Staring at the opposite side of the road, he could picture the little Merritt kid stepping down from the school bus, climbing the grassy rise, and looking around for his mother. He could feel the kid's apprehension. A hot pincer of fear clamped his gut and started squeezing.

It was the same feeling he'd had that day. He was twelve-years old again and back in the two-family house on Cove Road. It was late afternoon, and he was waiting for his old man's shift to end. Drum was cooking dinner, planning to surprise Big Matt and have everything ready when the old man walked in.

Drum was getting a major boot out of the idea. Usually, his father took care of the chow when he got home. But that day, Drum had fished one of his mother's recipes out of the wooden file box on the windowsill. He'd pulled some squashed bills out of his bank and walked to the small market near the town beach two blocks away for the things he needed.

He'd decided to make his old man's favorite: beef stew with vegetables. Standing at the sink, Drum had peeled the spuds and carrots, sliced the onions into neat canoes, and plunked in a can of chopped tomatoes and the necessary pips and dashes of spice. Fragrant steam tinged the air as the pot simmered and the fresh loaf of Italian bread from Tony's Convenience warmed in the oven.

The smell reminded him of better times, when his mother would be waiting for him after school, and the three of them would sit down to dinner together.

So where was the old man? As Drum waited, the prickle of worry turned to dread. His father always walked in on the minute or gave him a call. 'Jeremiah?' he'd say. 'Looks like I'll be running late, son.'

Drum stared at the phone, willing it to ring. He imagined his father's gentle, resonant voice. But nothing broke the oily silence.

The sky went still, black as death. Drum kept a dry-eyed vigil out the window. Kept looking half the night until the doorbell finally rang, and he was faced with the sick heaviness in Uncle Oliver's eyes. London couldn't get the words out, but words weren't necessary. Drum already knew.

Now he shook off the memory and checked his watch. Still too early to make his move. He dug into his briefcase and killed five minutes skimming the medical reports he'd filched from the hospital. The jargon was hip deep, but he managed to get a decent fix on the kid's injuries.

Twenty-five pages of high-priced jabbering. Came down to a broken leg, a variety of minor cuts and bruises, and a skull fracture. At first, the kid's vitals had gone screwy, but they'd managed to stabilize him within the first day. Now he was in a persistent, light coma. Improving, but slowly.

Something about all of it didn't add up, Drum thought as he put the sheets aside, but it wouldn't come to him. For now, the puzzle would have to wait. Time to roll.

Squinting through the haze, Drum tuned his mind to the day of the accident. Identical sky. He'd wait for the same time. The kid's scheduled bus stop was noon sharp. Drum had factored in a five-minute wait before the little guy would have given up and crossed on his own. Three minutes after twelve now. He used up one minute driving back to the intersection of Cascade and sat there waiting for another round of seconds to pass.

The minute hand closed in on five past twelve. Closer . . . now! He squeezed the accelerator, and the beauty kicked into gear. Gaining speed. Screaming. He shot around the blind curve and bore down harder on the gas. As he neared the pillars, the accident replayed in his head in garish stills. He felt the shock-hard impact of metal on flesh. Saw the spray of spattered gore on the windshield. Heard the strangled scream.

Drum lurched the beauty to a stop across from the entrance to Tyler's Grove. His heart thundered in the electric silence. He could see the huddled form on the side of the road. The little boy lay still and broken, his shattered leg dangling at an impossible angle. The little mouth was drawn in a grimace, trailing a trickle of blood.

Drum was sinking, slithering like a greased snake into the driver's skin. He'd hit the kid. Killed him. Damned kid was dead.

Panic gripped his throat and squeezed. Sparks of terror singed his mind. His gut was a bug swarm of guilty horror. Had to get away.

His toe found the accelerator, and the beauty leapt into action. Mill Road dissolved in a blur. Suddenly, he was on Cascade speeding. Faster. Racing mindlessly away.

He'd intended to slow down before the road patches, but the feeling took him over.

Further, faster. No way to stop. Couldn't let the horror catch up with him. Had to get away.

His breathing was low and ragged, heart stuttering. There was a sick rumble in his bowels. He was nearly to the center of town on Elm before he was caught behind a dawdling truck hauling a wide load of lumber. A solid steam of traffic was coming at him in the other lane, and he was forced to hit the brake.

Drum veered onto the edge of the road and parked the car. He resisted the inhuman draw of his own terror. 'It wasn't me. Wasn't real. None of it's real. Just a frigging case.'

The panic began edging away. Easing a tortured inch at a time.

He felt sore, wasted. Stepping out, he gave the beauty an affectionate pat on the snout. Poor old girl sputtered and coughed a shot of sour exhaust.

Shoving his hands into his pockets, Drum took a walk around to work out his fisted muscles. The sun baked the back of his neck. He felt clammy, his head pounding like a sledge.

Slowly, he sucked in a stream of cool air. Steady. Releasing it in an invisible curl, he felt himself easing up. Letting go. Better.

Looking around the street, he half expected the hit-run

driver to crawl out of hiding and throw himself on Drum's mercy. Creep had to be near empty by now.

Running took a giant load of fuel, Drum knew. No one could ever guess how big unless they'd been there. And Drum had been there. He'd learned the hard way how you could break your butt running and wind up exactly where you didn't want to be in the first place.

He dragged on an invisible smoke and walked back to the beauty. Flipping on a soft jazz station, he gunned the engine and aimed toward home. He was sorely in need of a little recharging. Maybe a nice matinee if Stella was home. There was a quickening in his groin. He could almost taste the creamy mounds of her flesh, feel himself sinking in her sweet, moist, secret spots. Best places in the world to get lost.

And getting lost for a while was exactly what he needed. Climbing into the sewer was getting easier all the time. Too easy. The hard part was hauling his butt back out and trying to shed the stench.

Drum rubbed his eyes and worked a kink out of his neck. It all goes with the territory, Jerry, old kid, he chided himself. All in a day's work, pal. So quit whining.

A giant yawn rode over him like a wave. His mind was socked in a fog. The beauty was flying on automatic pilot, and so was Drum. But a persistent notion kept teasing at the edge of his brain. A whisper on the wind.

He shook his head, trying to clear it. Whole thing made no sense.

Drum tuned back to the image of the kid at the edge of the road. Scared, hesitating. Then screwing up his courage. Stepping into the street. And from nowhere . . .

A whisper on the wind. Crazy idea, Drum thought, trying to kick it out of his head. But it kept inching back. Teasing.

That was another one he'd have to remember to tell Booker. You need answers, keep your mind wide open, hotshot. It's what you learn after you know it all that counts.

Drum imagined the kid's bright, trusting eyes and the

respect in them as he recited Drum's canned advice. And he felt a bitter catch of sorrow. Sooner or later, Booker was bound to learn the truth about his two-bit, tarnished hero.

Drum hoped it would be later. Later would be more than soon enough.

15

James had been jabbering in staccato bursts since the insurance man left. 'Pop the weasel. Shadow man. Green man tunnel! Mrs. Wheel.'

Paul, who'd made a quick visit between appointments at the studio, was convinced that the gibberish was a positive sign. Cinnie was too worn out to argue. Anyway, there were far more critical things for them to battle over, if she could ever find the nerve and energy.

Dr. Ferris and Dr. Silver had stopped by on separate morning rounds and caught snatches of the rambling. Neither one had any idea of what might be causing it or how to get James to relax.

Cinnie tried to calm him with strokes and pats. She tried playing soft music on the Walkman. Finally, in desperation, she started singing one of his favorite silly songs, 'There Was an Old Woman Who Swallowed a Fly.' He was out cold by the second chorus.

Cinnie kissed his cheek and smoothed the covers over his chest. 'Works every time, Jimbo. My singing is enough to make anyone unconscious.'

Convinced that he would sleep soundly for a while, she trudged down the hall to the patient bath for a shower. Afterward, she dressed in the clothes she'd asked Paul to bring from home: a navy skirt, red sweater. She shoved her reluctant feet into stockings and pumps, even smudged on a little makeup.

After a week of incarceration in this joint, she felt like she was in awkward disguise and about to stage a daring jailbreak in broad daylight. Looked as if this getting back to normal business was going to be a major adjustment.

Leaving the patient bath, she almost tripped over Hanky Moller, the creepy, omnipresent volunteer, pushing his cart. He looked her over as if she were an offering on a buffet table and he hadn't eaten in days.

'Nice outfit,' he said. 'Going somewhere?'

'To work.'

'Oh. When'll you be back then? I'll stop by and see if your boy needs anything.'

'Thanks anyway. I told you, James is all set.'

He shook his head and chuckled. 'Never know. I'll check later. Got some new stuff you might like.'

Exasperating creep. An angry flush scaled her neck as she walked back to James's room. She couldn't say why the man got to her, but she didn't like having him anywhere near James. Or near her, for that matter.

Dr. Ferris was at James's bedside. He looked up and appraised her. 'Good morning, Mrs. Merritt. Is everything all right.'

'Yes. Just a question. What's the story with that guy, Henry Moller?'

'Hanky, you mean? He's one of our most loyal volunteers. Logged something like a thousand hours already.'

'I'm sure he means well. But is it normal for him to spend so much time on pediatrics? I see him here nights, mornings. Doesn't he ever leave.'

Ferris shrugged. 'Happens with some of our most dedicated volunteers, Mrs. Merritt. They get very attached to the place. Want to spend all their time at Fairview. No harm in it I can see.'

'I guess.' Cinnie felt foolish. There was no real reason for her animosity toward the man. She kept telling herself he was harmless. 'Big day for James today.'

He allowed a minuscule nod. 'I'm sure he'll do nicely.'

'I hope so.'

'Not to worry. He's ready for this next phase of treatment. No doubt we'll see positive changes.'

When he left, Cinnie took a deep breath. The man didn't allow a trace of emotion, but if he said James would make good progress, she was more than willing to believe him. She *had* to believe him.

James was scheduled for physical therapy at ten, speech at eleven, and then an hour of occupational therapy, which in his case would amount to attempts to stimulate him to fuller consciousness. After a break for lunch, he'd spend an hour in the rec room with the other kids on the unit, and then he was on for a battery of follow-up tests.

Cinnie had been able to handpick his therapists, so she knew he was getting the best. Still she was nervous about the whole business. Had James really recovered enough to handle all this? And even more questionable, had she?

On the theory that keeping busy was the best defense, she'd booked herself solid with patients during the morning. Her father had called to say he'd be stopping by at lunchtime with Madeline to see James, so Cinnie was determined to be elsewhere.

There was nothing wrong with her stepmother. In fact, the woman was warm, sweet, and singularly well-intentioned. Cinnie also knew that having a new wife was good for her father, the best thing. Madeline had hauled him up out of the bleak well of resignation he'd fallen into during her mother's long illness, especially at the end.

But knowing all that didn't make it any easier for Cinnie to ward off the sudden swipes of resentment, the bitter feelings. It was all her problem, she knew. The strident child in her couldn't stand seeing another person in her mother's place. Easy to analyze. And she intended to get past it as quickly as she could. But in the meantime, she knew it was best to keep her distance.

There were plenty of ways for her to fill the rest of the day, so she'd have no time to worry. Much. She was getting James ready to go when Karen Sands from physical therapy breezed in pushing an empty wheelchair.

'Is there a Mr. James Merritt in this room?' Karen said with an impish wink. 'I have a large hug delivery for a Mr. James Merritt in five-fourteen.'

James shot her a goofy grin. Karen had always been a favorite of his. She was tall and rangy with a salted bob of straight brown hair, a ready smile, and infinite patience. Karen would know how to distract James when the exercises got painful, Cinnie thought. It was critical to keep his muscles loose and to maintain the normal range of motion in his limbs.

So it would hurt. So stop thinking about it, and let Karen do her job. At least James had calmed down.

Cinnie finished dressing him in his striped robe and Yankee slippers, passed a comb through his hair, and rubbed blots of color in his cheeks. 'You be a good boy for Karen, Jimbo. See you later. Okay?'

'Mom?'

'Yes, sweetie?'

'Cookie, Mom.'

'Chocolate chips on the brain, huh?' Cinnie said. 'You must be feeling better.' She wrapped him in a careful hug, breathing in his scent, then forced herself to let him go. She waited until Karen had wheeled him off to the rehabilitation wing before leaving pediatrics for her first appointment.

She found a basket of fresh flowers on her desk and a welcome-back sign taped to the bulletin board. The files for her morning sessions were waiting in a neat pile. She reviewed the top chart and buzzed Sandy at reception to send in the first patient.

He was dressed in a gray suit and a starched, white shirt. His paisley tie was knotted clumsily and tugged off center. A slick of pomade formed a crooked road down the center of his head. She caught the scent of Old Spice.

'Good morning, Mr. London. Aren't you looking spiffy today?'

He made a grunting noise and reached his good arm slowly behind him. From the utility bag, he extracted a lumpy package. 'Buh,' he said and frowned. 'Buh . . . boy!'

Cinnie's eyes widened. 'Did I hear you say, "boy"? Again, Mr. L. Say it again.'

'Buh . . . Booooy,' he said. A triumphant grin claimed his face.

She restrained herself, not wanting to get him over-excited. 'You got something for James? Aren't you a sweet-heart!'

'Boy,' he said and scowled. 'Gug . . . ' He reddened, struggling to form another word, but he couldn't get it out. In frustration, he pounded the armrest.

Cinnie put a hand on his. 'It'll come, Mr. London. Wait it out. Don't push so hard.'

He took a few deep breaths, and his lips started working again. 'Gug . . . ' He chewed the air and coughed hard. 'Gug . . . get. Get!'

'Great, that's it. Take your time now. Easy.'

'Get. Bigger. Boy . . . gug . . . bigger?'

He was beaming. Cinnie smiled. 'Good job, Mr. L. You want to know if James is better?'

'Bigger, yup.'

Typical path to recovery. Many aphasic patients went through a period of substituting similar, opposite, or associated words for the ones they wanted to say: 'Chair' for 'table', 'up' for 'down', 'bake' for 'oven'.

'James is much better, thanks. And so are you, I see. I want the truth now. Have you been seeing another therapist behind my back?'

He looked indignant. 'Nah!'

'Okay I'll take your word for it. How about we get down to business? Something tells me you're going to turn out to be my star prisoner.'

For the rest of the hour, they practiced the names of common objects and recited the key words and phrases London would find most useful. 'Hello', 'Good-bye', 'The food stinks'.

'Food . . . bluch,' was the closest he came.

'Good enough. No question you'll get your point across with that,' Cinnie assured him.

She asked him to supply the missing words in stock sayings and had him identify pictures of common objects. The work was slow and difficult. London's color deepened as he fought to find each word, and his body tensed with the effort to make the sounds fit the fractured thought patterns. Often, his attempts failed, but he kept at it. Cinnie watched for signs of serious fatigue but spotted none. Stubborn old mule looked like he might outlast her.

'Well, that's it for today,' she said finally. 'You were terrific.'

'Boy?' he said.

She tapped the package. 'I'll see that he gets the present. I'm sure he'll love it.'

'Boy.' He smacked his armrest and worked an imaginary steering wheel with his good hand.

'The driver, you mean?'

Affirmative nod.

'No luck yet, but the police are working on it.'

London cocked his head and looked quizzical. Cinnie couldn't guess what he was after until he tapped his lapel where his shield would have been and molded his fingers into a mock pistol.

'You want to know which cops are on the case? Good question. The guy in charge is Deputy Chief Charles Allston, but, to be honest, I'm not convinced anyone's really on the case. Allston's what you'd call the high profile, low performance type.'

London's face went smug.

'What's that look about, Mr. L.? You know something I don't?'

Half his mouth curled in a contented smirk.

'C'mon. Give.'

London held up a chiding finger and swiped it back and forth.

'All right. Chief Carmody keeps telling me the same thing, to keep the faith. So I'm doing my best to stay out of it. But it's not easy.'

He smiled his crooked smile.

'Tell you what. I know you never got that pastrami sandwich I promised you. So in honor of your tremendous work and fabulous progress, how about I get you a pass and take you to Deliworld for lunch tomorrow?'

He squeaked and pounded the armrest. 'Buggup. Booooy.'

'That's sweet. But James isn't well enough to join us. Maybe next time.'

He smacked the rest three times and shook his head.

'Not about James? What then?'

He pinched his nose. 'Bluch . . . World.'

'You trying to tell me Deliworld stinks?'

He nodded vigorously and smiled. 'Boooy.'

'Boy's name? . . . Al's you mean? You want me to take you to Al's Deli?'

London saluted.

'Al's it is, Mr. L. Anything you say.'

The rest of the morning went quickly. At noon, Cinnie left the office and forced herself to keep walking out of the rehab suite. She was sorely tempted to stop by and check on James. But she knew he'd adjust better to the therapy routines without her. And according to her legion of spies, consulted frequently during his earlier sessions, James was doing fine.

Far better than she was, Cinnie knew. Then maybe it was time for some serious therapy of her own.

16 She left the hospital planning to drop in on Dal at work and persuade her to go out for one of their infamous lunches. In third grade, when Dal had moved to Rockville Centre from exotic Houston, the two had discovered a shared passion for rich desserts and serious philosophizing. More than two decades and thousands of empty calories later, they'd managed to resolve the majority of the world's major issues and were in the process of tackling some of the stickier small ones. A fresh favorite, before James's accident, had been the cosmic significance of Dal's perennial struggle with an extra five pounds.

What Cinnie needed today was the comic relief of watching her friend stare with longing at a piece of chocolate mousse pie on the dessert cart as she wondered aloud: 'You know, sometimes I think that with my luck, I'll finally lose the damned five pounds and they'll turn out to be my best ones. I mean, who's to say they won't be five pounds of wit or sex appeal or raw intelligence.'

Cinnie would tell her she agreed. No reason to risk such a tragic consequence. And Dal would order the pie with a double scoop of whipped cream for insurance. Dal had a way of helping Cinnie keep things slightly askew of normal perspective. Exactly where she needed to be at the moment.

But a stronger need drove her past the entrance to Dal's market research firm, and she headed north on High Ridge toward the Grove. On the way, she stopped at the Cheese Shop and Vic's Liquors for supplies. There was another old friendship that needed attention at the moment. And emergency resuscitation if necessary. It was time to put the useless anger and recriminations behind them. At least, it was worth a try.

By the time she turned through the stone pillars, Cinnie

had outlined a detailed plan of attack. She pictured a crackling fire. Soft blanket spread out over the plush rug. Nothing cozier than an indoor picnic: crusty chunks of french bread slathered with butter and cheese, slices of a perfect apple, all chased back with a chilled glass of Chardonnay. Paul for dessert.

The house was bristling still. Cinnie set a match to the trio of logs in the fireplace and left her bundles in the kitchen.

Trampling over the frozen lawn to the studio, she rebuked herself for not doing something like this sooner. As long as they got to a better place, what did it matter who did the pushing?

She noticed a trio of cars and a battered pickup in the lot behind the studio. With a sinking sense of disappointment, she cracked open the door and peered inside. Paul was at the sound board wearing a serious set of earphones. His fingers skittered over the keys and levers as he tracked the winking lights and made adjustments. A group was performing behind the soundproof glass partition. There was no hint of the restless inattention that signaled an impending break.

She waited a few minutes, hoping Paul would notice her and read her lewd intentions. No such luck.

Retreating, she skirted the house and headed toward Grove Street. She followed the road as it snaked its lazy way through the neighborhood. Her feet crunched in the small mounds of dead twigs and leaves left over from the municipal cleanup.

Had it only been two weeks ago that James spent half a Saturday tracking the giant, yellow vacuum trucks as they lumbered from house to house, sucking up the mountains of autumn debris that had been raked or blown onto the pavement?

He'd come home flame-cheeked and chilled, redolent of earth and engine fumes. Papery leaf fragments were twined in his thick, copper hair and matted on his sweater. With a triumphant smile, he'd presented Cinnie with a bouquet of desiccated maple leaves. She wondered if they were still in the empty peanut butter jar on the kitchen sill.

Halfway down the street, she spotted Todd Holroyd coming toward her on a Big Wheel. He moved with the plodding resignation of an inchworm.

'Hi, Todd. No school this afternoon?'

'Teacher conferences, so we got off. How's James doing?'

'Okay. I'll tell him you asked.'

He gave her a dull, quizzical look. 'You'll tell him?'

'Yes.'

'But my mom said he can't . . . '

The boy bit his lower lip, dropped his eyes, and pressed on.

Cinnie swallowed a bitter lump of envy. Even Odd Todd could do so many things James no longer could. Things James might never do again.

Walking on, she spied a quartet of neighbor women huddled beside the DeRosas' gazebo: Lydia Holroyd, Ellen Podhoretz, Lucy Pavan, and Vivian Goldblatt. From half a block away, she could read their intent expressions and the protective tilt of their bodies as they talked. Obviously, it was a serious discussion. They stood with folded arms and hitched shoulders, their eyes bound and serious.

Lucy Pavan noticed Cinnie and motioned for her to join them. Cinnie hesitated, but after an awkward beat, she traversed the distance.

'How's it going?' Lucy said. She was a tiny woman with a Dutch boy hairdo and the large, curious eyes of a deer.

'Coming along.'

'Oh? Is James more alert, then?' Lydia said. She smoothed her pleated skirt and pulled up the collar of her starched white blouse.

'A little.'

Lydia ticked her tongue. 'Must be so terribly difficult for you, Cinnie dear. James was such a clever child.'

Was. Cinnie couldn't find the words or the stamina to answer the bitch. Why bother? 'You'll have to excuse me,' she said. 'I've got to get back to the hospital.'

On her retreat toward the farmhouse, she remembered

113

being on the other side, part of the smug circle whose earnest discussions had been strained by the awkward appearance of one of the unfortunate ones. There was no graceful way to deal with the impossible pain, no right thing to say.

She remembered running into Marion Druce soon after Laurel's accident. Cinnie had wanted to be comforting and supportive, but her tongue was tied in hopeless knots. Nothing came out the way she intended. After that uneasy meeting, Cinnie had felt so ashamed, so inadequate.

So now it was her turn to be shut out. She was positive the women had been talking about James, Paul, and her. She could all but hear the words: *'Such a pity. Poor James. Poor family. Can't imagine how they're managing to deal with it all.'*

Cinnie also knew the guilty subtext beneath the veneer of studied concern. The women were thinking: *Better them than me.* They were wondering what Cinnie and Paul had done to deserve the tragedy, certain on some level that it had to be deserved. They were recoiling from the threat of contagion.

An occasional car drove by. Otherwise, the street was idle. Midday, and the neighborhood symphony was muted to a hum: dim voices on a distant television, a barking dog, an engine idling in a closed garage.

Cinnie's ear filled with the tides of her own breathing and the crackle of her footfalls. Shivering, she noticed that the blazing sun was strangely lacking in warmth. She closed the top button on her coat and tipped up the collar.

Nothing had changed, but everything was different. It was as if the place had been gutted, the exterior a cruel joke. She imagined giant hands slapping the walls of this hollow world together, nothing to lose but a loud rush of emptiness.

James's imprint was on every tree and hillock. Cinnie could see him up at the makeshift plate in a neighborhood stickball game, plastic bludgeon poised on his shoulder, tongue boring in his cheek. She imagined him catching frogs in the shallow pond behind Mrs. Zielinski's and then straggling with a crew of other small ones to 'secret' head-quarters, the moldy weatherbeaten packing crate that had been dumped behind the Pavan's screened porch and forgotten.

When she and Paul first came to see the farmhouse, the realtor had prattled on and on about the virtues of the Grove. 'Plenty of kids for your little boy to play with. And you couldn't ask for a safer place.'

She found herself turning onto the Druces' flagstone walk. The house was an asymmetrical cedar contemporary with broad spans of twinkling glass and patios that jutted off the main house at unexpected angles. Marion Druce was a free-lance graphic artist who worked out of the sunny attic loft.

The doorbell echoed in the cavernous interior. Cinnie heard footsteps descending the circular staircase and caught a flash of Monster, the Druce's golden retriever, bounding toward the door.

Marion held the dog firmly by the collar while she flipped the locks. 'Put a lid on it, Monster,' she said. 'Cinnie? What a nice surprise. Come in.'

'Hope I'm not interrupting anything. I stopped at home to pick up a few things, and I had a question. Got a minute?'

'Sure. Coffee? You have lunch yet?'

'No, but I'm fine. Don't bother.'

'It's no bother.' Marion led her into a square, sunny kitchen with a gleaming wood floor and Mexican tile counters. 'Tuna fish or turkey?'

'Whatever you're having's fine.'

She led Cinnie to a bentwood chair at the oak table and fixed the sandwiches. 'Dal tells me James is coming along fine.'

'Getting better. It's slow.'

'And not easy, I know. It's good that you're able to get away for a while. I remember how those hospital walls had a way of closing in on me.'

She brought the sandwiches and two mugs of instant coffee to the table and sat opposite Cinnie. Monster

115

plunked down his giant muzzle in the vacant span between them. His licorice eyes were solemn and filled with pleading, his nose twitched.

'Down, Monster,' Marion said. 'This lunch isn't worth begging for, believe me.'

The beast sighed and withdrew to the floor in front of the stove. His tail wagged with the steady insistence of a windshield wiper.

Marion had aged, Cinnie noticed. Before Laurel's accident, Dal, Cinnie, and Marion had made it a point to get together once a week or so with the kids. Marion had been the resident parenting expert, most years logged on the job.

Cinnie and Dal had always prized her logic and practicality. Marion had helped Dal through several of her more critical crises with TeeJay including the time Teej wanted a doll carriage and Lydia Holroyd had warned that it was a sure symptom of gender confusion. Marion's response was to lend TeeJay Laurel's carriage, which he'd promptly upended and used as a fort.

Now there was a slackening in Marion's firm features and some of her ruddy color had leached away. Not surprising. In the eleven months since the accident, Laurel had been through five operations on her injured leg, rounds of intensive therapy, and a number of harrowing medical crises. Twice, there had been talk of amputation. The child still suffered chronic pain.

'You had a question?' Marion said.

'Yes. I wanted to know if you ever wonder about all the accidents?' Cinnie pleated her skirt between her fingers. 'Laurel's and the others?'

'Sure I do. I wonder why any of this had to happen to any of us. . . . But that's not what you're getting at, is it?'

'I'm not sure exactly what I'm getting at. I just keep thinking that there must be some explanation, rational or otherwise.'

Marion shrugged. 'Accidents, Cin. You said it yourself. The world is full of accidents and weird coincidences. Unfortunately, we've had a run of rotten ones in the Grove.

Nothing anyone can do about that but hope the streak is over.'

'Maybe so. But what if it's more than simple coincidence? What if there's some reason all these horrible things are happening here?'

Marion sipped her coffee. 'Like?'

'Who knows? A curse, a jinx. I know it sounds ridiculous, but I can't shake the feeling that there's more to all this than coincidence, Marion. There has to be.'

Marion stared into her coffee cup and traced a slow circle along the rim. 'Look, I'll be honest with you, Cinnie. I've had thoughts like that. But where do they get you besides crazy? What's the point of beating it to death? It won't change anything for Laurel or James.'

'The point is to try to understand why all these terrible things are happening here.' .

'No. The point is to get past it. Believe me, it's the only way.'

As Cinnie left the house, the words reverberated in her mind. Marion was right. It was best to put the doubts and questions behind her. Best, but impossible. She couldn't shake the conviction that there was some explanation for all the terrible accidents.

Her logical side told her all the wondering was futile. Even if she could prove there was some malevolent force behind the tragedies, what could anyone do about it? Move away? Have the Grove condemned and evacuated like a spook-infested Love Canal?

She started toward the farmhouse. It would only take her a few minutes to pack up the things she wanted to get for James and some fresh clothing for herself. That would get her back to the hospital in plenty of time to sit and wait for James to finish the scheduled afternoon tests. Sit and wait and worry her fool head off.

Or, she could hang around the farmhouse and dwell on all the haunting *if onlys*: If only she'd asked to see TeeJay at home on the day of the accident. If only Paul hadn't been so careless, had bothered to check his wristwatch against the studio clock. If only the school bus had been early or late or someone from the neighborhood had happened by to help James across the street . . .

Enough.

She kept going back to *why*. Logical or not, there had to be a reason for what had happened. And she was convinced that once she found it, she could somehow use the knowledge to help James recover.

Passing the Sanders' house, she noticed Lois's Chrysler in the driveway. On impulse, she rang the bell. Lois was a physics professor at Columbia, a stony, intellectual pragmatist. Not at all the type to take well to Cinnie's groundless feelings and suspicions.

Or so she thought.

Lois answered the door and ushered Cinnie inside. The woman's eyes were full of unspoken feelings. She was more than ready to talk.

17 The stairwell was dim and musty. A single caged bulb cast a wavering puddle of light over the stained cement walls and garnish metal railings.

Four steps below the pediatrics floor, Malcolm Cobb sat hunched on a grainy, gray riser and listened. His keen ear caught an occasional flurry of footsteps. There was the piteous mewling of a frightened child. A hacking cough.

The nurse was several rooms past the boy's by Cobb's calculations. He had tracked her foot strikes and her grating voice as it pierced the solitude. He imagined the blinding jolt as she snapped the lights on and doused them again with jarring suddenness. In this place of cruel indignity, it was routine for sleep to be rudely rent and left gaping like a wound.

Foul venue.

Foul woman! Save for her unwarranted presence, he could be satisfied and long departed now. A live wire of fury sizzled in his gut. And an angry tic worked his cheek like nervous fingers snapping an elastic.

He forced his attention back to the sounds. There was the ebb and flow of steam in a mist tent, the stertorous exertions of a ventilator. A scream. More footfalls. Retching.

At last, a silence formed and solidified. Cobb held his breath as he climbed to the fifth-floor landing and opened the door.

No one about.

Cautiously, he made his way back to the child's room. Steps echoed down a remote corridor. A door slammed. All at a safe distance. Nothing to hamper his approach.

The boy's door was agape. Cobb edged into the room. No sound emanated from the woman. Excellent. He settled his gaze on the object of his yearning, and his heart swelled.

The child's eyes blazed in the darkness. Cobb felt their heat.

'Be still, my treasure,' he whispered. 'All is well.'

He took a step toward the slatted bed. Another. 'Gooooood boy,' he crooned. 'Nothing will harm you. Not to worry.'

Plucking the needle and tubing from his pocket, he approached the foot of the bed. The child's eyes stretched and sparkled with fear.

'That's marvelous, James. Perfect. Stay as you are. Be still.'

Cobb was even with the child's arm now. All he had to do was lower the covers to expose the harvest site. That done, he slipped his fingers around the boy's wrist and clamped down.

'No. No green tunnel. No, Mrs. Wheel. Mommy. *Mommy!*'

The woman grimaced and moaned. Cobb ducked out of sight at the foot of the bed. His heart stammered in the sharp report of automatic fire.

Slowly all settled in stillness again and the tension dissolved. Cobb tuned his breaths to the rhythm of the woman's. Deeper. Softer. The metronome of Morpheus. Sweet serenity. Silence divine.

He was preparing to rise when there was a sudden creak of bedsprings and the soft concussion of the woman's bare feet on the harsh linoleum. She approached the bed and leaned over the boy.

'You okay, sweetie?'

'Mrs. Wheel. *Wheel*, Mom.'

'Ssh. It's okay, Jimbo. Just a bad dream. Try to get some sleep now. Okay?' She tugged up the blankets and prodded the ends under the matress. 'There. All tucked in tight and cozy. Better?'

Cobb heard three kissing sounds and then padding steps retreating across the room. There followed the weary rush of her breath and the squeal of bedsprings as she settled heavily on the cot. 'Sleep tight, baby. See you in the morning.'

Slowly, a fresh shroud of silence settled and held. Cobb

waited a prudent interval before emerging from the shadows. His legs were cramped, back knotted. As he stood, his knees crackled like dried twigs. Rubbing away the soreness, he looked at the child.

Impudent thing was staring at him again. Eyes glistening, defiant. Evil, feline eyes. A blatant challenge, a threat.

Cobb squelched a murderous rage. He forced himself to consider the painstaking weeks of preparation, the moment of assumption so aptly planned and executed. All that remained was the milking. The precious yield. Only a fool would jeopardize his just reward when it was so close. A breath away.

He had to wait, to let the specimen steep and mellow. A while longer.

Control.

'There there, James,' he rasped. 'I shall be going now, and you must rest. Rest and heal, my child. Salve of my soul. Wellspring of my salvation. Good night, James. Good night, my child.'

He felt the eyes following him as he crossed the room and peered out to check the corridor.

Safe.

Head ducked, Cobb dashed past the row of darkened patient rooms and turned down the narrow hallway at the far end. Beyone the storage and utility areas was an unmarked black door. He paused and rummaged through his pockets. He needed to think, to plan a fresh, bold, infallible strategy.

His fingers found the stolen key, and he quickly worked the lock. Checking again to make certain he was wholly unobserved, he let himself into the sanctum.

18 By the flickering spire of a wooden match. Cobb scrutinized the narrow chamber. Everything was precisely as he'd left it. In the center of the floor, the blue thread remained coiled in the serpentine symbol that was Cobb's designated sentry. The slightest movement would have deformed the gossamer shape. His refuge remained unviolated.

He sniffed, flaring his nostrils. There was a pleasant trace of mint from the essence he'd dabbed on the radiator to counter the musty pall of disuse. Crossing to the far end of the room, he found the pull cord that turned on a pink bulb of spare wattage. Gentle, serene.

She would approve, he thought and felt a shiver of pride. He imagined how she would purse her lips and press her graceful hands together as she assessed the fruits of his toil. He pictured her languid nod of affirmation.

Finding a safe haven had been critical to Cobb. On his last mission, he had suffered mightily for the lack of one.

The memory of that hideous experience throbbed like a festering sore. He had been on his way to the specimen's room when there was a flurry of approaching motion around a near corner. Lacking a suitable alternative, Cobb had shut himself in the tiny supply closet to avoid detection.

An unusual volume of activity on the floor had held him imprisoned in that stifling tomb. Trapped.

After a gelid mass of time, the walls had begun to quiver. Near the ceiling, a row of eyeball jets had materialized and slithered open to permit the leak of blue, noxious fumes. As his meager air supply was exhausted, Cobb had felt a dizzy wash of fear, felt himself yielding to the black descent.

Sinking through time.

He was a child again, locked in the broom closet. The

122

two of them were standing outside in the pantry, tittering. Cobb could hear the rise of excitement in their voices as they plotted his humiliation. The reptilian darkness looped around his neck and began to squeeze.

'Let me out! Please let me out!'

'Malcolm? Stop that insipid whimpering this instant. You act lazy and stupid, you know the consequences. You asked for this, Malcolm. You brought it upon yourself.'

'Let me out!' Fists pounding. Bones splintering. The blood of his desperation splattering the walls.

'Please! Please! Let me out. I can't breathe! Have to go to the bathroom. Can't hold it much longer. Please.'

Always the same. The two of them would wait for his silence. Wait until the darkness had grown to a multitentacled beast and begun to consume him organ by organ. Nothing he could do but cower in mute, paralytic despair.

Cobb could hear the tearing teeth of the darkness, feel the grinding dissolution of his flesh and sinew. Piece by piece he was swallowed. Foot, leg, knee. Hand, arm, shoulder. Nearing the end. Soon.

And then the door would swing open, unleashing a cruel avalanche of blinding light. When his sight was restored, they would be poised, one on each side. Flushed with pleasure, giggling in gleeful anticipation.

Heedless of his mutilation, they would shove him outside and force him to sit on the tall punishment stool in full view of the busy street beyond. They would slip the elastic holding the muzzle around his neck, shove on the cruel band with the floopy paper mule ears. And then they'd drape the tail around him, drooping from a length of cord around his waist so it pointed accusingly at the dark stain spreading across his lap.

And then they would set out the sign on the large wooden easel and ring the bell of shame. Only the rear of the placard was visible to him. But the words were etched in his mind. 'Come one, come all and see Malcolm Cobb, the world's stupidest ass.'

Hiding in the supply closet that time had brought it all back. Cobb struggled to squelch the razor scream rising in his throat. Bit hard on his tongue. Tasted the sweet metal of his own blood.

Beyond the door, he could hear the staff and patients milling about. Like giggling women in a pantry, plotting against him. Delighting in his mortification. Savoring his inner death. No! No more!

The scream was slithering through his clenched teeth, pressing at his lips. Stop!

He had come perilously close to giving himself away. Too close.

After that, he'd vowed to anticipate, to warrant against all contingencies. If the need for a refuge arose again, or if such a place eased his enterprise in any fashion, he would have a proper one prepared. He remained vigilant, haunting the silent halls, examining the hospital structure for abandoned or forgotten spaces he might claim as his own.

Then, on one of his preparatory visits before the taking of this latest specimen, he'd noticed the slim, unmarked, black door at the terminus of the narrow corridor beyond pediatrics. That night, when the guard had abandoned his post to indulge in a smoke in the cafeteria, Cobb had snatched the hospital's master key and had it duplicated in an all-night locksmith downtown.

Opening the black door, Cobb had discovered a small room cluttered with dusty supplies. From the basic furnishings, he divined that it had once served as a lounge where on-duty staff could sleep between calls. There were several like it scattered throughout the hospital, though the rest, Cobb noted, were far more commodious.

He recalled that Fairview had severed its relationship with a medical teaching facility some years earlier. Likely, this space with its spartan furnishings and paltry ventilation had been deemed suitable for the lowly interns and medical students but held laughingly inadequate for licensed staff.

Fortunate snobbery, Cobb thought. To him, it was the perfect sanctum. Close to the child. A breath away. And entirely his.

Over the course of weeks, Cobb had emptied the room of its superfluous debris, depositing useless items in various trash receptacles around the hospital. And then he'd set about fashioning the space to his liking with items he'd brought from the cabin or commandeered from hospital supply.

He'd mounted a small, framed mirror over the sink, placed a spare pen and tablet for his exercises on a stool beside the bed, and settled Mother's ancient rag rug in the centre of the floor.

He had dressed the cot with fresh linen and left three soft blue blanket rolled at the foot of the mattress. In the slim metal locker beside the door, he'd stored a shoe box filled with a spare set of toiletries. The uniforms he'd pilfered from the hospital laundry hung in a reassuring row: lab coats, green surgical scrubs complete with masks and shoe covers, the yellow gown and mask ensemble used for dealing with contagious patients.

In the corner under the window was a carton filled with his emergency survival supplies: extra candles and thread: soda crackers in plastic packets; a water jug; a shrink-wrapped patient bundle containing a plastic urinal, bedpan, soap dish, and pitcher; bandages and antiseptic, reading matter including his own precious volume. In a metal trough were several single-use syringes containing a variety of essential drugs.

All in readiness.

Any number of times during the preparatory phase, he'd elected to spend the night in the sanctum. In the morning, he'd donned one or the other of the several staff uniforms he'd managed to procure without effort and strode boldly about the hospital corridors. Not once had his appearance been challenged.

Fool drones.

But since the assumption of the specimen, he'd endeavoured to remain as inconspicuous as he could. More difficult, to be certain. But far more judicious as well.

Weary, he settled on the lean mattress and pondered alternative approaches to the harvest.

It would all be so simple save for the vile obstacle – the woman. She stood as a menacing impediment to his very survival.

Which left him with only one sound alternative. His dear one had warned him that the woman should be eliminated. But he had not divined a way to dispose of her without casting suspicion on his primary enterprise. Puzzle of grand perplexity, its solution teasing beyond his reach.

But he would not think of that now. It would come. Her reckoning, his resurrection. Bound together in a seamless, gratifying whole.

A pleasant warmth invaded his limbs as he imagined her disposal. His mind soared on a gossamer bubble. Flesh tingled.

Lovely.

He slipped his hand beneath his belt and insinuated his fingers in the tangle of velvety down and hardness. He was unbound. Rising. Riding the exhilarating crest. Soaring beyond!

Cobb ignored the leaping flame of warning. Silenced the strident caw of admonition. In a glorious rush, he reached the perilous peak and sank in a blessed gel of oblivion.

19 Cobb awoke with a start. Tentacles of dawn had slipped through the narrow window and were oozing across the sanctum walls. He detected the escalating activity that presaged a shift change. Footsteps, a percolator pulsing, voices.

'Morning, Gladys. Hope you're ready for the post-appendectomy in twelve. Kid's hell on wheels.'

'Bad as that foulmouthed little double-hernia in three?'

'Close.'

Wretched dolts were absorbed by their petty enterprises. How could they bear the burden of their mundane obligations with such brainless obedience? A swell of contempt filled him, centering his energies and mobilizing him to confront the day.

Better.

He could not make another safe attempt at the milking until tonight. Tonight, he would take what was rightfully his and be renewed. Meanwhile, he would have to utilize his reserves and find the will to play out the cruel charade of his normal existence. He must avoid suspicion at all costs. Now more than ever.

Cobb donned his vile uniform and forced himself to report to his job.

Fortunately, he was not confronted with any significant challenge. Nothing but routine mechanical inspections. Minor repairs and adjustments. The standard assembly line of fouled, repugnant parts he was mandated to test and restore to good condition.

He avoided all but the necessary contacts with his fellow workers and the customers, kept his movements spare and controlled. Still, by the time he was able to sign out and slip away, he was numb with exhaustion.

All because of that wretched woman. She had stood in his path, endangered him. Now his powers were dimmed to a vapor trace. Cobb caught a whiff of the repugnant scent. Vile residue of his own demise.

After work, he drove toward the cabin, hoping to find a message from his dear one. By now, she must be ready to patch their rift, to apologize. Perhaps she would be there when he arrived, waiting to surprise him. He imagined her seated on the rocking chair, her visage humble as a penitent. The possibility buoyed him, but only briefly.

As he drove, the muscle fibers in his left arm, shoulder to fingertips, went suddenly slack and insensate. Desperate, he groped for a way to battle the weakness and restore the waxen limb. Mental recentering, biofeedback. All useless.

Then, he happened upon a comforting incantation. Over and over, he recited the roster of treasonous elements: clavicle, scapula, humerus, scaphoid, trapezoid, pisiform, hamate, triangular, metacarpals, phalanges. It was an entreaty. A prayer.

Pectoralis major, latissimus dorsi, trapezuis, pectoralis minor, deltoideus, teres major, biceps, coracobrachialis, brachialis, triceps. Each a separate urging.

Control!

The words blunted his terror, but there was no real redemption. Nothing but further, relentless decline. He should never have yielded to the Flesh. How many times had she warned him? They had both warned him, Mother and her. Punished him lest he forgot and be damaged further. The Flesh was a deadly demon, a seductive trap.

He had always endeavored to resist temptation, and to follow their wise counsel, but every so often the Flesh would manipulate him, lure him like a painted harlot.

Later he would suffer the dark spells, his thoughts fluttering in and out of reach like capricious insects, his brilliance dimmed to the paltry sizzle of a spent bulb.

It was then that he would make the unforgivable errors, suffer the failures. Unthinkable grades. The ignominious descent from his proper position at the intellectual apex. Desperation would force him to commit the heinous acts. Then would come their revulsion and reprisals.

'Malcolm Cobb, stupid ass. Come see the world's stupid-est ass.'

As he drove down the ribbon of country road toward home, a sudden paralysis claimed the right side of his face, leaving him purblind and dribbling like an imbecile. A mockery. A grotesque!

Stumbling into the cabin, he caught sight of his monstrous visage in the mirror over the maple chest. In a storm of rage, he smashed the glass with one of Mother's bronze lion's head bookends until the battered frame yawned empty and a ring of glinting slivers lay at his feet.

Better.

He felt himself rising by meager degrees. Gaining.

He would not be ruled by the fear. Somehow, he would find the energy to complete the harvest and be healed. Next time he approached the child there would be no heinous impediment.

Patience.

Until the weakness subsided, he decided to seek distraction in the fifth-phase exercises. He believed ardently in the regimen of his group. The exercises outlined in their procedure manual had sustained him through the years of relentless assault by the blue vapor.

Peak mental conditioning required daily review of the sequential challenges leading to the tenth phase. Some never achieved that pinnacle of intellectual excellence, Cobb knew. But when he'd first joined the circle of brilliance, he'd been ready to commence with the fourth phase and quickly passed to the ninth and tenth.

For him, the fifth phase was almost soothing in its simplicity. So basic. Simple memory and recitation in two or more antiquated or exotic tongues. From his vast store of mastered idioms, Cobb decided on the classical Latin forms first. Then middle English. Virgil. Chaucer. All as familiar as his palm. But he kept stumbling. Losing his place and concentration.

Cobb shuddered. To have sunk so far. So quickly.

For once he was pleased that she had not come to heal the breach between them. Not tonight. She must never see him in such a state. He shivered knowing how her face would warp with revulsion and loathing.

What if she suddenly arrived? The thought sent him in a reeling panic.

And then he remembered the treasures. Trembling with need, he pressed his weight against the bedstead, and it yielded the necessary distance. Displacing the loose board section in the floor, he pressed his unafflicted hand into the cool darkness and emerged with one of the precious remnants. A portion of the child's shirt. Tattered and soiled. But to him a thing of wonder. Incomparably beautiful. Priceless.

He pressed his lips to the rigid mass in the centre of the fabric. His tongue worked over the healing humor. Softening and drawing forth the balm.

Instantly, Cobb felt the infiltrating charge of vigor. The warm wash of sweet deliverance.

Mere moments and he was restored. Robust. His muscles thrummed with vibrant renewal, face reveled in its own elastic symmetry. Magnificence!

Lord of the moment! Dark moon rising.

But his relief was fleeting. Soon, too soon, the vapor would begin to enfeeble him again. He needed grand stores of the pure healing reserves. Needed to begin milking the specimen. Nothing would stand in his way.

20 Drum awakened to the sound of the front door slamming and Booker's voice trailing up the stairs.

'Hey. Anybody home?'

The position of the sun said somewhere around three-thirty. Spokes of light leaked through the angled blinds spotlighting Stella's face. Still fast asleep.

Drum loved to look at her. Woman had a great puss. Strong bones. Generous, sexy features. Solid frame with terrific springs and incredible upholstery. Whole picture made Drum hungry all over again. But the kid was home, so he'd have to behave himself. He pulled the sheets up over her shoulders, nuzzled the downy triangle at the back of her neck, and was tugging on his pants when the knock came.

'You in there, Mr. Drum? Mrs. Drum?'

'Yeah, Book,' Drum whispered through the door. 'We were taking a nap. Stella's still zonked. I'll be right down.'

He found the kid at the kitchen table studying his spelling list over a glass of milk and a plate of cookies.

'So, how's it going, hotshot? Have a good day?'

'I ain't complaining.' He looked up from the list, and his lips spread in an impish grin. 'A nap, huh? You expect me to believe that, Mr. Drum?'

'Yeah. I do.'

'You was getting it on, wasn't you?'

Drum frowned. 'That kind of thing is between me and Stella.'

Booker rolled his eyes. 'It's cool, Mr Drum. You could tell me. Ain't no big deal.'

'Let it go, Book. You heard me. You're out of line.'

'Everybody does it, Mr Drum. It's normal. Ain't nothing to be ashamed of.'

'I said *can* it!'

131

Booker's face went dark, and he nibbled a hangnail. 'Don't have to treat me like some little kid.'

'Yeah I do. You are a little kid.'

'Ain't no baby though.' His mouth was set, eyes sparkling mad. 'Tell you that much.'

Drum knew the act. Booker still had his shell of defenses from the bad, old days. Slipped back on real easy.

'No, Book. You're no baby.'

'Well you treat me like one, man. Treat me like a damned baby. Pisses the hell out of me.' Booker shot to his feet, knocking the chair over. Crumpled his spelling list and flung it on the floor. Then he stomped across the room and out the swinging kitchen door. 'Don't have to take none of this shit, no way. I'm out of here, man. I'm gone.'

Drum heard kid clumping up the stairs and the sound of drawers smacking. Waiting for the storm to blow over, he leafed through the local paper and downed a couple of Oreos dunked in the remains of Booker's milk.

News of the unsolved hit-run had been demoted to a quarter column on page five. The Elks had added five thousand to the reward offered for information leading to the driver's arrest. Brought the pot up to twenty-five grand. Nice round number, especially adding the bonus five from Carmody. If things fell his way, Drum would ask old Danny boy to deliver the take in tens. Chief could definitely use the exercise.

There was a quote from Mayor Schippani trashing Carmody for the department's failure to crack the case. According to Schippani, the chief was guilty of mismanagement, lack of direction, poor use of the force's resources, tensions in the Middle East, and the hole in the ozone layer. Obviously, the blast was a direct feed from that snake Charlie Allston. Drum figured the guy was already having himself fitted to fill Carmody's shoes.

The kid came shuffling back into the kitchen when Drum was skimming through the classifieds. Hard habit to break after so many years of looking for something. Booker made a listless pass around the kitchen, slammed

132

a couple of cabinet doors, and stood with folded arms and a tight expression.

'Sorry I blew off like that.'

'No big thing.'

'Shot my fool mouth off. Lost my temper.'

'Happens,' Drum said. 'Forget it.'

Booker's face was full of feelings Drum understood too well. Shriveled, old feelings. Tough and bitter.

'I'll try to keep a lid on it, Mr. Drum. But I ain't promising. Sometimes I just blow off. Just my way.'

'So that means you're staying?'

'Guess I will, if it's cool with you.'

'Yeah, it's fine. Tell you the truth, Book, I'm kind of used to you having you around.'

'Guess I'm kind of used to you too, Mr. Drum. You ain't so bad.'

'Neither are you, hotshot.' Drum held out a hand, and Booker gave it a few strategic slaps.

'So we okay, Mr. Drum? We cool?'

'You bet,' He checked his watch. 'Listen, I'd better get back to it, kid. Catch you later.'

'How 'bout I go with you? Got no homework.'

'Not today, Book. Another time.'

Kid went glum again. It was like that with a kid sometimes: one step forward, two back.

Stella trudged in wearing a white terry robe and quilted pink slippers. She took the kid by the ears and bussed his forehead. 'Hi, handsome. Have a good day at the salt mines?'

'Yeah, fine. Hey listen, Mrs. Drum. Didn't you say I could hang around and goof if I don't have no homework? Didn't you say it was okay long as I was home by dark?'

'Yes, I did, honey. But today I need you stick around. Mrs. Bergmuller from social services said she'd be stopping by between four and five to say hello.'

She was trying to sound breezy, but Drum caught an edge of worry.

'What's she want?' Drum had never liked the broad. She was too young, too bouncy. Had way too many teeth.

Stella shrugged. 'She wouldn't say. Told me she had some news for us. Wants to explain it in person. That's all.'

Drum didn't like the smell of it. 'I'll wait then.'

'No need, Jerry,' Stella said. Drum could see she meant it. Knew he should be out there trying to earn his keep. 'You can go.'

He raised his eyebrows at her, double-checking. She nodded in that way of hers that said, yeah, she could handle it, whatever it was. Drum let her boot him out the door.

Driving north in the beauty, Drum kept thinking how you could never figure things. About this time last year they'd been mad as hell that social services wasn't on the case. The Bergmuller broad was in charge of Booker's file, but they hadn't heard a peep from her in months. Drum had called her office and left a stack of messages, but she was obviously ducking him. When he'd finally cornered her on the phone by posing as an old boyfriend from college, she'd finally admitted that Booker wasn't going to be easy to place for adoption: too old, too poor, too much baggage, way too dark.

Which had turned out to be more than okay with Drum and Stella. They were doing fine with the kid. Better than fine. The last thing they needed was some bouncy, shark-toothed, officious baby broad looking over their shoulders. Scorched him to think about it.

Maybe it was nothing. Drum shelved the infuriating thoughts and got himself ready for the next round. Time to drop in at the houses on his curious neighbour list.

He decided to go with his census-taker routine. Most people were willing to cooperate when Drum produced the ten page form he'd printed on the press in his basement and flashed his laminated ID card with the bogus official government business stamp. Once he got into a house and started people talking, the rest came easy.

No one answered at his first stop. At the next, a mock Tudor a half mile east of Cascade on Ponus Ridge, the door was tugged open by a seventyish couple named Marvin and Binnie Proust, who looked like flip sides of the same sort, portly, moon-faced coin and moved in the tortoise tandem of twins joined at the hip.

They were more than willing to answer his questions. Binnie pulled out a fat family album to put faces on the jumble of relatives she found cause to mention. Meanwhile, Marvin poured generous measures of Chivas Regal for himself and Drum.

Drum protested that he wasn't supposd to drink on duty, but he allowed Marvin to twist his arm and joined the old guy in a couple of belts to avoid an insult. Anything for the cause.

When Binnie mentioned her five-year-old grandson from Phoenix, Drum grabbed the opening and asked them if they'd known the local kid that age who'd been involved in the hit-run.

They went grim with honest interest. But when Drum gently pressed them to remember if they'd seen any speeding cars pass by around noontime on the day of the accident, he sent them into a hopeless spiral of confusion.

'The twenty-first? Wasn't that the day we went for the root canal?' Binnie said.

'Eye doctor, I think. I needed a new reading prescription, remember? Remember how I was looking at the *TV Guide*, and I couldn't find Tuesday?'

'Right, yeah. And then we had lunch at the diner on Summer Street? Tuna on whole wheat and you had the turkey breast with Russian, right?'

'It was Friendly's, Bin. Remember the eggs were cold?'

'Oh, yeah, and tough as rubber. And the fryolater was out of whack, so I had to have chips instead of fries, right?'

'Wait a minute, wait a minute. Wasn't that the day Aunt Sadie came for lunch, and she kept going on and on about how mad she was at Rose for not inviting her to Effie's wedding?'

Binnie let out a rush of breath. 'Sadie's dead five years now, Marvin. how many times do I have to tell you?'

'Oh, yeah. A stroke, right? Slipped my mind.'

'Not a stroke. A coronary. Milton had the stroke.'

'Oh, yeah.'

At the next house, near the intersection with Cascade, the door was answered by a young woman holding an infant. The baby was starched with anger, screeching like a tripped alarm. Drum tried to pinch his spiel over the ruckus.

The mother was shaking the kid like a cocktail, but it didn't help. After a couple of minutes, she shrugged her shoulders in apology and said that this wasn't a good time. Drum caught the word 'colic' and her asking him to come back later when the kid might be calmer. Eighteen or twenty years, he figured.

His next hope was a sprawling gray ranch on Mill. He judged Helen Silberfeld, the woman who answered the door there, to be in her late fifties. From her responses to the fake census survey, Drum learned she was a widow who lived alone with three calico cats, a pair of Irish setters, and a mouthy cockatiel. No kids. She'd worked for years in the reference department of one of the branch libraries, but she'd given it up when her husband got sick, and she hadn't gotten around to returning.

Mrs. Silberfeld was attractive and intelligent. Plenty of vintage class. But she had lonliness written all over her. Talked too much and too quickly. Gave too much away too fast, which suited Drum fine.

He turned the conversation to the day of the hit-run, and she was able to dip into her mental files with all the methodical clarity of a trained researcher. She did remember hearing a squeal of brakes and going to the window to investigate. She'd gotten there just in time to catch a fast glimpse of a dark car rounding the hairpin curve toward the High Ridge spur.

Drum coaxed, but she stayed foggy on the details. The car color could have been any dark shade or even a dirty medium. The driver had been out of sight around the curve before she made it to the window. Her first impression was of a van or a station wagon in brown or dark green, but after reading that another witness had mentioned a maroon sedan going in the opposite direction, she had to admit to herself that the whole thing had happened too quickly to leave her sure of anything.

A policeman had stopped by a couple of days later to see if she had information about the accident, but the incident had seemed too insignificant to mention. And reluctantly, Drum was beginning to agree. Woman was no star witness. He finished the cup of coffee she'd pressed on him and left.

Two hours work, and, so far, all he had to show for his troubles was a full bladder.

21 Drum had one last card to play. He made another slow swing through Tyler's Grove. Almost five o'clock and the place was finally starting to look lived in. Clumps of kids were playing noisily in the street, hopping around like beads of water on a hot skillet. Silent images danced on television screens. Smoke belched from several chimneys and wafted ghostlike on the frigid air.

Determined to interview the one witness on record, Drum pulled into the bluestone drive at the Holroyd house on Melon Patch Lane and rang the bell. He wanted to hear the broad's story about the speeding car with his own ears, see how it played live and in person.

No answer.

The house was a stock, center hall colonial with a weathered shake exterior and russet trim. Drum peered through a broad bay window into a pin-neat living room filled with fat English antiques. No junk, no tossed shoes or rumpled magazines. Crocheted doilies guarded the backs and arms of a plump sofa and a ring of side chairs done in pink cabbage roses on a field of ivory chintz. The end tables were clean except for a couple of family treasures propped against squat wooden stands: a hand-painted plate, a kid's book. The only island of friendly disorder was an old walnut school desk in the corner. Its pocked surface was piled with papers and a couple of texts. Drum studied the scene as if it might have something to tell him. It didn't.

One of those days.

He walked back to the beauty, stomping out his frustrations in the broad stream of bluestone on the driveway. Time to let out the slack and widen the circle.

He drove north on High Ridge and took Trinity Pass Road into the half-horse town of Scotts Corners, New York. The place came down to a scatter of clapboard houses and a single strip of understated shops: appliance store, kitchen design, health spa, Irish handknits, beauty parlor, Italian resaurant, combination stationery-deli-pharmacy with an unadvertised side business in football bets. Drum pulled into the gas station half a block past the main drag and strode through the cramped front office to the service bays.

He spotted Billy Driscoll's feet poking out from under a disemboweled Pontiac. The crusted, toeless work boots were a dead giveaway. So where the blackened toes poking through the gap with their inch-long grimy talons. Drum caught the rope trailing from the wooden dolly and yanked the body out until he had a view of the whole sad story.

The eyes blinked. Oily black eyes floating in a pool of sludge. Once, Drum had seen Driscoll spiffed for his mother's funeral. Turned out the guy had an actual face under all the filth. Long nose with pinched nostrils, full mouth, thick eyebrows, sharp cheekbones, cupcake chin. Standard equipment. But you'd never guess to look at him under ordinary circumstances. Everyday Driscoll was filthy cords of tangled hair, skin the color of raw sewage. Predictable stench. Real elegant.

The eyes stayed on Drum until they'd done their job and blinked a code of recognition.

'That you in there, Jerry? What's the deal? Halloween's over.'

'Yeah, Driscoll. Thanks for telling me. How's it going?'

Driscoll whistled. 'That's some damned good getup you got there, Drum. I wasn't a genius, I wouldn't have known you.'

'You *don't* know me.'

Driscoll stood and stuck out a hand. 'You'll still do anything for a buck, huh Jerry? Just like the good old days.'

Drum narrowly avoided the proffered shake. Pumping Driscoll's handle was like dipping your mitt into a sewer.

'I didn't come here to be insulted, Meat.'

'Why then?'

'I'm working on this little matter for a guy. I wanted to run the thing by you. See what you think.'

Driscoll wiped his palms on his denim overalls. The crusted lips spread to reveal a dilapidated fence of rotting teeth. Drum knew that some of the cracked ivories and blackened stumps were casualties of Driscoll's strange pre-dilection for eating things whole -- bones and all. Raw or cooked, alive or dead, made no difference to Billy, which was how he'd come by the nickname Meat.

Driscoll was a mechanical and scientific genius. As a kid, he'd gotten real interested in taking things apart to see how they worked. Started with radios and toasters. Ended with an old one-eyed guy who'd lived in a fleabag hotel in downtown Bridgeport. Drum had heard all about the incident from Driscoll himself when they were next-door neighbours at the Long Lane Youth Correctional Facility. Meat was real sentimental about that one-eyed guy.

Driscoll led Drum into the back office, a roach resort wedged between service and the employees' can. He cracked a fresh fifth of Jim Beam, poured a hefty measure into a glass of sweet cream, and slugged the mess back. Then he wiped his mouth with the back of his hand, refilled the glass, and held it out in Drum's direction.

Drum passed, but he was real polite about it. Last thing you ever wanted to do was hurt Meat's feelings.

Fortified, Driscoll folded his arms and nodded. 'Shoot.'

Drum described the kid's injuries: compound fracture of the left tibia, fracture of the left anterior skull. Persistent mild coma. Not wanting to influence Driscoll's read, he didn't mention that the victim had been a child. Avoided saying anything about a car or an accident. Brain like Driscoll's needed plenty of room for taxi and take off. Never knew where the guy would land either. Probably wouldn't come up with anything, but Drum figured it couldn't hurt to let him try.

Driscoll thought a minute, then he started firing ques-tions. Any tearing of vascular channels around the brain? Any scalp lacerations? Did the brain lesion cross the middle meningeal artery? What was the nature and size of the skull fracture? How did the victim score on the coma scale?

As usual, Drum was impressed. Driscoll would have made a helluva doctor if he hadn't been caught playing butcher.

'So?' Drum said. 'What's your read?'

'Wait a damned minute, Jerry. You know I don't lay my hand until I have all the cards.'

Driscoll asked a pile of additional questions about the posttraumatic condition of the victim. Vomiting? Pupillary asymmetry? Had there been a need for endotracheal intubation? Was the victim put on assisted or controlled respiration? What were the blood gas values?

Drum knew he was in way over his head at this point. He went out to the beauty and fetched the copies of the hospital reports from the trunk. Pulling off the identifying information on the top sheet, he handed the pile of paper to Driscoll and watched the cesspool read.

Driscoll chewed on a knuckle. Scratched his filthy head. At one point, he pressed one nostril shut and shot the contents of the other one into his shirt pocket. Guy's manners had improved.

When he finished, he tossed the papers aside and went into one of his stupors. Drum had seen it before. Guy turned blank and still as a rock. Only sign of life was the low humming noise that seemed to come from Meat's entrails. Sounded like he'd swallowed a bee hive. Then with Driscoll, you could never tell.

Drum waited until Driscoll came around and shook off the fog like a wet dog. 'Got it,' he said. And he started reeling off the facts and suppositions.

The injured party was a male child, aged somewhere between five and six. Driscoll recited the Merritt kid's vital statistics as if he'd just finished fitting the kid for a suit: thirty-eight pounds, forty-three inches tall, medium hair, light eyes, no prior injuries or serious illnesses. No allergies. No siblings. Parents well educated. Both employed. Professional or creative fields. Mother was in one of the helping professions. Meat was a little cloudy on the father's gig, but the man was definitely over six-feet tall and talented.

Drum knew Meat was only warming up. Driscoll could easily get all that information by working from the medication and equipment orders, the anecdotal notes, and the grainy copies Drum had made of the kid's X rays. Driscoll could read a person's life story in an X ray.

When they were at Long Lane, a vet from Belmont used to come up to visit Driscoll once a week during the racing season. All Meat had to do was look at the horses' X rays, and he could tell the guy exactly where to lay his loot.

Vet got rich, Meat got richer. And he'd invested his winnings wisely. Drum knew he owned a dozen stations like this one in various parts of the country, a fleet of cabs, a limo operation, and a chain of walk-in clinics and medical labs.

'All confirmed as far as you've taken it, Meat. Now tell me something I don't already know,' Drum said.

Driscoll's eyes narrowed. 'You always were an impatient sonavabitch, Drum. Hold your water, will you? I'll tell you plenty.'

The broken leg had been caused by sharp, sudden impact with a piece of curved metal. Probably a steel alloy. Approximately six inches high over a spring-mounted rubber base.

Translation, car bumper with a late-model crash damage control system. Car had a steel chassis, automatic transmission, power-assist steering. Either a foreign model or one of those American cars with Tokyo-made parts that had been slapped together in Michigan. The weight Meat estimated would make it a midsize sedan or a wagon with plenty of crap in the trunk. Steel-belted radial tired. Snows on the rear. If the car hadn't been laundered, there'd be blood on the right front fender and traces on the hood and windshield.

The head injury was not so easy for Driscoll to read. It was a depressed skull fracture with none of the accompanying tearing of the vascular channels Meat

142

would have expected to find. The circular scalp laceration was also surprising.

'You see, Drum. If the kid was hit by a car and tossed so his head hit something round and hard like a rock on the ground, you'd get a different kind of picture altogether. The blood vessels and membranes around the brain would be trashed. You'd have swelling, bleeding.' He held the X ray up to the light and pointed a soiled finger. 'Look at that head shot, my man. Squeaky clean.'

Other things didn't fit either. Given the injury profile, there was no reason Meat could see for the boy's cardiac symptoms. The kid had gone into arrest three times, and his vitals had remained erratic for the first twenty-four hours after the accident. Even after that, he'd had several bouts of tachycardia, rapid heartbeat so severe they'd had to put the kid on an antiarrhythmia medication called Inderal. Strangely, even that had failed to control the problem at first. Made Driscoll wonder.

Meat looped his grimy paws behind his equally grimy neck and paused for effect. ' . . . So what I'd say we've got here is a couple of interesting questions. How come the head injury was so clean? And why the heart symptoms?'

'So you have any ideas?'

'My mama, may she rest in peace, told me never to read in the dark, Jerry. Only one way to know for sure what we're dealing with.'

Drum scowled as Driscoll explained what he'd need to take the next step. 'Tell me you're joking, Meat. How the hell am I going to do that?'

'That's your problem, pal. You want me to make tea, you gotta bring me the tea leaves.'

Drum listened to Meat's instructions, picked up the kid's hospital reports, and walked back toward the beauty.

The last of the sun had dipped beneath the horizon. His shadow wavered and strained over the greasy blacktop, and his breath rode the air in angry puffs.

He hadn't been able to get Meat to make any guesses, but Drum was itching to come up with a few of his own. So how did it all fit together? He tried to find a place for all the odd pieces. Unexplained heart symptoms? Injuries that didn't add up? Strange medication reactions? What in the hell was Meat thinking?

Drum pictured the driver hitting the kid and flying into a blind panic. And after that, nothing. All he kept imagining was running and more running.

But then that weird image came back to him.

Whisper on the wind.

Why did he keep thinking about that? What did it mean? He could almost feel the pulse of air. A phantom projectile streaking through the silent sky.

Drum shook his head to clear it. Reading in the dark. Meat's mother was right. Definitely not the best way. The trick was to follow up, be methodical. He could almost hear Big Matt's voice. *Use what you have, Jerry. Everything you find can tell you a story if you take the time to listen and learn, son.*

Drum gunned the engine and turned the beauty around. A playful little smile worked over his mouth. Even though Meat had refused to lay out his guess, the guy had obviously smelled something, and Meat's nose was legendary. Funny how the people who try the hardest to disappear always manage to leave behind a calling card.

22 By the time Drum arrived at the hospital, visiting hours had ended. Entering the lobby, he heard a nasal voice over the loudspeaker urging the final stragglers to leave. Which called for Plan B.

Drum ducked into a phone booth near the coffee shop and asked the hospital operator to connect him with the family waiting room on the labor and delivery suite. A hoarse-sounding guy answered there, and Drum inquired if there was any news yet about Mrs. Rodriguez. Drum heard the receiver clatter on its cord and the hoarse guy asking around. No Rodriguez.

Drum hung up, waiting half a minute, and called again. He could hear the raspy guy's patience eroding. Four more calls, and the man was shooting sparks.

'Listen, buddy, I told you there's nobody here named Rodriguez. There's a Frasier and a Mahoney and a Minotti, period. Now will you stop ringing the damned phone? Happens we're waiting for important news.'

At the security desk, Drum stopped and asked directions to the delivery suite. 'My daughter's having a baby. Name's Minotti.'

The guard was a ruddy giant with Chiclet teeth and a salted walrus mustache. He took in Drum's misbuttoned trench coat, jittery stance, and the huge basket of flowers he carried, and grinned. 'First grandkid?'

'Shows?'

'Know it well. My first, I was out of my head. Got four now. Two more on the way. Everything works out fine and dandy. You'll see.'

'Yeah. Hope so.'

Drum shoved a cigarette between his lips, wrong end out. Thing felt peculiar. He'd copped it from a pack he'd hidden in his sock drawer for emergencies and managed not to need so far. The guard chuckled and punched a few keys on the computer terminal at the main desk.

'Minotti hasn't delivered yet. Go on up, grandpa. Be over before you know it, and you'll have yourself a nice little baby to spoil rotten. Nothing like it.'

When he was out of sight down the hall, Drum shrugged out of the coat, rolled it into a taut cylinder, and slipped it behind a trash can.

Underneath, he wore an ink-blue jumpsuit with 'Joe' sewn over the breast pocket and 'Property of Fairview Hospital' embroidered on the back. Carmody's tailor, Luigi, was far from the best needleman in the game, but he had to be one of the quickest. Drum had called in his order to Luigi's shop first thing this morning, and he'd found the package of costumes waiting when he went home for his afternoon nap.

He lifted the flowers out of their basket. Inside was a metal bucket, a measure of powdered soap, and a sponge. Drum replaced the flowers and set the basket on the windowsill at the far end of the hall. Then he filled the bucket in the nearest men's room and took a quick hike through the glass bridge and down the rear elevator to the laboratory. The door was double locked with a serious deadbolt, but Drum and his picks managed to convince it to open.

The place was exactly as Meat had led him to expect. He passed through a generous reception area, silent except for the angry hiss of the overhead clock. Inside, the work areas ran like spokes off the narrow central corridor. To the left was a rabbit warren of tiny, windowless offices. A series of labs separated by glass dividers jutted off to the right. Their specialties were stenciled on the glass doors: hematology, toxicology, cytology, genetics, chemistry, and other names that made Drum's tongue feel tangled.

The polished steel counters were crammed with intimidating machinery. Drum took a stroll around the place and checked out the gamma counters, the flourescence polarization machines, the variable rotators, centrifuges that looked like the eggs of giant aliens, the prothrombin time analyzer. He was hard-pressed to spot a microscope or much of anything that required a human hand.

He ended his tour in the hematology section. Along one wall was a line of steel-doored refrigerators. They held specimen racks by the hundreds, each jammed with dozens of labeled glass vials.

According the Meat, the Merritt kid's chart indicated standing orders for daily blood work. The docs wanted to check for infections and monitor any glitches in the kid's metabolism that might signal impending system failure. Standard procedure given the nature of the child's injuries, Meat had assured.

The orders didn't call for a fasting specimen, Driscoll had noted, so it was likely that the kid would be on the list for a late collection. According to Meat, that meant the samples would probably be stored for next-day analysis. There would also be a refrigerated baseline sample, drawn at the time of admission, and held for later comparisons. Perfect for Meat's purposes.

According to Driscoll, the daily draw would likely be divided into five vials. He'd instructed Drum to siphon a half inch or so off each sample and substitute the draw for the baseline sample Meat needed. Complicated, but the only way to ensure that nothing would be missed.

Drum started ruffling through the specimen racks. The samples were arranged by floor, which made his job easier. He culled the racks from the fifth floor and started searching for the ones bearing the Merritt kid's name and six-digit patient number.

Drum was down to a few final possibilities when he heard a key working in the door to the lab. His first instinct was to disappear, but he couldn't spot any promising hiding places. The room had too much glass, too many polished surfaces. He took a breath and stood his ground.

The key belonged to a stern-faced doctor in green scrubs. Guy stopped short when he spotted Drum sponging tight circles on the steel counter. But after a quick glance and a dismissive nod, he turned away, tugged open the warmer in the adjacent bacteriology lab and started rifling through the culture dishes. Not the type to waste much time on a mop jockey, Drum figured. Lucky thing.

Drum caught the doc's reflected image in a glass-fronted equipment cabinet. Something familiar about the guy, but Drum couldn't pin it down. Hopefully, the amnesia was mutual. Even in full camouflage, the right set of eyes could see through him.

The doc was staring at the cultures. On several, Drum could see where slimy green splotches had infiltrated the gum pink surfaces and spread to resemble the maps of emerging African nations. The doc made notes to himself in a leather pocket organizer and returned the glass dishes to the cooker.

Guy was taking his sweet time. Made Drum antsy as hell. The steel counters were already so clean they squeaked when he wiped them. He took a drag on the antiseptic air and let it out by degrees.

Finally, the doc was finished. His rubber soles squished across the checkerboard tile, and he closed the door behind him with a resolute click. Drum waited until the guy had plenty of time to get gone before resuming his search.

Three more racks to go. The names and numbers on the vials were faint and hard to read. Drum had to hold several up to catch the light at a better angle. Took him five minutes more to eliminate the rest of the first batch.

He was halfway through the second rack when he spotted the name Merritt. The kid's other samples had to be nearby. He was checking the rest of the specimens when he heard the knock.

There was a sharp rapping at the locked laboratory door. Too insistent to ignore. Cursing under his breath, Drum answered.

A plump, sandy-haired nurse was on the other side. She beckoned him with a cocked finger. 'Got an upchuck for you in five twenty-seven, friend. Doc was checking a kid's throat and back came dinner. No answer at maintenance. Where is everybody?'

Drum shrugged. 'I'll go get my mop. Meet you on five.'

'Uh, uh,' she said. 'I got you, I'm not letting you get

away. We have a beautiful mop upstairs with your name on it, Joe. Come on with me, I'll introduce you.'

She looped her meaty fingers through Drum's elbow and escorted him up to pediatrics. He swabbed up the mess, breathing through his mouth to avoid the stench. This was definitely going to cost Carmody something extra. Maybe that portable Nintendo game Booker had his eye on. Maybe more.

On the way to the elevators, he was stalled by a spilled glass of juice in five-thirty and a jammed Venetian blind in five-seventeen. The door to the Merritt kid's room was closed. Passing in slow motion, he picked up a muffle of voices from inside, but he couldn't make out the words.

Drum took the elevator down and went directly through the lab to the rack of vials. He found the kid's number again in the middle of the pack, located five other specimens with matching labels, and drew off the samples into the sterile tube Meat had given him to switch with the baseline sample from the refrigerator. Delicate operation. He was out of the lab, and the door had locked behind him before he noticed the pox of red flecks on his fingers.

He strode through the lobby wearing the trench coat. His hands were thrust deep in his pockets. The guard flashed him a silent question. Drum answered with a slow nod and held his grin steady until he was out in the parking lot. He'd smile for real when he had the right brand of blood on his hands.

23 Ten minutes after Cinnie returned to the hospital, Karen Sands wheeled James back from the last of his tests. Poor sweetheart looked exhausted, arms dangling, lids at half mast, chin lolling near his chest.

'He did great, Cin,' Karen said. 'Worked his cute little butt off.'

Cinnie kissed him on both droopy eyelids and slicked a ribbon of fallen hair back from his forehead. 'How's it going, Jimbo? You look like overcooked spaghetti.'

'I bet he won't sleep for more than a week or so,' Karen said. 'You get a nice rest now, handsome. No more Devil's Island boot camp for you until first thing tomorrow. Okay?'

They transferred James to the bed and settled him under the covers. His eyes fluttered shut, and his breathing settled in a light snore.

Karen patted Cinnie's hand. 'He really did well, Cin. Much better than I expected, in fact. You want my amateur opinion, he'll get over all this way faster than you will.'

'Testing went all right too?'

'Fine, from what I heard.'

'Come on, Karen. You know what I'm asking: numbers, conclusions, prognosis. Don't give me any of that "fine" crap. I want to know how he is – really.'

Karen flopped down on the visitor's chair and spewed a rush of air. 'Therapists make the worst patients and *absolutely* the worst patient's mothers, Cin. That's the truth.'

'Don't change the subject. Tell me.'

'There's nothing you don't already know. It's going to be a long haul. Everyone's reasonably optimistic about where he'll wind up eventually, but he's going to need a lot of intensive therapy. And he's going to need it for a long time.'

'So?'

'So as soon as Dr. Silver can put it together, everyone on the case will sit down to hash out the treatment options and figure out the best way to get from here to there.'

'I want an invitation to that meeting.'

She shrugged. 'You know patient conferences are strictly for case staff, Cin. Silver will never allow you to sit in. You and Paul will be consulted before anything's decided. That much I can promise.'

'I want an invitation, or I want a transcript or a tape recording. This is my kid, and I have a right to know what's said about him. How the hell are we supposed to make an informed decision if we're not informed?'

'Why do you always have to be so damned logical?'

'Word for word, I want to know what's said and who says it.'

Their eyes locked. Karen blinked first. 'I'll see what I can do.'

After Karen left, Cinnie settled in the chair next to James. Watching her son sleep, she felt her bones melting. Her mind drifted. She was nearly asleep herself when his voice pierced her bubble.

'Book, Mom.'

'Ssh, honey. You rest now.'

'Book, Mom. Book!'

'Sudden craving for literary enrichment, sweetie? Okay then.' Yawning, she walked over and picked several books from the stack on the windowsill.

'Okay, I've got *Mr. Angelo, The One in the Middle Is the Green Kangaroo*, and that classic epic poem, *I Can't, Said the Ant*. What's your pleasure, sir?'

James shook his head. 'Book, Mommy.'

'Not any of these?' She returned the first bunch and brought another pile to the bed. He kept shaking his head in the negative until she held out a slender beige volume called *Garden of Weeds*.

James nodded and patted the cover with his hand. 'Book.'

Cinnie opened to the first page and started to read. It was an odd, unpleasant story about a wicked woman who lived in an old stone house. She planted her garden with weeds and plucked out any stray wildflowers or sweet berries that poked up through the thorny tangle.

Eventually, her weeds grew tall and strong and began to invade other gardens in the village. The woman's neighbors pleaded with her to get rid of the mess, but she refused. So one night, the neighbors stole into the ugly garden and sprinkled weed killer over everything.

In the morning, nothing remained but two young, sturdy weeds named Dove and Elegant. The woman took them in and nurtured them as her own son and daughter. By supporting each other, the weeds thrived through a long, difficult winter full of harrowing threats by the angry neighbors, and the next spring, the old woman set them out again to flourish and spread.

The weeds were connected by some weird bond. When one had a good day, the other grew stronger. When one suffered adversity, the other one weakened and bled a bitter green sap. The ailing weed could only be restored by sucking the sap from a healthier weed in another garden. Charming.

Cinnie finished reading and set the book aside.

'Book, Mommy.'

'How about this one, Jimbo? It's an Encyclopedia Brown mystery. Your all-time favorite super intelligent little sleuth.'

But he picked up the book about the weed garden and thrust it toward Cinnie. 'Book.'

Reluctantly, she read it again. Creepy story. Homely little volume. The pages were yellowed at the edges, the pictures grim and unappealing. With a prickle of annoyance, Cinnie realized that her father's wife, Madeline, must have brought the book for James along with the ribbon-wrapped bag of chocolates on his night table and

152

the new pair of mud-brown pajamas she'd spotted in his drawer.

Cinnie's stepmother was a bargain fanatic. No doubt the pajamas and chocolates had been on sale. The book was obviously used. The name 'Malcolm' was scrawled inside the front cover; Cinnie's nose wrinkled at the musty scent rising from the pages.

Cinnie had nothing against bargains, but markdowns were Madeline's Holy Grail. Didn't matter how homely the pajamas or how creepy the story or how antique the chocolates. No matter if the pajamas were chocolate colored and the chocolates tasted like pajamas. As long as the price was right. Made Cinnie furious. Then everything about Madeline made Cinnie furious. At least no one could accuse her of being inconsistent.

'Book, Mom.'

'Come on, Jimbo. Enough of that putrid story. How about I read you *Curious George Goes to the Hospital*? It's got everything: suspense, romance, high adventure.'

She shoved the offensive little story under a pile of toys and found several more attractive alternatives. But James would not be deterred. He flushed, stiffened, and pointed in the direction of the hidden volume. 'Book, book! *Book*, Mom!' He was whimpering. Desperate.

'Okay, sweetie. Okay, you win. How come I'm bigger, and you always win?'

She read the weed story half a dozen times more, but still James wasn't satisfied. Nor did familiarity make the tale any more endearing to Cinnie. She had a sharp fantasy of sprinkling weed killer over Madeline and watching her shrivel and turn brown at the edges. Dreadful book.

By the time James finally fell asleep, Cinnie was tempted to toss the weed book out the window or stash it someplace suitable like the bedpan. But she had the grim feeling that James would be asking for it again as soon as he woke up. At least he was asking for something.

He slept soundly through Dal's visit. She brought Cinnie up to date on neighborhood news, including the delicious gossip that Lydia Holroyd's husband had given up his job that involved sixty percent travel for a new position in which he'd be out of town almost full-time.

'Can't say I blame him,' Dal said. 'If I was married to that know-it-all bitch, I think I'd become an astronaut.'

Dr. Ferris stopped by to see how James had fared in therapy. He passed a delicate hand over the little boys' forehead and smiled. Cinnie was touched by the unusual display of affection.

Being on the hospital staff, Cinnie knew enough to pick her doctors by skill rather than personality. She'd ignored all the nasty asides about Ferris from colleagues who resented his medical genius and his standoffishness. He'd committed the mortal sin of refusing dinner party invitations and refusing to attend hospital benefit dances.

Cinnie knew that socializing with the medical community didn't make anyone a better doctor. But she'd often longed for the vaguest show of warmth from Ferris, for her or James. For anybody. Most of the time, he reminded her of something shrink-wrapped. But now she had a teasing glimpse inside the careful packaging.

Ferris met her eyes. 'Can't tell you how pleased I am, Mrs. Merritt. How relieved. For a while there . . . '

'But he's not entirely conscious yet, is he? He still seems to be drifting in and out.'

The doctor frowned. 'Not entirely, but close. Anytime now, I think we'll have him fully alert. James has always been such a bright, animated little boy. So outstanding. You must be very proud.'

He looked softer than Cinnie could ever remember. Man had nice eyes. Pale, artistic face. Intelligent eyes. Gentle hands. She'd never thought about his age before, but he couldn't be much more than midthirties. Wouldn't be a shabby catch, she thought and wondered how he'd react if she mentioned Dal's single sister from Norwalk. Funny to consider Ferris as anything but a medical machine.

'Yes, I am proud of him, Dr. Ferris. And thanks for the vote of confidence. I can't tell you how many people refer to James in the past tense or pretend he's turned invisible.'

He waved away the sentiment and cleared his throat.

'If there's anything I can help you with, at any time, don't hesitate to call on me, Mrs. Merritt. I know all this must be terribly difficult for you.'

He scribbled his pager number on a prescription form and handed it to her. 'Call anytime.'

Dr. Silver, the neurologist, showed up shortly after Ferris left. The contrast between the two men was overwhelming. Silver was a brusque bigmouth with all the finesse of a lowland gorilla.

Cinnie had had plenty of professional run-ins with Silver over the years. He was vehemently opposed to therapy for older stroke patients, referred to anyone over sixty-five as beef jerky. Said treating them was a waste of money. In Silver's view, precious dollars should be reserved for more critical things, like fat salaries for baseball players. It struck Cinnie that he certainly knew jerky. Firsthand. She'd only put up with having him on James's case because he was the best neurologist in town. Strange talent for a simian.

Silver peered at James and cleared his throat. 'Zonked, huh? How's he coming along?'

'You tell me,' Cinnie said. 'You're the doctor.'

Silver squinted in her direction and frowned. His teeth were cigar chewer's yellow, his nose a spongy mushroom of large pores and broken capillaries. 'You look like hell, kiddo. When's the last time you got a decent night's sleep?'

'James is your patient, Dr. Silver. Not me. How did the testing go?'

'Don't you worry your pretty head about that, mommy. You just take care of yourself, and we'll do the rest.'

'Don't patronize me, Marty. I want to know how he did.'

Silver chuckled. 'Now, now. I know all this is hard on you, but really it's better if you relax and let us take care of the medical issues.'

'Of course, you're right, Dr. Silver. I must've lost my head. Wanting to know about my son's progress, what could I be thinking?'

'Look, you've been on the other side. You know it's not good to ask too many questions. Only gets you upset.'

Cinnie's teeth ached from clenching them. 'Just one question then, Dr. Silver. Do you know how to screw yourself?'

She was able to keep James awake through dinner, but he was out cold before dessert. When Paul arrived, she tried to wake the little boy long enough for a hug and a hello, but no chance. James was down for the long count.

She and Paul sat on opposite sides of the bed and talked awhile about work, the weather, topics so light Cinnie imagined them dancing in the air like dust motes. She thought of broaching her concerns about the upcoming meeting to discuss James's future treatment. She considered telling him about her visits with Marion Druce and Lois Sanders that afternoon. But it all seemed like way too much work.

A decent interval had passed, and Paul was getting ready to leave. He tuned his air guitar and sang a chorus of his traditional good-night song: 'See You in the Morning, Jameser, Unless I Sleep 'til the Afternoon.' After the final flourish, he returned the invisible instrument to its imaginary case, kissed James, who snored in response, and shot a questioning glance in Cinnie's direction.

'Need me to bring anything tomorrow?'

She responded by packing a few phantom things in an imaginary suitcase, closing the locks, and standing.

'You're coming home?' Paul said.

'Yup. Breaking out of this joint. You bring the salami with the file in it like I told you?'

'No, babe. Will baloney do?'

'Whatever you've got. I'm prepared to nibble on it.'

Nice lascivious leer. 'Your dish is my command.'

They rode home in an easy silence. In the farmhouse, Paul lit the fire and poured two glasses of dry sherry.

Settled on the plush rug in front of the stove, Cinnie sipped and stared at the flames. A delicious drowsy feeling overtook her, and she felt her muscles slacken. Paul lifted her hair and settled a kiss on the sensitive spot beneath her left ear. He snaked a hand over her shoulder and fiddled with the on-button in her right breast. He played her like a well-tuned instrument: stroking, teasing, coaxing out her hidden tones and rhythms. She floated on the feelings, felt her head expand, her mind bobbing free like a runaway balloon.

Later, she lay with her head on Paul's shoulder, their limbs tangled like unsorted laundry.

'That was nice,' she said. 'Friendly.'

'I was afraid I wouldn't remember how.'

'Nah, it's like riding a bike.'

Paul laughed. 'You must've had a helluva bike.'

So nice, Cinnie thought. Closeness, warmth. Her body reduced to tapioca, brain idling in neutral. She could have stayed like that indefinitely. Probably would have, if only she'd been able to keep her big mouth shut.

But she kept thinking of her discussions with Marion and Lois earlier in the afternoon, especially the one with Lois. And she yielded to an irrepressible urge to tell Paul about it.

She felt his body stiffen. 'Not that nonsense again.'

'This is different, Paul. Please hear me out.'

He got up, muttering. Cinnie watched him wrestle into his pants and slip on a sweatshirt. 'I'm going to the studio.'

'Can't we talk this through, Paul? Do you always have to run away to the damned studio?'

'The *damned* studio happens to be my work, my business.

'Your life.'

'Whatever you say.'

'I say if you weren't so selfish and preoccupied none of this would have happened in the first place.' She bit her lip, but it was too late. The words were out. The air between them went sour.

Paul's eyes narrowed. 'Christ. How the hell can you blame me for the power going out?'

'You have a watch, Paul. You could have bothered to check.'

His face darkened. 'Damn it, that's not fair. I love that kid as much as you do.'

'Maybe as much, Paul. But not the same.'

'What the hell does that mean?'

Her eyes were burning. A bitter swell closed her throat. 'I can't explain. It's just different for you.'

'You don't have to explain. I get it completely. You're wonderful and perfect, and I'm an irresponsible screw up. No way you'd ever let James have an accident, right, Cin? No way anything would ever happen to him with Mighty Mom around.'

'No. That's not what I meant. Please, no more. I don't want to fight.'

'Fine. At least we agree about something.'

'Look, I didn't mean to blame you. It's just . . .'

'It's just that you think I hurt our son on purpose.' His voice broke. 'You don't have to bother beating on me, Cin. I've been doing a good enough job on myself. A thousand times I've gone over it. A thousand times I've prayed to have that day back so I could do it over and make it turn out a different way . . .'

'I'm sorry. I didn't mean – '

'No, don't bother. It's all my fault. I accept that. I'm a selfish, unreliable jerk, and as a result, my kid may never be the same. And you're so goddamned perfect, it's hard to look at you without sunglasses. Does that about cover it?'

His expression went from pained to grim to empty. Cinnie could almost see him pulling down the shades, shutting her out.

'I know it wasn't on purpose, Paul. I'm not blaming you. Please try to understand.'

'I understand perfectly.'

Cinnie could feel the gulf between them, a dark, dangerous chasm.

'What's happened to us, Paul? I feel as if we're going under for the third time. And I don't know what to do about it.'

He sat on the edge of the bed and met her eyes. 'I don't either. Maybe we've got to concentrate on James for now and put our problems on hold for a while.'

'I miss you, Paul. I miss *us*. Especially now.'

His look softened, but after a beat, he stood and nodded. 'See you tomorrow.'

As he walked toward the door, Cinnie considered stopping him with a flying tackle. She toyed with the possibility of a really unfair seduction. Paul had always been a sucker for her lavender teddy and a splash of Chanel 19. The last thing she wanted tonight was to be alone right now. She had never felt so alone.

But she didn't move. She listened to the sound of the front door slamming and Paul's feet crunching over the frozen ground toward the studio. And before he'd had time to traverse the grassy span to the cottage, her mind was back on the hurt children.

24 Cinnie spent an hour staring dry-eyed at the ceiling. She craved sleep, but her mind was a whirling blender. After a call to pediatrics, where she was assured that James was still fast asleep and fine, she got up, dressed, and left the house.

The neighborhood was still. Lights winked through a few shaded windows. Otherwise, the houses were a scatter of hulking silhouettes framed by the velvet sky.

Everything looked so deceptively serene. Tyler's Grove, the model American neighborhood. Sculpted shrubbery and towering trees, gentle driveways and meandering fieldstone walks. Shadows were tossed like downy comforters over the slumbering lawns.

All so peaceful on the surface. But at every turn she was confronted by a gruesome shrine to one of the terrible incidents.

There was the broad pond halfway down Grove Street where Ricky Dolan had fallen through a thin patch of ice. It had happened on a Sunday afternoon a year and a half ago.

A group of neighborhood kids had been playing ice hockey. It had been a prime winter for the sport, three months of persistent record cold had carpeted the Grove Street pond with a dense frozen layer.

The children had dispersed at dusk, and seven-year-old Ricky was halfway home when he realized he'd forgotten his new ski mittens. He ran back to the pond to look for them, and bad luck had directed his steps to a freak thin spot in the frigid crust.

A neighbor heard the child's screams and called for help. By the time the emergency squad was able to pull the little boy out of the freezing water through the pond's cracked skin, he was gray and lifeless. The paramedics had managed to get him breathing again, but not soon enough to prevent the brain injury that had left Ricky with halting speech and a faulty memory.

Passing the Wilder's sprawling colonial, Cinnie shivered, thinking of Billy Wilder's nocturnal animal wails and the hollow-eyed creature he'd become. Sometimes, when she took a walk with James, she'd spot him cowering in the corner beside the den window.

Billy's disappearance and the epidemic of local hysteria that followed had been in June, a few months after Ricky Dolan's accident. Billy had been out riding his bike around the neighborhood at the time, something he did almost every day after school. Later, when his mother went looking for him, she'd found the bike propped against the towering oak tree in the front yard. Not a sign of Billy.

The recording studio had been booked solid with outside bands at the time, and Paul was spending most nights in the converted cottage overseeing the operations.

Determined to protect James from the child-snatching lunatic, Cinnie had slept on the floor at the foot of James's bed, startling at every creak and shudder in the arthritic frame of the old farmhouse until Billy was found a week later, wandering in the Arboretum a mile away.

Passing Pumpkin Patch, she spotted the McArthurs' sprawling brick ranch. Tragedy had visited here too, just last spring.

Cinnie, James, and Paul had been on the shady span of lawn behind the farmhouse when it happened. Paul was flipping burgers on the grill. James stood beside him, flipping grass clumps in imitation. Cinnie could still hear the child's melodic voice as he aped Paul's customary grillside patter. 'Who wants 'em roar? Who wants 'em well dunned?'

'One of each for me,' Cinnie said. 'You're such an excellent cook, I just can't get enough of your delicious burgers, Mr. Chef.'

'James berbers,' he said. 'Come and gettum.'

Perfect family scene.

And then came the inhuman shriek. Cinnie could still feel it piercing her bones.

Time froze for a bristling instant and began again at a

surreal pace. Paul sprinted down the block to investigate. Cinnie scooped James up and held him tight to her chest.

In moments, the Grove was aswarm with police and emergency vehicles. Neighbors congregated in nervous clumps. Rumors spread in a garish contagion of fear and speculation.

James went limp in Cinnie's arms, his head resting on her shoulder. His breathing gentled, and a flush warmed his cheeks. She swayed and hummed a soothing tune as she was drawn in a near trance toward the commotion. Maybe he'd sleep through it all.

Down the block, she saw Paul talking to a group of the men. She drifted past them, the horror compelling her like a giant magnet.

The dead boy lay in the gutter on a bed of grass clippings and pink dogwood petals. He was a tall child, Cinnie noticed with dull detachment. Pale and poorly built. The thick tube of fat around his middle poked out from under his T-shirt, and his limbs were milk-white and flabby. He had chunky cheeks, a formless chin, and a tiny uptilted nose.

A few feet away, a hysterical woman was being comforted by an obese man with brilliantined hair, dark glasses, and a garish Hawaiian shirt. Probably the father, Cinnie thought.

'It can't be,' the woman screamed. 'He was just standing there. Right there on the lawn, Larry. Right there. No. No!'

There were other voices, deep and rumbling like an underground train. Cinnie tightened her grip on James and walked toward home. The drive of the car that struck the boy had never been found.

Cinnie would never forget that scene. Or the similar shock and anguish after Laurel Druce was hurt. She'd been home that day too, baking cookies with James when the rescue sirens sounded down the block at Marion's house.

After the ambulance left to take Laurel and Marion to the hospital, Cinnie had turned to walk James home. She didn't realize how tightly she was holding his hand until he squirmed and wrenched himself loose.

Halfway home, they saw the furniture truck. The driver was slumped behind the wheel, mumbling to himself. 'She just came flying into the street out of nowhere,' he kept saying. 'Like someone threw her. I didn't do anything wrong. I swear I didn't.'

And then there was little Jason Sanders.

Cinnie was still shocked by the discussion she'd had with Lois Sanders after leaving Marion Druce's house. The last person she'd expected to share her suspicions was Lois with her cool, enormous intellect.

But Lois had surprised her. She'd opened the door and ushered Cinnie into her pristine living room like a guilty conspirator.

When Cinnie asked if she had any theories about all the hurt children, Lois had led her out onto the desolate redwood deck and pointed at a large square of railroad ties filled with colored stones halfway across the yard.

'That was Jason's sandbox,' said Lois. 'He used to play there for hours. We used to joke that he'd probably grow up to be a lifeguard or a politician. Both professions where you get a lot of sand blown in your eyes.

'That day, Jason was home with Stacy, my regular sitter. The phone rang, and Stacy ran inside to answer it. Turned out to be a wrong number, so she wasn't gone for more than a minute. But it was enough time for him to find the firecracker and set it off.

'EMS arranged to have Jason helicoptered to Bellevue. The microsurgery team there worked on him for almost twelve hours, trying to reattach the two fingers, but there was too much burn damage. Same with the eye. They told me he was lucky he didn't lose both of them. Lucky, can you imagine?' Lois said.

'Jason's a great little guy,' Cinnie said. 'I can't get over how he plays Little League with the prosthetic fingers. James is convinced he's going right to the majors.'

'Thanks. I know he's done well. He doesn't even seem to remember the explosion. Problem is I don't think I'll ever get past it.' Lois stared out at the box of stone. 'Strange how nothing will grow in that damned thing. Every summer I try, but anything I plant goes belly up. It's become my 'life's quest to win out over that stupid little piece of Earth.'

Cinnie followed her gaze. 'Jason's doing fine,' Cinnie said, more to herself than Lois. 'That's what counts.'

'True, but to answer your question, I do have a theory. More than a theory, in fact. I know that what happened to Jason was not an accident. That firecracker was planted deliberately.'

'What makes you say that?'

'The morning it happened, Jason thought he'd lost one of his favorite little plastic people in the sand. Major catastrophe. Before I left for work, Stacy and I sifted through every inch of the damned sandbox, but we couldn't find the stupid thing. Turned out Jason had stuffed it in the pocket of his jeans.'

'Did you tell that to the police?'

'Of course, I did. I told everyone who'd listen and plenty who wouldn't. But all I got for my trouble was patronized. "There, there, Lois. You're just upset, dear. So hard for you, sweetheart. We understand." ' There was a terrible look in Lois's eyes. Cold fury.

'No one took me seriously,' she went on. 'Even Stacy decided we must have simply missed the firecracker when we did the search. She went along with everyone else. Much more comfortable to believe the thing had been there since the Fourth of July.'

'But that is possible, isn't it?'

'No, I don't think so.'

The discussion left Cinnie unnerved. Who would hurt Jason deliberately? Made no sense in her wildest imaginings. But what did?

And what if Lois was right?

Could there possibly be a human connection between the terrible events in the neighborhood? If someone had planted the firecracker, may be the other accidents weren't accidents either.

164

She shivered and shook her head. Impossible.

Or was it. She had no better explanation, only this terrible, prickling conviction that something was horribly wrong.

Superstition, Paul called it. He spat the word like it was a rank obscenity. 'You must be out of your mind to think someone could be behind these accidents,' he said. 'Completely nuts.'

Cinnie's thoughts were pierced by the sound of a car braking to a sudden stop. She placed the din somewhere near the stone pillars on Mill Road. Stuck in place, she waited for the screams and sirens.

Nothing.

She struggled to clear her mind of the horrific image. But she could see the faceless child lying broken and bleeding at the side of the road. The anguished parents huddled nearby. The ring of anxious neighbors, closing the unfortunate ones out of the privileged circle. Protecting themselves from the fresh tragedy. Shutting out the pain.

She listened to the steady rush of the wind, the surge of distant cars passing, the fierce beating of her heart.

Slowly, she turned and started walking again toward the farmhouse.

25 Malcolm Cobb stepped on the broad sensor pad, and the hospital doors slid apart to admit him. Inside the deserted lobby, he sniffed and scowled. There was the repugnant stench of soiled flesh. Rancid perfume. Despair.

Cobb had observed the guard pacing about the entryway. He knew from prior scouting expeditions that the addicted sloth slipped off at regular intervals for a cigarette. Five minutes later Cobb watched him amble away and felt a swell of contempt. Wretched mass of putrid entrails. He pictured the tar-streaked lungs, the blood vessels reduced to a mass of shriveled worms. The heart a pulsing prune of impotent slime.

Striding through the lobby toward the stairs, Cobb dismissed his revulsion and focused on the impending harvest. Caressing the sweet specimen with his mind, he conjured the velvet skin, the fine features, the thrum of power and intelligence. Beautiful bounty! Soul of my deliverance!

His heart soared. He was the dark moon rising. Slipping up from the stone horizon. Emblazoning his brilliance on the somnolent sky.

The reward was inching closer, moments away. Time ticked joyously in his veins. Charged him with electric anticipation.

Climbing to the fifth floor, he ignored the steady sapping of his meager energies. Soon the limitless stores would be his.

At the fifth landing, he paused and prepared to claim his treasure. Gradually his breathing settled and his pulse gentled to a rhythmic purr. All in order.

But as he touched the knob, he realized that his right hand had gone numb again. He tried to grasp the metal orb, but his fingers were sodden bands of worthless flesh. They hung from the drooping wreckage of his dead hand, the flaccid hinge of his wrist. The entire arm was a maggot's feast of dark decay.

Impossible!

He swallowed his rising gorge. Struggled to suppress the panic roiling in his veins.

Stumbling down the corridor, he felt the weakness spreading. Suddenly, his knee buckled, casting him against the wall in a lurching stagger. His skull was pummeled, jaw battered against the cruel cement. An exquisite spike of pain penetrated his core.

Damnable vapor. Wretched treachery!

Cobb was sinking, melting to oblivion. A vicious pulse squirmed in his head. The darkness was building behind his eyes. Pressure of pain. Power of the terrible blue flame.

The phantom voice emerged, taunting. 'Stupid ass. World's stupidest ass. Throw one of our rotten apples at him, dear. There, now, go ahead. Enjoy yourself. He's too dumb to feel a thing.'

Splat and the acrid rot oozed its tortuous way down his face. Insinuated itself under his collar and slid its loathsome fingers over his flesh. The flies followed. Lazy, derisive.

Wretched invasion. Bounce and land, bounce and land until they pierced his hide and swarmed in his entrails.

Then came the screaming within. Sharp, hideous voices. Needle-edged. Puncturing, bleeding him to dust.

Through his agony came a match strike of warning. Cobb strained to listen, to understand.

A humming voice. Footsteps. Someone approaching. He must not be discovered. Lurching, stumbling, he struggled down the hallway and slipped out of sight.

26 The dream bubbled up from the silence. So vague at the beginning, it was little more than a shudder. A breath. Then came a harsh sigh that grew to form the wheezing rhythms of an approaching engine.

At first, James was oblivious to the danger. He was running. Washed by sunshine. Buoyant and unbound. Laughter welled up from his belly and settled on the air in a froth. He was running faster. Racing in wide, jubilant circles. Chasing the sun.

Then came the plaintive howl. Shrill whistle of warning. It licked him like a playful flame. Began to encircle him. then it cast around him like a vicious whip, caught him at the knees, and sent him pummeting headfirst to the ground.

James tried to get up, to escape. But his legs had turned to sand. His breath came in ragged gasps. The whistle shrilled louder. Screaming.

He was caught. The monster loomed closer. He felt its searing breath, the heat of its venom. Had to get away. Couldn't move!

Help me!

He startled awake. His heart was leaping like an eager puppy, pulse racing. James craned his neck to catch a comforting glimpse of his mother sleeping on the cot.

Nobody there.

Then he heard the door opening and the throb of approaching footsteps. Flashlight beams wavered across the room and settled below his chin.

'You up again, child? We got us a night watchman around here, you know. You trying to take the poor man's job away, or what?'

James watched as the cocoa-skinned nurse neared the bed. He caught a whiff of a flowery smell as she plucked the white sensor thermometer from its electronic housing and planted it under his tongue. While she waited for his temperature to register, she grasped his wrist in her meaty fingers and trained the light beam on her watch.

The tension from the train dream subsided, and James felt a tickle of amusement. He still saw two of everything. There were two dark nurses holding his wrist, two beeping thermometers, two stuffed bears in wrestling garb seated at the foot of his bed. The bed had two footrails and two mattresses. A double water pitcher with twin cups sat on his double nightstand. Two bunches of identical balloons hung from the privacy curtain. Both of the bunches needed air.

The nurse looked perplexed when he giggled. Both of her looked perplexed. Her double mouth twisted and her right eyebrows peaked at the center to form a pair of flying seagulls. James suppressed his mirth and attempted to explain.

He pointed at the stack of volumes on the radiator. 'Book, book.'

She flapped both of her right hands. 'You kidding me, James Merritt? It's the middle of the night, child. This is no time for you to be worrying about reading no books or nothing else for that matter. You go on and get to sleep now, hear?'

James sighed and tried a different tack. 'Bear, bear.'

'No playing either, mister. Bedtime. Night, night. You read me?'

She scribbled on the chart at the foot of James's bed and turned to leave. He gazed back at the cot.

Still empty.

Where was Mom? James struggled to remember her leaving, but could not. It wasn't like her to go without a proper farewell. Still, it was obvious that she'd been absent for some time. Her pillow was fluffed smooth, the blankets drawn taut under the slender mattress. Her purse was not in its customary spot on the floor beside the night table, and her suitcase was missing. He was forced to conclude that she'd decided to spend the night at home.

James attempted to ignore a flicker of unease. He assured himself that he was more than capable of dealing with her absence. No reason to worry. He would simply find his way back to sleep and remain there until she arrived in the morning.

He was foraging for a comfortable position when his eyes fell on the open closet door.

Impossible. The nurse was nearly out of the room now. He searched for the words to stop her. But he couldn't separate the ones he needed from the unruly mob of labels swarming in his head. She was almost entirely out in the hall now, her hand pulling at the knob. Desperate, he puckered his lips and made a loud kissing sound.

The nurse paused and poked her head back into the room. James could see the stark whiteness of her teeth as she grinned in response. She raised a hand and blew a kiss at him. 'Aren't you the sweetest thing? Nighty night now, Mr. James. You sleep tight, sweetheart, hear?'

James stiffened and tried to speak. But before he could force out the word she was gone. The door edged toward the frame and clicked shut.

Lying in the darkness, James worked to thwart his burgeoning panic with reason. This was not his room at home. It was highly unlikely that his monster had the wherewithal to relocate to the hospital closet. In fact, Vinton probably hadn't the slightest notion where James had gone.

All reassuring in theory. But James could feel the searing gaze of an evil observer emanating from the open closet. If only he could somehow make it across the room to shut that door.

He tried to lower the metal side rail on the bed, but it was locked in place, and he could not figure out how to unlatch it. He strained to lift himself high enough to vault the metal barrier, but his muscles quavered and lapsed, and he sprawled against the mattress in a clammy heap, his chest heaving.

Three kisses, covers to the chin, close the door hard, and no more Vinton. So simple, but he could not accomplish the protective ritual alone. His eyes welled with bitter frustration, and his lip began to tremble.

But wait, she was coming back.

The door opened with exasperating slowness. James had the word ready. 'Door.' He rehearsed it again and again in his mind, formed the sounds with his lips. Focused on it fiercely, so it would not elude him when she finally appeared. He would tell her what he needed done, and the monster would be incapacitated.

'Door,' he said with a burst of satisfied relief as the light from the hall fluttered in and she slipped inside. 'Door.'

But wait, it wasn't the nurse.

'Excellent, my child. You are recuperating precisely on course. Communicating purposefully now I see. And you understand me as well, don't you, James?'

James fell silent. The shadow man again. What could he possibly want in the middle of the night?

He seemed to read James's mind. 'The moment for the harvest has come. The time of grand reckoning. Rejoice!'

James felt a stab of fear. An involuntary protest escaped his lips.

'There, there. You mustn't be concerned. It's a very elementary procedure, as you'll see. A simple transfer of assets. Restoration of the divine cosmic balance. Right and renewal.'

James squeezed his eyes shut. Maybe if he pretended to be asleep, the shadow man would go away. His insides were churning. All he wanted was to be left alone.

'Excellent. Relax. Go to sleep. This won't hurt a bit.'

At that, James's eyes snapped open of their own accord. The shadow man was drawing closer, pulling something out of his pocket. James recalled the man's last visit. He anticipated the glint of the needle.

'No!'

'Now, now. No need to fear. This is your destiny. You shall be a catapult to greatness, James. Servant of the dark moon. Yours shall be the noblest of sacrifices. A glorious bequest.'

'Mommy? Mom!'

The man hissed for silence, and his face metamorphosed from dark to deliberate light.

'Your mother has departed, my child. Left us to our noble enterprise. She respects what I must do. Her wish is for you to cooperate with me in every way, James. You must lie perfectly still and make your offering now.'

James peered into the shadow man's eyes, searching for signs of guile or sincerity. But they were like the bowls of polished spoons: vacant, shiny. James saw nothing but his own distorted reflection in their gleaming centers. So eerie and confusing.

'She wants you to do as I say, James. She asked me to come and assist you in fulfilling your obligation. My healing is the path to your own, my son. My resurrection shall signal your full awakening.'

Another treatment? James thought about all the bizarre things they'd put him through in therapy. Rocking him over giant beach balls, dangling him from a net, strapping him into an odd, metal frame and shining lights in his eyes.

Thoroughly perplexed, James watched as the shadow man used his teeth to tear open a plastic package. Some clear spaghetti fell out and slipped to the floor. The man muttered and bent to retrieve it with awkward, lurching movement.

'Mrs. Wheel? Pop?' James was eager to understand.

'Quiet now! Be still.'

The voice was an angry blade. James demurred, chewing his lower lip. The shadow man rose and drew closer. The clear spaghetti was hanging from his mouth. A needle protruded from between two fingers of his left hand.

James detested needles. The sight of the shiny missile terrified him. He bit his lip harder and felt his muscles tense.

Silently, he chanted his mother's standard assurances. *A second and it'll be over, Jimbo. Pinch and it's done.*

So what was taking so long? The shadow man's face was drawing tighter. He dropped the tubing again and took forever to crouch and retrieve it. Then, trying to thread the fine spaghetti onto the needle, his fingers began to quake wildly like a cartoon character on the brink of explosion. James almost laughed, but restrained himself.

Then he had an intriguing notion. Maybe the shadow man was doing all this to amuse him. That would certainly explain the weird gestures, the strange speeches, the fun-house faces and awkward pitching movements.

All a joke.

James relaxed and watched as the performance continued. The shadow man had the needle nearly into the tubing now, but then he dropped the needle. His color deepened, and he spat a curse as he knelt and fished for it on the dark linoleum.

The forbidden expletive uncorked the trapped laughter. James felt it bubble up from the nervous hollow in his belly. He surrendered to it. Giggling in giant burst. So funny. So ridiculous.

Funnier still, the shadow man's face looming over him. Animal mad. Broad fiery blotches were climbing up from under his collar. His eyes bulged.

'That's enough, James. Enough I say!'

James tried to stem the mirth, but it had taken him over. His eyes were streaming tears, nostrils twitching like a rabbit's. His ribs were starting to ache.

'Stop it. Cease this instant!'

And then came the slap. A shock of pain across his cheek.

The man's eyes narrowed and sparked hatred. 'How dare you mock me? How dare you!'

His cheek stung. James felt the heat spreading from the site of the assault. A bitter lump filled his throat, making it hard to breathe and impossible to swallow.

The man's voice dropped to a poison rasp. It crept up James's spine, freezing him in place. 'Not another sound! Stay still, or I'll teach you.'

Again, the man tried to affix the needle to the tubing, but his hand was trembling wildly. His chest puffed and held as he tried to still the tremor. But he was unable to make the fine connection. He spat his disgust, flung the needle and tubing in the trash barrel near the door, and returned to the bed in a clumsy hobble.

He drew a penlight from his pocket and drizzled the beam over James's arm. The light perched on the taped IV line in the back of his left hand. A hep lock, it was called, James remembered. Left there in case of emergency, his mother had explained, though she'd assured him that no emergency was anticipated.

The shadow man tugged at the adhesive holding the device in play, but he was unable to disengage it. Then he leaned hard over the rail, lifted James's hand to his mouth, and caught the edge of the tape with his teeth.

There was a fire of triumph in his eyes as the tape yielded to reveal the capped intravenous line. James winced at the sight of the bared needle poking into a distended vein, but he managed to keep silent.

Now the shadow man used his teeth to pull at the protruding plastic cap above the needle. James felt a dreadful sting as the needle popped loose and fell away. A trickle of sticky warmth flowed over the top of his hand and dripped on the blanket.

Better. Done. Now go away. James's mouth was dry, and he was sweating ice.

But the man was not satisfied. A strange look came over him as he pressed James's hand to his lips and started to suckle at the open wound like a starved infant.

James felt the lapping tongue, they rhythmic suction. The man emitted a contented humming sound.

There was no pain now. Nothing but the tickly sucking and the shadow man pretending to be a tiny baby drinking from his mother's boob. So absurd, James thought. The man had to be crazy.

He'd have to tell Mom about all this in the morning. Knowing Mom, she'd have some logical, reassuring explanation. James busied himself with that comforting prospect until the shadow man withdrew his mouth, pulled the covers to James's chin, and made his way out of the room.

He was nearly gone when the stored word emerged

unbidden from his mouth. 'Door,' James said and worked his eyes toward the closet.

'Certainly, my child,' the shadow man said and tapped the cubicle shut. James watched him peer out into the corridor and slip away.

Alone in the dark, he tried to make sense of the strange incident. But a fog of exhaustion rolled in, clouding his thoughts.

'Mrs. Wheel,' he said in a lame whisper. 'Shadow man. Pop the weasel.' All so difficult to sort and comprehend. So confusing. 'Flying green tunnel. Blue coat lady.' Nothing made a bit of sense. No matter how he tried, he was unable to fit the unwieldy pieces together. 'Pop. Mommy? Mrs. Wheel. Book, Mom.'

The words swirled together in a muddy soup. James tried to place them in logical sequence, but they were too slippery.

A pleasant tingle overtook him. His eyes were so heavy. Allowing his lids to drift shut, he gave up the impossible effort and slept.

27 Drum was back at the service station ahead of schedule. He spotted Driscoll under a Mercedes wagon in the center service bay. Smartass had wedged the dolly out of reach and tucked the cord up under his legs. Meat's version of a Do Not Disturb sign.

Drum called, but Meat refused to acknowledge him. For a few minutes, he waited as patiently as he could, but Driscoll gave no indication that he was planning to come up for air anytime soon.

Drum slipped into the Mercedes, gunned the engine, and blasted the horn loud enough to get Driscoll's attention. When he got out of the car, he saw Meat's hand sticking out from under the car, shooting the bird at him.

'Sorry, Meat,' Drum said to the protruding finger. 'But you know how I hate waiting.'

'Keep busy then, Jerry. Go fuck yourself or something. I got a bleeder here. It's gonna take a few minutes. Like it or not.'

Drum fidgeted the time away. Smoked a couple of invisible cigarettes and paced the greasy floor. About ten minutes later, Driscoll emerged. Rising, he spotted the blood vial poking out of Drum's shirt pocket and nodded his approval. Motioning for Drum to follow, he loped out to the front lot.

Driscoll climbed into a jacked-up black truck decorated with dragon flames and fired her up. Thing roared like Stella when Drum had done something to light her fuse. Drum slipped into the beauty, fell in behind the truck, and braced himself.

Driscoll led him on a high-speed chase out of Scotts Corners, down High Ridge Road, and onto the westbound Merritt Parkway. They breezed past the Stamford and

Greenwich exits, jolting to a near stop every time there was a warning beep from Driscoll's fuzz buster.

Over the New York State line in the town of Purchase, the truck exited onto King Street and headed north passing a string of old mansions that had been converted into private schools, convents, dancing academies, and nursing homes. At the next light, Meat veered left and barreled down the approach road to the Westchester County Airport.

A twin engine Cessna was circling in toward the landing strip as Meat careened through the parking lot. He jolted the truck over the grassy fringe at the perimeter of the lot, toppled a span of link fence, and raced onto the tarmac. Drum braked the beauty at the edge of the blacktop and settled down to watch the show.

A startled guy whose fat ear protectors made him look like a Mouseketeer, started waving his signal lights at Driscoll in a frantic parody. Meat waved in response and killed the truck's engine smack in the center of the ring of lights set to welcome the approaching plane.

The Cessna was down now and speeding on a collision course with Meat's pickup. A little smile played at the corners of Drum's mouth. Driscoll wasn't much to look at, but he could be entertaining.

The guy in the earflaps was jumping up and down and screaming. Drum could see his mouth stretch in a broad oval and the cords bugging out in his chicken neck, but his shouts were swallowed by the noise from the Cessna's engine. The pilot had pitched the thing into reverse, and the plane roared like a tornado. A trail of sparks spat from the rear wheels.

As the Cessna jolted to a stop, Drum caught the stench of burnt rubber. Hard to tell whether it was coming from the plane or the little guy with the ear protectors.

Meat hopped down from the truck's cab, which was close enough to kiss the Cessna on the cheek. The little guy was gesticulating and sputtering some apoplectic noise. Ignoring him, Driscoll fetched a set of movable stairs from the line near the equipment hangar and rolled it out to the pilot's door.

A tall, round-shouldered guy in a leather bomber jacket and a baseball cap climbed out of the cockpit and strode down the steps. He was followed by a short, bigheaded character with a monk's tonsure and a serious squint.

Meat led the pair over to where Drum was standing and made the introductions. The tall guy was Jeff Harkavy, a Vietnam vet who piloted Driscoll's company plane and helicopter and ran a flying school on the side.

The Mr. Magoo look-alike was Alvin Greenglass. Meat explained that Greenglass had been in Honolulu for a couple of days, attending a seminar on the analysis of tropical microbes.

'After you left the station, I remembered that big Alvin here was on his way back tonight. So you're in luck, Jerry. Getting my best man,' Driscoll said.

Drum nodded. 'And your quickest?'

Driscoll made a face. 'Mr. Drum's ass is on fire, Alvin. Think you can put it out?'

Greenglass cocked his outsized head. 'What do you need?'

'Just a little blood work and a read on a piece of fabric,' Driscoll said. 'Nothing you can't handle in your sleep.'

'Good thing,' Greenglass said. 'It's been a long day.'

They drove in caravan to the lab, which was located near the sprawling Cornell-New York Hospital medical complex in Valhalla, New York. Driscoll's operation was housed in a sleek building done in steel and smoked glass. The interior was stark: polished tile floors, ice white walls, harsh lighting. Driscoll butted open the swinging doors leading to one of the immaculate laboratories and led Greenglass and Drum inside.

The lab was an oversized square packed with electronic gadgetry. Everything was slick and imposing. Made the setup at Fairview look stone age by comparison.

While Greenglass got started, Meat took Drum on a short tour of the facility. A line of interior passages connected the labs. Greenglass was working in the area devoted

178

to radioimmunoassay. When Drum and Driscoll returned, the chemist was hunched over an intimidating machine, loading vials of yellowish fluid onto a miniature conveyor.

'Basically, I'm playing musical chairs with molecules, Mr. Drum,' Greenglass said. 'I'm separating the free molecules from those bound to radioactive atoms. That way I'm able to compare the free molecules to a series of previously calibrated serums. If we find the analysand we've postulated in sufficient amounts, all we have to do is eliminate the substances that cross react, and voila! You understand?'

'Yeah, sure,' Drum said. 'Exactly how I'd do it myself.'

Driscoll and Greenglass traded shop chatter while the chemist worked.

'You ready for the gamma counter?' Meat said.

'Almost. Guess I'll use the Isoflex twenty-four well. Save a little time.'

'Good thinking.'

'Think I'll go take a leak,' Drum said. 'You guys be okay without me for a couple of minutes?'

'We'll survive,' Meat said. 'But hurry back, will you, Jerry? Never know when we might need your expert advice.'

By the time Drum returned, the machines had gone quiet, and Greenglass and Driscoll were in a tight huddle. Drum tried to break in, but Meat waved him off.

When they finished talking, Driscoll left Greenglass in the lab and led Drum to his private office at the opposite end of the building. It was a large, corner suite strewn with litter and filth. Meat was a devotee of the early landfill school of interior design.

Driscoll sat on the brown leather sofa and plunked his feet on a coffee table laden with old coffee cups, greasy doughnut wrappers. and worse. He wriggled his blackened toes through the holes in his boots and stretched. Drum took his chances and sat on a scummy-looking recliner.

'The fabric scrap had the same blood type as the kid, for whatever that's worth. The rest is sort of what I expected, Jerry. Only not exactly.'

Meat explained that Greenglass had found traces of a digitalizing agent in James Merritt's blood sample. Exactly what he'd thought they'd find, given there was no other reason for the child's cardiac irregularities immediately after the accident.

'No internal injuries, no major bleeding,' Driscoll said. 'So I figured the kid had to have been slipped a dose of some heart-hyping drug.'

'You saying the paramedics screwed up at the accident site?'

Driscoll kneaded an earlobe. 'Could be. Though it's real rare for paramedics to administer drugs. By the book, all they're allowed to do is start lines and monitor monitors.'

'So you think maybe there was a doc on the ambulance?'

'Plenty of possibilities, Jerry. You know the list. Someone could have screwed up on the way to the hospital or in emergency. Or the normal saline solution they hung on the kid could have been messed up at the factory. Or someone could have injected an amp from the wrong vial in the heat of the moment. Hate to say it, but it happens all the time.'

'All sickening and interesting, Meat, but none of this is going to help me figure who ran down that kid.'

'Maybe so, but there is an interesting hitch. Like I told you, I found what I expected, but not exactly.'

'Meaning?'

Driscoll hitched his brow. 'Meaning that what Greenglass found wasn't any of the standard heart drugs. We both figured he'd come up with one of the regulars like digoxin, but the drug traces he managed to isolate in the kid's blood sample don't match anything we're familiar with.'

'So you're saying it wasn't a heart drug after all?'

'Not one we know of. Greenglass guesses it was probably experimental. The good news is it's not something you'll trip over every place you look. Identify the substance, and it probably won't take much to figure out where the kid's dose came from.'

Drum scowled. 'Where does that get me?'

'Well, it's one thing for a regular, lying-around drug to find its accidental way into a patient. Something rare makes me real curious.'

Drum couldn't get his head around it without a lot of hard stretching. 'But why? Who? Makes no friggng sense.'

Driscoll chuckled. 'You looking for things to make sense, Jerry? Bet you still believe in elves and fairies, you cute thing.'

Drum wasn't going to hang around and argue. You never knew what was going to crack a case. Trick was not to toss anything unless you were sure it was worthless.

'Okay, I'll run with it. How long will it take Greenglass to dope it out? I can wait.'

'You'll wait a real long time, Drum. We don't have the equipment to run it here. You're going to need a fully equipped tox lab and someone with a good handle on rare compounds.'

'So who do I see?'

Driscoll hitched his shoulders. 'You want to get to Kansas? Guess you'd better go directly to the Wizard.'

28 The sky was pebbled with clouds, the moon a specter. Drum shared the dim road with a scatter of night crawlers. He passed one snub-nosed man in a Trans Am and a couple of woozy-looking kids in a dented Honda. A ragged line of bikers zoomed by. And he was forced to swerve around a sluggish van with blackened windows. Only two kinds were on the road at this hour. People looking for trouble and those who'd already found it. Drum figured he fit neatly in both categories.

Easing off the High Ridge Road exit in Stamford, Drum tried to kick the day's events to the back of his mind. He was eager to get home. Anxious to slip into bed beside Stella. All he wanted was to cuddle up in her creamy hills and hollows and check out.

Turning onto his block, he was surprised to see his house ablaze with light. Nearing the place, he ran through a string of comforting possibilities. Maybe Stella had gotten in later than usual and decided to wait up for him. Or maybe she'd worked herself half dead at the club and forgotten to shut things down. Or she could have left the place lit up on purpose, so he wouldn't have to stumble around.

What he didn't expect was to find her in the kitchen with Booker. They were faced off at opposite ends of the room like boxers between rounds.

'What gives?' Drum said.

'Tell him,' Stella said. 'Go ahead.'

'Got nothing to tell.' Booker gnawed at a cuticle and eyed the floor.

'Oh, is that so?' she said. 'Well I do. Want to hear how I spent my evening, Jerry? I had a charming tour of the West Side. I saw all the sights: shooting galleries, open-air drunk tanks, flesh peddlers of both and indeterminate

182

sexes. I was manhandled, hooted at, offered every illegal act and substance known to man. Risked my fool neck looking for this little character who thinks it's fine to take off whenever he happens to feel like it.'

'Nobody told you to come after me, Mrs. Drum. You didn't have to go do that.'

She spewed an angry breath. 'I *care* about you, you little jerk. You think I'm going to let you run around all night and maybe get yourself hurt?'

'I can take care of myself. My business what I do.'

Drum decided it was time to jump in. 'Wrong, hotshot. We're your family, remember? So it's *our* business what you do. Now what the hell got into you? Spill.'

'Don't belong to nobody. Ain't nobody gonna tell me where I gotta be or where I gotta go. Ain't no damned baby.'

Stella blew a breath. 'How many times do I have to tell you, Booker? There's nothing for you to get so upset about. It's nothing but talk.'

Stella explained that Ms. Bergmuller from social services had stopped by to report that a couple from New Haven had shown some interest in adopting Booker. They were both successful black lawyers in their early forties who'd been searching for some time for the 'right' child. According to Bergmuller, they were after a boy with exceptional intelligence. Kid with ivy growing out of his ears.

Stella imitated the woman's chirp to perfection. Even got down the broad's perky movements and the perpetual smile. Drum was so busy admiring the likeness, it took a few seconds for the words to sink in.

'You saying they're gonna take Booker away from us?'

Stella shot him a hard look. 'It's all preliminary at this point, Jerry. Probably won't come to anything.'

'I ain't going to New Haven or Old Haven or any damned Haven, Mr. Drum. Tell you that much.'

'What do you mean *preliminary*?' Drum demanded.

Stella tossed another loaded look, but Drum wasn't catching. 'I *said*, what do you mean?'

'I mean it's just talk. This couple read that article in the paper about Booker winning the school spelling bee, and it got them thinking. At this point, they're asking to have a look at his school records. If they're still interested, they'll arrange to meet him. See if the chemistry's right. Bergmuller said they've gone this route with several other kids, and none of them worked out. She said they've been impossible to please. So it probably won't come to anything.'

'You bet it won't. Booker doesn't have to put up with any damned dog-and-pony show. I'm going to call that Bergmuller bitch first thing in the morning and tell her so.'

Stella's teeth were clenched, hands fisted. 'You'll do no such thing. You'll keep your fat mouth shut and your feelings to yourself. Chances are this whole thing will blow over, and Ms. Bergmuller will crawl back in her little hole. That is unless you shoot your trap and make the lady mad. Then she might just decide we're not suitable to care for Booker under any circumstances. You catch my drift?'

Drum bit his lip. 'Yeah, okay. Guess you're right. Stella's right, hotshot. Best thing is to sit tight, and it'll pass.'

'Ain't going to no Havens of any kind, Mr. Drum. That's final.'

Drum took the kid by the shoulders. Their eyes locked. 'I said it's going to be okay.'

Booker lowered his eyes and mumbled some angry jive. Drum held on tighter.

'You heard me, hotshot. It's not going to happen. That's a promise.'

Booker's face changed. Kid was still wary, but Drum could tell he was easing up.

'Get to bed now. Night's half over.'

'Yeah, okay. 'Night, Mr. Drum, Mrs. Drum.'

''Night, Book. Sleep tight.'

They listened as he climbed half a flight, stalled, and trudged back down to the kitchen.

'Sorry, Mrs. Drum,' he said in a grudging whisper.

Stella gave him a hug. 'That's okay, handsome. Forget it.'

'You tell me who bad-mouthed you, I'll put out the word. Get their asses fried for them. I got friends.'

'Thanks, but I don't want that. It's over with. The important thing is everyone's home safe.'

'Yeah, but ain't nobody got the right to treat you that way. You're good people.'

'You too, kiddo,' Stella said and kissed him in both cheeks. ''Night now.'

Drum tried to look properly furious. 'You ever pull a stunt like that again, you'll have me to answer to. You hear?'

Kid dipped his eyes. 'Sorry, Mr. Drum. Guess I wasn't thinking.'

'Yeah? Well next time you'd better, or I'll give you something to think about – hard. Now get to bed and give it a rest.'

This time, Booker took the stairs at a trot, and there was the sound of springs whining as he flopped on his bed.

Drum's face darkened. 'So what's going to be?'

Her eyes shimmered with unshed tears. 'I wish I knew. Worst case, this lawyer couple falls in love wth him and takes him away. God, Jerry. I don't want to lose that little boy.'

Drum took her in his arms. She smelled wonderful, felt better. 'Don't worry. I'll think of something. Book's not going anyplace.'

Stella fell asleep immediately, but Drum's gut was churning. He couldn't let anyone take Booker, couldn't imagine life without that kid.

So what could he do?

The Bergmuller bitch had made it clear to Stella that if the black couple wanted the adoption, it was as good as done. Drum couldn't hope to battle them by trying to adopt the kid himself. That would mean a full background investigation. All social services had to do was get a whiff of his history and Booker would be taken away no matter what the lawyer couple decided.

Drum searched for a solution, but his head was teeming with useless regrets and recriminations. If only he'd done things differently. If only he could have that one night back agan.

Thinking about it now got him boiling. The loathsome face wormed into his consciousness. So like his father's face, but there was a hard edge to the elegant features and an ugly chill in the emerald eyes.

Uncle Liam.

Before his father's death, Liam had been a near stranger. Big Matt had never talked much about his older brother. And Drum hadn't seen much reason to ask questions.

After the funeral, Drum had gone home with Oliver London. Seemed like an okay arrangement to Drum, but a couple of days later a tall guy in a suit showed up and told them that Drum was going to be placed in Liam's custody.

Drum couldn't figure it and didn't want to go. But the suit-guy had handed London some official papers. Uncle Oliver read them through and shrugged.

'Liam is your next of kin, Jerry. He's petitioned for guardianship, and it's been granted by the court. Nothing we can do.'

So Drum went along. And Liam had seemed all right at first, though he didn't know the first thing about caring for a kid. He took Drum along on outings to his favorite pubs and strip joints, left him alone, sometimes for days at a time. There were no rules, no boundaries. Drum kept looking for the walls, but all he found was silent, endless space.

Liam's house was a rambling green Victorian with imposing turrets and gingerbread trim set on a lonely stretch of land overlooking the Long Island Sound. It was much grander and many multiples larger than the modest two-family Drum had lived in with his parents.

There was a game room complete with pool tables, Ping Pong, and pinball machines; a fully equipped gym, including steam room and sauna; a movie theater complete with commercial popcorn maker.

After Drum moved in, Liam had installed a soda bar, a

candy dispenser, and a jukebox in the oversized den. Drum's friends were bug-eyed jealous. But there was a cold empty feeling about the place that echoed the icy void in Drum's life.

At first, Drum tolerated his new circumstances with the numb curiosity that had become his central emotion since his father's death. He was especially curious about his uncle.

Liam did no particular work that Drum could see, but the guy had a bottomless cash supply. Liam was forever slipping big bills into Drum's palms or pockets. And Drum quickly learned that wherever he went, he could settle his tab by simply asking the proprietor to charge it to Uncle Liam. It was as if the man owned the world or, at least, held the mortgage.

Having everything he wanted was the one part of his new life Drum found an easy adjustment. Problem was everything didn't feel like nearly that much.

Drum's loneliness was like a fat, ugly cloud. It refused to yield to the noisy invasions from his friends, who loved to hang around his uncle's house enjoying the freedom and indulgences. Nor was it lightened by the steady parade of oddball friends and acquaintances who came to call on Uncle Liam.

The most intriguing people arrived at all hours to visit or court favor or seek advice. 'Types,' Drum's mother would have called them, meaning they were the sort who caught your eye and made you wonder. Drum had tried to size them up in every imaginable direction, but all they seemed to have in common was age. Drum had them all figured for high school, college age at the most. Funny for Liam to have so many young friends.

Liam's houseman, a willowy blond named Kurt, ushered most of the visitors into the office in the rear of the first floor. Generally, the meetings were concluded at the front door with Liam peeling bills from the fat roll of hundreds he always carried.

The private office was the only place in the house that was off limits to Drum, which naturally made him ache to get inside. Passing the heavy oak door, he never failed to rattle the knob, hoping Liam might have neglected to lock it for once. One night, when Liam was out of town and Kurt was gone for the day, Drum spent several hours rifling through his uncle's bureau drawers, hoping to find the key. No luck.

For months, the office remained a mystery to Drum. Then one night after supper, Liam appraised him with an odd look in his eyes. 'Half a man already, aren't you Jeremiah? Suppose it's time you were treated like one.'

He led Drum down the hall and into the hallowed office. The room was nothing near what Drum had imagined. One wall was mirrored in smoky squares that fractured Drum's face and made him feel strangely disoriented. There was a black leather couch, twin chairs upholstered in plush white fur, white fur throw rugs, an antique trunk with leather fittings, Liam's desk and a line of locked closets.

Liam poured hefty measures of brandy from a crystal decanter and held one out in Drum's direction. 'Here's to a fine young man. Go on now, drink up.'

The booze seared Drum's throat, but he managed to empty the glass. Matter of pride. He was half a man already, whatever that meant. At least, he liked the sound of it.

Almost immediately, he felt warm syrup infuse his bones, and his eyes went foggy. Next thing he knew, he was trying to climb out of a spinning well. Slick sides, nothing to do but keep sinking to the inky bottom.

He awoke to the sight of Uncle Liam lying with his head on the armrest of the leather couch. His silk robe was splayed open. Drum was startled by the whiteness of his uncle's skin, the distended belly shot with a rash of veins. The thatch of dark hair beneath the swell.

In mortified fascination, he watched as Liam played with himself, working his angry member in slow, languid strokes. His uncle's mouth was agape, eyes gleaming. He made low, moaning sounds like a hurt animal.

Drum stifled a nervous giggle and tried to pretend he

was still asleep. His head was thumping, mouth parched and sour. Hung over?

He pressed his eyes shut, but the pounding in his head worsened and the room started to buck and spin. Allowing his lids to open a crack, he chanced another peek at Liam. The man's flush was deepening, flesh slick with sweat.

Liam was transfixed, staring at something on the wall. Drum tracked his gaze to the pair of figures projected on a portable screen. The bigger one on top was writhing in passion, working over the smaller character Drum could hardly see.

A blue movie. Drum had heard about such things in the schoolyard. One boy claimed he'd found several steamy reels in his father's handkerchief drawer. For a week of lunchtimes, he'd entertained a pack of kids including Drum with the play-by-play.

The focus was poor, and Drum squinted for a better view. The bodies shifted. The camera zoomed in closer and fixed on the faces. Drum recognized the larger of the two figures as Uncle Liam himself. He was touching the smaller one, kneading at the naked flesh. Drum felt a slap of shock. He wanted to turn away, but he was caught, held.

The second, smaller person loomed larger and closer. His eyes were closed, features limp as melted wax. Drum's shock turned to raw, crawling horror. It couldn't be. His eyes had to be playing a vicious trick.

Liam's lips spread in a cruel, lazy smile. 'Like being a star, Jeremiah? Like the pretty pictures? Hot off the presses. Developed them myself.'

Drum lunged at him, started pounding the milky flesh in a rage. 'I'll kill you. You touch me again, I swear I'll kill you.'

Liam caught his wrists. Drum was shocked by the strength in the pale, portly limbs. Liam's smile twisted. 'You'd best behave, Jeremiah. Better mind or I'll have to arrange a nice private showing of your movie debut. Invite all your little friends. How would that be?'

Drum tore loose. He yanked the film reel from the projector. Tugged the celluloid off the reel and crushed it.

Gasping, he turned to face his uncle. The creep stood with his robe still gaping. His fat gut heaved over his dying erection. 'There,' he spat. 'Now you can go to hell.'

'Fine, Jeremiah. I'll go, but you're going with me. You see, all you ruined was a copy, my boy. The original is locked in my desk. And there it's going to stay as long as you behave.'

29 The morning was drab and shot with drizzle. It was near eight-thirty when Drum finally finished his round-trip run to Philadelphia and limped the beauty into his garage.

He found Booker sitting cross-legged on the kitchen floor. Kid was munching on a buttered bagel and poring over the business section of the *Times*. Runt had an eye for investments, sound and otherwise.

'Hey, Mr. Drum. What's up?'

'Not me, that's for sure. Hey, check the time, hotshot. You'd better hustle or you'll miss the bus.'

'Ain't going to school today.'

'Law says you have to go, kid. School or jail.'

'Hell with that. I'm spending the day with you, Mr. Drum. We gotta talk.'

'Get your butt to school. We can talk after.'

Booker shook his head. 'Can't wait for after. Trust me.'

Upstairs, Drum splashed cold water on his face and put on a fresh shirt. Stella was still sleeping. He took a long, longing look at her. Watched the ebb and swell of her bosom under the bodice of her white lace gown. Admired the way her dark hair fanned over the pillow and the flush on her cheeks. Took everything he had to keep from diving under the covers and drowning in that beautiful broad.

The kid had his coat on and was waiting at the door. 'If you got to work today, it's cool, Mr. Drum. I'll be glad to help you out.'

'How about we hit the diner first? I could use some breakfast.'

'That'd be good. I already had some, but I'd be glad to watch while you fill up. No problem.'

At the Greek place on High Ridge, Drum ordered a toasted English and coffee. The runt pored over the menu and asked for a stack of pancakes, two eggs over, a side of bacon, home fries, and a large orange juice.

'Wouldn't want you to eat alone,' Booker said.

Kid sucked up the food like an Electrolux. Pity Stella wasn't around to watch, Drum thought. Nothing made that woman happy like the sight of the kid making a pig of himself.

Drum kept waiting for Booker to spill what was eating him, but the kid was in no hurry. Figuring he wouldn't waste the time waiting, he decided to run a couple of errands.

First, he dropped by the headquarters of the Volunteer Ambulance Corps on Long Ridge Road. Posing as a new guy in town interested in serving on the emergency rescue squad, he managed to get a copy of the procedure book and a lecture on what EMS technicians could and couldn't do.

Absolutely no drugs were administered. No docs ever rode on the local ambulances. So it wasn't likely that the heart drug, whatever it was, was accidentally slipped to the Merritt kid on the way to the hospital.

Next, he swung through Tyler's Grove, hoping to find the Holroyd woman home. Still no luck. But when he swung around to the Merritt's place, there were encouraging signs of life in the recording studio behind the farmhouse. Drum spotted a pack of cars in the driveway, silhouettes dancing on the translucent shades. He left the runt in the car and trudged over the lawn to the cottage.

No answer when he rapped at the door, but it wasn't locked either, which was Drum's idea of an engraved invitation.

Inside was one cavernous room buffered by heavy-duty acoustical tile and vault-thick walls. The space was divided by a glass partition. On the far side was a stage setup and a crowd of microphones. The side nearer the door was jammed with electronic gadgetry and enormous speakers. Drum noticed the clock, a flashing red digital readout on the sound board. Hard to miss.

A solitary guy sat on a stool in front of the main controls.

He was listening to something through a fat set of earphones. Something mellow, Drum could tell. Guy's head was bobbling like a rubber duck in a bathrub, and his eyes were hooded.

Drum recognized the character from the hospital: the kid's father. Guy did fit Meat's description exactly: tall, involved in a creative field. Made Drum's tongue itch to watch the character enjoying himself while his kid was laid up in the hospital. Not a fair reaction. But his allergies had no sense of justice.

He went around and stood where the guy couldn't miss him.

'Mr. Merritt?'

The man took off the earphones and blinked. 'Yes. Sorry, I must've lost track of the time. Do we have an appointment?'

Drum had put on a three-piece suit, an upstate accent, and blue contact lenses. With his hair parted on the other side and his personality set at extra pushy, he could see that the father didn't recognize him.

He introduced himself as Larry Tympani, an account supervisor for Young and Rubicam, and tossed the guy a business card. He said his firm was considering a local advertising shoot and needed to hire a sound studio for the vocals. So he needed to see samples of dubbing tracks the studio had done for other videos.

Drum sized the father up while the guy made his spiel about the quality of the studio's work. Man obviously had Stella's passion for music. You could see it in his face when he talked about tracks and tunes and arrangements. His eyes glistened like fresh snow.

Drum had mixed feelings about the guy. He looked okay, talked a good story. But he had the kind of smooth, boyish good looks that sometimes turned up on the wrong kind of poster.

Paul Merritt pulled a couple of tapes from a metal rack. Drum caught the dates on the labels and asked to see the one made on the day of the accident. He sat back in a swivel rocker while the guy set up the viewing equipment.

Good, comfortable chair, Drum noticed. Too bad no pop-corn.

The tape featured a smoky-voiced woman in a black knit skirt the size of a Band-Aid. Her tits were so big they looked as if they were meant to be continued on the next woman. But it wasn't the giant jugs that held Drum's attention.

He was glued to the digital time running at the bottom of the tape. The hour, minute, second, and millisecond ticked away under the singer's tapping spike-heeled shoes.

Drum watched for a few more minutes, long enough to be polite, and promised to get back to the guy when the firm made their decision. His smile faded as he stepped outside.

The running time on the tape started at ten to eleven, so the bit about a power outage making making the guy late to meet the kid's bus could be genuine. But that still left a fat end dangling.

To double-check, Drum traced the outlet for the main power line from the cottage and tracked it as it ran beneath the eaves and dropped down the rear of the build-ing to connect with an underground feed to the farmhouse. Drum trailed the line from the source again, but there was no mistake. The farmhouse and the cottage were on the same line. A power outage in one place had to mean the whole system was down. But the Merritt woman had been real clear that the blackout had been restricted to the cottage.

Made no sense. He kept working it like the dial on a combination lock. Turning and turning. Listening until his ears ached for the sound of those sweet tumblers click-ing in place.

Only two possibilities he could see. Either someone else had altered the studio clock, by accident or on purpose, or the kid's father had done it himself. Could be he'd changed the time accidentally while he was messing with the board. But it could also be he'd wanted to create an excuse for being late to meet the bus.

That led to a couple of thoughts Drum didn't enjoy considering. What if the guy had set the kid up for the accident and tampered with the clock to give himself an alibi?

Crazy, yes. But Drum had seen way crazier. Maybe the father had a chickie on the side who didn't like kids. Maybe the kid had life insurance or a trust fund that would revert to Daddy in case of the child's death?

The only thing Drum knew for certain was never to be sure of anything. He scribbled a couple of notes to himself. Does the kid have any inheritance? Insurance? Is Daddy involved in extracurriculars? How's the marriage?

Continuing north, he took a turn through Scotts Corners. Driscoll wasn't at the station, so Drum left a note saying that he'd been to see the wizard and the guy had promised results in a couple of days tops.

Back in the car, Drum could see that Booker's brain was running at full throttle. Soon as he gunned the engine, the kid was full of questions.

'So where'd you go to last night, Mr. Drum. Heard you take off, must've been pushing three in the morning.'

'I had to see this Chinese scientist guy in Philadelphia. Couldn't sleep, so I figured I might as well get the trip over with.'

'Middle of the night you went to see the guy?'

Drum nodded. 'Best time. Guy's nocturnal.'

'Thought you said he was Chinese.'

They were headed south again on High Ridge when Drum felt the kid tense and stare out the window. He kept his peace.

The silence paid off after a few long minutes.

'We got it pretty good, don't we, Mr. Drum? I mean, we got us a nice life the three of us, ain't that so?'

'Yeah. I'm not complaining.'

'Me neither . . . So that's why I decided I'm gonna make sure things stay just the way they are.'

Drum scowled. 'What's that mean?' He looked over and noticed the smug look on the kid's face. 'Talk to me in English, hotshot.'

Booker patted Drum's hand. 'No big thing. I got a plan

guaranteed to keep me clear away from that New Haven place.'

'Which is?'

'Don't you bother yourself about it, Mr. Drum. I just wanted to let you know you can leave it to me. Everything's under control.'

'Don't be a smartass, Book. You don't want to go getting yourself in trouble.'

'Trust me, man. I ain't no fool.' Kid whipped a paperback book out of his jacket pocket and started reading. Case closed.

If only Drum had been able to put a lid on his childhood demons and trash them as easily. But they'd been way too big and ugly.

After that night in his uncle's office, Drum kept waiting for Liam to try to touch him again. One finger on him, and swore he'd kill the sonavabitch. Drum had spent a thousand hours rehearsing the murder. His dreams were full of Liam's blood. Visions of knives slashing the spongy white flesh, the recurring image of Liam's brains spattered over the walls by a gun blast in his fat mouth.

But Liam didn't come near him. Didn't look at him. Shut Drum off like he was dead and forgotten.

Drum was left with nothing but the fury and the fear. What if Liam showed that film to anybody? The idea froze his flesh, turned his bowels to water, left him raw and empty inside. Drum had dread flashes of the grainy images playing on the side of the school building. Everyone watching.

He tried desperately to find the original film. Every time Liam wasn't looking, Drum was pulling things apart. Looking. But he knew the damned thing was in Liam's office. Locked in the desk where he couldn't get at it. Eating away at his life.

Remembering, Drum felt the wrath building again, consuming him like a wisp of paper in a raging fire. His hands were balled in iron fists. The nails bit his flesh. *Stop it, Drum. Let the damned thing go.* There was a hot sword in his throat and the taste of bile.

'You okay, Mr. Drum? You look funny.'

Drum forced a couple of breaths. It took all his strength to push the anger back a centimeter. Heavy bureau full of poison hatred. Damned thing sitting in the dead center of his existence, so he was always having to walk around it.

'Yeah, hotshot. I'm fine. Daydreaming, that's all.'

Booker shook his head. 'Even sound funny, man. You could tell me, Mr. Drum. Whatever it is. Probably feel better if you was to talk about it.'

'It's nothing, Book. Nothing to tell.'

Better, the anger was backing off like a challenged punk. Nothing left but a hulking shadow and the feeling that someone had iced his bones.

Drum kept up the deliberate breathing until the rage was half a block away. Almost back to normal, not that his normal was anything to write home about.

Driving toward home, he turned his thoughts to business. Best way to keep his mind off the rest. Driscoll's hotshot scientist friend in Philadelphia had told him that it would be a couple of days before he'd have a definite answer on the kid's blood sample. Drum knew he couldn't afford to waste the waiting time.

But what next?

He closed his eyes and rummaged around for an idea. The other big hole was the damned car. There had to be a way to find it. Made no sense that the hit-run vehicle had made its way through a sprawling neighborhood like Tyler's Grove in the middle of a sunny day and managed to elude all but one witness. So maybe the trick was to figure out who else had seen something and maybe not even realized they had.

One witness with one sketchy description wasn't much to go on. Drum considered the librarian again, but even if the car she saw was the one they were after, she didn't have much to add to the mix. Not nearly enough.

Drum considered what Big Matt would do under the circumstances. What he would not do was try to play out the hand while he was only holding half a deck. *If you don't have what you need, you go out and find it, son.*

He eased back to a better time, when he was a real kid with all the trappings: love. security, big eyes. Funny how you never appreciated those simple things while you had them. Never thought about them until it was way too late.

Drum draped an arm across Booker's shoulder and settled into the rhythms of the ride.

30 An icy mist was falling. Cinnie parked the Volvo in the Fairview staff lot and raced across the blacktop to the hospital's rear entrance. She'd checked in several times with the night shift, but she was anxious to see James for herself and confirm that he was fine.

When Cinnie got to the room, a young nurse with a bouncy ponytail was giving James a sponge bath. He looked as soggy as the towel.

'Well, look who's here, Jimmy. It's your mom.'

He managed half a grin.

'Hi, sweetheart. Sleep well?'

'Mom?'

'Yup. How's my trooper? Feeling better today?'

His voice was a zephyr. 'Shadow man. Mrs. Wheel. Book, Mom. Pop the weasel.'

The nurse frowned. 'He keeps saying those same things over and over. What's it mean?'

'Wish I knew.'

The nurse removed James's left arm from his hospital gown and dipped the washcloth in a bucket of soapy water. Cinnie's eye was drawn to a livid bruise on the back of his hand.

'What's that?'

The young woman eyed the wound. 'Looks like an old IV site.'

Cinnie remembered the hep lock. 'Oh, right. They left one there in case of an emergency. Guess we're finally past that. Nice.'

'Guess so. All done now, Jimmy.' The nurse slipped his arms into a fresh gown, rinsed the washbasin in the sink, and left the room.

Cinnie sat on the edge of the bed. 'You okay, Jimbo? Anything hurting?'

At that, he tensed. 'Shadow man, Mommy. Baby man. Door, Mom.'

She stroked back his hair and pulled up the covers. 'Ssh. Get some rest now, sweetheart. Karen will be coming by to get you for therapy in a little while.'

In moments his eyes closed. Restless, Cinnie went out to the nurses's station and thumbed through his chart. If anybody questioned her, she was prepared to claim she was checking on a patient, which was true enough.

She found nothing out of the ordinary in the nurses's anecdotal entries. Paging back through the physician's scribbles, she winced at some of Dr. Silver's gems. 'Patient condition unchanged. Mother agitated and unreasonable.'

'I'll give the creep agitated and unreasonable –'

'Everything okay, Cin?'

The concern was courtesy of Evelyn Larwin, the head pediatric nurse who'd been on the Fairview staff since the hospital's opening in the early sixties. Evelyn was also Fairview's unofficial housemother: warm, soothing.

'Everything's fine,' Cinnie said. 'Just talking to myself.'

The nurse cast a meaningful look at James's chart. 'We're all keeping an eye on that cutie pie of yours, Cin. Giving him star treatment. Try to ease up a little, will you?'

'I am trying. That's why I want to know what's going on. Keeps me saner.'

'Guess I'd be the same way. Any particular questions? I'll do my best to answer.'

Cinnie shrugged. 'No, nothing particular. Just fishing, I guess. I was glad to see they removed the hep lock. That's progress at least.'

The nurse hesitated. Something odd crossed her expression. 'Listen, I'd better get hopping. We're short-handed today. If you need anything, holler. Okay?'

Cinnie watched Evelyn's bustling retreat. She spent a few more minutes with the chart, long enough to convince herself that nothing ominous was lurking in the stack of pages, and went back to James's room to watch him sleep.

Dr. Ferris stopped on morning rounds. Trailed by a covey

of residents and interns, he pointed to James in a proprietary gesture.

'This young boy is the kind of patient who makes it all seem worthwhile. He was gravely injured in a car accident. But the child has the kind of fortitude that can help restore anyone to health. And, of course, the strong family support helps as well.' He nodded in Cinnie's direction as if soliciting applause.

'Thanks, Dr. Ferris.'

'Thank *you*, Mrs. Merritt. When James wakes up, tell him I said, "hi".' He motioned for the ducklings to follow and left to continue his rounds.

James was still dozing when Karen Sands showed up almost an hour later to take him to therapy. Cinnie shook him gently awake and helped him into his robe.

'Wheel, Mom.'

'Okay, sweetie. Ready to go now?'

'Vinton, Mom. No more Vinton!'

'That's what he kept telling me yesterday,' Karen said. 'What's a vinton?'

'Vinton is James's personal monster. Lives in his closet at home. Don't you worry, Jimbo. Vinton's not here, and he's not coming. Even he knows they don't have decent closets in this place.'

'Vinton came, Mom. Last night.'

Cinnie was taken aback. That was more clear language than she'd heard from James since the accident. If she didn't know better, she'd swear he was making sense.

Karen wheeled him out of the room. Cinnie took the stairs up to her office and locked the door. She had ten minutes before her first scheduled patient. Enough time to call Deputy Chief Allston.

Allston was a tall, pallid blond with dull blue eyes, an aquiline nose, and a personality like coarse-grade sandpaper. He might be one of the top men on the force, as he himself had been quick to inform her, but that didn't mean Cinnie had to like him. From her first interview with the man, she'd found him abrupt and unsympathetic. Now, after several more unpleasant run-ins, she knew her first impression had been wrong. Allston wasn't disagreeable, he was positively repulsive.

'What is it, Mrs. Merritt? I'm very busy.'

She refused to let him get to her. 'I'm missing James's backpack and his favorite T-shirt. He had them both on the day of the accident. Could you please check to see if they were claimed for evidence?'

The phone clattered against a hard surface, and Cinnie heard Allston squawking into the intercom. Moments later, there was a squawked reply, and the deputy chief came back on the line.

'Property has the backpack, but no shirt. Check with the hospital, why don't you? Docs in emergency may have taken it off and trashed it.'

'But . . .'

'Have to run now, Mrs. Merritt. I told you, I'm busy.'

The phone disconnected with a jolt. Cinnie glowered at the dead receiver. 'One more thing, Charlie dear. As soon as you can make time in your busy, busy schedule, do me a favor and go to hell, will you?'

She hung up fuming. Jerk wouldn't even listen. No question James's shirt was gone by the time he was placed in the ambulance. Cinnie had a clear picture of his bare chest under the sheet. The police or EMS workers had to have taken the shirt off at the scene.

Which was very strange, when she thought about it. All hospital personnel were required to take first aid training, and rule one was to avoid moving an accident victim any more than was absolutely necessary.

She remembered the ambulance driver handing her James's jacket on the way to the hospital. 'Had to take it off to start a line,' he'd said. The T-shirt wouldn't have been in the way. And even if they'd chosen to remove it for some reason, why wouldn't it have found its way to Cinnie or the property clerk like the rest of James's things?

So many questions. So much frustrating speculation.

Seeking a distraction, she took the top chart off the pile on her desk and flipped through the records. Mrs. Hibbel was her first scheduled patient. Good. Mrs. H was one of

Cinnie's favorites, a retired singing teacher in her mid-eighties with a severe case of vocal polyps, also known as 'screamer's nodules'.

Mrs. H had a gentle voice. Good pitch, proper volume. Cinnie had been mystified about the source of the voice abuse until, after several sessions, the woman had sheepishly admitted that for years she'd belted Ethel Merman numbers in the shower with no ill effects. But recently her grandson had turned her on to Tina Turner.

There was a knock. When the door opened, Cinnie was surprised to see Evelyn Larwin. The nurse sported a plastic smile.

'Sorry to interrupt you, dear. I was wondering if you happened to know who took out James's hep lock.'

'No idea. Why?'

Evelyn's grin evaporated. 'No big thing. I couldn't find an order for the removal in the chart, so I thought I'd check it out.'

'It was gone when I came in this morning. Are you saying someone took it out by mistake?'

Evelyn flapped a hand. 'Don't give it another thought. I'm sure there's some simple explanation. I'll get right to the bottom of it and let you know.'

As the nurse ducked out, Mrs. Hibbel arrived for her session. Cinnie tried to focus on the delightful old woman. But her thoughts kept shifting to James and the missing hep lock.

Could someone have removed the line without orders? She knew only too well that even the top hospitals committed their share of calamitous errors. Given that she was on staff, she'd counted on James getting the best care Fairview had to offer. But maybe their best wasn't good enough.

Terrible, chilling thought. She wished she could slip James out of this place and take him someplace where he'd be safe and protected.

If only such a place existed. Funny how she used to believe it did.

31 The morning seemed to evaporate. Cinnie's case schedule was booked solid, which left her blessedly short of fretting time. There were two new evaluations, an hour spent teaching a postop throat-cancer patient to talk with the aid of an electronic larynx, and then she'd been called to the emergency room to do sign language interpreting for a deaf girl who'd collapsed in the Town Center Mall and been brought in for an evaluation.

When the knock came, she was back in the office catching up on paperwork. She was surprised to see him in the doorway, dressed in a natty pair of tweed trousers, a cardigan, and a dotted bow tie.

'Mr. London? I told reception to let you know I had an emergency and couldn't reschedule you for today. Didn't they call?'

The working side of his face fell. 'Pick-uh?'

'Sorry, I didn't get that. Try again, would you? Nice and easy.'

He sucked in a major breath. 'Pick-illll.'

'Pick . . . ill? Pickle? Oh, of course, we have a lunch date, don't we? Stay right where you are. I'll get my coat.'

He set his jaw and started to pivot his chair toward the door. 'Bluch.'

'No wait. I'm looking forward to it, really. I've just been up to my ears this morning, so it slipped my mind.'

'Bluch,' he said again. With a dismissive swat, he started wheeling out to the reception area.

'All right. Have it your way. If you don't want to come, I can take Mrs. Hibbel or Mr. Levinson. I'm sure either one of them would be delighted to join me in a *delectable* bowl of chicken noodle soup, a *thick, juicy* hot pastrami sandwich on fresh seeded rye, an *icy, delicious* cream soda . . .'

London made another valiant push.

'. . . A *creamy* double scoop vanilla sundae with hot fudge and wet nuts . . .'

With that the old man stopped cold. He threw up his good arm and shook his head in surrender.

Cinnie came up behind him and started pushing the chair toward the elevators. 'You certainly play hard to get, my friend. Lucky I think you're worth the trouble.'

She drove north on High Ridge and angled the Volvo into a slim space in the parking lot fronting the deli. It took considerable maneuvering to get Mr. London transferred from the front seat into his chair. He leaned heavily on Cinnie's shoulders, but still his wasted leg wobbled like cheap furniture. She shifted his weight in an awkward stagger and set him clumsily on the plastic seat.

Flushed and perspiring, she flashed a high sign and worked to catch her breath. 'Bring on the pastrami.'

The proprietor, a bearish man named Ernie, led them to a small table in the corner and removed one of the bentwood side chairs to make room for London.

'Looking good, Officer London. So nice to see you out and around again.'

'Bluch,' London said. 'Bull-shit.'

'He's a little cranky,' Cinnie said. 'Forgive him.'

Ernie shrugged. 'No problem. Usually he's a *lot* cranky.'

They ordered, and London passed the time spearing sour tomatoes from the bowl in the middle of the table and popping them whole into his mouth. His cheeks bulged, and soon he was enveloped in a garlicky haze.

When the soup and sandwiches arrived, they ate for a while in silence. Cinnie noticed a softening in London's posture, and a mushy look of contentment came over his face. Simple pleasures.

After he'd downed the soup and three quarters of the sandwich, the old man finally saw fit to pause for a second. 'Good,' he said and unleashed a hearty belch.

'Glad you're enjoying it. Up for dessert?'

He belched again. Not a real answer, but the twinkle in his eye said yes.

By the time he'd plowed through half of his banana split, Cinnie had run out of small talk. Left idle, her mind wandered back to all the strange, troubling events: the missing T-shirt, the hep lock removed without orders, all the suspicious accidents, James crossing Mill Road on his own. When she looked over at London, he was staring at her with a questioning look.

'Sorry. I was just thinking about the accident for a change. Makes me crazy that they haven't found the driver yet. And there are so many things that make no sense.'

'Thiings?'

Cinnie hadn't intended to trouble London with any of it, but she started telling him about the missing T-shirt and wound up spilling everything. She talked about all the accidents in the Grove. All involving children.

So much didn't add up: Ricky Dolan falling through a freak thin patch of pond ice in the dead of a record cold winter, Jason Sanders finding a firecracker in his sandbox and somehow setting it off after his mother had searched the sand for a missing toy, Billy Walker's disappearance that had never been explained, three kids in car accidents in under a year.

'How could all that be simple coincidence? There has to be something going on in the Grove that no one is willing to recognize. And I keep thinking that unless something is done, there'll be more and more hurt kids. At least, we have to try to put an end to it, don't we?'

It was so nice having someone who was willing to listen for a change. London displayed none of Paul's caustic scepticism, none of Dal's sympathetic but disbelieving indulgence, none of Detective Allston's maddening lack of interest.

Ever the cop, London waited until she'd finished and then strained to fill in the blanks in her story.

'Ice?'

'It was only thin in that one little patch where Ricky fell through. The cops checked over the entire surface the day after it happened, and they found four to six inches frozen solid everywhere else. So isn't it creepy that Ricky happened to step on that particular thin place? And it was so cold – why was that one spot thin in the first place?'

He formed a circle with his thumb and forefinger and held it to his eyes. 'Seeee car?'

'You mean did anyone witness the hit-and-run? Yes, in fact, a neighbor of mine saw a car speeding away right after the time James must have been hit. She gave the police a description, and she noticed the car had New York plates. So why can't they track it down? You know how the force operates better than anyone, Mr. London. Am I being unreasonable?'

London looked sympathetic.

'I don't understand it. The person who hit James didn't fall off the face of the earth. There has to be some way to track him down. All this time, and the police are no closer to finding him. This can't be the best they can do. I have to know who did this. I have to know what kind of a person could hurt my little boy like that and just leave him there to suffer.'

Tears puddled in her eyes and spilled over. She swiped them away furiously.

London patted her hand. 'Ssh,' he soothed. 'Ssssh.'

'Sorry. The last thing you need is my sob stories. It's just so aggravating. I'm starting to think they'll never find out who hit James.'

'Git . . . get. Yes,' London said with a firm nod and a solid fist on the table.

'You really think so? I wish I had your confidence.'

A sly look crossed London's face. 'Yooou . . . tell.'

'Tell? Tell what to who?'

'Tell . . . awllll.'

'Sorry. I don't get it.'

She tried to catch his confidence. But for some reason, she wasn't feeling very optimistic. In fact, she was starting to get that awful sense again that she'd had on the day of James's accident.

She mustn't let herself do this. 'Ready to go? I'll get the check.'

'Tell . . . boom boooom.'

London's face was flushing in dusky blotches. He hunched his back and rapped his fist on the table. 'Boooom . . . boom. Tellll. Awwll . . . tell.'

'Easy, Mr. London. Check please, Ernie. Let's hit the road, friend. I think it's time you got some rest.'

She helped London back into the Volvo and folded his chair into the trunk. Maybe taking him out hadn't been such a hot idea. Suddenly, Cinnie was eager to get him back to the hospital.

Slipping behind the wheel, she took an anxious look at him. He'd stopped pounding and gesticulating, and his color had dimmed to an innocent pink. Better. Whatever had upset him so had obviously passed.

He gave her a sheepish smile. She patted his hand and felt a swell of affection. 'Thanks for the company, Mr. London. And thanks for listening.'

He looked vague and distracted. 'Tell awwll . . . tell boooomm boom,' he muttered. 'Tell, go . . . shit.'

'It's okay, Mr. London. Don't worry about it.'

Cinnie pumped the accelerator, turned the key, and the cranky, old engine came alive.

32

Tunnel of smoke.

Malcolm Cobb narrowed his eyes and surveyed the shadowy street. Plume of foreboding darkness. Beckoning fingers of silent doom. Beneath him, the engine trembled like a frightened beast. The wheel shuddered in his grasp.

Breath held, he began another slow circuit of the block. The pavement was rutted and strewn with rubble. Driving without headlights, he was powerless to avoid the dross. Flying stones assaulted the undercarriage, and the tires crunched like giant's teeth in the drifts of putrefying matter. The concussion of the ride rattled his bones.

Tunnel of doom.

Her house was at the dark terminus. Cobb saw it as a seductress. A painted siren, simultaneously beckoning and repellent. Pillar of peril, precipice of dark demise.

A blush of light escaped the drawn curtains. The porch lamp blazed. A halo of heat cradled the roof, and a teasing curl of smoke escaped the chimney. Mesmerizing.

Approaching again, Cobb's mouth parched and a cruel pulse pummeled his temple. At the critical instant, doubt forced his foot to the accelerator, and he shot past the drive and back to his starting point.

'Dolt,' he muttered angrily to himself. 'Cowardly buffoon.'

Slowly, he marshaled his courage and started again. The car jolted over the scarred terrain. Cobb's apprehension built with the speed of a wind-fed fire.

This time, he kept up a running patter with himself. 'Nothing to fear. She will welcome you. How can she not? You are bound to her by flesh and destiny.'

He was nearer, approaching the drive again. 'Blood of her blood. Go, and be reconciled.'

Almost there now. Only few more yards separated him

from her sweet approbation. But before he could traverse the meager distance, a spasm jammed his foot hard onto the brake.

The car screeched like a wounded beast. The sound pierced his torment. Had anyone heard?

Casting his desperate gaze from side to side, he observed the neighboring homes. No shades fluttering, no peering accusatory eyes. There had been no deadly betrayal. Not yet.

But the seconds were seeping away, draining from the finite supply, dripping into the bottomless chasm of eternal regret. Fool!

He had to proceed without delay. Cobb invoked his firmest control. Lever of will engaged.

He eased the car onto her drive, rolled out of sight behind a stand of evergreens, and killed the engine.

Stepping out, he felt the rush of a stern wind. It prodded the clouds scudding across the solemn face of the night.

Cobb embraced the image. He was a cloud. Plump cumulus bobbling in the gentle arms of eternity. Vicar of the night sky. Lowering lord of lost vision and failed enterprise.

Brilliant!

Moon of night. Eclipsing the day's fire. Reigning in dark triumph. Dark moon rising over the cowering universe. Behold!

His doubt evaporated. Boldly, he strode to the door and rapped on the frame. There was a crackling silence, but Cobb was not to be denied. He knocked again. Louder.

Finally, he heard the deep concussion of footsteps overhead. They were followed by the light crackle of stair risers. More steps. A lamp flared in the front vestibule. The door opened.

His breath caught at the sight of her. She was radiant. Eyes glinting. Mouth bowed in a knowing smile. He'd never seen her so beautiful. She led him into the living room and bade him to sit.

'So,' she said. There was mischief in her gaze. 'Not a great success from the look of you, was it, Malcolm?'

Cobb struggled to remain calm. He longed to sound confident and appear commanding. But a tic danced beneath his right eye, and his throat jammed in an incipient stammer.

She frowned at him. Pursed her lips. 'What happened exactly, dear? What went wrong?'

Despite his urge to deny the failures, the story poured forth. The mistakes had not been his doing, he told her. The child's mother was to blame, constantly thwarting him, standing between Cobb and his rightful recompense until he was weakened almost beyond redemption. It was the woman who had aborted his proper harvest, left him to forage for scraps. All the woman's fault. Everything.

She listened without comment or obvious emotion. When Cobb finished the tale, she settled a harsh gaze on him. 'Then you know what you must do, Malcolm. Whimpering won't solve a thing.'

Cobb nodded. The threat of her ire had rendered him mute.

'And in the meantime, how do you propose to regain your strength, darling? You look dreadful.'

Cobb flushed with confusion. Endearment tainted with insult. She was a master at unsettling him. He struggled to speak, had to respond.

'I'm f-fine. Tired is all.'

Her giggle was a piercing awl. 'Oh, come now. I can see the weakness. Look at yourself, Malcolm. It's written all over you.'

He caught his reflection in the window. His features were beginning to sag, arm growing numb again. He gasped in horror. She must not see him in this condition.

'Think, Malcolm,' she said. 'There must be some way for you to overcome this little setback. You're a clever boy.'

His lip quivered. 'I'm trying, you know. It's not my fault, I told you. It's all her doing. That miserable woman.'

'Don't be a fool, I said. Get hold of yourself now, Malcolm.'

'I . . . I am trying.' His eyes welled up and spilled over. 'I am.'

'Listen to you. How ridiculous you sound. Put aside that mewling self-pity and think, you silly dolt. Use your head. Stop that slobbering this instant!'

Her rebuke was an icy wash. Cobb stiffened and caught hold of himself. 'I'm sorry.'

'As you should be. How perfectly useless to fall to pieces like that. What a perfect waste.'

'You're r-right, of course. I can divine a solution. I m-must.'

He fell silent. Evading her icy gaze, he endeavored to view the problem as a puzzle. Slick pieces, sharp-edged and singular. Using the technique he'd mastered in the seventh-phase exercises, he transmuted the parts, viewing them from subtly shifting angles like the play of evolving images in a CT scan.

Cobb could see each of the several faces of each of the several parts. Endless possibilities. Permutations ad nauseam.

Slowly, finally, the right one appeared. Perfect, priceless! *Ad astra per aspera!* He would struggle toward the heavens. Reach the stars!

'What is it, Malcolm?'

He stifled a giggle. She looked perplexed. Dear little muddlehead. Sweet little bumble-brain. Fearsome little bubble of poison fluff.

Cobb stood, pulled her to her feet, and danced her around the floor in a raucous waltz. She sputtered in dismay. 'Come now, Malcolm. Get a grip on yourself.'

Bright bursts of hilarity rocked him like a dinghy in a squall. 'I have it. I have it. It's so wonderful. You'll be astonished.'

She disengaged herself and faced him with crossed arms and a petulant expression. 'Tell me then. Don't behave like an ass.'

Cobb recoiled at the slur. 'Don't call me that.'

'Come now. Don't be such a silly boy. You know I didn't mean a thing by it.'

'You must never call me that.'

'Tsk, tsk. So sensitive, are we? Forget I ever said it, will you, Malcolm? Tell me. What's your plan? I'm dying to hear.'

He bit his lip and kept his eyes averted. He would bear no more of her insults.

Her face went coy. Flirtatious grin, fluttering lashes, voice an ooze of warmest honey.

'Come now, dearest. Please, please tell me. I can't wait to hear your clever plan. Such a genius you are, Malcolm. Such a giant of intellect and creativity. You can solve anything if you put your mind to it, you lucky boy. You simply must share it with me right now. This instant. I'll positively burst if you don't.'

He allowed her to cajole him awhile. Reveled in her discomfiture. She began to whine, so frustrated was she with his stolid denial. Served her right. How much frustration had he borne at her behest? How many torments?

'Malcolm, stop this! I can't bear it another minute. Tell me this instant. Tell me or . . . '

Her eyes went dark, rent him like skewers. He could not allow this to degenerate as it had the last time. That would be his undoing.

'All right. If it's all that important to you,' he said.

'Oh, yes, dear. Very, very important.'

Cobb explained his plan. So simple and elegant. And yet entirely foolproof, he was certain. All he needed to do was procure the vehicle. And he couldn't imagine that as more than a minor inconvenience.

Her expression changed as he spoke. Surprise yielded to respect, respect to awed pleasure.

'Brilliant,' she said at last. 'Truly brilliant. And you're sure the child won't even know he's being milked?'

Cobb shook his head. That was the incredible part. It could be done openly, and the specimen would not realize a thing.

'You're right, dear boy. It is perfect. Priceless. Oh, I'm so proud of you, Malcolm. So very proud. As soon as it's done, we must celebrate. Name the time, and I'll bring the refreshments. Finest champagne and caviar first, in honor of your triumphant recovery. And then a feast. Doesn't that sound lovely?'

She fluttered about the living room making plans for their repast. 'Oysters, I should think. And then that roast veal with the chestnut purée you're so fond of. A warm rhubarb pie with cream . . .'

Cobb smiled, satisfaction warming him like a beneficent sun. There was nothing on Earth he wouldn't do for her approval. Joy of joys!

Suddenly, she went silent. Her brow furrowed. 'And what about the woman, dear? I suppose you've thought of a brilliant way to see to her as well?'

The words pierced Cobb's elation. Sent him plummeting. The woman's disposal presented a complex of difficulties that he had not yet been able to overcome.

Then, if his brilliant plan for the specimen went well, the woman would be irrelevant. Cobb was buoyed by the thought, infused with fresh confidence. 'Certainly,' he said. 'The woman will be no issue.'

Her eyes narrowed to penetrating slits. 'You're not protecting her, are you, Malcolm? Sometimes I get the feeling you're afraid to deal with that dreadful woman.'

'Afraid? Don't be absurd.'

'I certainly hope it's absurd, dearest. It would surely be absurd for you to protect her as you did Mummy, wouldn't it now? Absurd and dangerous, Malcolm. Very dangerous as you know.'

Cobb stiffened. 'You needn't worry. I'm entirely in control of the situation.'

'I sincerely hope so, darling. For your own sake.'

Cobb wished to believe his own comforting words. The woman would not interfere this time. But if she somehow did manage to thwart him again, Cobb was determined to overwhelm all obstacles and make certain it was her final intrusion.

33 After a stop at home for lunch, they spent the rest of the day cruising. Getting the feel of things. It was one of the things Big Matt used to do when he'd hit a wall on a case. You looked around long enough, you might finally see something.

Most of the time, the kid was quiet, enjoying the radio and the day off. Over dinner at a little Italian place in Pound Ridge, Booker thanked Drum with a melting smile and a couple of high fives. Best return Drum could ever remember getting on an investment, and he'd traded from the cozy inside more than once.

Booker was out cold by the time Drum pulled the beauty into the narrow garage. Drum hefted the kid and carried him up to bed. Hotshot weighed next to nothing. Amazing given what he'd packed away that day alone. Kid had eaten a giant hero for lunch and downed most of Drum's lasagna at dinner after he'd inhaled his own. Runt probably sucked up helium when no one was looking. Maybe they'd better tie a string on the little bandit before he floated away altogether.

Drum felt himself grinning like a fool. Kid had that effect on him. Made him something he never imagined he had the capacity to be.

Drum settled Booker in bed, tugged off his high-top sneakers, and pulled the covers up to his pointed chin.

''Night, hotshot. Sleep tight.'

There was a neon vacancy in Drum's stomach. Anxious to fill it, he went to the kitchen and spent a few minutes with his head in the icebox. He found some leftover meat loaf, a bowl of cold mashed potatoes, two cans of Bud, and a wedge of Boston cream pie. Not the perfect snack, but close enough.

On his way to the table he spotted a note in Stella's firm hand propped against the phone. She'd been called to fill in for the night at a jazz club near the Sound. The regular singer had come down with laryngitis. It would be a late gig, she figured, so she'd see him in the morning.

The note mentioned that there had been a couple of calls from Carmody. Chief wanted him to leave a progress report with his friend Louis Packham at Failsafe Security. And Drum was to make sure Booker had a decent dinner and a hot bath.

Drum crumpled the note and tossed it in the trash. He'd done okay, he decided. Booker's day had been one long meal. Way better than decent. And as far as the bath was concerned, things hadn't turned out near as dirty as Drum had hoped.

Louis at the alarm company thanked him for the last batch of pirated tapes and agreed to pass a message to the chief. Drum considered how optimistic it made sense to sound. If he was too negative, Carmody might get disgusted and pull the plug on Drum's operation. On the other hand, if Drum's message was too upbeat, Carmody would probably expect an immediate solution and drive Drum nuts until he got one.

Drum decided to have Louis tell the chief that things were coming along as expected. That'd keep the old lard guessing.

'Okay. I'll tell him.'

'Yeah, and tell him there's no reason for him to go shooting his hose. You got that?'

'Sure, Jerry. No reason for the chief to shoot his hose. Got you.'

Drum had planned to cash it in for the night, but the message from Carmody made him feel ambitious all of a sudden. He called next door and got Mary Ellen to come over and keep an eye on Booker until he got back.

The roads had gone slick from a quick shot of frozen rain. Drum skidded turning onto High Ridge. The beauty did a wild three-sixty and then angled in to bash the curb. A car braked hard behind him, and Drum braced himself for a crash that didn't come. When he looked out the rear window, he saw a fat guy in a Lincoln sputtering curses and clutching his chest. Drum waggled his fingers and blew the guy a kiss.

After that, he headed north at a sensible crawl. Everything was moving in slow motion. Other cars inched along like languid snakes. Traffic lights hung forever in the red zone. As he approached the Merritt Parkway intersection, a rangy, slack-tongued dog loped across High Ridge in front of him and he was forced to a stop. Beast was in less than no hurry. Drum was stuck forever watching the one-pooch parade. Lucky he liked animals.

Finally, he was under the Merritt Parkway overpass and skating the beauty through the tricky turns on the way to Tyler's Grove. He turned in through the broken pillars and eased the beauty around until he was idling at the precise spot where the witness had been stopped when she saw the speeding car. All three police reports put her at the same place, in front of the first house beyond the left stone pillar.

He rolled down the beauty's window. The air had the damp, heavy feel of wet sheets. Not much in the way of noise. Listening hard, Drum picked up the vague crackle of frosted windows, music thumping from an over-wrought stereo system, a baby bawling.

Drum faced Mill Road and stared through the stone columns. Almost five minutes passed before a car approached from the High Ridge spur, slowly rounded the curve in front of the pillars, and continued north toward New Canaan. Drum watched without blinking, but the view was nothing near what he expected. Surprised, he waited until a second car followed the same track, crossed his vantage point, and disappeared up Cascade.

Real interesting.

Drum waited for one more car to trace the path along Mill toward New Canaan. He wanted absolute confirmation, and he got it.

Same story all three times. Approaching cars on Mill Road followed the curve in the street so that they remained invisible behind the left pillar at first and then swerved so a stand of trees quickly swallowed the image. With the way the road banked, there was no way to cut the curve and still hold the pavement. Especially not if the driver was speeding.

From where the witness had claimed to be, she could not have gotten more than a fleeting view of any passing vehicle. With all three cars, Drum had managed no better than a hazy glimpse of dark metal and a glint of glass. No way to be sure about model or body type. Impossible to get a read on the license plate or the person behind the wheel either, and the Holroyd woman had told the cops the driver was a young, blond male with cropped hair and blue eyes.

With the sun in her eyes as it would have been at the time of the accident, it would have been a trick for the witness to have seen much of anything. No more than a streak of passing glare.

Which made him more anxious than ever to hear the story with his own ears. He drove the beauty around the block and turned down the small cul-de-sac off Grove where the witness lived.

Broad was home, but not to Drum. He tried to coax an audience with the stiff, disembodied voice behind the locked door, but she wouldn't budge. Not even when he gave her the line about being a reporter with the *Times* on tight deadline and slipped his fake press pass through the mail slot. Thing came flying back out at him like a broken cash register drawer. No sale.

'Sorry. But it's quite late, and I'm busy. You really should have rung first. I'd have saved you the trip.'

'I only need a couple of minutes. All I want is to ask a couple of questions about the car you saw leaving the scene of the hit-run. The paper is willing to run a feature on the case, help get the word out and maybe nab the driver.'

'I've already told everything to the police. Call them, why don't you? I'm sure they'd be delighted to cooperate with the *Times*.'

'Right, only I'm sure you can tell it better, Mrs. Holroyd. You were there.'

'As I said, I'm busy. Good night now.'

Her voice was dead-bolted. Drum could hear it was useless to argue.

He made his way over the uneven flagstone walk toward the beauty. The woman doused the spotlights when he was halfway to the drive. Miss Hospitality.

The darkness gave Drum a chance to look around. Over his shoulder, he eyes the silhouettes moving behind the filmy drapes over the living room windows. There was a tall, slim one Drum made as the witness. She had her hair slicked back, posture like a palace guard. Broad was shaped like a raw ziti, Drum observed, but not the kind that'd make you the least big hungry.

There was a smaller silhouette halfway across the room. The son, Drum figured. Kid was also long and skinny but without the mother's starch. He was huddled behind the antique school desk cluttered with papers. Kid was clutching the desk as if it were a life preserver.

Drum could see the woman barking at the little guy and how the kid appeared to shrink from the words. His head was bowed, shoulders rounded. Drum had the impression of a regular kid who'd been put through a juice extractor.

The woman crossed the room and picked up an object from the end table nearest the desk. She held it so Drum couldn't exactly make it out, but he remembered it from the last time he'd stopped by when no one was home and peered in the window. Funny how she seemed to take the thing so seriously. She was pushing it in the kid's direction and spitting her words. The boy was backing off.

Drum watched until he was sure the kid wasn't in for a beating. A hint of that, and he would have found a way to butt in with a distraction. There was always the broken-down-car bit or the one about his emergency beeper sounding and having to call in. Kid definitely didn't look like he needed hurting.

But the ruse wasn't necessary. After a couple of minutes the woman flung the object back on the desk and stormed out of the room. The kid waited a beat and followed. Not what he would have done if he was afraid he was headed for a pounding.

Drum couldn't decide what to make of the broad. He didn't need to hear her fleeing driver story to know it didn't compute. She'd invented at least some, if not all, the details. But why?

He toyed with the options.

Could be she was so anxious to help the cops nab the runaway driver that she'd succumbed to wishful thinking. Imagined she'd seen what the cops might need. Woman didn't come across like the concerned citizen type, but you never knew. She did have a kid of her own, and Drum was learning firsthand how much having a kid could change a person.

Then there was the chance she'd made the whole thing up to get attention. Plenty of nuts around who craved microphones and spotlights. Never occurred to them they could be scuttling a case and letting some rodent run loose in the process. But if the broad had such a yearning for center stage, why would she refuse to talk to a reporter?

Drum had plenty of questions but only one definite answer. His own eyes had convinced him that Lydia Holroyd couldn't be definite about the hit-run driver, the plates, or even much about the speeding car. In other words, no matter what her reason for telling it, the woman's story was suitable for dumping.

Drum gunned the beauty and headed up the Mill Road spur toward High Ridge. Sifting through the cassettes in the beauty's glove compartment, he selected a big-band collection featuring the Duke and Stan Kenton and popped it in the cassette deck. Good thing it was a three album set. Looked like he was in for a lot of running around.

34 The doorbell rang as Cinnie was about to step into a steaming tub. She was sapped, but she perked up at the sight of Dal bearing one of her care packages of sample products from her market research firm.

Dal was wearing her hide-all-sins sweater, a green number large enough to sleep six, over a pair of baggy jeans and black high-top sneakers. She looked like an overgrown version of TeeJay in drag. Same impish grin, same electric vitality.

'This week we have the wonders of macrobiotic plant food, cotton wabs in designer scents and colors for the truly pampered belly button, and the pièce de résistance – ta-da ... colorless odorless chocolate syrup.'

'Sounds revolting. Who'd buy such a thing?'

'Good question. The manufacturer came to us convinced that there's an enormous untapped market of diet cheats out there aching to get their hands on invisible chocolate.'

'So what did you tell him?'

'I told him five thousand plus expenses, and he can expect the report in a month. Business is business, Cin. My mission is not to turn away customers, no matter how demented their products.'

Dal had also brought a chilled bottle of Johannesburg Riesling. 'I actually sprung for that myself. So open it quickly, before I come to my senses and remember what a tightwad I am.'

Cinnie uncorked the wine, and they sat in the den, sipping and catching up. The conversation soon turned serious and drifted to James.

Cinnie had suffered a serious blow to her optimism. She needed to talk to someone about it, and Dal had always been the person she could tell the impossible things.

'I'm starting to think he may never get over this thing, Dal.'

Earlier in the evening, Dal had smuggled TeeJay into James's room for a quick visit, and the contrast between the kids had been devastating. A few weeks ago, James had been the bigger, stronger, more advanced kid by several years and all the right margins.

TeeJay had always looked up to James. Cinnie could remember how the little guy had watched his older friend with reverent eyes and unflinching attention. She and Dal used to get a grand kick out of the way TeeJay imitated James's every move and mannerism.

But the accident had turned everything upside down. At James's bedside, it was TeeJay who'd chosen the activities and patiently explained the rules and procedures. TeeJay was the one who'd spoken slowly and carefully in a higher than normal voice, instinctively trying to help James understand. James had been the one struggling to imitate and keep up. Broke Cinnie's heart to watch them.

It also had forced her to take a hard look at the possible future. And she'd had to admit to herself that there might be some virtue in Paul's tendency to steel himself for the worst.

'I used to believe James could be anything he set his mind to, Dal. Now I feel like I'd better get used to the sound of lost options and doors slamming in his face.'

'Wait a minute. That doesn't sound like the Cinnie I know and love. What have you done with my friend, lady? Come on, I'm wise to you, you miserable impostor.'

Cinnie shrugged and forced a feeble smile. 'Can't help it, my Pollyanna suit is at the cleaners.'

The words brought back her conversation with Detective Allston. She felt a ripple of anger remembering how he'd dismissed her concerns and ignored her questions.

Cinnie should have let the creep know what she thought of him. Maybe that was part of the reason she was feeling so down. She'd been allowing herself to be a doormat. Play victim, you become a victim. When had she forgotten that important bit of truth?

The odds might be against James, but she wasn't going to improve them any by moaning to Dal.

'Mind if I kick you out?' Cinnie said.

'Nah, I've been bounced out of way better joints than this. Everything all right?'

'Not entirely, but I just remembered there is something I can do to make myself useful. Maybe drag myself out of this putrid funk while I'm at it. And I really should get started before I collapse for the night.'

'Okay.' Bless Dal. She knew when to ask questions and when to disappear.

Cinnie walked her to the door and flipped the lock behind her.

In the den, she found a blank legal pad and a pen. Curled up on the sofa, she nudged her mind back to the morning of the accident and started writing. If that adjuster from the insurance company thought an account of that terrible day might be useful, why not give it to him? What had Mr. London advised? Tell all. Couldn't hurt, could it? At this point she was willing to try almost anything.

The day came back to her in a vivid reel. Everything had seemed so routine: James eating instant oatmeal for breakfast, she and Paul munching on wheat toast. Cinnie could see the table jumbled with plates, coffee cups, and newspapers. She pictured James crouched on his haunches, prattling on between mouthfuls about soccer and how his team was going to win the championship of the world in the indoor season.

There was that particular smile on Paul's face, the one only James knew how to evoke. Thousand-watt smile, full of pride and pure amusement. Cinnie had always found it contagious and incredibly sexy.

Since the accident, there hadn't been a trace of that look on Paul. She wondered if she'd ever see it again.

No more playing sob sister, she rebuked herself. Pay attention.

They'd all left the house at eight-thirty. Cinnie had dropped James at the bus stop and driven on toward the hospital. She'd caught a last glimpse of his ruddy cheeks and sunlit copper hair in the rearview mirror as she approached the intersection of Cascade.

Paul had gone to the studio, where his schedule was packed as usual. He'd mentioned the lineup to Cinnie, and she reconstructed it now as best she could: a couple of demos, a sound track for a music video, and then the afternoon had been reserved for a new group under contract to Polygram. Paul was producing their first album.

Cinnie felt a little foolish detailing her routine morning at the office, but the adjuster had been clear about wanting her to go back over everything to refresh her memory.

She wrote nonstop until she'd covered all that she could remember about that terrible day. In painful detail, she recounted her trip to the Grove from the hospital. She recalled the delightful sense of well-being that had enveloped her on the ride. And then came the horror as she approached the tangle of emergency vehicles on Mill Road and found out they were there for James.

The memory caught and held her as if she were a startled deer. But she forced the feeling away. She wrote about the terrible ride in the ambulance: James spewing gibberish, the horrifying wail of the heart monitor.

And then came the hideous time she'd spent sitting outside the emergency room, waiting for someone to come and tell her that it had all been a dreadful mistake. James was fine. James *had* to be fine.

It had taken forever for Paul to get there. With the studio's soundproofing, he hadn't heard the sirens on the corner. He'd been totally unaware of the accident until someone in the studio turned on the local radio station during a break and they heard it reported on the news. By the time he finally arrived and finished sputtering his impossible excuses, all they could do was wait together in mute terror.

Dr. Silver had been called in for an emergency consult, and he'd been the first to emerge through the swinging doors to the waiting area. The man had the touch of a typhoon. 'It's bad,' he'd told them. 'Could be worse than bad. First twenty-four hours will be crucial.'

'What can we do?' Paul had said.

Silver shrugged. 'Know any prayers?'

Thank heaven for Dr. Ferris who'd shown up moments later. In his cool, rational way, he'd taken over. After assuring Cinnie and Paul that things weren't as dire as Silver made them out to be, Ferris had collected the early diagnostic test results and the professional opinions of everyone who'd examined James so far. Then the pediatrician had distilled the information and gave them a clear, reasonably encouraging picture of what they could expect in the short run.

'We're going to monitor him very closely until we can assess the extent of the injuries.'

'Is he . . . is he going to make it?' Paul said.

'Yes, he is.'

In that quiet certainty, Cinnie had found her anchor. Ferris would take care of James. Ferris wouldn't let anything happen to her baby. She would have embraced the man, but he was as cuddly as a porcupine.

Thinking back, Cinnie wrote about the power outage in the studio and Paul being late to meet the bus. She waited for the usual stab of fury, but it didn't come. So maybe she was finally through with it. Or too numb to feel anything.

The narrative rambled on for fifteen written pages. The insurance adjuster was going to get a lot more than he bargained for, Cinnie thought, and probably nothing he'd find worth his time.

She stapled the pile of pages together and stuffed them in an envelope. As the insurance man had suggested, she called his service and told the man who answered that the letter was ready. She hung up and went outside in her robe and slippers to deposit the account in the curbside mailbox.

Back inside, the warmth of the farmhouse seeped under her skin and turned her to mush. She yawned. Now she was absolutely ready for a long soak in the tub and a night's sleep, preferably in good company.

On a hopeful whim, she dialed Paul's number at the studio. No answer, which meant he was in the middle of a session and had switched his calls to his service. The operator finally picked up on the fifth ring, but Cinnie didn't bother to leave a message. No way she could induce Paul to leave the studio before he was entirely ready. Another woman she might be able to handle, but she didn't have a clue about how to compete with a sound board.

The bath water was too cold. Cinnie drained it and started over. She flipped the taps on full and poured in a packet of scented salts. Waiting for the tub to fill, she undressed and wrapped herself in an ancient blue robe. With a few minutes to waste, she picked up several papers and magazines from the neglected pile on the desk and started leafing through them.

The world had continued to turn in her absence: plenty of murders, political coups, economic upheavals, deaths, divorces, major scandals in the wings waiting their turn for tabloid space.

Her eyelids gained weight as she tried to catch up on three weeks worth of local politics, favorite cartoon strips, goings on in Central America and the Middle East, recipes for Tex-Mex concoctions.

A tickle underfoot jolted her alert. She looked down to discover that her bath had overflowed and was forging a soapy river on the bedroom floor. She raced into the bathroom, sloshing in the flood, and turned off the faucets.

It took over an hour of baling and mopping to tame the tides. The plank floor was still soaked through, and ancient layers of wax were lifting in ugly white blotches. The small oriental rug that she'd inherited from her mother was saturated. Cinnie wrung it out and draped it over the tub to dry.

Finished, she surveyed the mess and mused at her own lack of reaction. After all that had happened, she couldn't get too worked up over wet wood planks and a soggy hunk of woven wool. James's accident had shifted the world into different focus.

Which reminded her to call pediatrics and see how her sweetheart was doing.

She recognized the voice on the other end as the young

nurse who'd given James his bath this morning. Double shifting, Cinnie thought. No wonder they made mistakes.

'This is Cinnie Merritt. How's James doing?'

There was an awkward pause.

'What is it? What's wrong?'

'Oh, I'm sure it's nothing really, Mrs. Merritt. Poor Jimmy just seems . . . unhappy to me. Kind of upset or something. Not the way he usually is.'

'What do you mean? What's he doing?'

'It's hard to explain. Look, I probably shouldn't be bothering you with it at all. He'll probably drop off to sleep in no time and be just fine in the morning.'

'Of course you should bother me with it. You did exactly right. Do me a favor, will you? Tell him I'm coming right over.'

'Oh, I'm sure there's no need.'

'Fifteen minutes, tops. Please tell him.'

'Really, Mrs. Merritt. We can take care of him. No reason for you to . . . '

'Be right there.'

Cinnie tossed on a sweatsuit. The Volvo refused to start, so she grabbed the keys from Paul's dresser and took the Porsche.

Maybe it was silly, but instinct nudged her to make the trip. And from now on, she was determined to listen to those inner voices, no matter how unreasonable they sounded.

Traffic was thin on High Ridge, and the lights had been switched for the night to a series of yellow warning blinkers. She wanted to hurry, but the slick roads held her to a frustrating crawl.

The radio surrounded her with a comforting cushion of sound. Cinnie concentrated hard on the icy road. All she wanted was to get to her little one and ease whatever was troubling him. She was so focused on her destination that she never saw the accident coming.

35 Cobb was jubilant. Procuring the vehicle had been far simpler than he'd dared to hope. A single phone call made with the appropriate modicum of guile had sufficed. As planned, he explained that he was conducting a crucial experiment and required immediately delivery.

He had suffered no tiresome queries, no hesitation from the source, though he had been prepared to deal with both, if necessary.

But all had proceeded apace. And the brilliant means to resolving his dilemma had been forthcoming in hours, conveyed directly to his cabin by a fawning courier. All that remained was the installation and retrieval.

As he approached the entrance to the hospital parking lot, the arm of the wooden sentry made its deferential ascent. At the far end of the desolate blacktop, he eased his car into the shroud of shadow cast by a ring of evergreens.

Stepping out, he was caressed by the vibrant night sky. Spurred by the wind. Silently, he traversed the dark sea of pavement and claimed the cover of a privet hedge near the entrance.

He was a few spare feet from the guard. Cobb narrowed his eyes and appraised the vile creature: scaly skin with a bilious cast. Eyes the dull yellow of overboiled eggs, mouth puckered and dry like an anus. Cobb observed the man's blunted fingers and edematous paunch. With rising abhorrence, he catalogued the bold signatures of the creature's impending demise.

Failing health aside, the moronic sloth still craved his putrid vices. Cobb caught the stench of stale tobacco rising from his rumpled uniform. He was visibly agitated. His head flailed from side to side, limbs pulsed in a clonus of nervous need.

Perfect.

As expected, the guard soon abandoned his post and vanished around the corner of the building. Cobb rejoiced. The munificent fates were urging him on his mission.

The lobby was empty save for three ancient women. He winced at their aura: a ripe ooze of decay. The dust of their putrefaction trembled in the stifling air and settled about them in a savage halo. Heedless, they prattled on. Voices an impotent shrill. Cobb masked his revulsion as he passed near them *en route* to the stairs.

He climbed on cat feet, lithe and limber. Anticipation had overwhelmed his debility. He was the moon rising, fountain of celestial splendor. Spikes of warmth radiated from him, brightening the dank stairwell.

Fifth floor.

Cobb paused at the landing. He peeled open the lid of the plastic container to peer inside. The vehicle remained hail and plump.

Glorious.

With the certitude of high resolution film, he reviewed all that he'd read in the seminal three-volume Oxford University Press work on the subject of his chosen vehicle. Species Hirudo medicinalis. Variation on the common swamp leech.

Ancient physicians had employed the cunning creatures to rid ailing patients of what were presumed to be tainted humors. But with the advent of so-called modern medical practice, therapeutic bleeding had fallen into disrepute. For centuries Hirudo had been reviled and grossly undervalued, to the point that several subspecies now faced the imminent threat of extinction. Only in recent years had the pharmacological virtues of the species been reconsidered and acknowledged.

Cobb was conversant with several promising new treatment modalities involving the lowly leech. After microsurgical limb reattachment, the creatures had demonstrated the unique ability to resorb small clots around the surgical field without harming delicate tissues.

But that was far from Hirudo's sole value. Leech saliva had been found to contain a protein called hirudin that had grand potential as an anticlotting agent in the treatment of cardiovascular disease. Hementin, a substance produced by the Amazonian leech, had proven effective in dissolving blood clots. And orgelase, also a byproduct of Hirudo metabolism, was under study for its potential value in the treatment of glaucoma and certain circulatory disorders.

But Cobb had still another, grander enterprise in mind for the humble Hirudo. Plan beyond reckoning. Triumph of ingenuity.

He pressed his ear to the fire door and listened. Footsteps clacked like frozen teeth over the cold linoleum. Voices chattered. An anguished child begged for respite from his pain. The wails pierced Cobb's fragile font of patience.

Be still! Silence!

Anxiously, he willed the clamor to subside. But the noise and activity were incessant. A telephone rang. There was the staccato clatter of a linen cart and the low rumble of a gurney returning a patient from surgery.

A sudden draft invaded the stairwell, and the lights dimmed. Strident voices echoed up from the bowels of the building. Cobb felt the crackle of menace before his ear caught the approaching threat.

Footsteps on the risers below.

He held his breath as the interlopers ascended to the third landing and commenced toward the fourth. Silently, he bade their immediate arrest. Come no further. Cease!

But the footfalls persisted. Resonant, determined. Drawing closer. On the fourth landing now, and still approaching.

He could not be discovered cowering in the stairwell. What reasonable excuse could he offer? He would be exposed, humiliated. The intruders were drawing nearer.

No choice, no time.

Cobb threw open the fire door and forced himself to stride boldly down the bustling corridor. He averted his eyes, refusing to return any curious glances. Only a few yards to the sanctum. There, he could safely await his opportunity.

When he was certain he was unobserved, Cobb let himself in and quickly shut the door behind him. Crypt darkness. He searched through his pockets but found no matches. Arms outstretched, he made his way across the span to search for the light cord. He groped and fumbled, his fingers recoiling from objects he was powerless to identify.

In the center of the room, Cobb stumbled and cursed. His strength was evaporating. Panic reduced him, sucked him into the maelstrom of oily ruin.

Stop!

Cobb clenched his teeth and struggled for control. He invoked the rudimentary first-phase exercise. Mental mapping. Universal, global, and internal maps were all dependent on the same elementary device.

Eyes shut against the dark invasion, he extended his mind's eye to a postulated focal point on the unseen wall. Through complex calculations, he divined the formula for placement of any given object within the remainder of the meager space. He had only to extend a finger then and find one object. He touched a slick framed rectangle: his shaving mirror.

With renewed confidence, Cobb turned and moved toward the obvious position of the lamp. There, he felt the shade and grasped the dangling chain beneath. A triumphant tug and the room was awash with soft pink illumination.

Cobb scanned the space. All appeared to be in order. The serpentine thread had been deformed, but that had likely been his own doing.

Waiting for the commotion on the floor to subside, Cobb opened the plastic container and stared at the wriggling vehicle. He was spellbound by the creature's luxuriant movements. Slither and writhe. Squirm in mindless pleasure.

Precious specimen. Cobb imagined the lustrous body engorged with the child's blood. He would then be able to extract the precious humors directly. in the fresh form he required. There would be no evaporation of the essential humors as there was when the specimen's blood was stored in those ruinous vials in the laboratory. He required pure infusion and he would have it as soon as . . .

Cobb's reverie was pierced by the silence. All activity had ceased in the corridor. A precious lull.

Stealing forth, clutching the vehicle, Cobb made his way toward the specimen's room.

36 The dingle nurse had returned. Real names continued to elude him, but James had managed to apply alternate labels to the jumble of people he saw regularly in this noisy bed world. There was the dingle nurse, the pebble nurse, nurse heighdy-ho, the goo-goo doctor, Mister blah, the shadow man.

The shadow man. The thought slithered up James's spine and made him shiver. He had a horrific image of sharp needles, evil teeth gleaming in the darkness, tunnel eyes.

He nudged the terrible thought aside.

Dingle nurse was plumping his pillow now, turning it over to the cool side. Nice, pretty dingle. Her hand on his cheek was warm pudding. She had a sunshine face and eyes like pool water.

Double sunshine face. Double pool water eyes. Now she moved to the head of the bed to straighten his sheets. James observed her twin upside down mouths from his queer perspective and attempted to enjoy the absurdity.

She began talking. Her words were reminiscent of the melody bells James had been assigned to play in music class because he was the only one who could read music. Light, tinkly sounds without substance issued from her inverted lips.

After so many tries, James recognized the probable futility of the effort. But he decided to make one last attempt to explain his concerns to the dingle nurse.

'Shadow man. Vinton. Pop, Mom. Door.'

'There now, Jimmy. That comfy?'

'Green tunnel. Mrs. Wheel.'

'Easy now, honey, guess what? I just got off the phone with your mommy, and she said to tell you she's on her way to keep you company for a while. She'll be here real soon. So how's about you settle down and get a little rest in the meantime?'

James attempted to heed her counsel. He watched her effervescent double image as she left the room and closed the door behind her. A fist of foreboding gripped him as the lock clicked shut.

What if the shadow man came back?

He vowed not to entertain that dread possibility, but the idea kept snaking back into view. The shadow man could appear at any moment.

James started at the slightest sound in the corridor. Any hint of an approaching intruder and he tensed.

Where was his mother already? He listened for the glad ping of the elevator, imagined the sharp cadence of her approaching stride. He could almost feel the door fling open with a cool rush of air and visualize her walking toward him. 'Hey, Jimbo. How's the world's best small person?'

The thought of her voice warmed him and made him smile. She would sit on the bed beside him and tell him a story.

'Once upon a time there was a monkey-faced little boy named James. And he lived in a house in the woods with a garden full of weeds.

'The two strongest weeds were a brother and a sister named Dove and Elegant . . .'

No. Not that story. He didn't want to think about that.

James had mentioned the book in the hope that he could convey it's significance to his mother, that it had come from the shadow man. James had wanted to inform his mother about the shadow man's weird visits, all the strange, scary things. But she had misunderstood.

She'd thought he wanted the book read again and again. After so many hearings, he though he could probably recite the narrative from memory. ' . . . And the strong weed, Elegant, made sure her ailing brother, Dove, got the sap he needed to get well. When she was ailing, Dove went out and found the healing sap for Elegant.'

Stupid story.

So stupid he would not give it another thought. James ordered all vestiges of the tale from his consciousness and filled the fragile void with soothing mechanical utterances: 'January, February, March . . . ; summer, fall, winter, spring. Mary, Mary quite contrary, how does your garden grow . . . ?'

' . . . With silver bells and cockleshells and pretty maids all in a row.'

James froze at the voice and the cackle of mirth that followed. The shadow man had slipped in without his notice.

'Feeling better all the while, are you not, my child?'

James went mute with fear. The shadow man's face was stretched in a grotesque grimace.

'I have a surprise for you, James. A simple means to fulfill your obligation. It doesn't even require a needle, isn't that grand?'

James couldn't move. He watched the shadow man from the corner of his eyes. There was a glint of mischief in shadow's expression. The man peeled back the cover from a cloudy plastic container with a sound like paper tearing. And then came a slurp as he dipped his hand deep into the cylinder and had to wrench it loose.

When the hand emerged, James saw a fat black blotch squirming on the palm. The shadow man raised the blotch toward his lips and crooned lovingly. 'Dear little cleverness. Cunning beast of my salvation.'

A nervous giggle bubbled in James's throat. But he remembered the last time he'd laughed and the slap that followed. He bit hard on his lower lip.

The man's voice was changing, growing dangerous. He was still addressing the blotch. 'You are the moment. Creature of great enterprise. Servant of the dark moon. Behold.'

The shadow man came nearer and leaned over so James could look into his empty eyes. 'Be still now.'

James stifled a tremor. The shadow man pulled down his covers. He felt a hard pull at the top of his leg cast and a pressure verging on pain as the man forced his fingers down the tight plaster tube.

'Still my child, almost finished.'

There was an odd, clammy sensation as the man withdrew his fingers. James wanted to scratch it away, but the best he could do was rake the plaster.

'All done. See the magnificent simplicity? Sleep now, James. Rest.'

The shadow man slipped out of the room. James still felt the clammy tickle under the cast. He forced his flattened hand down the top as far as he could, but his fingers were too short, and he couldn't get close enough to scratch the tickle.

Then he thought of the blotch. Had the shadow man put that blotch thing on his leg? James tensed and squirmed at the notion. He wanted it out, gone. Whatever it was, he didn't want it *on* him.

He whimpered a protest. The sound generated another and another and took on a frightening power of its own. He could hear the shrill of his own terror, but it seemed to be coming from someone else. He couldn't reach it, couldn't find the way to stop the screaming.

Where was his mother? Why wasn't she here?

37
'Name.'

'Cinnie Merritt.'

'You okay, Mrs. Merritt? Want me to call an ambulance?'

She told him no. An ambulance was the last place she ever wanted to be again. Anyway, nothing hurt more than a dull shot. Plenty of bumps and bruises, but nothing to merit bouquets or exceptional sympathy. Arms folded over her chest, she surveyed the wreckage.

The road was strewn with jewels of shattered glass. What remained of Paul's cherished car looked like a battered red accordion. It was wedged against the curb at an improbable angle, spewing acrid fumes and making a noise like hot grease.

Cinnie knew she was badly shaken. Her voice quavered, and she felt a numbness she self-diagnosed as mild shock. Her mouth was chalk, heart jumping.

Ten yards away, another cop was chatting with a truck driver, a blond giant with a walrus moustache, an orange hunter's vest that capped several comic strips worth of tattoos, and an incendiary expression. He was claiming at the top of his considerable lungs that the whole thing had been Cinnie's fault. There was one clean dent in the side of his produce truck, a dimple between the painted apples and bananas.

'That woman came streaking out of nowhere in that fancy car of hers. Thinks she owns the damned road.'

Cinnie tried to keep calm. 'Look, officer. I'm on my way to see my son in the hospital. This character came turning onto High Ridge from the parkway ramp without bothering to look or slow down. But I don't have the time to argue right now. The important thing is, nobody's hurt. So please, can we have our insurance companies hash this out or something? I have to get to my son.'

'Merritt?' the cop said. 'Was it your little guy in that hit-run?'

'Yes. Please, I have to get to the hospital. I spoke to his nurse, and James is having a rough time right now.'

The cop turned to the trucker. 'You were turning onto High Ridge from the parkway, the lady says. That right?'

'Yeah, but she . . .'

'But she nothing, buddy. No trucks allowed on that parkway. You aware of that? And would you happen to remember who has the right of way at a parkway ramp, if you were supposed to be on it in the first place?'

The guy started sputtering. The cops rolled their eyes and got on with it. One began writing citations for the traffic violations while the other opened the patrol car door and offered to drive Cinnie to Fairview. Sweetheart was even willing to call a wrecker and have the Porsche towed away. Nice to know how caring and efficient some cops could be.

By the time the officer dropped her at the hospital entrance, Cinnie had put the accident behind her. Despite his devotion to the stupid hunk of metal, Paul's car was only a thing. It could be fixed, replaced, forgotten if necessary. If Paul chose to have a tantrum or go into mourning over it, that was his problem. James was all that mattered now.

The sound hit her as soon as the elevator doors opened on five. Desperate screams. At once, Cinnie knew it was James.

She raced to his room. Two nurses and a resident were trying to calm him. Everyone looked flustered and worn out, especially James. His face was blotched, swollen, and streaked with tears. His mouth distended as he continued to scream. His voice was fading and full of static.

'It's okay, Jimbo. It's all right, baby. Ssh, now. Stop.'

She took him onto her lap, cast and all, and pressed his cheek to her shoulder. He was drenched with perspiration, body heaving in hysterical pulses.

'Stop, sweetie. Ssh. Tell me what's wrong. Let me make it better.'

238

Slowly, he calmed down. She held him tight until the last tic of anguish shook his little body.

'There, that's better. Want a drink of water?'

A nurse handed her a cup, and James took a sniffling sip. Cinnie wiped his face and neck with a cool, damp washcloth and changed him into fresh pyjamas. Settled back in bed, he looked like a deflated balloon.

'Better now, sweetheart? Can you tell me what happened?'

Cinnie gestured for the troops to retreat. The nurses and young doctor nodded and left the room. They all looked ready for early retirement.

She sat on the edge of the bed and stroked James's forehead. Poor monkey had been through a giant emotional wringer.

'Tell me, sweetheart. Did you have a bad dream?'

He shook his head no.

'Are you in pain then? Is that it? Can you show me what hurts?'

He touched his leg cast at a point just above the knee.

'Your leg is bothering you? That's what all this was about?'

He nodded.

'Oh, sweetie. I'm so sorry. I'll go call the doctor. Probably the cast is too tight or some dumb thing like that. I'll take care of it right away, honey. Hold tight a minute. Okay?'

There were no phones in the pediatrics rooms. Cinnie hated to leave him, even for a minute, but she had no choice. And James was much calmer now. She imagined how frustrating it must have been for him, in pain and not able to tell anybody.

'I'll be right back.'

On her way to the pay phones she passed one worried face after another. She wanted to shriek at every one of them, maybe wring a couple of necks. Why should James have had to suffer like that? Someone should have taken the time to try to figure out what was bothering him.

She dialed Dr. Rosenquist, the orthopedist who'd set the leg. Service answered. Cinnie explained the problem, but the operator told her Rosenquist was off for the night. Dr. Terry was covering.

Cinnie knew Terry only too well, and she wouldn't have trusted that jackass to set her hair. One thing about working in the hospital, you got to know which noble healers to avoid.

She tried a couple of other bone men, but no one was willing to see an inpatient under the care of another private physician. Cinnie was running out of ideas when she thought of Dr. Ferris.

Ferris's service picked up on the second ring, and Cinnie explained the urgency of the problem.

'He's in terrible pain. Someone has to come tonight and take a look, and I've run out of orthopedists.'

The operator assured her that Ferris was on call and available by pager.

'I'll beep him and make sure he gets right back to you, Mrs. Merritt. One thing Dr. Ferris can't stand is seeing a child in unnecessary pain.'

'Thanks. I'll wait right here.' Cinnie gave the woman the number of the floor phone and hung up feeling better. Ferris was dedicated and competent. He'd get here as quickly as he could and take care of it. Cinnie knew you didn't have to be an orthopedic surgeon to cut a window in a plastic cast and see what the problem was underneath.

'Oh, how's Jimmy? Calmer?'

It was the young nurse who'd answered Cinnie's call. She was stepping off the elevator. Probably back from a break and missed the commotion.

'His leg is hurting him. I couldn't get hold of Rosenquist, but I'm waiting for a call back from Dr. Ferris.'

'That's good. Ferris knows his stuff. I have a problem with a kid. I'm always glad to see that man.'

'Yes. Me too.'

The phone shrilled moments later. Ferris hadn't answered his page yet, but the operator was positive she'd be able to reach him in a couple of minutes.

'He's always available when he says he'll be, Mrs. Merritt. Probably caught him in the shower or something.'

'You're sure?'

'Absolutely. You go visit with James, and I'll fill the doctor in as soon as I can reach him. Don't worry. He'll be there very soon.'

Cinnie's insides were still churning. On the way back to James's room she made a quick stop at the restroom to splash her face with cold water and compose herself. She wasn't going to do her little boy any good if she was cracking at the seams.

Everything was going to be all right. Ferris would show up and do whatever it took to make sure James was comfortable again. Soon.

Sooner than she could possibly imagine.

Even as she stood at the bathroom mirror and resolved to put on a confident front for James, Malcolm Cobb was back in the child's room. He'd heard her at the phone trying to get help for her son. He had to retrieve the vehicle before it could be discovered.

38 Drum was out before dawn, threading the beauty through swags of low-lying fog. His breathing was labored, heart clunking like a gummy carburetor. Damned case was wearing him out. When all this was over, he'd have to find a way to swing a family vacation in the Caribbean. What he needed was a week on one of those islands so quiet the fish died of boredom. He'd have to figure a way to get Carmody to spring for it. Drum couldn't imagine a better use for the department's sunshine fund.

He followed the maze of streets leading to Tyler's Grove and drove in through the broken stone pillars. The neighborhood was out cold. All the houses were dark, shuttered, and still. Only sign of life was a striped tabby whose stalking shadow played over the frozen ground.

Drum stopped in front of the Merritt's farmhouse and retrieved the bulging envelope that Louis at Failsafe Security had told him would be waiting in the mailbox. Looked like the kid's mother had found plenty to say. Some of it surprising, he hoped.

High Ridge Road crossed the New York State line five miles north of the Grove and continued through the sprawling Westchester town of Pound Ridge. Drum drove past a pristine town park, a line of ancient white clapboard buildings given over to municipal use: library, historical society, post office, hall of records. Place reeked of New England. Drum had the uneasy sensation he'd slipped off the real world and landed in a Norman Rockwell painting.

He tracked the main road for a while, checking out the few gas stations, body shops, and chop operations on the list he'd put together. Not much industry in this town, he'd noticed. Then most of the types who lived here had already done their most important life's work: gotten themselves born to rich parents.

Eventually, the road veered left toward the village of Bedford, New York, and Drum did likewise. The properties stretched and the houses grew larger and more distant until they disappeared like shy giants behind towering iron fences and manicured hedgerows. From then on, the only hints of life were the carefully chiseled estate signs and the posted warnings about mad dogs, ferocious burglar alarms, and the high cost of trespassing. He stopped at the town line and turned around.

On the return trip, he covered the few side streets on his list. There were a couple of auto operations tucked into the rows of shuttered stores, one next to a small private school, and another half hidden behind a garden supply place dotted with specimen shrubs and fledgling Christmas trees.

At each stop, he drove the beauty in a slow loop through the lot and then got out to peer through the body shop windows. Remembering Driscoll's assessment of the Merritt kid's injuries, he looked for right-side front fender damage on a late-model, foreign-make midsized sedan or wagon.

Nothing matched Meat's description, but the car he was after could well be long gone.

Thinking that Driscoll might be able to pin the missing car down further, Drum swung left and headed through the center of Scott's Corners.

No lights were on in Driscoll's service station. Drum knocked, but couldn't raise anyone inside. Then he climbed the rickety back outside stairs to the apartment Meat kept over the garage and pounded on the door. No answer, but the thumping had dislodged a note wedged between the storm door and the frame. It was an order to the milkman to hold Driscoll's deliveries until further notice.

Meat's peculiar eating habits had left him with an ulcer the size of Hoboken, which he treated by drinking fresh sweet cream out of the carton (often laced with a shot of bourbon to cut the cholesterol). Driscoll was never without his sweet cream, so the note meant Meat had to be out of town. Maybe visiting one of his favorite vacation spots: Attica or Sing Sing.

Still an hour or so until the earliest businesses opened. Drum settled back in the beauty, poured himself a short cup of coffee from the Hulk Hogan thermos he'd copped out of Booker's lunch box, and opened the envelope.

The Merritt woman's account was very clear and detailed. Interesting how the worst days got etched in your memory. Burnt in like the scars on Drum's face.

Snap, and it all came back. Snap, and he could relive every stinking minute. Stroll down memory frigging lane.

That filthy loop of celluloid had been Drum's cage. He was terrified of crossing his uncle, afraid the old man would pay him back by showing the film at the Avon Theatre. The air in Liam's house was too thick to breathe, rancid. But Drum couldn't leave, couldn't go anywhere as long as that movie reel was still around.

He spent all his time searching for a way out. His nights were full of toxic dreams and murderous fantasies. Drum ached for Liam to drop dead. But even the old turd's death wouldn't release him. He knew he would never be free until he got rid of the damned film.

The plan came to him weeks before he had the guts to pull it off. A simple way to cut loose. It would work. Risky, true. But there were way bigger risks in not taking care of it. Risks so big, Drum couldn't see past them. The threat was a huge range of black mountains blocking out his life, leaving him cold and empty. Whatever the possible consequences, he had to destroy that film.

Drum waited for a time when he was sure Liam would be out of the house. He'd checked with Kurt, the houseman, who'd assured him that Liam would be spending this particular night in Manhattan.

Kurt left after dinner. Drum sat awhile listening to the silence, letting the hatred build and consume him. He thought about the film until he was too full of rage to feel fear or anything else.

Earlier, he'd taken the can of charcoal lighter fluid from the garage and copped a box of kitchen matches.

Nobody home, but Drum still stole silently through the dark house toward the office. His blood was frozen, heart wriggling like a hooked worm.

He soaked sheets of looseleaf paper with the ligher fluid and eased them under the office door. Enough flame, and the carpet would catch. Drum was counting on that. First the carpet, then a slow spread of flames until the drapes went up and the wood paneling caught.

No one was expected until Kurt came back in the morning. By then, there'd be nothing left in the damned office. And Drum would be long gone.

He lit a match and touched it to the protruding tail of one of the sheets of paper. Thing went up with a reassuring pop. Drum could hear the flames leaping on the other side of the door, and he caught the stench of burning wool.

A couple of minutes to make sure the fire had taken hold, and Drum planned to get the hell out. He had no idea where he was going. Didn't care either, as long as it was far enough away from this place. So far, he'd never have to look at that fat, ugly monster again.

He caught the first whiff of gathering smoke. He decided to wait a minute more to be absolutely sure the fire wouldn't go out. A few more seconds.

Satisfied, Drum turned to leave. His hand was on the doorknob when he was stopped by the shot. Turning, he saw Liam in the foyer archway, his face twisted with rage and loathing.

'Next time, I don't miss, Jeremiah. Next time I start killing you off a bit at a time, you scum. Start with that sweet, little sausage of yours. See how it looks grilled.'

He aimed the gun at Drum's crotch. 'You don't want to make me do that, do you? Wouldn't want me to make you a girl, Jeremiah. That's been your worry right along, hasn't it?'

Liam shook his head and sniffed. 'Here I take you in, give you everything. And this is the thanks I get.'

Liam kept the pistol level with Drum's groin and edged him toward the kitchen phone. Raising the receiver, he flashed an evil smile. 'Seems you've left me with no choice, boy. First, I call the fire department. And then I'll have to report all this to the cops. It's my civic duty to help them understand what sort of a boy you are, what sick appetites you have. Pity it is, what's become of my dear brother's son. Poor Matthew would roll in his grave if he knew, wouldn't he, Jeremiah? Matthew never would countenance certain types of appetites, you know. He'd make these little fag jokes, your father did.'

The fury was building in Drum like a trapped head of steam. Growing until it was too large to contain. An inhuman sound ripped from his throat. Drum knocked Liam down with a flying tackle and started pummeling the bobbling flesh. He kept punching. Pounding. A monstrous rage fueled him, drove his fists like metal pistons.

Liam deflated like a stuck balloon. Went still. Panting, Drum looked down in horror to see his uncle's pale, wasted body. A trickle of blood flowed from the distended nostrils, and there were livid welts on the puffy limbs. Otherwise, the old man looked like a huge empty pelt.

Paralyzed by shock, Drum staggered back. He was so sure Liam was dead, he couldn't fathom the hand that shot out and caught his ankle. He plummeted to the floor, slamming his head on the polished wood. Sparks erupted behind his eyes, and the air rushed out of him.

Struggling against unconsciousness, he rolled over onto his back. There was a flash of metal as Liam smashed the pistol down toward his face. He felt a crack across his nose and tasted blood. Then came an exquisite pain as Liam brought the gun down and shattered his wrist. Another searing blow across his knee, and everything went black.

He came to in a hellish inferno.

Through the forest of flames came the stink of his own burning hair and flesh. Dark billows of acrid smoke filled the foyer, stealing the air. The house was a nightmare of heat and boiling fire, furniture going up like sparked paper, beams crashing down.

He stumbled, his legs reduced to numb stumps. Half crawling, he continued toward the door. Ragged breaths burned in his chest. A snake of horror wound around his neck and started squeezing.

Finally, he managed to reach the door. But the knob was scalding metal that melted his palm like candlewax. He recoiled in an electric shower of pain. Desperate, he struggled back through the curtain of flame toward the window.

Closer, there, a light.

Drum ran through the ragged glass like it was a spray of cool water. Felt nothing but exquisite relief.

The night air was unbearably sweet. He filled himself and felt dizzy from the sweetness. The sky was ablaze, rent by approaching sirens. Looked so much like the real world, Drum's eyes swelled with grateful, bloody tears.

But he knew everything was changed, ripped into unrecognizable fragments. Nothing anyone could do to save him now.

Liam was dead. Drum had killed him. He had to get away before the cops showed up, had to run.

Drum snapped out of the dread reverie. Not now. No more, Drum. Shut it away. Lock the frigging door on it already.

His throat was chalk. He downed another little red cupful of sweet coffee and started out at the misty dawn. The cords around his neck eased up a little. He picked up the pages again in a trembling hand and forced himself to keep reading.

Fifteen minutes later, he was finished. A couple of things had caught his attention, and he added them to his growing list of loose ends.

But first things first. Drum had decided to start searching for the car up north. Way fewer shops to check in that direction. And the lonely ex-librarian had seen a car speeding toward the High Ridge spur, which fed the northbound lane.

If nothing panned out on this round, he'd have to turn south toward the endless possibilities in downtown Stamford, Greenwich, and the dense Westchester, New York towns further along. Not a happy prospect.

But Drum had a hunch it wouldn't be necessary. If a guy with a bloody, dented fender wanted to disappear in the middle of the day, he wasn't likely to head through the congested center of Stamford. Not when the end of the world was only a few miles in the opposite direction.

Drum started with the auto body shop nearest the accident. He introduced himself as an investigator for the triple A. Metal-maulders were very anxious to stay on the good side of the auto association. Plenty of referrals came that way. Could be even more efficient than chasing ambulances and monitoring the police band.

Drum claimed he was conducting a safety survey, looking at recent accident rates by make and model, covering the last three weeks as a random sample.

He knew exactly what he was after, but he came up empty at the first four shops he visited. Last on his list in the area was Bud's Auto Body near Bedford Center.

Drum was beginning to lose faith. There was always the chance that the hit-run car was languishing in a barn or garage or rusting among the bottom weeds in some sleepy river. But he was counting on the driver wanting the evidence erased. Permanent solution, everything neat and tidy.

Bud's Auto Body looked more like a movie set than a real garage. Drum pulled the beauty in front of the immaculate glass-walled shop. Mostly exotic imports in the lot. Drum figured Bud did a land-office business in door dings and upholstery stains.

Three mechanics were having coffee in the office when Drum walked in. There was a big guy who had *boss* written all over him, a younger clone Drum made for the head honcho's son, and a third young guy who had actual dirt under his fingernails. The big man flashed Drum a challenging look. Drum guessed he didn't pass for the shop's standard customer.

He danced through his triple A routine, and the boss took the bait. Big guy said he'd be glad to cooperate, but he didn't have many accident cases to report. Most of the shop's routine work was detailing, he explained. For two hundred dollars, they cleaned customers' cars fender to fender by hand, Q-tip, and toothbrush. Drum didn't comment, but for two bills he'd expect to get a whole lot more taken care of than his ashtrays and hubcaps.

The boss hauled out a ledger and gave Drum a rundown of recent jobs. In addition to a long roster of weekly detailing customers, there had been three accidents in the past three weeks: a black Corvette with a dent in the passenger-side door, a flipped beige Jeep, and a baby-blue Rolls with a dimpled rear bumper.

While Drum listened, he worked his eyes and picked up something real interesting. Thinking this might be his lucky day after all, he kept the boss talking until the phone rang in the immaculate office. When the big guy ambled in to answer, Drum waved good-bye and headed for the exit.

Perfect. The boss's son was busy buffing the trim on a Jaguar. Drum motioned for young Mister Dirty Fingers to follow him out and held the door open for him.

'Got some rust I'd like you to take a look at, pal,' Drum said loud enough for anyone interested to hear. Then he caught the young guy by the elbow and steered him toward the beauty.

The kid caught a glimpse of Drum's shark grin and started to look a little nervous. When they were next to the Mustang, Drum patted the hood and winked. 'Something tells me you do a little work on the side, am I right?'

'What do you mean?'

'Work, pal. You know, a little repair business just between you and me. You fix up my sweetheart here. I pay you direct and get a real reasonable price. We both make out, so what's the harm, right?'

The kid shrugged and went cute. 'Wouldn't be right for me to make side deals, mister. I work for Bud.'

'Yeah, that's right. You do. Until I tell him you've been scamming him, that is. Then I bet you're an independent contractor full-time, wiseass.'

'Hey, come on. You got nothing on me.'

'Like hell I don't.' Drum grabbed one of the kid's dirty

paws and held it up so it caught the sunlight. 'Let's see. Here we've got a nice domestic metallic silver, a spatter of Ferrari red, a touch of Lincoln sapphire blue, vintage eighty-nine. Want me to go on? Or you think Bud won't need to hear the whole sad story before he cans your crooked ass?'

The guy started whimpering. 'Please, mister. I can't get by on what he pays me. Nobody could. So once in a while, I do small jobs after hours. Like you said, what's the harm?'

'Exactly.'

Kid perked up. 'So okay, fine. I'll be glad to fix you up. Nice old girl you got here. What night you want to bring her in? Name it. On the house.'

Drum put an avuncular arm across the kid's shoulders. 'All I want from you is a little information, buddy. You tell me something real interesting, and I just may forget all about blowing my whistle to big Bud.'

39

Thoroughly disgusted, Drum reared back and pitched the receiver low and inside. It smacked against the plastic wall of the phone booth and left a satisfying web of cracks.

Better.

He hurled the thing several more times until the booth wall looked frosted and the phone's entrails were dangling from the metal cord. The exercise dimmed his anger to the low flame of a pilot light. Too bad that jackass shrink from the department wasn't around. Drum would show him displaced aggression like he never imagined.

Why was nothing ever easy?

The big hot lead was turning out to be a big hot pain in Drum's butt.

The young mechanic from Bud's had been the ticket after all. Kid had patched up five cars on the sly in the last three weeks. Two met Drum's basic specifications: a brown Audi 5000 and a green Peugeot wagon. The winner had been real easy to pin down.

The Audi had belonged to a middle-aged guy who claimed to have skidded into a phone pole. The dent had been consistent, according to the mechanic. Large even bruise in the right front fender.

But the Peugeot was another story. Stranger had come in late in the day three weeks ago and told the mechanic he needed work done right away. Kid had agreed to meet the guy back at Bud's an hour after closing.

When the character showed up, he'd acted real nervous. There was a big ding in the Peugeot's right front bumper, a spatter of dried blood on the bumper and hood and more blood traces on the windshield. Guy claimed he'd hit a deer.

The damage had been easy to fix. All it took was a mallet on the fender dent, a little rubbing compound, and a quick shot of spray paint. The driver had come back for the car in a couple of hours as they'd agreed. Acting like he was in a hurry, he'd paid cash and left without wasting any words.

Kid told Drum he'd suspected right away that the deer story was a phony. He'd seen plenty of wrecks after deer collisions. Cars usually looked as if they'd slammed into a brick wall, much more than fender damage and way more spattered gore. But he hadn't thought to take issue with the guy's story. Way he saw it, people had plenty of excellent reasons for keeping their business to themselves.

Drum had pressed for a helpful description of the driver, but the guy had been too damned ordinary. Medium everything: hair, height, eyes, build. According to the mechanic, the driver had no distinguishing features except the hundreds he'd used to cover the tab.

The kid hadn't made note of the license plate number and hadn't noticed anything out of the ordinary about the car. Drum was about to cash his chips when he thought to ask whether the kid had happened to notice anything inside on the seats or the floor.

Drum could see the light snap on in the mechanic's eyes. There had been a strange-looking booklet on the passenger seat. Kid remembered it because of the peculiar picture on the front. It showed a head sliced open above the ears so the brain was exposed. Underneath was a single word, *Braintrust*.

A couple of calls, and Drum had learned that the name belonged to an L.A.-based organization whose membership qualification was a stratospheric I.Q. Made ordinary geniuses, like those who joined the far better known Mensa, look dumb. Naturally, it was a very small, very exclusive bunch.

It was only couple of minutes past dawn L.A. time but Drum called anyway, hoping the group might be administered out of somebody's house. Drum wasn't worried about waking the character. Anyone with brains that big could afford to be groggy.

Jackpot. He'd been prepared for a service or a tape, but

a wispy, male voice answered instead. Drum didn't bother apologizing for the hour. He didn't see it as his responsibility. Anyway, the guy didn't sound all that sleepy.

'Braintrust. *Mirabile visu.*'

'Yeah sure, same to you.'

The wisp chuckled. '*Mirabile visu* means "wonderful to behold." That's our organizational motto, Mr. –?'

Drum passed himself off as Fred Conga, a researcher for *Donahue*. They were planning a show on geniuses and wanted to contact some possible guests from Braintrust in the New York metro area.

The response was an obnoxious giggle. It went on long enough to make Drum's teeth itch. '*Donahue*, no less.'

'What? You got a problem with Phil? He's a sweetheart, honest.'

'You misunderstand. It's just that our membership eschews publicity at all costs. None of us would be willing to expose or exploit our gifts in such a trivial fashion.'

Drum was getting a teensy bit miffed, but he managed to hold his reigns. 'Nothing trivial about it, I promise. Phil's planning a real quality presentation. Very educational.'

'Oh, my, look at the time. I'm off to the gym now. Have to run.'

'But wait, I have to . . .'

'*Tempus fugit*. Toodle-oo.'

Drum tried to stall the jerk by asking about the group, but all he got was a disgusted sigh and an offhand mention that the trip to the gym would only take half an hour or so.

Drum assaulted the phone one last time, left the booth, and stopped at a nearby coffee shop for a shot of wake-up juice. Counter girl kept looking him over. Drum couldn't tell if it was interest or disgust. Finally, he stuck a finger up his nostril and did a little mining. Broad got real busy on the other side of the shop. Cleared up that mystery in a big hurry.

But there were all those others. Drum still couldn't make sense of the Holroyd broad's story about seeing the hit-run car. He still wondered about the kid's father. What made the guy tick? And was it the kind of ticking that should make Drum consider calling the bomb squad? And what in the hell was Charlie Allston doing to keep busy? The deputy chief had spent the entire three-week investigation running in place. Then, maybe screwing up, if you raised it to an art form, was a full-time job.

What Drum figured he needed was fewer questions or a way bigger brain or maybe both. Bigger brains. Got him thinking about that wispy-voiced guy from the egg-head group again.

Drum kept thinking as he drove south. His mind was elsewhere as he sped past the pay phone at the Gulf station north of the Merritt Parkway. Spotting the booth from the corner of his eye, he made a lunatic U-turn, stopped in the lot, and got out to dial the L.A. number again.

The wispy guy was back from the gym, but he refused to budge. 'As I told you, our members respect their unique intellectual aptitudes. They wouldn't dream of giving public performances on the subject. It would be sheer exploitation.'

'Isn't it possible they don't all agree with you, pal? They don't want to do it, they'll tell me no, right? So what's the harm if you give me the names? I won't even say where I got them. Scouts' honor.'

'*Abyssus abyssum invocat*, sir. One misstep leads to another. I cannot violate the trust of my brothers. That would be unthinkable. Good day now.'

Drum heard a click, and the line went dead. He dialed again, managed to keep his tone even, and tried to reason with the jackass. He tossed in all his aces, flattery, bribes, threats. Got nowhere. Hanging up, he sentenced the phone to die a gruesome death, but he noticed that the station manager was watching.

Temporary stay of execution, he muttered as he walked back to the beauty. But only temporary. First thing when he got back from L.A., he'd take care of it.

40 The tape Karen Sands had made of that afternoon's staff meeting was barely through playing when Cinnie stormed out of the rehab suite, took the stairs to the second floor, and strode past the startled receptionist into Dr. Silver's private office.

Silver was leaning back in his desk chair, staring at a magazine he obviously was not proud to be caught reading. Flustered, he shoved the thing in a desk drawer and shot Cinnie a sour look.

'Okay. What's the hysterical matter this time?'

'In case it's slipped your tiny, little mind, Dr. Silver, James happens to be my son. You have no right making plans to have him transferred without Paul's and my consent.'

He blew a breath. 'Lighten up, lady. Blythedale is the best place for James to do his long-term rehab. A space opened up, so I grabbed it. I was going to tell you.'

'You're not supposed to *tell* me. You're supposed to ask me. And if you had, I'd have given you our answer: No way.'

He clacked his tongue and sighed. 'Now, now, Cinnie. Let's be reasonable. There is no medical reason to keep James at Fairview any longer. His head injury is healing nicely. And after all his carrying on last night, they did X-rays and a visual inspection of the fracture site. Everything's coming along fine. So it's time for him to move on.'

'Fine, no argument. I'll take him home first thing in the morning.'

Silver puffed his disgust. 'The kid needs intensive rehab, Cinnie. Every day for months. Don't be a mule about this. Blythedale is an excellent facility.'

'I agree with you.' Cinnie had been to the Valhalla, New York, hospital several times to visit patients who'd been transferred there for long-term treatment. Blythedale was a chronic-care facility for kids: bright, cheerful, good reputation, fine staff.

'Great,' Silver said. 'I'll call administration and set things up. We'll have James transferred tomorrow.'

Cinnie shook her head. 'You misunderstand, Dr. Silver. I agree that James's follow-up therapy should be done at Blythedale, but it will be on an outpatient basis. He'll stay home.'

Silver bullied and argued, but Cinnie was not about to be pushed. She knew that therapy sessions were restricted to regular business hours. She could drive James to Blythedale before work and pick him up at the end of the day. No question in her mind that he'd be better off at home the rest of the time.

Silver finally pushed back from his desk and threw up his hands. 'Okay. You win. I'll write the discharge orders for tomorrow morning.'

Cinnie's triumph was tempered by a sudden attack of insecurity. What if something went wrong? Would she be able to take care of James?

She rebuked herself. They wouldn't be considering any kind of discharge if he needed medical monitoring. And she could certainly care for him better than anyone else.

'Fine. I'll cancel my morning appointments. What time can I take him?'

'That's up to Dr. Ferris. He'll want to do a final checkup and write the home-care orders. Want me to call his office?'

'No. I'll speak to him.'

Cinnie took the elevator to pediatrics. After Ferris finished with the patient he was seeing, she was ushered into his office. It was scrupulously neat, antiseptic, and controlled, like the man. On entering the office, Ferris exchanged his soiled lab coat for one of the dozen hanging in his closet. He washed his hands at the sink under the window and sat behind his polished desk with woven fingers and a noncommittal expression.

Cinnie explained her plan to keep James at home during his rehabilitation.

'Makes no sense to have him stay at Blythedale, Dr. Ferris. They can't do anything for him that I can't. I'm sure James will be more comfortable in his own bed with his own family.'

'I'm sure you'll manage things.' Typical Ferris. Flat and even as new pavement.

'So you don't think it's a mistake?'

'You have to do what you think best. I can't tell you what arrangement would best suit your family, Mrs. Merritt.'

Cinnie searched for a pin of encouragement or disapproval, but if Ferris had a stronger opinion he wasn't prepared to part with it. She pressed harder, anxious for his blessing. 'But you think James will be all right?'

'Yes, Mrs. Merritt. I think James will continue to recover nicely. As I told you, he's a strong child. Highly intelligent and vigorous. Try not to doubt yourself. What greater medicine is there than a mother's love?'

Leaving, she was still vaguely uneasy, but feeling better all the time. It had taken some doing, but Ferris had approved. It was okay for her to take James home. She tried Paul and Dal to give them the news, but she couldn't reach either of them.

Madeline answered at her father's apartment. Cinnie told her stepmother about the impending discharge, and she couldn't have been lovelier or more supportive.

'I'll be glad to come stay with him whenever you like, dear. And if you need help getting him back and forth to therapy, just holler. Wait until I tell your father, he'll be so thrilled.'

Cinnie was disarmed, and she felt a pang of guilt. She had never thanked Madeline for all the visits or the gifts she'd brought for James in the almost four weeks since the accident. Sheepishly, she apologized for the oversight and tried to sound enthusiastic about the pajamas, candy, and book.

'I didn't bring a book, dear. That must have come from someone else.'

Cinnie hung up perplexed and more than a little chastened. She was always so quick to find fault with her stepmother. The fact was, Madeline had always been patient and kind, even though all she'd gotten from Cinnie in return was frostbite. And she'd embraced James as her own grandchild, even though Cinnie had done everything in her childish power to get in the way.

Time to stop the nonsense.

She dialed again. Madeline answered. 'I'm sorry.' Cinnie said.

'For what?'

'Everything.'

There was a pause. 'Don't be silly, dear. You haven't done anything.'

On an impulse, Cinnie invited Madeline and her dad to come to a party at Fairview late that afternoon in honor of James's release. She made a few more calls to arrange things and went back to give James the good news before he was taken to therapy.

'Imagine it, Jimbo. No more hospital food, no more nurses waking you in the middle of the night to see if you're sleeping comfortably. Tonight will be your very last night in this joint, kiddo. Tomorrow, it's over the wall.'

'Shadow, Mommy. Shadow!'

'Come on, sweetie. Forget all that junk. One more night, and we're out of here. Isn't that enough to take your mind off your troubles?'

He shook his head from side to side, looked like he was on his way to another major tantrum. His color deepened, and his hands were balled in fists. 'Book, Mom. *Book*!'

'Okay, anything. Even that awful thing if you'll calm down.'

She found the weed book and pulled the visitor's chair close to James's bed. Revolting book. She wondered who'd brought it. She thought of weird Hanky Moller, the volunteer. It would be just like that creepy character to foist off a hideous story like this on James when she wasn't looking.

Flipping to the beginning of the story, she noticed the name penciled inside the front cover. *Malcolm.* It sparked a tickle of recognition, but she couldn't make a clear connection.

Turning the page, she noticed that the copyright was more than ten years old and that the book had been published in London. Someone had probably donated the dreadful volume to the hospital. How many times had she told Hanky that James didn't want or need anything from his damned cart? But that infuriating man would not listen. At least, if he was going to ignore her wishes, he could have come up with something more pleasant than this heinous book. Almost anything else would have been an improvement.

'All right, Jimbo. Here goes absolutely nothing.'

By now, she knew the story from memory and wished she could get away with a condensed version. A few sentences were way more than the tale deserved. An old woman grows a garden of weeds that start to spread to other gardens in the neighborhood. That neighbors protest. The protests fall on deaf ears, so the neighbors do what they have to do. Form an antiweed vigilante committee.

Two weeds survive, a brother and sister named Dove and Elegant. Pretty stupid names for a couple of weeds, Cinnie thought. At least the book was consistent in its dreadfulness.

The weed siblings have this weird sap dependence, and they're able to pull each other through a series of ailments by taking sap from healthy weeds. So they make it through the winter. And everyone lives strangely ever after. The end.

Cinnie closed the book and kissed James on both eyelids, both cheeks, his nose and chin.

'Now please, O best little boy in the history of little boys, don't ask me to read that stupid thing again. Okay?'

His eyes were full of pleading. He bit his lip, whimpered, and turned his head toward the wall.

'I'm sorry, Jimbo. I didn't mean it. I'll read it as many times as you want. No big deal.'

He shook his head and whimpered again.

'All right, honey. Let's forget everything except how

great it's going to be to have you back home again. One more night, sweetie. Isn't that the best?'

Tears glistened in his eyes. One spilled over, and Cinnie brushed it away.

'I know, honey. I can hardly believe it myself. Tell you what. I'll go home a little early tonight and make sure everything's all ready, so I can come for you the very first thing in the morning. Okay?'

Another tear trickled down his cheek. Cinnie felt a sympathetic stinging in her own eyes and scooped him up for a hug. It was going to be all right. One more night and James would be safe at home.

41 Drum had planned to fly to L.A. later in the afternoon, give himself a day to take care of things, and head home the following morning. But when he called Stella to fill her in, she reminded him that he had promised to be at Booker's big event the following evening.

Drum had always kept his promises, except one. And that book wasn't closed by a long shot.

He called for flight information. There was a ten-thirty on American out of Kennedy that would get him to the coast at about one Pacific time. He'd do his arm-twisting this afternoon and check in someplace for the night. To make Booker's gig, he'd have to catch the first bird back in the morning.

It was past nine-thirty by the time he eased the beauty onto the Merritt Parkway. Normal to the airport was an hour and change give or take traffic. Drum waited until he was through Greenwich and fished for the red plastic gumdrop he always kept in his glove compartment. The thing stuck to his hood by four suction cups and connected to a nine-volt battery under the driver's seat by a thin filament of clear wire threaded through the window gasket.

Ready, he flipped on the light and activated the siren he'd had installed to scream through the Mustang's four speakers. Traffic parted. Moses at the wheel.

He made it to JFK with more than ten minutes to spare and bribed the guy supervising the lot nearest the American terminal to keep a real close eye on the beauty. Drum slipped him a twenty up front and promised him another bill or a full set of dentures if anyone touched a hair on his car while he was gone.

The terminal was jammed. Drum busted through a long line of Spanish-speaking people with tons of luggage waiting for who-cared-what. At the ticket counter, he walked directly to the only unoccupied clerk, who just happened to be selling first class. Drum requested a seat on the L.A. flight.

The clerk told him that the ten-thirty was booked solid. Oversold in fact. Drum had no time to argue. He asked what was available, and the clerk punched at the keyboard for a couple of minutes until he came up with a single first class slot on the next flight out to Phoenix. Drum took it and ran.

He looked up at the posted gate for the L.A. flight and hustled to the security checkpoint. Damned metal detector went off three times, and Drum had to go back through the archway, stripping away his watch, chain, metal belt buckle, and keys until they finally discovered that the problem was his sunglasses.

Another three minutes gone.

The L.A. gate was at the far end of an endless row of departure areas. Drum took the distance at a jog. By the time he arrived at the departure lounge he was looking for, his lungs were screaming and his calf muscles were hot fists.

The last of the passengers were heading through the boarding door, and the gate clerk was closing up. Drum rasped at her to hold it, said he had to make the plane. When she started to argue that it was full and he didn't have a boarding pass to L.A. anyway, he took a surreptitious look around and told her he was a safety inspector from the Civil Aeronautics Board.

Fortunately, he always carried an impressive set of federal credentials in his wallet. Chief of the Bullshit Bureau. He flashed the papers at the broad. She hesitated a half second and picked up the phone at the desk.

'Don't let on,' Drum mouthed. 'It's supposed to be an unannounced inspection.'

'Oh, of course. I wouldn't say a thing.'

He smiled. Three seconds after he was through the door, she'd be on the horn to the flight crew, warning them to cross all their *t*'s. Drum knew he'd have to deal with a truckload of bowing and fawning. If only Carmody knew how he sacrificed for the cause.

She had a muffled conversation with the plane, hung up, and smiled. 'They're offering a free round-trip to anyone who'll volunteer to take a later flight, sir. I'm sure we'll have a seat for you in just a minute.'

'I'm sure,' Drum said.

Five and a half hours later the DC 10 touched down at Los Angeles International. Not a bad flight, considering. Drum had been installed in first class, waited on like he was somebody. Before the plane landed, the main cabin attendant had slipped him a bag with a couple of bottles of champagne and a life supply of midget scotch bottles. At the cabin door, she'd given him a kiss that made Drum wonder if maybe they'd been closely related in a former life.

He'd used the in-flight phone to call for the stretch Lincoln that was waiting at the curb. A gorgeous broad was at the wheel. Drum was surprised for a second, then remembered where he was. Everyone in this burg was killing time, waiting for that big break. Drum grinned, thinking of the one unsuspecting sucker who was about to get his break in spades.

Drum gave the driver the address and settled in for the ride and the view. From where he sat, he had a good angle on the woman's profile: nice features until he got to the chest. There the hills were too high, too round, and way too firm. Again Drum remembered where he was: silicone valley.

He turned his thoughts to the creep at the genius organization. Like it or not, the guy would have to part with his precious member list. Up to him which way he was going to do it, hard or easy.

The driver took the San Diego Freeway and exited at Sunset Boulevard. She followed Sunset to the Pacific Coast Highway and aimed north.

Drum took in the cliff dwellings on his right. Many of the sprawling houses were perched like overweight birds on the rocky precipice. Others clung to the heights like barnacles. On his left were sandy expanses punctuated by an occasional surfside restaurant. State beaches. Drum watched the roiling breakers and thought how weird it was for the ocean to be on the wrong side of the car. Gulls circled in the hazy sky, and the sharp, briny smell made his eyes water.

Farther along, small clusters of homes cropped up on the ocean side of the road. From Drum's angle, they looked like nothing much, could have been storage garages or workshops. But he knew they were the incredibly pricey digs of characters like Johnny Carson.

The driver turned into the last row of beach houses in the famed Malibu Colony and stepped out to open the door for Drum. 'This is it. Want me to wait?'

'May as well. Shouldn't take more than a few minutes.'

Drum spotted a double mailbox next to the front door. It was the guy he was after, all right. There was a small plaque under his name with the legend, 'Braintrust, *mirabile visu.*'

'I'll give that creep something wonderful to behold,' Drum muttered as he stuck his finger in the bell and held it.

A bearded, gray-haired guy with unnaturally white teeth and a trim, tanned California physique answered the door. He blinked at Drum as if he'd been expecting someone else. Drum muscled his way inside before the jerk had a chance to react.

'Excuse me! You can't come barging in here like this. Who are you?'

Drum took in the posh digs. Panoramic glass wall overlooking the ocean, vaulted ceiling with a lazy rolling fan in the center of a line of suspended baskets hung with ferns, white leather furnishings accented by large abstract oils from the likes of Motherwell and Hockney, white marble floors. There was a cutesy collection of gilt-edged ceramic teacups propped in an open glass case on the far wall. That would do fine.

'I'm the guy you wouldn't help out on the phone this morning. So I had to come all the way from New York to explain how important it is for you to give me those names, pal. Phil wants those names real bad.'

Guy's eyes got a touch wider. 'I told you it is strictly against Braintrust policy to reveal our membership. I simply can't give you the information. *Volo, non valeo.* I am willing but unable. I'm sure you can understand.'

'Let me get this straight, buddy. You're telling me no? Is that it? You're saying no to Phil frigging Donahue? I'm shocked, honest.'

'If I could help you, I would. I am a mere servant of my brethren in the group. We function in support of one another, devising challenges, sharing experiences. We are not a performing society.'

'Yeah, sure. I read you. You'd help me, but your hands are tied.'

Guy's shoulders dropped. 'Exactly.'

'Guy's gotta do what a guy's gotta do, right?'

'Right.'

'Exactly.' Drum picked up one of the teacups and dangled it by the delicate handle.

'Please. That's a priceless antique. Put it down.'

Thing was weightless, edged in gold, way too fancy for Drum's taste. Made him itch, fancy things like that. He tossed it up and caught it. Thing wasn't even any fun to play with. So what was the point?

'Put it down, I said! Put it down!'

'Yeah, sure.'

Drum did like the guy said. Put it down. Thing shattered against the marble floor with a nice crystalline splash. Left a dusting of shiny splinters. Much more interesting that way in Drum's estimation.

The guy started to sputter, his face was turning scarlet. 'Those cups are irreplaceable. They date to the court of Louis Quatorze. Please don't . . . '

Drum picked up a cup in each hand. One slipped right through his fingers. 'Tsk, tsk. How clumsy of me.'

The guy lunged at him. Drum let the other cup fly and deflected the creep with a head butt. Guy went reeling backward, staggering toward the glass wall.

He hit the glass with a sick thwacking sound and let out a startled little cry. His legs gave way, and he dribbled to the floor like the runny innards of a cracked egg.

Drum lifted two more teacups.

The guy held up a hand. He spoke between gasps. 'No more, please. No more. You win. I'll give you the damned list.'

Guy stood and brushed off his bruised dignity. His lip quivered. Cutting a wide swath around Drum, he crossed to the white lacquer desk, rolled back the cover, and turned on his Compaq PC.

His fingers danced on the keyboard, and a series of displays flashed on the screen. There was a whoosh as the laser printer spat out a page.

'These are our only members within fifty miles of New York City. Now, if you'll kindly leave me in peace.'

Drum eyed the list and scowled. 'What the hell's this? Machiavelli? Sir Arthur Conan Doyle? Rasputin?'

'All our members are registered by mailing address and a historical pseudonym that reflects a special personal interest. It's a long Braintrust tradition. That is all the information I have.'

Drum expressed his dismay by tossing another cup. The guy flinched but didn't sing another chorus. So Drum could see the phony name story was genuine.

More work, more trouble.

Drum got into the limo, sat back, and put his feet up on the opposite velvet seat. He had the driver use her cellular phone to call ahead to the Four Seasons Hotel on Doheny. He'd intended to cash it for the night at one of the airport flophouses, but after all the aggravation, he figured he deserved a nice, comfortable place to stay. Executive suite with a Jacuzzi would do nicely, room service dinner with a little sevruga and a chilled bottle of bubbly to drown his sorrows.

So Carmody would see the expense chit and spit fire. The chief was so damned cute when he was mad.

42 James's friends departed in turn, and each was replaced by a mass of emptiness. The blank spaces loomed as cold and frightening as the yawning grave at grandma's funeral.

It was a long time ago, but the memory was clear as yesterday. James could still see his own startled eyes reflected in the coffin's polished surface. He could still hear the straining sound of the lowering pulley and the terrible concussion as people tossed shovelfuls of pebbles and dirt on the box to close grandma in.

What if he slipped and fell in with her? James had stationed himself behind his father's solid frame and clung fast to the sturdy legs to avoid such a dread possibility. But even when the service had ended and they were safely ensconced in the car on the way home, he had continued to gulp greedy mouthfuls of air, imagining.

Now he shivered and fought the draw of sleep. His mother had not yet left for the night, and James was determined to convince her to stay. It was imperative that he be alert and at his most persuasive when she returned from depositing the party trash in the large barrel down the hall.

He decided it would be prudent to ease into the subject. First, he'd thank her for the party. All his favorite people had come: TeeJay and his parents, Grandpa and Madeline, Laurel and her mom, Jeremy Heckerling and Mike Marchand and Bobby Moon from his class, even Mrs. Tella, his teacher.

There had been gifts, laughter, flattering comments about how well he was doing and how wonderful it was that he was being discharged.

James was hopeful that the event had left his mother in excellent spirits. And he was reasonably confident that she would accede to his wishes. Still he intended to broach the subject with all due discretion.

His eyes were so heavy. Elephant feet stomping on the lids. He decided to rest for a moment until he heard her coming. Then he would be fully awake and ready to make his pitch.

He would explain that, even though he realized it was unseemly for someone his age, he would dearly love to have her company tonight. He would appeal to her soft center, the part of her that he had always been able to melt with his most calculated pleading looks. He'd make no mention of his compelling concerns that the shadow man might reappear in her absence. He knew nothing would be gained by that approach.

For reasons beyond James's ken, he'd been unable to make his mother appreciate the peril from the shadow man. How many times had he patiently tried to explain his dilemma only to see that same taut, uncomprehending expression claim her face?

So he'd avoid that issue. As soon as she came back from dumping the trash, he would simply tell her he needed her to stay. It was a pure, visceral, undeniable need. Childish yearning. How could any mother fail to be moved by that?

But where was she?

He forced his eyes open a crack. The light stung. Objects undulated in a vexing rhythm: bedstead, bears, balloons, toys. James felt an unsettling in his stomach. Hard to discern whether it was a rumble of hunger or a protest of overindulgence.

He decided on the former, and he was drawn to the tantalizing bouquet of chocolate chip cookies. Turning toward the nightstand, he spotted the leftover pile of home-made double-sized, double chunkers on a doily-lined plate. They had been a gift from Dal, Rick, and TeeJay.

His mouth watered, and he yielded to a sudden surge of appetite, downing several of the cookies. He chewed with his eyes closed, savoring the sweet crunchiness: chocolate, walnuts, brown sugar, a pinch of vanilla, purest flour snowing from an ancient red sifter, warm butter beads like drops of sunshine. James squeezing the silver handle, adding the baking soda, baking powder, pinch of salt, and cook them for an hour . . .

Rise of delicious aromas, fingers of warm comfort stroking away his fear, enveloping him. Floating him away on a puff of a lovely dream so thick nothing could pierce it. Not the first invading light of morning. Not even the door squealing open in his room or the muffled steps of the approaching stranger.

In the dream, he's sitting on his dad's high stool at the sound board, using a pencil to conduct the band behind the glass wall. The singer croons to the beat of his bobbling eraser. The drummer answers with a rapid roll that escalates into a wild, pulse-pumping riff. James feels the rhythm thumping in his bones. He's dancing, flying.

Sound of drumbeats, arms hefting him skyward, joyous feeling lifting him like the upward spring off a trampoline.

He's so absorbed in the dream, he barely notices the tiny stick of pain. Minuscule gnat bite in a carnival universe. His attention flits to it for a split instant and flutters back to the dream.

The pain does not alarm him. In his wildest imaginings, he has never considered that death could come in such a tiny, innocent way.

43 Cinnie had set the alarm for seven and was ready to leave for Fairview by half past. In the garage, the Volvo shuddered and stalled, but she managed to persuade the old bomb to turn over. Several hard stomps on the accelerator and the threat of a trip to the local crusher had done the trick.

Leaving the Grove, she thought fondly back to yesterday's farewell party at the hospital. James had obviously enjoyed the attention and commotion. As soon as the final guests were out the door, he'd fallen fast asleep with a smile on his face.

Cinnie had straightened up the majority of the mess and sneaked out of the room to avoid waking him. She'd been surprised to find Paul waiting for her in the lobby. She'd thought he was anxious to get home. Saw him leaving with Dal and family and assumed he was going to hitch a ride with them so he could get back to his precious studio. For once, it was lovely to be mistaken.

He'd driven her home in the bomb. On the way, there was only one minor explosion. Stopped at a light, Paul bashed the steering wheel and started muttering angry nothings under his breath.

'I know, it's no Porsche, Paul. But it gets you there.'

'My car gets you there better.'

'Not right now it doesn't.'

She could feel him smoldering.

'Look, I'm sorry. It was an accident, and not my fault, but I know how much that precious car meant to you. If they can't fix it, you'll get the insurance money and buy a new one. No big deal.'

'No big deal to you. No big deal, because it was my car. Is that the way it goes?'

Cinnie swallowed hard. 'No, Paul. No big deal because

it was a thing, a stupid hunk of macho metal and glass. It wasn't our kid.'

They fell silent. Cinnie went cold inside. Stayed that way until he put a gentle hand over hers and spoke in a hushed voice. 'You're right. I'm sorry. How could I be so stupid?'

'Years of practice.'

He chuckled. 'I deserved that. I love you, Cin.'

'Oh, yeah? When I kick off will you grieve for me the way you're mourning your dumb car?'

'Well, maybe. But you've got a lot more mileage in you.'

They fell into a comfortable torpor. Sentimental tunes wafted from the radio. By the time they turned into the Grove, both of them were in a very friendly mood.

They'd walked hand in hand from the garage to the farmhouse. Paul lit the fire, and they spent a cozy while staring at the flames, sipping at glasses of port. And then they'd made the kind of slow, lazy love that used to turn Sunday afternoons into Monday mornings before James and the rest of reality came along.

Afterward, Paul hadn't even felt the need to vault out of bed and trek back to the studio. They'd slept like cradled spoons, the way they used to at the beginning.

Cinnie yawned and did a languid cat stretch, remembering. She found herself daring to consider that they might be on the brink of becoming a real family again. James was coming home, Paul cracking out of his blasted shell. She realized she hadn't thought about the accidents or the hit-run driver since before last night's party. So maybe her obsession was curable too. Things were definitely looking up.

Paul had even volunteered to cancel his early morning recording session and accompany her to the hospital, but Cinnie had assured him she'd be fine picking up James by herself.

She could hardly wait. In an hour, James would be home in his own bed, surrounded by silly toys, watching pure garbage on the tube, learning to be a regular, little kid again.

Traffic above the parkway was moving at an exasperating crawl. Early commuters snaking toward the Merritt, Cinnie thought. Restless, she inched along, the speedometer needle barely wavering out of the dead zone.

It was after eight when she finally turned into the Fairview staff lot. She wound through the packed lines of parked cars searching for a vacancy. Nothing. Disgusted, she finally created her own space at the edge of a grassy divider. Worst she'd get was a ticket. And she couldn't stand to keep James waiting another minute. Or herself for that matter.

She felt wonderful in a hyperactive, apprehensive sort of way. Reminded her of the day she and Paul took James home as a newborn. She could still picture him swaddled in blue blankets. Nothing visible but those wide, navy blue eyes and the vague look of concern on his tiny features. Cinnie had caught the solemn expression and decided the kid was smart enough to be worried about her parenting abilities. She'd offered a studied, reassuring smile in return, but James hadn't been fooled for a minute.

Paul had brought the car around to the hospital entrance, and she'd sat in the back with the baby, feeling about as relaxed as she would be cradling a lit stick of dynamite. Paul had driven home at about three miles an hour, stopping altogether when he spotted a bump in the road.

They'd thought that James was so fragile then. His vulnerability had seemed so terrifying. And yet neither of them had really understood how fragile everything was, until this. The solid-looking world could be ripped to paper shreds and scattered to the wind.

But now she could envision an end to the nightmare. Only a few more minutes, and they'd be civilians again.

'Morning, Cin.'

Cinnie waved and smiled at the colleagues she passed on the way to the elevator. She made the highly scientific observation that everything looks ninety percent cleaner, brighter, and more attractive when you're on your way to spring your kid from a hospital bed.

The elevator took forever to come. Cinnie was toying with the idea of a five-flight run up to pediatrics when one of the three cars in the main bank finally showed up. But inside, one of the maintenance men was fiddling with the light panel in the ceiling.

'Better take another car. I've got to get this thing fixed.'

The next arriving car was jammed with a linen cart and a stretcher-bound patient headed down to X ray. Cinnie was halfway to the stairs when the final elevator in the bank materialized. At a run, she managed to make it inside before the doors closed.

Typical morning chaos on pediatrics: babies crying, televisions blasting. A flushed hellion raced buck naked through the halls trying to escape his morning bath. Cinnie's smile kept broadening on the way to five-fourteen. This was the last time she'd have to come here to visit James. Last visit, last walk down this blasted hall, the end of it.

She considered what James might want for lunch. Maybe she'd have Paul pick up a pizza. How long had it been since that kid had some good old American junk food? Probably teetering on the edge of a serious deficiency by now.

Cinnie was nearing James's room when she saw Nurse Evelyn Larwin's considerable rump poking out through the door. Probably saying good-bye.

Closer now, she noticed another, slimmer uniformed butt wedged in the doorway. Then she spotted the wall of people inside the room.

It didn't click at first. All she could imagine was that everyone had come to say good-bye. So many docs and nurses at once? Didn't they have anything else they had to be doing? She hoped James wasn't overwhelmed by the glut of people.

Cinnie raised her voice to be heard above the clamor of voices.

'Hey you guys, can I get an audience with the star, please? I have an appointment.'

No one seemed to notice her.

'That's my kid in there, pals. How about letting me in, okay?'

What the hell?

Standing on tiptoe, she managed to catch a glimpse of the knot of people hovering nearest James's bed. She couldn't catch what they were saying, but there was a sharp edge to the voices. And what was that at the foot of the bed?

'Hey, what's going on? What's the matter?'

Evelyn Larwin turned and put a hand to her mouth. 'Oh, Cinnie. It's so crazy. He was fine. I just looked in on him ten minutes ago. But when Ferris stopped by on rounds, James was cyanotic.'

Blue, not breathing.

Dead?

The word stuck like a sword in Cinnie's throat, she couldn't say it. Couldn't think it. She tried to shut it away, pressed the iron door against it. But the word edged into her mind and erupted in a blinding shower of sparks. The world was wavering out of focus, turning black. She was sinking. Slipping away.

Suddenly, hands were around her, setting her down. The sharp sting of ammonia spirits shot up her nostrils. She opened her eyes to a swarm of anxious faces.

Dr. Ferris suddenly appeared, edging the others away. 'Give her some air now. Back off, people.'

She felt fuzzy, padded by shock. 'What happened? Where's my baby. James? James!'

'Easy now. It's over. He'll be all right.'

Now Cinnie didn't trust her ears. 'He's not . . .'

'It was touch and go there for a minute, but he's okay now. Stable.'

He helped Cinnie to her feet. She was shivering, her legs unsteady. Ferris walked her to James's room, and she sat on the chair next to the bed.

She watched James breathe, stared at every hitch and fall of his chest. His face was deathly pale. Cinnie wiped the sheen of cold perspiration from his forehead. There was a fierce tremor in her hand that worsened when she tried to contain it.

She could feel Dr. Ferris standing behind her. 'What happened?'

'I honestly don't know, Mrs. Merritt. We're running some tests. Should have an answer later today.'

'I don't understand. He was fine.'

'The accident was a major assault to his system. It's rare, but there can be delayed reactions. Setbacks.'

Cinnie remembered Ferris voicing some objections to James's discharge on the tape of the team meeting. But he'd given in so easily.

'Then why didn't you insist he stay here? This could have happened at home. James could have been . . . '

'But it didn't. And he's not.' As always, Ferris was the voice of reason: soothing, sane. 'If I'd thought there was real danger to James, you know I'd never have agreed to his going home. This was a one-in-a-million thing. No one could have predicted it. I thought I was being overcautious having any doubts when the others were all in favor of the discharge. Given the odds of a problem, I *was* being overcautious. None of us has a crystal ball, Mrs. Merritt. You know that.'

Cinnie's anger was crumbling. Ferris was as careful as they came. Even the deadly scourge of hospital politics and Dr. Silver's blowhard bullying wouldn't have moved him to agree to James's release against his will. His crime was not heeding his own best instincts, putting reason, training, and statistics above the far more trustworthy mindless reaction. Deadly flaw.

But the worst hadn't happened. Cinnie would have to hold on to that for the time being.

'Where do we go from here?'

Ferris's mouth pressed in a seam. 'Several steps backward, I'm afraid. I'll order a complete battery of tests. Make sure we're not missing anything. I think we should suspend therapy for the time being also. Give him a chance to rest and recover.'

'You'll let me know the test results?'

'Of course, as soon as I get them.'

'I'll be right here.'

He shook his head. 'Do yourself a favor, Mrs. Merritt. Go home and get some rest. You've had quite a shock to your system too.'

'I want to stay with James.'

'I understand. But I've given him a sedative, and he's going to do nothing but sleep for a good, long while. Anyway, I'll be right here in the building, and the nurses are going to keep a very close eye on him.'

'I'm staying until I know exactly what happened, and I'm sure it won't happen again.'

Ferris clacked his tongue. 'Please, Mrs. Merritt. You're not going to do James any good if you become hysterically overprotective.'

So she had another vote for hysterical mother of the year. So what? Cinnie didn't bother to argue. No matter what anyone said, she was staying right where she was until she was damned sure James was out of danger.

She took James's limp hand and held it. Ferris turned on his heel and strode angrily from the room. Cinnie felt a twinge of regret. She'd always had a cordial but positive relationship with Ferris, always felt there was solid, mutual respect.

But that wasn't important anymore. This was far bigger than image or attitude. It was a matter of life and death.

44 The sanctum was dim and suffused with a penetrating chill. Cobb lay shivering on the bare mattress. His knees were pressed tight to his chest, head bowed as if braced for an assault. No sound pierced his fear but the sharp, relentless ticking of the clock.

Only ten hours remaining.

Cobb strained against the dizzying dissolution of the milliseconds. The lapsing time dripped like acid, pitting the surface of his strength, eroding his flesh. He chafed at his own putrid odor, the stench of hopeless surrender. That, mingled with the acrid scent of the blue vapor, made his stomach heave in dry rebellion. He endeavored to quell the queasiness with slow, measured breaths.

Less than ten hours.

Time was trickling away with the dread inevitability of death. Dark dissolution. Pain beyond reckoning.

In his mind she was already arriving at the cabin, crossing the stone patio, tapping lightly at the door. He could see her delicate arms laden with sackfuls of succulent delicacies, her face flushed with anticipation.

She would breeze in and set the tins and wrapped dishes on the table, and then she would bustle about collecting the necessary implements for their celebratory feast.

While she prepared, she would prattle on about fluff. But all the while, that coy, expectant expression would play upon her face. Goading him. Waiting for his declaration of success.

Waiting for what he could not deliver.

Cobb wished he could deceive her in this one instance. But no matter how heroic his attempt at guile, she would know he had failed. She would sense his humiliation, *smell* it. And then she would seize the chance to bludgeon him with his ineffectuality. Taunt and upbraid him. Leave him to bleed his shame and impotence until nothing was left of him but desiccated bark and a core of putrid decay.

He seethed at the injustice. His plan had been inspired. None of the failure was his. It was all the woman's doing.

That vile woman had deemed herself the guardian of *his* child. Contemptible shrew. Usurper of his salvation. She had foiled him with her vicious meddling, brought him to this hideous impasse. If only he had disposed of her earlier. Lethal indecision.

Cobb struggled to sit. The sanctum walls tottered. A harsh ringing erupted in his ear. Pressing his finger to the tragus, he attempted to block it out, but the sound worsened, building to a cruel, electric crescendo.

The sensation tracked a sharp descending pathway, triggering a series of jolting alarms in his cochlear nerve, the glossopharyngeal, the visceral efferent fibers of the accessory, crossing the dendritic processes of the hypoglossal, and driving like a spike into the spinothalamic tract.

His body went rigid, back arched, limbs splayed, head wrenched back so hard his throat constricted, and he felt the first strangling heat of asphyxiation.

The pressure mounted. Screamed in his skull. His lungs swelled toward rupture. Cobb held his breath. Strained against the white-hot pain building inside him.

At last, the spasm eased. In a reflex of survival, he dropped to the floor and crawled out of harm's way before a second wave of rigor overcame him. It was weaker this time. Shorter in duration.

He wrenched his mind from the horror. Anything but this. Groping for escape, he turned to the second-phase exercises. Focus.

Focus!

Cobb grappled with the simplest mental challenge—permutations to infinity of an increasing spire of digit forms. No more than mechanical busywork, and still he failed to achieve perfection. But the exercise had the intended effect. By the time he'd completed the requisite series of calculations, the second seizure had passed.

He opened his eyes and strained to focus. A soft glow bordered his conscious perspective. His sensations were swaddled in an insulating foam. There was a torpor in his limbs, not entirely unpleasant. And the clamorous clanging in his head had been supplanted by a low-pitched hum.

Afterglow.

Cobb exploited the false aura of well-being. Lifting himself to the edge of the cot, he sat and assessed his dilemma with clinical detachment.

He knew that the seizure meant his stores had sunk dangerously low. He was far too feeble to renew himself by direct assault on the specimen. But there was one more reserve in the secret place in the cabin. One final supply of healing humor. His emergency store.

His only chance.

After he renewed his strength, he would dispatch the woman. Without her, nothing would impede his mission. He could use the child at will. The specimen would not be leaving the hospital. He had seen to that by injecting the insulin.

Marshaling his strength, Cobb donned one of his disguises and strode toward the elevators. He could not afford to fritter his meager energies on the stairs.

Each step was a conscious effort. Deep flexion in the rectus femoris and gluteus followed by femoral extension through the hamstrings, heel strike to firm dorsiflexion of the foot. Sizzle of the firing nerve bundles, blaze of spent neurons.

He drew no suspicion. Nothing but offhanded nods and automated greetings from those he passed. How could they fail to perceive the ghastly aura of his steady expiration? Fools were purblind and deaf. Cobb could herald his contempt in their fool faces, and still they remained unaware. Duped.

Even now, he could fool the fools. Even in death, he was the dark moon.

Temporary death.

He had only to get to the cabin. The emergency reserve would allow him to overcome this heinous adversity. By the time his dear one arrived for their celebration, he would be ready.

Driving was hellish. Cobb's vision was constricted to an overwrought pin of glare in a sphere of glimmering distortion. His grip was uncertain. The car lurched and flailed in his limited control like a child in tantrum.

Further on, the road narrowed and began to swerve in unexpected directions. His unblinking eyes went dry, fingers clutched the wheel in spasm.

By the time he turned into the long, winding dirt drive leading to the cabin, he was bathed in sweat. Stumbling over the patio, he entered the dark main room and engaged the row of locks behind him.

Cobb turned on a single lamp and sat in the rocker waiting for his racing pulse to subside. There was much to be done before her arrival: his own ablutions, a final tidying of the cabin.

He would soak in a lavender-salted tub, perhaps, and then scent himself with that lemon water cologne she so admired. He planned to dress in a white-on-white shirt, silk paisley ascot, the tan vicuna jacket with suede elbow patches, pale tweed trousers or perhaps the brown cashmere. Tasseled suede slippers over the hand-knitted argyles she'd given him for his last birthday.

So much to do, the prospect exhausted him further. And still cruel time dripped away.

Cobb tuned his attention to the final scrap of fabric from the specimen's bloody shirt. He had to move the bed to get to the precious remnant hidden under the floorboard. No meager feat given his debility.

He pressed his shoulder to the bedstead and applied the force of his weight. The floor groaned, and the bed yielded a paltry inch or two.

Several more exhausting attempts, and the bed still occluded the secret compartment. Cobb leaned against the wall and struggled to catch his breath.

To think.

The bed would yield far more easily if he could find a way to reduce the friction of the legs against the plank floor. He thought of stuffing the edge of a tangled sheet underneath, but he was unable to lift the bed enough to wedge the fabric below. Next, he sprinkled talcum around the base of the bed, but when he attempted to stand and push, his feet slid on the velvety powder, and he was unable to gain solid purchase.

Bristling with frustration, he tried wiping up the talc with the bedclothes, but only succeeded in spreading the lubricant and extending the slippery area. He dampened a rag in the kitchen to wipe up the mess. But the liquid turned the powder to beads of pasty sludge that he was powerless to disperse.

In a fit of desperation, Cobb flung the filthy rag out the bedroom door. It splattered against his row of precious books, marking them indelibly with the stain of his worthlessness.

Cobb sank to the floor and wept. After his grief was spent, he stayed sprawled there for an indeterminate time, worn as the saturated rag, lame as the filthy slick of talc.

Hopeless.

He might have remained in that piteous heap indefinitely. But his ear caught the prickle of approaching disaster. The familiar concussion of her tires on the long drive, the wavering beams of her headlights.

She could not see him like this. With a Herculean effort born of fear, he shoved at the bedstead again, and it yielded the necessary distance. Cobb pried up the loose section of floorboard and found the precious scrap of soiled fabric underneath.

Gasping, he staggered to the cabin door and opened the locks.

Too late.

Her headlights were bearing down on the cabin. He would be trapped in the glare and exposed.

Cobb tore a page from his tablet and scribbled a note claiming there had been a sudden emergency at work and a colleague had come for him. His fingers were quivering, thoughts tumbling together. She must believe him. Mustn't suspect.

There was a rumble of engine sounds beside the patio. She parked and doused her lights. He heard her car door open and close again with a resonant ping.

Cobb hastened to the bedroom, slipped out through the side window, and dashed to the cover of the woods.

There he crouched, shivering with the cold and terror. He heard the sharp strike of her heels against the patio stones, the light tap of her knucles on the cabin door. The melody of her voice.

'Malcolm? Malcolm, are you in there? Anybody home?'

There was a silence. Cobb imagined her fiddling in her purse for his keys, letting herself in.

'Where are you, you silly goose? Come now, Malcolm. I'm in no mood for games.'

A light flamed on in the cabin. And another.

'Look at this godawful mess. What is all this powder? My god. And I've brought such a lovely meal. You come out here, Malcolm. Come clean up this instant.'

Cobb shuddered. The black wind tore through him. He pressed the fabric scrap to his lips and worked his tongue over the stiff stain at the center.

Instant wash of warmth. Rush of vigor.

'Malcolm Cobb. Stop this. You're acting like a goddamned ass. This is stupid now. Crazy.'

The insults glanced off his heightened sensibilities and fell away. Nothing could wound him. He was inviolate. Charged with the night air. Vicar of the darkness.

Cobb slipped deftly through the brush toward the distant roadway. Soon he would return triumphant.

He could think of nothing else. There was nothing for Cobb beyond the crackle as his feet crushed the underbrush and the ripe scent of impending conquest. Her mocking voice had been swallowed by the wind. He would paint the echo.

45 Drum's day had started off on a rotten foot. The cashier at the Four Seasons had taken an American Express imprint on check-in, but when Drum went to settle up, the money man wasn't able to squeeze enough juice out of Gertie Gold Card to cover his considerable tab. Same problem with Vicky Visa and Marjorie MasterCard. Seemed all Drum's best girls had been putting in way too much overtime and were begging for vacations.

Drum was more put out than embarrassed. He was a goddamned good customer. Okay, maybe too good. But the way he saw it, the whole point of plastic was to let you overextend yourself.

The cashier was starting to lose patience when Drum remembered the department A.E. green card he'd neglected to turn in when he was suspended. Actually, Dan Carmody had only ordered Drum to surrender his piece and his shield. Not a word about the company card, so Drum had figured he might as well hold on to it. American Express had always been his weapon of choice.

When he handed the cashier the department card, Drum knew he was taking a big chance. If the charge happened to clear before the case did, Carmody would hang him out to dry. But any more delays, and he'd miss his plane. The slightest hitch on the next flight out, and he could be late for Booker's big deal. So he tossed Carmody's plastic on the counter and hoped for the best.

Still he had to hustle to catch the eight o'clock flight out of L.A. International. By the time he wheezed through the departure gate, the plane had already boarded and was pretty well packed. Nothing was available in first or even business class, so Drum was forced to take the center seat in a five-across. Sardine central.

On his right side was a broad who should have been

required to buy a second seat for her mouth. Woman kept harping at the bald guy next to her until Drum wanted to send her tongue out for bronzing.

The guy on his left was months overdue for his annual bath. Drum had already seen the movie, and it hadn't been worth viewing once. Breakfast was typical airline fare: Alpo and eggs.

Not very conducive working conditions, but Drum didn't want to waste the time. He'd stopped at the main U.C.L.A. library late yesterday afternoon and wangled a rush on the computer search he wanted. If the genius group members chose their historical pseudonyms by special interest, Drum figured it couldn't hurt to get a handle on the three characters on the list: Machiavelli, Rasputin, and Sir Arthur Conan Doyle.

The university mainframe had coughed up way more than he'd bargained for. Drum skimmed through the hill of pages, window shopping.

'Niccolò Machiavelli had been a Renaissance statesman and political writer. In his most famous book, *The Prince*, Big Mac had argued that it was okay for a ruler to do whatever it took to seize and hold power.

Reminded Drum of a couple of the young Italian toughs from the old neighborhood. There was this one punk especially, also named Nicky by funny coincidence, who'd strutted around the Cove section of town like the whole area was registered in his name.

Guy was heavily into being right all the time. You didn't agree with him, Nicky would bust up your father's car or trash your family's pet or toss a little Sunoco daiquiri through your living room window. All very convincing ways to make a point as Drum remembered.

He flipped to the section on Rasputin. Guy looked like another piece of work altogether. He'd started out as your average peasant in the late eighteenth century. Then one day he's slopping the pigs or doing other peasant stuff, as usual, and he gets it in his head that he's got these astonishing mystical powers.

Drum concluded it was probably a nasty hay allergy or

the side effect of sucking up too many manure fumes. But this Rasputin character is completely convinced that he's become a major hotshot. Goes to monk school. Starts to think he's got a direct pipeline to the big man upstairs. Guy's even nervy enough to show up at Tsar Nicholas's palace in St. Petersburg, shopping for power.

Turns out the tsar and tsarette have a kid with hemophilia, which, as Drum remembered, was this bleeding disease that royal families tended to get because they insisted on marrying their cousins.

That number Drum had never been able to understand. His cousin Lucy, on his mother's side, had had an obvious thing for him when they were kids. And Lucy wasn't half bad: round, sexy, not at all shy or short of real interesting ideas.

Drum had been tempted, true. Especially this one Thanksgiving after dinner in the broom closet at Aunt Jeanette's. But he'd thought about the possibility of having two-headed kids who bled all over the place, and there went the mood.

Anyway, Rasputin does some hocus-pocus with the tsar's kid, and claims the bleeding problem is cured. Tsar Nicholas and his wife are so grateful, they practically hand Rasputin the country, which he proceeds to practically run into the ground.

This Rasputin character gets so carried away with himself, he thinks he can pull off anything. Starts handing out pink slips to some of the tsar's top ministers. Predictably, he steps over the line, offends some hot-headed types, and they set him up in a brand-new career – pushing up daisies.

Drum had saved Sir Arthur Conan Doyle for last on purpose. Big Matt used to be a giant fan of Sherlock Holmes. Drum still had the old, falling apart, volume of Conan Doyle's collected works that his father used to read aloud. Still remembered some of his favorite stories: 'Three Broken Threads', 'The Man on the Tor', 'The Adventure of the Red Circle'.

Now he learned that Sir Arthur had been educated at

Stoneyhurst and Edinburgh. Guy became a doctor, but his head stayed in fantasyland. In addition to the Sherlock stories, he had written a bunch of historical romances, history books, and plays.

Four pages of the printout made a big deal out of the relationship between Holmes and Watson. Claimed there was way more between those two guys than clues.

Drum tossed the material down in disgust. Watson maybe. But no way was his man Sherlock bent. And even if he was, Drum didn't want to know about it.

He leaned back, closed his eyes, and mulled over the three historical figures. Nothing jumped out at him. No obvious reason to put one of the three eggheads at the top of the list of people most likely to run down a kid and panic. He spent a few minutes concocting a way to approach the geniuses, and then he caught a quick snooze.

The plane touched down at Kennedy ten minutes ahead of schedule and slid right into a vacant gate. Drum jostled his way down the crowded aisle and out the door. No luggage, so no waiting at the claim area. He was in the beauty and on the road by ten to five.

Booker's gig wasn't until seven. Traffic was thick but moving. Drum decided to skip a stop at home and see how far he could get with his eggheads before he was due at the kid's school.

Machiavelli's address was half a mile from the Hutchinson River Parkway exit in Scarsdale. Town reeked of money. Giant houses stood shoulder to shoulder like beefy linebackers. The lawns were so stark perfect they looked fake. Kind of place where weeds couldn't afford the rent.

He turned the beauty into a circular drive paved in brick chevrons and parked in front of the massive double doors. Waiting for someone to answer his ring, he stared through one of the Tiffany glass panels flanking the entrance and took in the cascading chandelier in the entry foyer, the soaring marble staircase, the oversized Aubusson rug, and the scatter of oriental antiques. A Shar-Pei trotted in at the heels of a white-gloved, uniformed maid. That breed cost five big ones minimum, Drum knew. Looked like something forgotten at the bottom of the laundry basket. Had a collar on him covered with genuine fake rubies and diamonds.

Real understated.

Drum pitched the maid that he was an independent investigator for the MacArthur committee. Told her that someone in the family had been nominated to receive the genius award, which paid big chunks of cash for five years with no strings. The prize committee looked at the nominees' potential. It was Drum's job to make sure the candidates were kosher.

The maid hesitated and ushered Drum in to wait in the library while she passed the word.

Room was furnished in burgundy leather pieces and rich mahogany. There was an oversized fireplace with a carved granite hearth. Drum strolled around checking out the shelves jammed with leather-bound first editions. He took in the ripe scent of lemon oil and pipe tobacco. Soft music wafted through the paneled walls.

A couple of minutes later a paper-thin blond broad in a purple silk caftan showed up. She moved like something on wheels, held herself in a model's pose: jut-hipped and round-shouldered, one hand floating on the air. She introduced herself and started babbling about the nomination.

A couple of sentences, and Drum could tell she wasn't the brightest of bulbs. He pushed for a introduction to the nominee, and she floated out to fetch the family genius.

Drum was hoping for a nondescript guy of medium height, weight, etc. If Machiavelli matched the man who'd brought the bloody Peugeot to Bud's Auto Body, Drum could put a hold on him and call Carmody to take care of the packaging and delivery.

But the skinny blonde came back with a pudgy pigtailed kid in tow. Girl was about ten with a plague of freckles and a mouthful of braces. She wrenched loose from the woman's grasp and stood with her stubby hands on her hips. Her chin was tipped forward, mouth pressed in a hard line.

'I told you, I am not interested in awards, Mother. I

am, as the great one said, "the class of intellect which comprehends by itself." So good-bye and good luck, Mr. Whoever-you-are. Have a nice life.'

Kid went storming up the marble stairs. The woman followed Drum to the door. Carried on all the way about how Melissa Ann was high-strung and impulsive. She begged Drum not to hold it against the child. Kid's I.Q. had been estimated at two-twenty. So difficult for a young child to deal with an intellect of such awesome magnitude, she said. Everyone misunderstanding her. Expecting so much.

'They don't realize what a strain she's under. So they pressure her to conform, and naturally she acts out. Please don't judge her by this one little meeting. How about coming back tomorrow for dinner? Or lunch?'

Drum nodded all the way to the door. The broad's voice followed him out to the car. He revved the motor and turned up the radio to drown her out.

He spent the distance to the next step appreciating Booker. Kid was plenty smart enough by anybody's standards. But he wasn't angling for a Ph.D. in obnoxious like that speckled fat kid.

One night away from home, and Drum was missing the runt already. He wondered if Stella had heard anything more from the social service bitch about that New Haven couple. Thinking about it made him spit flames. No way anyone was taking that kid away from them.

The address for Arthur Conan Doyle was a dilapidated rooming house over a deli in downtown White Plains. Drum checked the number twice to be sure. Didn't look like fitting digs for an Einstein.

Whole building smelled like pickle brine and stale pumpernickle. Drum climbed to the first landing above the deli and started knocking on doors. No one home at the first three. At number four, he managed to raise a Howard Hughes look- and smell-alike. But the guy was a little under the whatever, speaking in tongues.

As Drum was about to climb to three, he nearly collided

with an old geezer carrying a sack of groceries. Drum gave the guy the genius award story. And he bit hard.

Old guy knew right away whom Drum was after. He led him back to the first door at the top of the stairs and knocked.

Drum had already tried that one. No answer. But the geezer didn't give up so easily. 'Open up, Artie. I got someone here may want to give you some money.'

Grumble inside.

'Big money, Artie. Don't be a schmuck.'

Took a few minutes more for the old guy to wangle their way in. Drum spent the time imagining his average-looking guy. Hoping. More than ready to be done with this damned thing.

But when Artie finally relented and opened the door, Drum could see it was strike two. Artie was done up like Sherlock himself, double-peaked cap, manor-house tweeds. Everything fit except the motorized wheelchair the guy was sitting in. He controlled the thing by sipping and puffing at a mouth stick. Had a trained monkey to fetch and carry for him. Monkey's name was Watson. Real original.

The old guy walked Drum back down to the deli level. On the way, he told Drum that Artie (guy had actually changed his legal name to Arthur Conan Doyle) had been paralyzed from the neck down in a high-school football accident. Good bet Sherlock Junior hadn't strolled into Bud's Auto Body or anyplace else for over twenty years now. Hadn't done any fancy running away either.

Brilliant deduction, Drum.

Which left Rasputin and the problem of having to track the guy through his listed address, which was a box number.

After six-thirty already, so the post office would be closed. Anyway, Drum wouldn't make the kid's big event if he did any more digging right now. So the last great hope would have to wait.

Drum didn't want to think about it, but there was always the chance that he'd strike out with Rasputin too.

The Braintrust booklet could have been left in the car by anybody. Maybe a visiting relative or friend, maybe a stranger who'd hitched a ride. Anyone.

Worse, it could be the Peugeot wasn't even the car he was after. Guy in that car might have hit an actual deer like he said. Or for all Drum knew, the moonlighting mechanic at Bud's might have made up the whole damned story. No Peugeot, no dent, no booklet, no nothing.

Not a pretty thought.

If he didn't bag a pigeon soon, Carmody would pull the plug on his operation. He'd have nothing to show for his trouble but egg on his face and a couple of lousy bucks that wouldn't begin to fill the gaping hole in his pocket.

There'd be nothing more for him to do but contemplate his inadequacy full-time. Wait out the suspension. Probably spend the rest of his cop career as a crossing guard on a slow corner.

Turning into the lot at Davenport Ridge Elementary, Drum tried to get past the doomed feeling. He had too much riding on this, too many people he cared about letting down – himself included.

But the case was looking more and more like a terminal situation.

Drum tried to block out the gloomy feeling and get himself in the mood. Tonight was for the kid, and the hotshot deserved to be put center stage for the duration. All that hard work, and he'd earned at least that much.

People were streaming into the auditorium. Drum locked the beauty and joined the crowd.

46 A line of gunmetal folding chairs stretched across the auditorium stage. Drum spotted Booker in the clump of kids milling in front of the vacant seats and waved. Hotshot didn't see him.

Place was near capacity. He looked around for Stella. Took him a few to spot her up near the front. She was standing in the middle of the row chatting with some people Drum couldn't make out from a distance. He was halfway down the aisle when he realized who they were. Made his skin crawl.

Stella was flushed, running at the mouth.

'Jerry, hi. See, I told you he'd make it on time. He wouldn't let Booker down for anything. Those two are like this.' She twisted her fingers together so hard they blanched white. 'You remember Ms. Bergmuller from social services, don't you, honey? And these are the Duncans from New Haven.'

The Bergmuller bitch held out her little paw, which Drum treated like a hot stove. 'Hello, Mr. Drum. The Duncans wanted to come and meet Booker. Get acquainted. So I thought this was the perfect opportunity.'

Right away, Drum could tell they weren't his type. Guy was way too tall. The woman's smile was all teeth. Nothing behind it. Hoop jockey and an empty cage. No way they were right for Booker.

Drum caught Stella's warning look and tried real hard to keep a lid on it. 'How come you want to get acquainted with *our* kid?' he said. Stella shot him another hard look, but Drum couldn't see her problem. He was smiling, wasn't he?

Ms. Bergmuller issued a nervous giggle and pointed at the stage. 'Oh, look, they're getting ready to start.'

Drum was steamed, but he tried not to scorch anything.

He sat next to Stella as the lights dimmed and watched Booker claim a seat smack in the middle of the line of chairs. Finally caught the kid's eye and flashed a high sign. Book answered with a grin and hitched his thumb.

Runt looked to be on top of the situation. Drum was another story. He felt nervous for the kid. Hotshot had worked so hard for this. Studied that damned spelling list until he could practically recite it by heart. Kid deserved to win.

First round started, and Booker's turn came. Drum held his breath as the kid approached the mike and waited for his word. Drum fired silent darts at the English teacher holding the list. Give him an easy one, scum, he chanted in his head. Make it real easy.

Guy said, 'elephant', and right away, Drum relaxed. Piece of cake for Book.

Hotshot was looking around, acting antsy all of a sudden. His glance flitted toward Drum, and Drum nodded his encouragement.

Kid knew the damned word. No question. So why didn't he get going already? Drum started mouthing the letters, trying to help him along. But Booker wasn't looking his way.

'Elephant,' Book repeated finally. His chest puffed and held. 'Ee . . . el . . . ee . . . ef . . . '

A razzing buzzer sounded. Drum felt his elevator plunge. It's okay, kid. No big thing.

Hotshot looked confused for a second. He blinked and opened his mouth as if he wanted to say something. But no sound came out.

It's okay. Don't take it too hard.

Drum kept beaming the subconcious message to the stage, hoping the kid would pick it up. But Booker looked stuck there at the microphone. Guy with the list leaned over and said something to the kid, but Book still didn't move. So the guy put a hand on the runt's back and gave him a gentle nudge.

The push set the kid off like a nuclear warhead. Booker

spun around and caught the guy in the midsection with a flailing arm. Then he started stomping and screaming.

'You can't do this to me, man. Didn't give me a goddamned chance. You think I'm a dumb nigger, don't you? Think I don't deserve no chance.'

Guy with the list looked like his eyes were going to pop out of his head. The principal and a couple of other teachers hopped to the stage and practically carried Booker to the wings. Kid was a screeching dervish.

'Get your damned hands off me. I ain't your nigger, man. You got no right.'

Drum was in a tight bind. Half of him wanted to race out to help the kid, but the rest didn't want to make the scene any bigger. After a few more kids got their words tossed at them, Drum decided he'd sneak out to find Booker. Best way.

Waiting for things to settle, he caught the grumbling down the row. The Duncans were huffing at the Bergmuller bitch. Carrying on about how they'd been led to believe Booker was free of emotional problems. What was she trying to pull here? They certainly weren't interested in a child with such poor impulse control or such rotten upbringing.

They fumed out of the other side of the row and bustled up the aisle toward the exit. Bergmuller chased after them.

Stella stood to go out and find Booker. Drum pulled her back down beside him. 'Wait a minute.'

'I have to go to him, Jerry,' she said in a rasp. 'Poor kid is really hurting. I've never seen him so upset.'

Drum chuckled and shook his head. 'Kid's too much.'

'What are you talking about?'

He turned and saw the auditorium doors close behind the Duncans and Ms. Bergmuller. Rising, he signaled Stella to follow. 'You'll see. Come on.'

Book was waiting on one of the cool-off chairs outside the principal's office. He was smiling and jiving to a tune in his head when Drum and Stella walked in.

'Hey, Mrs. Drum, Mr. Drum.'

'Hey,' Drum said.

'Booker, honey. You okay?' Stella hugged him and held him out for inspection. 'You shouldn't have taken it so hard. It wasn't that important.'

'Yeah, I know. Just blew off a minute. It's cool now.'

She smoothed his hair. 'Well you look much better. Good. You shouldn't take things like that so seriously. It was just a game.'

The principal had edged out of his office. He clasped his hands and nodded. 'Exactly what we talked about. Isn't that so, Booker? Competition is difficult for many young-sters Booker's age, folks. I'm sure he'll learn to deal with it much better as he goes along, won't you son?'

'Oh, yeah. I go along. I'm gonna be something else. You'll see.' Wall-to-wall grin.

'And no more outbursts, right?'

'Eighty-six on the outbursts, man. You got my word on it.'

Principal gave Book a pat on the back. 'That's the spirit. All done and forgotten. You people run along now. See you Monday, son.'

'Yeah. Later.'

Booker was all shake and swagger on the way out. Half-way to the car, Stella's puzzlement yielded to a glimmer of understanding. 'You mean to tell me that –'

Booker's eyes went real innocent. He cast an anxious look in Drum's direction.

'Go on, you little con. Tell Stella the truth.'

'Truth is, I ain't no dead chicken hanging in a window.'

'What's that mean?'

'Means I ain't for sale like some goddamned dead chicken hanging in the butcher shop. Ain't going no place I don't want to go, and ain't nobody telling me different.'

Stella shook her head. 'I told you, it was only prelimi-nary, Booker.'

'I ain't for sale, Mrs. Drum. Preliminary or no other time.'

Drum shrugged and bit back the smile pulling at his mouth. 'I'll take Book home with me, Stella. Okay?'

'Take him. Be my guest.' Stella was trying to look mad. Failing miserably. 'That was some performance.'

In the beauty, Book leaned back and wove his fingers behind his neck. 'Saw to that, didn't I, Mr. Drum? Took care of it like I said I would.'

'Didn't I tell you to watch it, kid? Didn't I tell you not to come up with some crazy scam and maybe get yourself in trouble?'

'Yeah, you did. But I pulled it off, Mr. Drum. Told you not to worry.'

Drum fell silent. For once, he had no bottled advice for the kid. Instead, Booker had given him a fat dose of what he should have remembered himself. You want something bad enough, you go after it. Use whatever it takes. Keep going until it's yours. Basic.

But for a while there, Drum hadn't been thinking that way. He'd been ready to give up, cash it in because things weren't falling in his lap.

'Yeah, hotshot. You pulled it off.'

'*Miz* Bergmuller brings around any more people like those Duncans, I'll take care of them too, Mr. Drum. You'll see.'

'Bet you would, kid. But a bigger bet you won't have to.'

Pain pinched the child's expression. 'Guess you're right. No way nobody's ever gonna want to adopt me. Ain't no cute little baby no more. Ain't easy either. Just as well.'

Drum didn't answer. He'd give the kid the words when he had the ones he wanted.

47 While Stella was tucking Booker in, Drum called Louis at Failsafe Security for his messages. There had been couple of nag calls from Chief Carmody and one from Lindy Tang, Driscoll's big-shot scientist friend from Philadelphia.

Drum dialed the number Tang had left for the Bethlehem, PA, lab. Turned out to be the guy's private line.

'I have evaluated the sample, Mr. Drum.'

Tang told Drum he had isolated an organic poison in the child's blood. It was a glycoside from the seeds of a tropical plant in the foxglove family that was indigenous to Africa. The poison mimicked digoxin in its tendency to cause erratic heart rhythms.

'A poison, you said?'

'Correct, Mr. Drum.'

'Is this one of those poisons that has some value as a medicine?'

'As I said, it is a heart stimulant, so it is feasible that it could be employed medicinally. But its historical use is as an arrow or dart poison.'

Drum asked the scientist the obvious questions and got exactly the answers he didn't want. The poison shrub was readily available from any number of tropical greenhouse suppliers across the country. No major skill or fancy equipment was necessary to extract the plant's venom from the seeds.

Nothing to narrow the field.

He hung up feeling like he'd lost another round. Meat had suggested that the substance in the kid's blood might be an experimental medicine. If he had to canvas all the tropical greenhouse suppliers and every drug manufacturer running experiments on heart drugs, it was going to be a real long winter.

He called Carmody and gave him a line about how well things were coming along. Drum kept it in code in deference to the chief's telephone paranoia. Made it sound like he'd had a stomach problem, and it was almost cured. 'So all that gas is almost gone, Chief. You can't imagine what a relief.'

Drum knew he wasn't any closer to nabbing the creep, but there was no reason to let Carmody in on the secret. He had to try to keep the chief interested long enough for his luck to turn.

Stella ducked her head into the den to tell him there had been a message from Oliver London on the phone machine. Drum played it back three times. 'Boooy . . . good,' the old guy had said. There was obvious effort in the voice. Big deal for the poor slob to get the message out. And for what? So the Merritt kid was doing okay. Drum didn't make that as a major news bulletin.

Disgusted, Drum was ready to call it a night. Figured he'd start at Stella's left ear and work his way down. Nothing he liked better than a nice, lazy, nature walk. All scents and scenery.

He was dawdling at one of her more interesting foothills when the phone rang. Stella made him answer. Woman had a mean streak.

It was Dan Carmody again. He'd just gotten a call from American Express asking for approval on the Four Seasons chit.

Carmody was spitting fire. Drum held the phone out to keep from burning his ear. He caught snatches of the tirade. Enough to know the chief was not a happy fellow.

Drum listened, hoping Carmody would run out of steam. But the guy showed no sign of cooling. Came down to an ultimatum. Drum had forty-eight hours to tie up the hit-run, or he was dust.

Drum hung up and did the only logical thing under the circumstances. Tossed a lamp against the wall. Trashed four of the good crystal goblets they'd gotten as a wedding gift from Stella's Aunt Frieda. Then he stood back to survey the carnage. Didn't make him feel a bit better.

Used to be tantrums like that did him a world of good. But even the simple pleasures were turning on him.

Stupid, Drum. He knew he'd brought this on himself. Knew he'd been asking for it.

Stella had heard the commotion. She brought Drum a broom and dustpan and left without a word. She was right as usual. He'd made the mess, time to clean it up.

Ten minutes later, he was in the beauty heading for the Pound Ridge Post Office. Two days weren't much, but he was determined to make the most of them.

48 When Dr. Ferris stopped by on evening rounds, James was sleeping. The doctor took a cursory look at the little boy and turned to leave. 'Wait,' Cinnie said. 'I wanted to hear about the test results.'

He looked surprised. 'Test?'

'The blood work you did after James got so sick this morning. You said you'd have the results by this afternoon.'

'Oh, right. I did. But apparently the lab is backed up. One of the techs is out sick, I think. Probably hear from them tomorrow.'

'But this was an emergency.'

'Come now, Mrs. Merritt,' he snapped. 'Let's not overdramatize the situation.'

Cinnie felt slapped. 'How can you say that? James wasn't breathing. He could have . . .'

Ferris mumbled to himself. He seemed so strange and distracted. 'Sorry. You're right. Forgive me. I haven't been getting much sleep lately.'

That she could understand. 'You'll have the results in the morning?'

'Soon as possible. Excuse me, will you? There's something I have to take care of.'

On her way back from washing up in the patient bath, Cinnie almost tripped over Oliver London. He had stationed his wheelchair beside the door to James's room.

'Boooy?'

'You heard what happened to James? It was awful, but he's fine now, Mr. L. You're sweet to come check.'

He cocked his head and strained to get something out.

She put a hand on his shoulder. 'Honest, he's all right. He's fast asleep hugging that sweet teddy bear you brought him. See you tomorrow, okay?'

He shook his head, puffed his chest full of air, and unleashed a flood of gibberish.

'Tomorrow, Mr. London. Since I won't be taking James home, we have our usual date at nine-thirty. You go get some rest now, all right?' She went inside and put her things away.

She'd expected London to leave, but she could hear the squeak of his chair as he positioned himself directly in front of the closed door. There was the sound of the brakes clicking in place.

Cinnie decided to ignore him. Sooner or later, he'd get tired and leave.

James was still sound asleep. Cinnie smoothed his forehead and tucked the blankets closer around him. When she kissed his cheek, he stirred and muttered a few garbled words before settling down again.

'Night, sweetheart. Better day tomorrow. I promise.'

Cinnie curled up on the couch. Easy promise to keep, she thought. Today had been world-class miserable.

Why didn't Ferris have any answers yet? She had to know what had caused James's crisis.

Ferris had acted so strangely. Usually, he was cool and impossibly level, but tonight, there'd been a jittery edge about him. He'd seemed so distracted and eager to leave.

After he'd gone, Cinnie had called the lab herself, hoping to put a fire under them. But both of the docs she knew on the pathology service had already gone for the day.

The receptionist was new. When Cinnie asked her to check the status of James's blood work, the woman had trouble finding the requisition order. After about a five-minute wait, the receptionist finally put her hands on the form, but she couldn't make sense of it. She said it looked as if the order had already been processed. At the time, Cinnie had assumed the woman was simply mistaken.

Lying awake now, Cinnie began to wonder if Dr. Ferris had been evasive on purpose. Could it be that he'd found something terrible in James's blood sample and didn't want to tell Cinnie about it yet? She knew how doctors sometimes worked, put off transmitting the bad news until it was absolutely necessary. Or slightly afterward. That would certainly explain Ferris's jumpiness.

Then there was Oliver London's strange behavior. Maybe he'd heard something terrible about James, and that was why he was hanging around. Cinnie knew people tended to talk freely around patients like London. Hard to remember that the man was perfectly capable of hearing and digesting everything. But London was. And if he'd picked up any interesting information, she was more than ready to hear it, good or bad.

She knocked at the door and asked London to move his chair. When she could hear that he'd rolled a safe distance away, Cinnie went out to the corridor. London looked miserable. His eyes were rimmed with dusky circles.

'What are you trying to tell me, Mr. London?'

London struggled to speak. His eyes bulged, and the cords tensed in his neck.

'Easy. Slow and easy. It is something about James? Did you hear something about his test results?'

His mouth gaped, and he flushed crimson. Cinnie was afraid he was headed for another stroke.

'That's enough. Take it easy.'

He stretched his mouth, pushed a final time, and gave up. His breathing was harsh and ragged. There was deep sadness in his eyes.

'Listen to me, Mr. London. You're working too hard. Don't try to talk anymore for a while. A good night's rest and you'll be back to yourself in the morning. Whatever it is can wait until then.'

London looked bowed with defeat. He didn't protest when Cinnie wheeled him to the elevator and pressed the button. She waited until a car arrived, maneuvered him inside, and pushed the number for his floor.

As the doors slid closed, she stepped out and blew him a kiss. 'Take it easy, Mr. London. See you in the morning.'

Passing the nurses' station, Cinnie lifted James's chart, tucked it under her robe, and sneaked it into the room. She read until her eyes went hazy, studying every new entry and all the lab reports for the past week. There was nothing from today. So Ferris was telling the truth. If the results had been sent up, a copy would have been placed on James's records.

Cinnie took the chart back to the front desk and slipped it back in place. Then she padded down the hall to James's room, flopped on the cot, and pulled up the covers.

This time she dismissed the nagging inner voices. Sleep was her major need at the moment. Everything else would keep.

James shifted in his bed, tossed an arm over his pillow, and mumbled. Cinnie flipped off the bedside light and shut her eyes against the darkness.

49 Drum parked the beauty out of sight behind the historical society and made his way through a chink in the dividing hedgerow to the Pound Ridge Post Office. Place looked like an old country house: bright white siding, green tiled roof, black shutters, rusted iron eagle over the door.

He checked the windows for alarm tape and spotted nothing. But given that they were multipaneled casements, Drum knew shock sensors were the more likely trap. Six months on the repair staff at Precision Alarm Company, and he had picked up a few things about security systems. Next to locksmithing, working for an alarm operation was the best prep school in the world for a would-be burglar.

Circling the building, Drum was able to dope out the system in no time. All bets had been laid on the perimeter. No sign of motion sensors or ultrasonic beams. There were simple contacts on the exterior doors, shock sensors on the casements, fat silver snakes of conductive tape on the basement windows. Tracing the exit wires on their way to the phone pole, Drum spotted a junction box. So he knew that the library was hooked on a direct line to the police station.

Stepping back, he could see there was only one way to get in without tripping the system. Drum figured the pants were a sure sacrifice. Ditto the silk-blend shirt. Lucky thing Carmody was already steamed. Save him the trouble of working up a fresh head when he got Drum's final expense vouchers.

Treading carefully on the window frame, Drum hoisted himself to the second story and then onto the gabled roof. His shoes were leather-soled and slippery, so he was forced to sink to hands and knees and crawl up the steep incline toward the chimney.

The copper flashing at the base was green with age. When Drum grasped the edge to pull himself closer, a moldy sheet of copper snapped off in his hand. He slid backward, raking at the shingles to stop his fall.

Slowly, he regained the ground he'd lost and hoisted himself to the top of the brick-faced spire. He lowered himself feet first into the breech and let go.

Drum barely fit through the slim tube. He was jostled and bumped to the bottom. By the time he hit, his knuckles, elbows, and knees were scraped and bleeding. He was caked with soot and creosote.

Brushing away the worst of it, he crossed to the inner office and started rifling through the files. He found endless records of insured packages, color-coded forms in triplicate, stacks of booklets about mail fraud and postal regulations.

Nothing about P.O. boxes.

Drum busted into a couple of desks, rummaged through the drawers. He was about to give up altogether when his eye caught the computer terminal at the sales counter.

Last chance. Drum flipped on the system and fiddled around. He'd seen Booker doodling with the Apple IIC they'd bought him for his birthday, and it looked easy enough. Easy for the kid anyway. All Drum got for his trouble was a lot of angry beeping and a bunch of warning messages he couldn't understand.

Hotshot would probably be asleep by now, but this was an emergency. Drum called home collect, so there wouldn't be a record of his being in the place after regular hours. Using his best pitch, he convinced Stella to wake the runt.

A few minutes later, Booker picked up. Kid sounded zonked, but he snapped to when Drum explained the problem.

Kid talked Drum through the keyboard. Gave him a couple of suggestions: keystroke combinations, ways to persuade the system to sing his tune. Five minutes later, he was looking at the list he wanted.

'That's it, hotshot. Got it right here. Thanks, I owe you.'

'No problem, Mr. Drum. What you up to anyway? You need me to come help you out, be glad to. I ain't sleepy.'

'Not necessary. You were great. Go back to bed now before Stella works me over but good, will you?'

'Ain't tired, I told you. So what's it to her?'

'I don't know, kid. Point is, she'll boil me if I keep you up, so pretend you're tired and turn in, would you, please? It'd be a big favor.'

Big yawn. 'Yeah, okay. Going to bed now, Mr. Drum. I'm *real* pooped. See you in the morning, man.'

Drum scrolled through the post office box numbers until he came to the four-digit combination that belonged to Rasputin. Box was leased to a guy named Malcolm Cobb at an address a couple of miles out of town on Hollow Tree Ridge Road.

A few minutes, and he'd know whether he was back to square one.

Drum shut off the computer and took a look around. The keypad for the alarm was next to the front door. He couldn't disable the system without the entry code.

From the months he'd spent at Precision, Drum knew there was a way to rig a false contact that would allow him to open the door without setting off the bells. But that would take time he didn't care to waste. And there was no guarantee he wouldn't trip something in the process.

So he did the only sensible thing. Threw open the door and ran like hell for the beauty.

Seconds later, he rolled out of the entrance to the historical society and headed north. Half a mile away, he caught the flame of approaching headlights and a wail of sirens. Drum broke hard right, bolted down a slim driveway, and bumped the beauty out of sight on the swatch of lawn behind a private house.

After the commotion passed, he angled back to the road and continued the distance to Hollow Tree Ridge, a curving, narrow strip of backwoods blacktop. He found the number he was after, changed into respectable clothes, and ditched the beauty at the foot of the long, narrow drive.

50

A late-model green Peugeot wagon was parked at the mouth of the drive. Car had no bruises or blood spots Drum could detect. No obvious signs of repair work either. Thief at the body shop had done a decent job.

Crouched out of sight behind the car, he took a hard look at the cabin. No sign of anybody stirring, no curious eyes at the window.

Drum slipped into the car through a rear door. The Braintrust booklet was still on the front seat.

Drum left the car and took in the exterior scene. A homemade patio connected the cabin with the unpaved drive. Brown scraggly grasses poked up through the seams, and the fieldstone blocks were cracked and uneven.

Place was screaming for paint and a new roof. The cedar shakes were pocked with scaly patches and spreading fingers of dry rot. Swords of peeled paint clung to the window frames. Curled shingles topped the desiccated tar paper lining the eaves. The rusted gutters sagged under the burden of years of muddy debris.

Drum pressed his ear to the door and listened. The place was all lit up but dead still. No response to his knock. Using his pick collection, he worked the trail of locks and edged the door open.

The cabin had been trashed. Incredible mess, stench that made Drum gag.

He took a deep breath and started searching. Began with the bedroom. Stingy square. Nothing in it but an old maple dresser and a four-poster with a broken canopy. All the clothing had been dumped out of the dresser. The bed linens were a tangled, dirty mess. A ring of scum took the place of a throw rug. Drum ran some of the slime through his fingers, felt like glue, smelled like a baby's behind.

From the way the dirt on the floor was distributed, Drum

could tell the bed was not in its normal position. Staring hard, he noticed an unexpected pair of seams in the floorboards near the rear legs. He poked and prodded until a small rectangle lifted out.

Underneath was a hollow. Drum groped around in the dark space but found nothing.

The contents of the medicine cabinet had been dumped in the bathroom sink: a couple of physician's samples, a straight razor, and a half-used bottle of cologne with a cloying lemon scent.

Back in the main room, he traced the stench to two large paper sacks in the corner. One held two fancy china plates, two place settings of ornate silver, and a pair of crystal wineglasses wrapped in linen napkins. Peering inside the other, he saw that someone had opened an assortment of food containers and dumped the contents in the bag. Then the mess had been mashed together and crowned with a human turd.

Drum's stomach lurched and threatened to erupt. But he stayed on top of it and forced himself keep looking.

There was an old maple chest topped by a smashed mirror. Materials from the genius group had been pulled out of an antique writing table: intellectual exercise books, a procedure manual. At the bottom of the heap were two writing tablets. Drum flipped through them. Both were empty.

A dozen or more of the same slim book had been tossed from a shelf on the opposite wall. Drum stooped and picked one up. The cover was damp and streaked with more of the pasty mess from the bedroom floor.

It was a kid's book. Prickly garden scene on the cover. Needles of anticipation poked his neck as he opened to the inside back cover.

Yes! There was an author picture on the flyleaf. Young creep with long, scraggly hair and the face of a scared rabbit. The eyes were vacant and strange. Weak mouth, pale sickly complexion.

'I'm gonna get you, you scum. You thought you were going to get away with it, didn't you? Well, it's payday.'

He tossed the reeking paper sack out the open bedroom window and settled in to wait.

Drum sat on the rocker, staring at the cabin door. He tuned his ear to the road, willing the sound of approaching tires. Nothing but the wind.

'Come on, you shithead. I'm ready for you.'

Silence. The tortuous slow passing of scrutinized time.

Restless, Drum picked up the kid's book again and read through the story. Couple of weed kids shaking up the neighborhood. Sister and brother named Dove and Elegant. The young weeds come out okay after the neighbors try to destroy them, but then they get sick with this weird weed bleeding problem.

So this Rasputin character is real interested in blood, Drum thought. Even writes kid's books about it.

Bad kids books. Drum couldn't imagine why anyone would want to read their kid a creepy story like this.

But people did. He knew they did. Drum had seen the damned book before. No question. Where, Drum? Think.

He tried to bring it in focus. Went through the list of logical places where he might have seen children's books. Definitely wasn't one of Booker's. Drum could picture the runt's shelves.

So where?

He rolled it over and over in his head. Closed his eyes and tried to concentrate.

It came to him like a filmy scarf drifting on a breeze. Blew in and settled down until Drum could pick it up and run it through his fingers.

No need to wait around for the sicko creep to come home. Drum had caught his scent.

51 It took less than ten minutes flying time for Drum to get to Tyler's Grove. He turned in through the broken pillars and followed the curves of Grove Street to the second spur. He eased to the end of the cul-de-sac, and left the beauty at the curb.

Crossing the lawn, he saw a curtain move on the second floor. Drum could feel the eyes on him. But when he rang the bell and pounded on the door, no one answered.

Which definitely called for self-help.

Drum pulled the picks out of his pocket and went to work on the deadbolt. He wasn't trying to be quiet, but the noise of his jemmying was drowned out by the sound of feet clumping down the stairs and crossing the living room. Drum was in the house before she could finish dialing.

He wrenched the phone out of her hand and waggled a finger at her. 'You promised this dance to me, sweetheart. Don't you remember?'

'The nerve! What do you mean breaking in here like this?'

Drum looked her over and couldn't help smiling. Broad was in character, even at this time of night. Her hair was pulled back in a perfect chignon, stern school-marm expression firmly in place. She wore a prim robe over matching silk pajamas. Her feet were encased in pristine pink leather slippers with regal trim.

'I mean to find out who Malcolm Cobb is to you and where I can find him.'

Lydia Holroyd stiffened and pushed back an invisible wisp of hair. 'How absurd. I don't even know anyone named Malcolm anything.'

Drum took the kid's book off the stand on the antique

school desk and flashed it in her face. 'You don't know him? Then why do you display his frigging book?'

She didn't flinch. 'Because that happens to be my son Todd's favorite story. Now if you'll leave me in peace, I won't have to call the police or your boss at the paper.'

Drum's temper was flaming. 'I'll leave when you tell me what I want to know, lady. Who's Malcolm Cobb?'

'I told you, I don't know. Now get out of here.'

She was coming at Drum, a murderous expression in her eyes. Drum was enjoying the show, but he was distracted for a second by the sound of steps entering the room. When he turned to check who it was, the broad beaned him with a bronze lion's head bookend.

Drum staggered, but he didn't go down. He caught her hands, disarmed her, and shoved her down hard on the couch. She sat with a startled rush of breath. Flat tire.

'That wasn't very *nice*, Mrs. Holroyd. Not real *hospitable*.' Drum rubbed his head. A big lump had already risen, and a tropical pulse was dancing in his temples. He used everything he had to keep his temper from exploding.

'This is my house, and I want you out of it. Right this minute!'

Drum bared his teeth, kept his tone even. 'I want out too, lady. Only first I have to hear about Malcolm. I have a special present for him that I have to deliver in person.'

'You mean Uncle Malcolm?'

'Shut up, Todd,' Lydia Holroyd hissed.

Too late. Drum smiled at the kid. Walked over and ruffled his hair. The kid returned a shy little grin. Boy obviously wasn't used to much affection.

'Yes, pal. That's exactly who I mean,' Drum said. 'Thanks, you've been a big help. Run along now, will you, tiger? I have to talk to your mom alone for a couple of minutes.'

Kid looked at his mother, but she wouldn't meet his seeking expression. Catching Drum's wink and nod, he hustled up the stairs.

'Now, you're going to tell me all about *Uncle* Malcolm, Mrs. Holroyd. One way or the other.'

She eyed her lap. Drum watched her sigh and bite her lower lip.

'All right. I suppose I've no choice. Malcolm is my younger brother.'

'Just slipped your mind there awhile? Is that right?'

She caught his eye. Hers were frosty and filled with loathing. 'He's all the family I have. It's a natural instinct to want to protect him when I have no idea what you're after. What do you want with dear Malcolm anyway?'

Drum wanted to deck her. '*Dear* Malcolm ran down one of your neighbor's kids and nearly killed him. Took off and left the kid hurt and unconscious on the side of the road.'

She gasped. Her lip quivered and tears puddled in her eyes. 'This can't be. Not after . . . '

'After what, lady?'

'Nothing. You have to make them see. It's not his fault. He's not responsible.'

'Why the hell not?'

Drum watched her lips work and the nervous play of her hands. 'It's a long story. Terribly complicated,' she said finally.

'Then you better get started,' Drum said.

When she looked up, there was a slick of pleading in her eyes, but she stiffened and pulled the shade on it. Cool bitch, Drum thought. Should have a frostbite warning sign on her.

'All right. I suppose it will have to come out anyway . . . Malcolm was a brilliant child, not simply precocious but highly creative. Talented in art, music, writing. To think what he might have been . . .

'Our mother wanted to give him everything, all the right enrichment and stimulation. But it was so difficult for her. My father abandoned us when Malcolm was just an infant. Mummy was forced to work two jobs to make ends meet.

'Malcolm and I were alone much of the time. Being older, I was responsible for him. I tried to watch him, to make him mind, but I was only a child myself. And he was so terribly difficult. He would break things deliberately, hurt people.

311

'It worsened as he got older. Malcolm was forever getting himself into some dreadful trouble, and Mummy would have to drag him out of it.'

'What kind of trouble?' Drum said.

Lydia Holroyd flushed. 'He would . . . expose himself to other children. Threaten them into sodomizing him. Doing as he wished.'

Drum felt his gorge rising. 'Boys?'

'Mostly.' She met Drum's gaze for an instant and looked away. 'Mostly young boys.

'Mummy had to scrape and borrow, but she always managed to hire the finest lawyers. And they always found a way to get Malcolm off. She could never accept that he was seriously ill. Just bored, she'd say. A bored genius.

'After each of his messes was cleared up, Mummy would do what she thought best to discipline him, to make him see how naughty he'd been. And it would seem to work for a time. But then the awful behaviors would start again. Worse each time.'

'Worse how?'

Her voice dropped to a whisper. 'He became paranoid, fancied that evil spirits were after him, sapping his strength. He was so irrational, so frightening. The violence and abuse escalated.'

Drum had heard enough. Too much. 'Look, you tell me where I can find Malcolm, and I'll be sure the DA hears the whole story about his being sick and maybe not responsible.'

'I can't. I don't know where he is.'

Something in her expression changed. Drum could almost smell the lie.

'Yeah, you do. You know.'

She tensed. 'I thought it was over. I thought he was getting better. Honestly, I did. But now this . . . '

'Where is he?'

She started to cry. Her body heaved and tears streaked her face. 'Oh, God. It can't be happening again.'

'Where is he, lady? You have to tell me.'

She wiped her face with a hankie and blew her nose.

Folding her hands, she made a visible attempt to compose herself.

'You must understand, it was years before I was finally able to get him into treatment. I couldn't really help him at all until after Mummy died. She wouldn't hear of it. "No doctors," she'd say. "Malcolm is perfectly capable of turning around on his own."

'On her deathbed, she finally admitted why she hadn't been able to deal with Malcolm's illness. She told me that our father had been severely schizophrenic. When Malcolm started to act out, she suspected deep down that he'd inherited the sickness.

'Mother blamed herself, you see. She thought she should have realized how deranged Father was before she risked passing that terrible curse on to his children.'

Drum was losing patience. 'All real interesting, Mrs. Holroyd. But it doesn't help me find your brother.'

'I told you, he had delusions that spirits were pursuing him, ruining him. When I got him into therapy, Malcolm was able to tell the doctor that he'd found a way to fool his assailants. Each time they stole his precious humors, he restored himself by claiming the humors from a strong, intelligent child.'

Drum didn't get it and said so.

'Blood. He would hurt a child. Then he would go to the hospital, where he could sneak in and take the child's blood.' She shook her head. 'I thought it was finished. He's been functioning so well for such a long time. Working, pursuing his interests, making a life for himself. For a long time, he was so terribly reclusive, barely left that cabin of his except to go to work. But last year, he even managed to do some traveling.'

The tumblers were clicking in place. 'To Africa?'

'Why yes, how did you . . . ?'

'And is one of his interests archery, Mrs. Holroyd? Does your baby brother practice shooting arrows and darts?'

'He took it up at one of his treatment centers. Became quite proficient, as he does in all things. But how did you know that?'

Drum's head was reeling. All of it was beginning to come together. The Merritt kid getting zapped with some weirdo arrow poison. The odd round bruise on his head that Driscoll said couldn't have come from being run down. Whisper on the wind.

And then there was the clock in the recording studio running an hour behind the house. All of it made sense if the hit-run had been planned deliberately.

He felt a crawling in his gut. Rage building and a fat sense of urgency. He raced to the phone. The broad was all over him, pulling at his arm. Begging him not to hurt Malcolm. He shook her off like a bug.

Nobody answered at Carmody's house. Drum dialed the chief's direct line at the station. Three rings . . . four.

No answer.

Carmody had to be carrying his beeper, had to be. Drum dialed, left the Holroyd broad's number, hung up, and prayed until the phone rang half a minute later.

Not a second to waste. Drum spoke in a rush, gave the chief just enough to convince him to get rolling. Carmody promised to cordon off the hospital and conduct a room-by-room search. No one would get near James Merritt.

Drum felt a rush of relief. 'Meet you there, Chief.'

'No way. You show your face at Fairview, I'll suspend your ass for another six months. As far as this case is concerned, you don't exist. Jerry. Remember that.'

Drum didn't bother to argue. What the chief didn't know, wouldn't hurt him. And if going against Carmody's orders extend his time in Siberia, that was a price Drum was willing to pay. He'd eaten his frigging greens. Time for dessert.

Crocodile tears were streaming down the broad's face. Drum wasn't impressed.

'They won't hurt him, will they?'

'Don't you worry, lady. *Dear* Malcolm's gonna get exactly the treatment he deserves.'

52

Chief Carmody and Charlie Allston oversaw the search-and-destroy operation from a makeshift command post in the office of Fairview's chief administrator, Walter Kampmann. Kampmann, a stately septuagenarian, had arrived minutes after Carmody's call. Ever since, he'd been raking nervous fingers through his fine, white hair and pacing a rut in the cocoa carpeting beside the office window.

The final sector report came in less than forty minutes after dozens of cops had disappeared to canvass every room and cubicle in the ten-story building. Carmody listened to the squawking voice on the walkie-talkie, gave instructions to the sector chief, and signed off with a hefty sigh of relief.

'That's it then,' he said to the others. 'Not a creature is stirring.'

'So what now?' Kampmann said.

'So now, we wait,' said Allston.

'Exactly,' Carmody said and felt the tension building again. 'We wait.'

The chief leaned back in the gray leather desk chair, wove his hands behind his head, and considered the reception committee he'd arranged for Malcolm Cobb.

From the distance came the persistent slapping sound of helicopter rotors. The traffic chopper had been commandeered from a local radio station to sweep back and forth between the turnpike and the parkway and report on approaching vehicles. The sweep would deliberately avoid the immediate Fairview area to keep from arousing the pigeon's suspicions.

Five deserted-looking EMS vans were parked at planned intervals in front of the building. They were rigged with ultrasensitive listening devices and infrared video equipment to immortalize Malcolm Cobb's grand entrance. Each was manned by a pair of the department's top marksmen armed with Heckler & Koch MP-5 semi-automatics. Another five men with McMillan M-82 sniper rifles were stationed on the roof. Two unmarkeds with deep-tinted windows were covering the rear and emergency entrances.

Ideally, if Cobb didn't get wind of the trap, he'd be allowed to make it inside, where three men were waiting to take him out, down, or whatever it took. On the impossible chance that he managed to slip through the wall of perimeter security and tried to get anywhere near the Merritt child, Carmody had posted a pair of guards in the stairwell at each landing.

The gas-leak ruse had gone off without a hitch. No one had questioned the announced need to check every room for a trace of fumes. Most of the patients had slept through the sweep, and those who hadn't were satisfied with the canned assurances. The staff had been unruffled too. Not a raised eyebrow. Exactly what Carmody had hoped to accomplish.

So Jerry Drum wasn't the only one in the department who could pull off a successful con. Dan Carmody issued a wry chuckle in Drum's honor. The man was tough, talented, and hands-down the most exasperating cop Carmody had worked with in his forty years on the squad. Drum had inherited his father's pluck and instincts, but there the similarities ended.

Carmody could well remember Jerry Drum as a little kid. He'd had so much of Matthew in him then, it was uncanny. The child had mastered his old man's energetic stride, the distinctive vocal cadence and speech patterns. He'd even aped Matthew's courtly manners.

But young Jeremiah had coarsened over time. He'd developed a rough exterior and insides so bristling hot with anger it took next to nothing to set him off.

Though it hadn't been easy, Carmody had put up with the outbursts and the man's crazy spending for Matthew's sake, and his own. Jerry Drum used his wolf hunger to advantage, pushed way past the point when standard, sane cops gave up. Which made him an incomparable treasure in a seemingly hopeless case like this one.

An almost finished hopeless case.

Carmody tried to get a mental read on the stalking lunatic. From what Drum's had told him, they were after a crazy genius with a family history of severe schizophrenia.

The chief had encountered the type too many times before: wholly dysfunctional. Suffering from the kind of reality breach that leads to acts of desperate violence against unseen enemies and imagined threats.

He could tick off a list of the worst cases the department had ever handled; many were of that breed. There was the serial murderer who'd left a trail of decaptitated bodies strewn along the banks of the Rippowam River on the alleged orders of a minor character in a comic strip. There was the young man with a Jesus complex who'd visited a local elementary school playground carrying an Uzi for show and tell. He recalled the woman who fancied herself a savior of animals when she bombed the homes of corporate executives whose drug companies were conducting experiments on mice and monkeys.

The men scouting the fifth floor had come across an old, forgotten storage room that the guy had obviously commandeered as his own headquarters. Carmody had been called up to take a look, and the sight had made him shudder. Tiny, dim space. Compulsively clean and orderly. Stocked as if someone were planning to bunk here for a long siege, or already had. There was a strong, primitive stench.

Stifling his revulsion, Carmody took in the furnishings: cot, dresser. There was a row of staff uniforms hanging in the metal locker: surgical scrubs, a lab coat, the yellow jumpsuit used around infectious cases. A shoebox beside the sink was full of first aid supplies, rotting food, books, and loaded hypodermics.

Carmody had been horrified. To think that the madman had been so near the children. Able to move about the hospital undetected. He wondered how long this had been going on, how many other seeming 'accidents' had been engineered by Malcolm Cobb to satisfy his sick bloodlust.

Wally Kampmann was still pacing. Carmody watched the guy and felt a swell of sympathy. 'We'll get the bastard, Mr. Kampmann. It's all over but the shouting. Don't worry.'

Kampmann flashed a desperate look. 'I can't believe this, Chief Carmody. To think he was right here and nobody knew . . .'

'Try to put it behind you,' Carmody said. 'It's history. Malcolm Cobb is history.'

Allston started working on the incident report. Anything to pass the time. Carmody passed the time picking his cuticles. Unless Cobb was tipped, he would show up eventually. And with someone watching the sister's house and monitoring her phone calls, a tip was highly unlikely.

But nothing was worse than the waiting. And Carmody knew that nothing was certain until the waiting was done.

53 Oliver London tuned his breathing to the rhythmic rise and fall of the child's chest. After Cinnie had put him on the elevator, he'd waited a decent interval and come back up to keep an eye on things. His chair was pressed in the shadows in the corner of the room where he could watch Cinnie sleep and the sleeping boy and the door. Silent sentry.

When Peterson and Daitch had come through on their room-by-room search of the pediatric floor, London had seen enough to convince him that the sweep was not about any gas leak. The pair of detectives had approached each room with guns discreetly drawn. They'd gone in according to standard procedure for handling a perpetrator marked *armed and dangerous*: door shoved in, the men crouched in position, spring-ready for any nasty surprises.

When London tried to get the real lowdown from his brother officers, Peterson had handed him a patronizing line of malarkey about there being nothing at all to worry about. And didn't he need his rest? And why didn't he run along to his own room like a good boy?

London ached to tell the young snot what to do to himself and by what method, but he'd found his tongue tied in half hitches as it often was since the stroke, especially when he was angry or upset.

London was confident that Jerry Drum would be willing to tell him the truth about the operation, but there was no sign of him. So the old man had been forced to content himself with waiting until Peterson and Daitch were a few doors down. Then he'd slipped into James Merritt's room and settled in for the duration. Whatever was going down, he would not allow it to touch Cinnie or her son.

Anyone who thought of hurting either of those two would have to do it over London's dead body.

54 Hours passed, and a tense hush settled over the surveillance operation. In the EMS vans, the marksmen stared through the darkened windows at a somber sky. Behind emergency, two detectives in a Chevy drank tepid coffee from paper cartons and hid the glow of their cigarettes in cupped palms. On the roof, members of the sniper squad took turns ducking into the stairwell to warm hands and feet numbed by the bitter chill and the need to lie prone against the cold concrete to remain invisible.

The men posted in the lobby and at each landing were tight enough to snap. They sprang to action with every unexplained sound: a capricious turn of the wind, tapping tree branches, creaks and shudders in the building's facade.

No one knew when Malcolm Cobb would appear or from what direction. No one could predict what the madman would do when he realized he was cornered.

The waiting had taken its toll on Oliver London too. He'd struggled valiantly to stay awake, but his eyes were so heavy, he finally relented and allowed them to drift shut. Only resting, he told himself. If anything happened, he would hear.

But the figure moved in utter silence. He stalked the deserted corridor. Pressed out of sight in the cubicle housing the fire extinguishers, he peered toward the specimen's room and exulted.

Laughter bubbled in his throat, but he thwarted its escape. He had foiled the swarm of eyeless, mindless, malevolent pests.

Dark moon triumphant. Rising over all.

Cobb plucked three rubber-capped hypodermics from the pocket of the lab coat he wore, selected one, and injected its contents into his thigh. At once, he felt the heat of his escalating energies. His pulse began to race, and there was a ferocious thumping in his chest. Rush of sacred humours, power of the dark star.

Now he was ready.

A final look, and he started down the hallway again. He was halfway to the child's room when a pair of clucking nurses turned the far corner and came toward him. Cobb's urge was to turn and flee, but he resisted. His adrenalin-induced powers were at their peak, he could not afford to waste the charge or allow it to ebb. He knew that another dose too quickly could imperil him.

Control! Lever of will engaged.

Maintaining an even, unhurried stride, he approached the two nurses. They were engaged in petty discourse. Blessedly preoccupied.

But as they drew nearer, they went mute and foisted their full attentions on him. Cobb stifled his terror and kept walking.

Control!

They must not thwart him. He would have to dispose of anyone who stood in his way.

He was within a few yards of them now. Boldly, he cast his eye at the pair and acknowledged their presence with a curt nod. The wrong response would be their last. Cobb was beyond worry over consequences. He was the dark moon, soaring and inviolate.

'Hello,' one of the nurses said with a coy tip of her chin. Cobb nodded again.

'Hi, Dr. Ferris,' the other one said. 'How is it out? Look like snow?'

Cobb shrugged and kept walking. The hens continued on their way. He heard the ping of the elevator bell behind him and a breathy swallow as the doors shut the pair inside.

He was beyond harm. Prepared to dispatch the woman at last and have the specimen to himself.

Cobb paused at the door to the child's room and listened to the stillness. The moment had arrived.

The wretched masquerade and the waiting were behind

him. Now was the time to reap the dividends at long last. Cobb indulged in a moment of self-congratulation. He had fooled them all.

Dolts. He had duped them thoroughly and systematically. Overlooked nothing. They had been deceived by the falsified diplomas, the flaunted knowledge he'd absorbed from his readings, the laudatory references from invented colleagues overseas.

At this moment, at each moment of final fulfilment, it seemed well worth the years of waiting. He thought of all the vile filth he'd endured, the petty concerns of pinch-browed parents, the wails and protests of the loathsome children. So many of them useless little lumps of refuse. So few brilliant enough to serve his magnificent cause.

True, Lydia had helped. Cobb had found his finest specimens by listening to her. How she'd go on about this one and that one and how her Todd was the most brilliant of all. Of course, poor Todd didn't nearly fulfil his astounding potential. At least, as she saw it, the child did not. She was forever mewling about this child and that one pretending to be Todd's superior. She complained about the other ones and their duplicity. All trying to detract from her Todd's genius.

In all but one case, the children she'd touted had turned out to be perfect prospects. To be fair, the sole exception had been Cobb's error. He had been after a young boy at a particular house, but he'd damaged the child's visiting cousin by mistake. A rapid assessment had revealed that the injured child was not worth saving. The wounded boy had been fat, slovenly, and dull beyond forgiveness. Cobb had rectified the mistake by dispatching the child in the emergency room. The appropriate injection and the problem was remedied.

A minor travail, quickly forgotten.

A simple error. Cobb bristled remembering the punishments he'd endured over the simplest errors. Cruel tortures, humiliations beyond reckoning.

No matter what his accomplishments, they had been inadequate by her standards. Like poor Todd, he'd always been found lacking. The only time Cobb had won the unmitigated glow of her approbation was over the publication of his book. And then he'd been unable to produce its equal. The shame! The heinous ignominy.

But after this, he would be unfettered. Soaring.

He twisted the knob, pressed the door open, and slipped inside the specimen's room.

The woman was sleeping on the cot at the far corner. First, he would see to her. He could not risk her interference again.

Cobb plucked the rubber stopper from the second hypodermic. The reservoir was filled with Norcuron, a depolarizing neuromuscular blocking agent. The drug would paralyze the woman, render her incapable of speech, movement, breath. Her death would be slow and agonizing, fifteen minutes or more of terrifying awareness. She would be trapped in the useless shell of her vile being. Helpless.

No more than she deserved.

Once he had dosed her with the deadly extract, he would wrest the healing humors from the child. He had decided to sedate the boy to prevent an outcry. Cobb hadn't wished to risk any diminishment of the child's powers, but he was well beyond concern over optimal conditions. At this point, he would be content to begin his restitution by whatever means.

The woman stirred and rolled onto her side. Cobb observed her, and felt a swell of loathing. Anxious to be done with her, he approached the cot. The needle glinted in his grasp. His eyes blazed with madness.

Lowering the covers, he tried to spot a promising vein in the woman's hand or forearm, but the light was inadequate. He would have to settle for an intramuscular injection. It would take slightly longer for total paralysis to set in, but ultimately, it would be as effective, and as lethal. He was poised to administer the dosage when he felt the hand on his back.

Cobb spun around and was startled to see the old man in the wheelchair. The wizened creature was gnarled and nearly immobilized. He attempted to speak, but only succeeded in issuing a few porcine grunts. Cobb was moved to laughter.

What was this? The gargoyle was attempting to overwhelm him? The man was tugging at the hypodermic with a mangled claw.

'Get back. Get away from here. I'll kill you, you putrid ruin.'

Behind him was the sound of the woman coming awake. Rising. Cobb could not allow the deformed ancient to thwart his plan. With the full might of his fury, he shoved the wheelchair back against the opposite wall where it tilted and flipped on its side. Then he turned to the woman, caught her flailing arm, stabbed the needle into her forearm, and pressed home the plunger.

Delighted, Cobb stood and watched her begin to yield to the drug. Her voice faded, and she crumpled back against the cot. Satisfied, he left her to her horror and approached the child.

The boy was fast asleep, but Cobb decided to heed caution and proceed with the sedation. He extracted the final hypodermic from his pocket and injected a meager dose of valium into the child's buttock. Enough to ensure his docile cooperation.

Cobb risked a momentary flash of the bedside lamp to ease his efforts. In an instant he had inserted the hollow needle into a vein in the specimen's hand, and the humors were infiltrating the clear plastic tube. Cobb lowered his mouth to the end of the tubing and began to suck, trying to draw the humors more quickly. He was so absorbed in his enterprise, that he didn't anticipate the arm that coiled around his knees, tugged with all the might of a stubborn will, and sent him reeling.

He struggled with the old man, but his strength was failing. The familiar numbness claimed his arm, and he felt the sinking in his face. Inches away, the precious humor was dripping to the floor from the tube in the child's hand. If only he could get closer.

Cobb lunged for the tube, but only managed to dislodge

324

it. Sputtering in frustration, he turned and lashed at the old man. There was a blind struggle. Two weak hulks of rotting flesh. Each was fueled by foolish resolve and the last dying gasps of desperation.

But Cobb was winning. He rolled the old man on his back and pinned his good arm to the ground. Raking his fingers against the saggy flesh on the face, Cobb raised lines of bubbled blood. He pressed his weight against the ancient Adam's apple and began to squeeze. Soon, it would be over. Moments.

He wasn't aware of the old man's other hand as it struggled in a palsy toward the call button dangling from the child's bedstead. He heard the squawk of the intercom and the nurse's voice. 'Yes, James? Need something, honey?'

Startled, Cobb wrenched the button from the old man's hand. There was another squawk as the old man drew a torturous breath, and forced the words, 'Code Bluuue.'

55

The silence was a suffocating blob. Cobb pressed his hand across the old man's mouth and stared at the metal grate of the intercom. His breathing was shallow and labored. He willed it to settle, so he could trust his voice.

The intercom crackled and lit up again. 'Yes, James, honey? You want something. I didn't catch that.'

'Dr. Ferris here.' Cobb said. 'I must have hit the button accidentally. James is asleep and fine.'

Static and a pause. 'Yes, Dr. Ferris. Thanks.'

Cobb pressed a trembling thumb against the old man's jugular until the wrinkled lids fluttered shut and the man went still. He had moments to milk the child and be gone. They could not find him lingering here too long.

Clumsily, he retrieved the dislodged tubing from the floor and struggled to thread the fine edge over the needle that still protruded from the child's vein. His fingers quivered with weakness, head reeled from the effort.

There!

He watched as the healing fluid trickled into the tubing and oozed through with exasperating slowness.

Starving with need, Cobb bent over the free edge of the tube and pressed his lips to the cool plastic. He was waiting, sucking greedily, when the first blow came.

56 Drum raised the washbasin and bashed it down again on the lunatic's bowed head. There was a satisfying crunching sound and a rush of air, but the sonavabitch wouldn't go down.

'One for Mommy,' Drum said and beaned him again. 'One for . . . baby. And one for Uncle Oliver! Now crumple, you crazy sonavabitch. Give it the hell up before I get *really* peeved.'

The creep reeled around with an animal yelp and lunged at Drum's throat. Drum felt the iron fingers digging into his larynx, saw fireworks.

Getting light-headed, he brought his knee up hard into the maniac's groin. The pressure on his neck let up. Drum staggered backward and rubbed away the sore spot. 'That was *not* a good idea, buddy,' he gasped. 'Now you got me real *offended*.'

Catching his breath, Drum took a running start and butted the guy hard in the chest, knocking him back off balance. When he caught his footing, Drum balled his fist and gave the creep a nose job. Local anesthetic.

Cobb fell to the floor in a fetal ball, weeping.

'You go ahead and cry, sweetheart. Your privilege. The party is frigging over.'

Drum looked around and took in the damages. London and the kid were out but appeared to be okay. The kid's mother was another story. She was stiff. Even her eyeballs seemed starched. Drum flipped on the light and caught her ashen color. Leaning over the bed, he pressed the emergency buzzer and then he raced out to the hall to hustle things along.

They had to be able to save her. Damned story was supposed to have an happy ending.

57 The beauty was in a feisty mood as he drove toward the Sound. Drum slipped a Nancy Wilson tape into the deck and settled in for a bumpy ride. His part in the case was over, but he still had one large piece of unfinished business to see to. The thought of it turned his mouth to chalk, but he knew it was time. This debt was way past due.

Drum rolled down the window and felt the tear of the frigid wind. Dark night. No stars: no moon. Fine with him. Anything better would have felt like window dressing. Wouldn't have made this any easier.

On the four-lane abutting the Sound, Drum eased up on the juice and tried to pull it together. He had to keep remembering what he was after. Stick to the point, no matter what it cost him. Not going to be easy.

The house loomed like a hulking giant against the brooding sky. The sight of the place started a pulse knocking in his throat. He tried to push back the foul memories, but they kept at him.

He used one of his plastic chits to raise the electric gate and drove inside. Fifty yards down, he took the fork leading to the rear service entrance and parked.

He left the beauty idling and worked his way inside through the pantry door. The kitchen was dark, but he could see nothing had changed. A ring of dark pots hung like executed prisoners over the commercial stove. Everything cold and hard.

Treading down the back hallway, Drum was careful to keep it quiet. He wanted to surprise the old turd. Hold on to every advantage.

He stopped outside the study. The door was open a crack, and Drum had a view of the leather couches, the skin rugs, the wall of mirror tiles. Everything was back to the way it had been before the fire. Perfect restoration of the horror museum.

The old man was sitting at the desk, poring over some filth, Drum figured. He butted the door open and strode inside. 'Long time no see, Uncle Liam.'

Liam looked up and the color drained from his fat face. Drum could see the tremor in his hand. But the old creep forced a plastic smile. 'Jeremiah? How have you been?'

'Great. I've been just terrific. You?'

'Getting old, you know. Aches and pains. Slowing down. Usual crap.'

Drum chuckled. 'But you're not dead yet, are you, Uncle dear? Every day I read the obituaries hoping, but no luck so far.'

Liam was inching his hand toward the desk drawer. Good, Drum needed a little comic relief.

'Oh, I'll be gone soon enough, Jeremiah. Dead and buried so you can come by every Sunday and spit on my grave. That's what you want, isn't it? Never forgive a thing, do you, boy? Just like your father. Always disapproving of me. Making his little jokes.'

Time. Drum caught the old man's wrist as he was curling his fingers around a fat, ugly Lüger. 'Tsk, tsk. Don't you know it's dangerous to play with guns? You could get hurt real bad.'

Holding the flabby arm tight, he stared into the burnt-out eyes and smiled. 'Make a wish, sweetheart.' Then he twisted the hand until he heard the wrist crack.

Liam howled and hunched over in pain.

Drum sat on the desk and started counting on his fingers. 'Let's see. I owed you one broken wrist, which is all paid up. But I've still got to take care of the nose, carve a couple of nice, deep gashes on your ugly face, trash that fat knee of yours. We're gonna be real busy here for a while, aren't we, Unc? Hope you got no plans for the evening.'

'No more, Jeremiah. What do you want, boy? Name your price, and then leave me in peace.' Liam was blubbering like a scared baby.

'You don't get it, do you, shithead? I don't want your money. I want you to suffer the way I suffered. I want you to run and hide, so scared all the time, you can't see straight. And then I want to find you and fuck with your mind and ruin your frigging life.'

'Tell me, *Uncle* Liam,' Drum said. 'Was it fun for you? Did you enjoy telling the cops that I set the fire for no reason? Did you get a big bang out of testifying against me so they'd send me away for the maximum?

'I loved watching you up there on the stand. Mr. Squeaky Clean, talking about how you'd taken me in as a poor orphan, given me everything, love and affection, all the frigging advantages.

'What was it you said about me? Oh, yeah, I was incorrigible. That's it. I was the bad seed, right, buddy? Took me ten years to crawl out of the hole you dug for me. Truth is I'm still crawling.'

Liam was mewling. 'Please, Jeremiah. No more. I'm an old man. Have mercy.'

Drum laughed. 'Now, that is a real funny one. Hysterical almost. What the hell do you know about mercy? I was a kid, for chrissakes. You cut me up in pieces and chewed on my bones. And to you it was all a game, wasn't it? You had a wonderful frigging time watching me sink.'

'Can't let go, can you? Just like your damned father, may he rot in hell.'

Drum lunged across the desk and grabbed Liam's collar. 'All right, you fat shit. You want mercy, I'll give it to you. I'll put you right out of your frigging misery.' He squeezed until the old man's eyes bulged and his face turned the dusky purple of an old bruise. Drum was a fist of rage, quaking from the poison.

Liam's color was deepening. There was a gurgling sound in his throat. Death rattle. Drum forced himself to let go. The creep slumped back in his chair, breathing in ragged puffs.

'Now, here's what you're going to do, Uncle Liam. You're going to make a phone call to one of the many important people you own in this town and arrange something for me. Then, you're going to forget you ever knew me. And unless you give me a real good reason, I'm going to do the same for you. Get it?'

The old man's nose was running. A broad stain was spreading over his lap. Drum caught the urine stench and winced.

'Start dialing, shithead,' he said. 'I'll give you the details as you go along.'

58 The next night, Drum had the chess board set up when the kid came down from taking his shower. 'Up for a quick massacre, hotshot?'

'Yeah, sure, if you are, Mr. Drum. We playing for one hundred big ones like usual?'

'Pennies?' Drum raised a brow. 'Actually, I had bigger stakes in mind. Unless you're chicken that is.'

'No way, man. You name it. I'll cover.'

Drum fiddled with his king and regarded the runt from under his eyelids. 'I'm talking real high stakes, Book. Man-sized.'

'Ain't no chicken, I told you. Lay it out, Mr. Drum. I'm ready.'

'Okay. Here's the deal. Winner has to change his name, permanent-like.'

Booker's eyes went wary. 'Don't get you.'

'It's simple, kid. If you win, I change my name from Jeremiah to anything you choose.'

Booker laughed. 'You mean like Mary Lou?'

'If that's what you want, yeah.'

'And if you win, you get to pick my new name?' Booker said. 'Guess I can risk it, seeing as how you never win.'

'Okay, Book. But I want to warn you up front. If I win, I'm going to make you change your name to Drum. Booker Drum.'

Kid's face went through a series of changes: confused, caught on, coy. 'You saying you're asking to marry me, Mr. Drum? 'Cause Mrs. Drum ain't going to like that, no way.'

'No, Book. Not marriage.'

'Then you must be thinking about adoption. That right?'

'Yeah. That's what I had in mind.'

Booker let the grin flash, but reined it back in fast. 'What about that Bergmuller lady from social service, Mr.

Drum? She ain't gonna let that happen, you know. She likes black on black. Everything neat and tidy. You're way to pale, man.'

'Way too pale, way too ugly, way too lots of things. But it's all taken care of. Someone I know arranged it, Book. So it's up to you.'

Kid shrugged. 'Same to me either way, Mr. Drum. Like you said, why don't we play for it? See how it goes.'

Drum extended a hand for the runt to shake. Kid pumped it eagerly, with a nice squeeze of warmth. 'Fine by me, hotshot. Let's see how it goes.'

Drum was playing black. Booker opened with his queen's bishop's pawn.

59 Less than twenty-four hours had elapsed since the attack in James's hospital room, but already it had assumed the blunt, grainy guise of distant memory. The facts were so hard for Cinnie to absorb. Dr. Ferris, trusted physician and consummate professional, was in reality a deranged killer with a vampire complex. Stranger still, Malcolm Cobb, Ferris's alter ego (or was in the other way around?) had turned out to be Lydia Holroyd's phantom brother.

And then there was the weird business about some stranger no one could identify showing up to save Cinnie before the drug she'd been given had time to do its lethal damage.

Whoever he was, Cinnie would be in his debt forever.

She had just begun to feel the terrifying constriction in her throat and the oppressive weight of paralysis crushing her chest when the crisis team had burst in with the crash cart. Before he'd disappeared, the stranger had handed the labeled used hypodermic to the head doc, so they knew she'd been dosed with Norcuron.

The emergency team had administered an antidote, and the effects of the drug had been counteracted in seconds. Some of the longest seconds in Cinnie's life.

Thankfully, no one had been seriously hurt. Mr. London had suffered scrapes and bruises, but nothing worse. Cinnie had worried that the excitement might precipitate another stroke. But the old man had been kept under close observation overnight. And the impossible darling had shown no ill effects from the ordeal.

Mr. London had even managed to get one of the night nurses assigned to him to come back and sneak him a corned beef sandwich for lunch. Cinnie had caught the telltale scent when she showed up to thank him in person for risking his neck to protect her and James. So she'd decided to ditch the pastrami on rye she had hidden in her tote bag. Another time.

James had come through the nightmare unscathed. Because of the sedative, he didn't even have a clear memory of the episode. This morning, he'd reported a strange dream about the shadow man coming in to give him a needle. Exact words: 'Dream, Mommy. Shadow man come. Stick my arm. Ouch.'

Cinnie played the words over in her mind. It wasn't her imagination. James was better, clearer. Even wretched Dr. Silver had noted the change in his inimitable way: 'Kid's less of a dishrag today, Cinnie. Not ready for the debate team, but he's coming along. Encouraging.'

Yes, she was encouraged. Tomorrow, they'd be bringing James home. For real, this time. His so-called setback had been from a shot of insulin Ferris had given him. Luckily, James's blood sugar was up after the farewell party, so the drug's effect had been blunted.

Paul had insisted on canceling all his appointments for the day to be with James and her, and this time, Cinnie hadn't argued. It would be nice to have him around for the homecoming, but she knew that things were far from resolved between them. In fact, Paul was at his precious studio right now. He'd brought her home and hung around for a while. But then the old restlessness had drawn him away.

'I'll be back in an hour, I promise,' he said. 'Just have a couple of things to finish up.'

She watched him leave. She was forever watching him leave.

Cinnie was through straightening James's room. Paul wouldn't be back for more than a half hour, but she was determined to be ready for him. She might not know how to compete with that blasted sound board, but it didn't hurt to try.

She took a hot shower, dressed in her lavender teddy, sprayed a few strategic spots with Chanel 19, and slipped between the cool sheets. A wonderful torpor claimed her, and she allowed her thoughts to float. Her mind filled with lovely images: James playing soccer, flipping grass clumps at a backyard barbecue, doing his Springsteen imitation.

At the edge of her consciousness, she caught the sound of the front door opening. Paul was early. Good sign.

Lying on her side with her eyes closed, she listened as he closed the door and padded down the hall. He was walking so slowly and quietly, Cinnie thought he must be planning his own surprise.

The footsteps paused in the kitchen. Sweetheart was planning to bring her something. Taking so long.

Finally, the steps started again. He was coming into the room, getting closer. She turned to greet him.

It wasn't Paul.

A strange, flattened face was looming inches from hers. Cinnie felt the heat of its breath. Smelled its acrid odor. The creature emitted a feral shriek and lunged at her. She tried to fight, but the intruder had both her wrists caught in an iron grip. Flailing from side to side, looking for a way out, she spotted the knife. Razor point. Glinting in the lamplight.

'No!' she yelled. 'Let me go!'

She couldn't move. Her legs were pinned by the intruder. The monster was raising the blade, aiming it at her neck. Cinnie screamed again and watched in horror as the knife reached the top of the arc.

'No,' she said. 'No!' She struggled against the creature's iron grasp until her muscles caught fire. The blade was coming closer, plunging toward her throat.

But time stopped. Her assailant was letting go, turning to fight with someone else.

Cinnie raised her head and rubbed the soreness from her wrists. The assailant's features were blunted by a nylon stocking. One gloved hand raised the knife and tried to thrust it into Paul's back.

Numb with shock, Cinnie lifted her pillow and brought it down hard on the knife blade. The point stuck and the knife clattered to the floor.

Someone shrieked. Paul and the masked intruder were pummeling each other. They grappled to the floor, and both lunged for the fallen knife. Cinnie held her breath as Paul overpowered the monster and bashed the masked head hard against the wooden floor.

The assailant went still.

Paul looked up at her, his face ashen.

'Call nine-eleven,' he said in a breathless rush.

Cinnie made the call. The dispatcher took the vital information and told her to keep the line open. 'They're on the way.'

'Five minutes,' Cinnie told Paul. The figure on the floor stirred. 'Be careful.'

Holding the knife in one hand, Paul used the other to peel off the stocking mask. His jaw dropped.

Cinnie gasped. 'Lydia?'

'Christ, what's going on here?'

At that moment, a man burst through the bedroom door wielding a pistol. There was something vaguely familiar about him. But Cinnie couldn't make the connection.

'You okay?' he said.

'Yes, thank goodness my husband showed up when he did,' Cinnie said.

Paul came over and put his arms around her. 'I love you, Cin,' he murmured in her ear. 'If anything had happened to you . . .'

Cinnie touched his cheek and turned to the stranger. 'How did you get here so quickly?'

'Sorry I didn't make it sooner. You shouldn't have had to handle this load of garbage yourself.'

Lydia Holroyd snapped alert at the slur. 'You've some nerve, you wretched man.'

'Shut the hell up.'

'I'll *not* be spoken to that way.' Lydia started smoothing her crumpled and disheveled hair.

'Shut the hell up, *please*. That better, scum?'

'What's going on here?' Paul said. 'Why the hell would you want to hurt Cinnie, Lydia?'

'Tell her why you dropped by, *Lydia*.'

Lydia glowered at the stranger. Her mouth was a drawn seam.

337

'The gentleman asked you a *question*, Mrs. Holroyd. He asked real polite-like. So *answer* him.' The stranger caught Lydia's hair in a clump and pulled so hard her features were stretched like taffy.

'I had no choice, don't you see?' Lydia said. 'I kept warning Malcolm that she was dangerous, but he was so weak, incapable of dealing with her. She reminded Malcolm of Mummy, I suppose. He never could fight back at that bitch either. Malcolm always allowed Mummy to mortify him, to make him nothing. I couldn't allow you to do the same, Cynthia. I simply could not see you destroy everything.'

'What is she talking about?' Cinnie said.

'She's the other half of the dynamic duo,' the stranger said. 'It was her idea to have dear Malcolm hurt the children. She convinced her screwy brother that he needed the kid's blood to survive.'

The stranger turned to Lydia Holroyd. 'But you knew better, didn't you, slime? What you really wanted was to get all the smart kids out of the way so your Todd wouldn't have any competition. Since Mrs. Merritt was watching James too closely, you decided Malcolm had to get rid of her too. All that mattered were those A-pluses and awards, right, Lydia? Pretty sick pup, you are, lady. Sicker than old Malcolm even, and that's saying something.'

Lydia Holroyd sat up, squared her regal shoulders, met Drum's gaze squarely, and spat in his face.

He pressed the gun to her temple, and a terrible look came into his eyes. Pure rage.

'Don't,' Cinnie said. There was the shrill of approaching sirens. She caught the flash of cap lights.

'There's your royal escort, princess. But I can save you the trip, can't I?'

The stranger clenched his teeth, and his hand quavered with fury. Cinnie winced at the click of the safety. But he didn't shoot.

A trio of uniformed cops took a struggling Lydia Holroyd away in handcuffs. Cinnie and Paul watched as they shoved her into the back of a squad car and pulled away.

The stranger had disappeared during the arrest, but now

he came sauntering back into the bedroom. 'You two sure you're okay?'

'Yes, and thanks for showing up when you did. Mr. –?'

The name he mentioned wasn't familiar to Cinnie. But she recognized the voice. Same voice as that insurance agent who'd come to visit at the hospital. But the face . . .

He seemed to read her mind. 'I usually cover up the scars when I work, Mrs. Merritt. They tend to distract people.'

Cinnie couldn't get over how different he looked with the ragged depression in his cheek, the droopy eyelid, and the thick gray stripe running through his hair. She made a conscious effort not to be rude and stare. 'How did you know about Lydia?'

'My kid helped me put it together. He remembered some of the things I told him your boy kept saying when I came to the hospital. Last night, after I beat his butt in a game of chess, he started guessing what it all meant. He figured out that the "flying green tunnel" was Cobb's green station wagon. "Pop the weasel" was about Cobb hitting the kid with a dart full of poison to make it look like his heart was screwy so they'd be sure to admit him to the hospital. The "shadow man" was Cobb himself when he tailed James to get a handle on his daily routine. That left "Mrs. Wheel" and the "blue coat lady".

'My kid suggested that the "blue coat lady" must have been someone posing as you to lure James into the street. Wouldn't take much in a heavy glare like the one on the day of the accident to fool the kid into thinking she was you: curly wig, similar coat.'

'Your son figured all that out? Some smart kid,' Paul said.

'Yeah.' Drum couldn't help grinning. 'My son. And after they nabbed Ferris, I realized that "Mrs. Wheel" was one of those word substitutions like Oliver London makes. "Mrs. Wheel" was your boy's way of saying "Dr. Ferris."'

'Makes sense,' Cinnie said.

Dazed, Cinnie listened to the rest. Nothing was as it

seemed. Ferris had never trained as a physician, and Lydia Holroyd had never been your standard, suburban matron.

After Booker got the wheels rolling, Drum began to make the rest of the connections. He'd thought about the children's book Malcolm Cobb had written. Both weed kids had been major league screwy.

On the hunch that the names Dove and Elegant might tell him something, Drum had looked them up in a baby name book Stella had picked up years ago. Turned out Dove and Elegant were translations for Lydia and Malcolm.

After that, Drum had gotten one of his buddies to tap into an underground patient-claim data bank and confirmed that both Malcolm Cobb and Lydia Holroyd had done long, hard time at a variety of funny farms.

An hour ago, it had come to Drum that Cobb's weed story might be an allegory of Lydia's and Malcolm's real lives. Drum had reasoned that after Cobb was out of commission, the surviving weed would be real anxious to take over and make things right. That's why he'd come rushing over, to keep an eye on things in case Lydia came prowling for blood. Unfortunately, he'd been late.

'That's some good sleuthing for an insurance agent, Mr. Drum,' Paul said.

'Thanks, Mr. Merritt. Only I have to tell you the truth. I'm no insurance agent.'

Paul started to laugh. After a beat, Cinnie joined him.

60

Paul had gone downstairs to settle with accounts and bring the car around. Nurse Evelyn Larwin had gone off in search of the cart they'd need to haul James's collection of toys and other paraphernalia to the car.

James was dressed for the first time since the accident. They'd slit the leg of his jeans to accommodate the cast and gotten him a new Hard Rock Cafe shirt. Little guy was the most beautiful thing Cinnie had laid her eyes on in weeks.

She peered at her watch. 'Where's Evelyn already? I'm ready to blow this joint. How about you, Jimbo? You looking forward to going home?'

He went thoughtful a minute and gave her a wary look. 'Vinton?'

'He's gone, sweetheart. He got so tired of waiting around for you to get out of this place, he decided to retire from the monster business altogether and move to Florida.'

James looked at her and burst into giggles. 'Mom fooling.'

'No, honest. He took a condo in a new hotsy-totsy development at Boca Mocha West, which is right near Fort Whoknowswhere. They have a golf course and everything. Big rooms, terraces on every unit. Heated pools. The closets aren't so hot, but old Vinton decided he'd make do. You get to a certain age, you've had enough of the daily grind, Jimbo. Give it seventy, eighty years, and you'll see what I mean.'

'Evelyn coming?'

'She'll be right here. Getting restless?'

He eyed the stack of books, and something uneasy crossed his expression. 'Read book, Mommy?'

'Any particular book you have in mind?'

'Book,' he said. Cinnie knew full well which one he wanted.

She'd been sorely tempted to throw the awful story away, but much as she wanted to be rid of it, she'd decided to let James get tired of it on his own. Poor sweetheart had earned the right to work this nightmare through on his own terms. Slipping the ugly, little volume from one of the shopping bags, she opened the cover and started reading.

'Once upon a time, there was an old woman who had a garden full of weeds.'

She read about the angry neighbors and the weird, parasitic weed sister and brother named Dove and Elegant. She read about the long winter and the illnesses that kept afflicting the strange sibling pair. When she got to the final chapter about the following year, Cinnie paused and gave James a kiss.

'And then?' James said, wanting the ending.

'And then spring came and it was time for the weeds to go back out into the garden,' she said. 'But when the old woman went to set them in the ground, she found the garden was already too crowded and she changed her mind.

'You see, Jimbo, while she was all tied up with those ugly weeds, someone had sneaked in and planted rows and rows of chocolate chip cookies.'

James's puzzled expression yielded to a tentative grin. 'Happily after?' he said.

'Yes, sweetie. And they all lived happily ever after.'